Corvus

Eduardo Luengo

Published by Clink Street Publishing 2014

First edition.

ISBN: 978-1-909477-14-8
Ebook: 978-1-909477-15-5

Origins

"In ignorance there is bliss. In knowledge there is power. And power corrupts the greatest of minds."

I once valued the courage of battle. I praised the brave and the generous. There was a time when I sided with justice. There was a time when Mother Nature and the people were my concern. I was considered a hero, subject of legends and stories. Now, across the millennia, my name has been tainted by my own actions. My legend faded into myth. I share my name with the Sun, Antares, whose tender light caresses the realm of Dædali, and which means bright star in *Komundruum*, the Common Language. I am Antares, once hero of the people, now a villain...

The wind came in gusts that struck the belfry where I stood overlooking the vast grasslands at the feet of white towering mountains, whose jagged peaks harbored dark secrets.

The meadows, pure and virgin, would soon become the Valley of the Fallen. In the future, tombstones engraved out of respect and grief would rise all across the fields, over kilometers, commemorating the fallen heroes of that day to come. And, yet, I will not be with them.

What is this world in which we live and have lived for eons? What is this world we fight and die for everyday? I know not; I am ignorant; I do not have power, not just yet. But what I certainly know is that it is worth fighting for.

I consider myself a man of peace, and that all issues can be settled with diplomacy and that war is a last resort.

I waited for the arrival of the enemy; they would be here at any moment. I looked up from the tower to find the sun obscured by dark clouds that approached to swallow our last defenses.

Our enemy is swift; they are lithe and burly, as unlikely as it may seem. They are resistant to all four elements; they are immune to the deadliest of poisons and toxins. Their armor is hard to breach. Piercing and puncturing their thin and membranous wings should keep them bound to the earth. Dragons are loyal, greatly devoted to their leaders. Dragon blood is believed to bear a curse because wounds inflicted by swords dipped in it have been found to be incurable. But most remarkably, they are incredibly intelligent creatures that have evolved into thinking beings and established a complex hierarchy.

Centuries of contention against these marvelous beings have already passed. A long fight continues for survival and hegemony over Dædali.

Drákuvaar, the elder lord of the Fiery Mountain, prepared his legions of dragons to eliminate our race from the face of the world. And as the first stirring in the dark swollen skyline appeared, I pulled on the chains above me without a moment of hesitation. A mighty peal of the bell reverberated across the valley, its clamor making the mountains tremble. The battle had started.

Bedlam arose amongst my fellow warriors who had been impatiently waiting for the enemy to strike. Beneath the belfry supported by vaulted buttresses and thick pillars, within the high crenellated walls of the citadel, a turbulent throng of heavily armed warriors flooded out through the great front doors, brandishing swords, axes, hammers and crossbows. Archers waited, calm and steady, stringing their taut bows and nocking arrows in the rigid bowstrings as they surveyed the field from the top of the walls.

When the first dragon glided around the tower, I hurled my lance and it speared into its flanks. I did not hate the enemy at all, but wanted their and our species to unite and live together in harmony. The dragon plummeted into the hard ground in the middle of the raging battle with a painful bellow; and it hurt me too. I was not brutal, but war demanded a drastic change in me.

The dragons began to spit blue-tinged red fire from their maws. Others shot a frostbite breath that froze the ground soldiers alive.

Other inhaled the air and released it, sending out a whirlwind that sucked warriors into it and tore them apart.

I descended the tower and entered into chaos. I sprinted through the battlefields, my Arcadian armor bumping on my athletic body with my every movement, as I looked to engage my enemy, my Stygium sword already in my hand. Many dragons were already on the ground, taking on my soldiers. A large flock still swarmed in the air. Archers cast arrows into their wings. Eventually, all the dragons landed on their flanks, brought down by the arrows sticking out from their wings and sides, skidding to a halt, running over other dragons and soldiers that could not move out of the way. They stood back on their hind legs and began countering and parrying attacks with their sharp claws and fangs.

The battle lasted for hours. Most of my men were already dead, so were most of the dragons' forces. I, along with the few survivors, was already worn out. I felt my arms leaden because of the heavy and constant exertion of swinging the sword, hurling spears and blocking with my shield. Not only was exhaustion a problem, but also, seeing the blood spilled by the liter and piles of lifeless corpses heaped on the ground was demoralizing. The sight was simply heartbreaking.

We were finally about to claim victory, after eternal hours of distress, grief and weariness. It was finally ours when the last few dragons began to flee the battlefield, either by crawling away with agonized cries, or struggling to keep flight in mid-air, using their damaged spearhead tail as a rudder. We had finally defeated them. But there had been a drastic change inside me. I felt rage and despair. War had changed me. War had made me brutal and ruthless.

It was victory, until a calamitous roar boomed across the aftermath of the battlefield. I scrutinized the dark sky, in search of the source. Then I caught a glimpse in the distance of something stirring almost beyond sight. And so the outline of heavy beating of wings came into view.

I locked eyes with the elder lord of the Fiery Mountain, Drákuvaar, as he landed heavily before me, causing the earth to quake as his curved sword-like claws gouged beneath it. His snakelike gilded eyes drilled into mine as a new growing fear lanced through my body like a deadly toxin. Drákuvaar furled his monumental wings behind his ridged back and lowered his head. I was still out of range of his fangs.

"Surrender, puny Dwellers," he hissed in the Common Language, "and I shall be clement with your race."

As soon as I materialized the spear out of thin air, Drákuvaar's back arched defensively and he quickly discharged a fireball from his throat. For unknown reasons, I have always had a certain affinity to the element of fire. As I got engulfed in the firestorm, my spear lit red and I cast it against his throat.

Drákuvaar swiped it away with his claws, giving me time to move out of the fire and into him. With my sword drawn, I nimbly climbed all the way to his throat and found the chink in the armor, wrath flowing freely through my veins. My Stygium blade easily penetrated the dragon scales and dark red blood spurted out. Drákuvaar made heavy gagging sounds as he flailed his head to shake me off, but I had an iron grip on the spikes jutting out of his back. When he finally tumbled upon the bloody grasslands, I, still clinging to his neck, withdrew my sword and looked at my few surviving men, who stared at me in disbelief, dismayed and awe-stricken.

"Captain?" one stammered out. "He was still negotiating…"

"It was too dangerous to let him finish the sentence," I replied, with clear disdain. "His death was long overdue."

The dragon Drákuvaar was not evil at all, I came to realize with the passing of time. He was only the leader of the dragons; I was the leader of the Dwellers. Perhaps he feared us like we feared them. He probably feared that we would slaughter and exterminate their race—survival of the fittest. And probably, he was right. On the other hand, I wanted peace all along, but something within me dragged me into chaos.

Shortly after the battle, my own men began to avoid me. The story of my dishonor quickly flew through the entire world, how I had violated an ancient war protocol and killed the dragon hero Drákuvaar before he finished his negotiation. Soon after the battle was won, the feared Death herself appeared before me. The Corvus, death represented in the shape of a black crow, warped from her own dimension and gave me an unexpected visit. There was a deal. She told me there had to be a leader ruling the realms of the Underworld. I was dumbfounded. I did not understand what she meant by Underworld; I was too ignorant. Supposedly there was another world by which she referred to as the Overworld, where another race of men vied for survival as well. The Corvus offered me the eternal rule of the Underworld, granting me immortality and incredible powers beyond comprehension.

"In ignorance there is bliss. In knowledge there is power. And power corrupts the greatest of minds."

The immeasurable power she bestowed upon me corrupted my mind; every race of Dwellers and dragons despised my mandate. I quelled fires of the people that arose in upheavals against me. My everlasting years in power have been a nightmare to the denizens of the Underworld. And I never regretted it. One of my few commendable achievements was the peaceful unification of the two warring races: the Dwellers and the dragons. Aside of that, I was always feared.

There was a law the Corvus warned me to never break: the Universal Law of Nature, which imposed that no Dweller should ever cross the threshold into the Overworld. She warned me and I did not listen; she warned me and I ignored her. I wanted more power; I desired more power. As soon as I tried to open the portal into the Overworld, Death cursed me with slow and painful demise.

But I will resist. I will cling to life as long as I still have breath. When all my defenses have collapsed, as I lie on my deathbed, I will only be able to rely on my faithful Harbingers and my personal guard, the dragon Kronnix the Sovereign.

I am the fallen hero, Antares, who lived long enough to become a villain…

"In ignorance there is bliss. In knowledge there is power. And power corrupts the greatest of minds…"

A Menacing Call

It was the worst of times. There was a war on the way, one that threatened to ravage France and England. Conflicts and crises surrounded Europe as time reached one of its darkest epochs. Now at the brink of war, one new powerful threat had arisen to scourge humanity and bring an end to it. The year was 1337 Anno Domini.

The chilly wind whispered briefly at intervals, and then it blew again, through the desolated streets of Paris, which were deserted not only at midnight, but also at midday. The dirt and dust swirled upon the ground, and the branches of the trees whistled as the wind passed by. There was not a single voice.

Some streets were cobbled with stones and others were only covered by dirt. They were flanked on both sides by houses—shacks or manors, depending on the importance of the district. Peasants mostly lived either at farms or at the external edge of the city. Merchants, artisans and musicians lived in shacks or houses, depending on their popularity. Nobles or clergy members dwelt in their luxurious manors, surrounded by the trappings of wealth and the good life.

But nobody was there, outside, in the streets. Not since that fateful day, a couple of months ago, when the mysterious attacks began and corpses were found in Notre Dame.

The sun blazed upon the city, reflecting against the manors' and Notre Dame's shattered windows. The broad Seine river glittered blindingly. The green trees murmured dismally as the wind rustled their leaves. Besides that, everything was deceptively calm and silent.

The windows of Notre Dame and the surrounding manors and houses were all shattered, the doors and roofs were battered, and some of them had huge holes blown in their façades. There were blood-red stains all over the walls of the buildings and on the ground. Nobody was there, and nobody wanted to be there, except for two knights, whose obligation was to be there, exactly because nobody wanted to be there.

"Seems like a ghost town...," observed a one-hundred and eighty-five centimeters tall, burly man, of about twenty-four years, with blond hair and blue-colored eyes, now clad in the silver armor of the Order of the Knights, except for the helmet, which was on his lap. He was riding a magnificent jet-black stallion, which was wearing the silver armor as well. The knight's name was Arthur Montague.

"It's worse than that," replied a slim and athletic-toned girl, of about twenty-two years, strong enough to wield a war ax and bear her silver knight's armor, her helmet on her lap as well. She was one-hundred and eighty centimeters tall, thus Alice Houdin was considered one of the tallest female knights in the Order. She had a short wavy brown hair, emerald-colored eyes and an upturned nose. She was riding a chestnut mare, likewise wearing silver armor.

"Much has changed for ill, and, according to my last report, our Company will be the next one to be sent in," said Arthur. Notre Dame was where the attackers were believed to reside. Ever since a few months previously, masses in the cathedral had been suspended, and up until this day they had not been reinstated. The Scorpio Company was dispatched into Notre Dame, and a few days thereafter it was confirmed that they would not come back. Nobody survived the mission but one lethally wounded knight who could barely make it back to the White Bastion. In the infirmary, right before his death, he revealed what he had witnessed inside the cathedral. However, after two months, as usual, facts were warped by misinterpretation and skepticism. Nevertheless, what many did know was that what lay in Notre Dame was not human.

The Order of the Knights, founded by the wealthy Duke of Guyenne, Nicholas I, in the early 14th century, had the sole purpose of protecting France from both internal and external crises. It was a formal institution under the jurisdiction of the Viceroy, who was originally appointed by his Highness, the King Philippe V. And though it was an independent organization from the king's mandate, it still held allegiance to the great monarch. The backbone of the Order was the knights: elite soldiers who held higher prestige and had had more strenuous training than the conventional knights of the king's army. And equally important was the fact that the founder believed that women could serve a much better purpose than the population generally thought them capable of, since, at the time, they were considered greatly inferior to men. In the Order of the Knights, women were treated better than they would have been outside, although they were still considered inferior, and men vastly outnumbered them.

"Do you believe what he said?" asked Alice, glancing back ever so warily at Notre Dame. Even under the glare of the sun at its zenith, Notre Dame stood towering and sinister, its dark façade overlooking the ravaged buildings from where it lay isolated across the dismal Seine river, overshadowing the Cradle of Paris. "Do you believe what the Scorpio knight said before his death?"

"I have no doubt about it. I may not know what it is exactly, but I understand the general idea," replied Arthur. "However, we will have extra assistance, unlike Scorpio. They were on their own. Now we're two Companies."

"Still…it's a suicide mission…and nothing else," replied Alice, dejectedly looking down. "This is probably the last patrol we'll have."

"It is the reason why the Order of the Knight exists," said Arthur. "Because we are there to help when the King's army is unable to."

"No wonder. We are the ones responsible for dealing with attackers that are not even human. People say that they must be demons or the Catholic Devil himself," Alice responded. They were riding at a slow pace, beside each other, in the street along the River Seine, Notre Dame already behind them. Arthur thought Alice's term 'Catholic Devil' was odd, but then he remembered she had her own specific reasons for speaking in such a way. He knew she did not have any religious belief and he had sworn an oath to her not to tell anyone else she was not a believer. In most cases, atheism was punishable with death.

They remained silent for a long time, observing the somber avenues as they passed through them. Then after riding down another street, Alice spoke quietly:

"There is where your father found me. I remember because that's the alley I usually went to to sleep and hide from the rain," she said, pointing at an entrance to an alleyway between the wreckage of two buildings. "If it hadn't been for him, I would probably not even be alive today. Just after he brought me into the White Bastion he named me his page."

"That's when we met, at the time I was a novice squire," recalled Arthur, chuckling slightly, his voice softening. "When I could barely handle a sword."

"I'm sorry about your father," said Alice, looking down. "He was a father to me as well."

"Don't worry," he muttered. "I know we both share the same woe."

"Do you know how much time is left for the patrol to end?"

"It's around four, which means we are almost finished for the day. We have to go back to the Bastion before sunset," said Arthur.

"Bliss is weary, I can feel it," Alice murmured, stroking the mare's mane.

"We are, too," replied Arthur, tugging the horse's reins to the right and steering it to the end of the street, toward the edges of the city, where there were still a fair amount of people who had not yet fled the capital.

Alice nodded. "Where are we heading?"

"Someplace safe where we can have a drink in peace," replied Arthur, smiling at her.

They rode through more streets and avenues toward the limits of the city, which were less dangerous to wander around. They began to notice that farther ahead there were more people, but not that many. Wary merchants, peasants, artisans, or beggars scurried toward their destinations in a rush and hid again in the building they'd been heading to. Few sentries and watchmen were still alive, thus some citizens remained in the city. Carrying out duties as a sentry or guard meant early death.

The sun was starting to hide behind a huge gray cloud. Soon, the city was completely overcast.

The walls of the city loomed ten meters high over the adjacent buildings, giving rise to a sense of security from external threats that was now actually a false one. Next to the parapet, the knights came to a stop in front of a small building: it was a tavern, judging by the name of the place and the appearance. It had a wooden sign on top that read: 'The Drunken King', in rough handwriting. The windows were somewhat holed and covered with something that was not visible from outside, but suggested planks.

Alice and Arthur hitched their horses to wooden poles stuck in the sidewalk.

The tavern smelled foul, of mold and moisture, because nearly everything in there was made of wood, from the structure of the building to the plates, chairs and the counter. The humidity easily entered and deformed the timber.

Immediately upon entering the pub, Alice and Arthur received furtive glances from the people who were drinking inside. There were four men seated in a dim corner, talking in whispers while drinking pints of ale. The bartender, behind the bar, was seated on a chair, glancing at the quartet in the corner.

Slabs of wood were coarsely nailed to the frames of the windows for an improvised protection against the attacks, making the place look gloomier. There were dying candles scattered around the pub, half consumed and dripping wax.

"What can I give you?" asked the bartender as Alice and Arthur sat down across the counter. He had a surly expression and rose with difficulty from his wooden chair, carefully placing his hands on his back to straighten up.

"Just a gill of mead, please," answered Arthur.

"Milady?"

"The same," answered Alice.

The bartender turned around and took two pewter tankard mugs from the shelves and served the mead in them.

"Thank you," said Arthur. He took a sip from his drink and glanced at Alice, who was staring distantly at hers. "What's wrong?" Instinctively, he placed his hand on hers. Alice shot him a quick glance.

"It's hard to say," she said softly, moving her hand away. "Your father rescued me from the mire I was stuck in, during the dearth of food and shelter when I would probably have perished, and I am deeply grateful for that. I could never repay him for what he did for me. He gave me my first real home since my mother's death."

"Just don't let your past take control over your future, no matter how much it torments you. The only way to overcome it is by accepting it and living with it. Just as I did when my father was gone." He knew that phrase was not exactly encouraging.

"It is easier said than done," she replied.

"And yet, with all the experience we have, together, accrued, I can remark that you are one tough lass who is not easily daunted and who can overcome every obstacle set in her way," Arthur said, smiling at her and slightly squeezing her hand.

Alice smiled back and replied: "Perchance you might be right, Arthur."

"Just don't think about it. We can leave at any time you want."

Alice pushed her drink away. She snapped: "You do not understand. I cannot help but *think* about it. I want to *live*, live as though it was my last day," she insisted, turning to Arthur and looking him straight in the eyes. It was an intense gaze of want and despair. She lowered her voice to a quivering whisper. "The Order, all it does is set conditions and constraints. I don't feel like I have ever truly *lived*! I only have three options: I die at the hands of the Inquisition, or by famine and illness, or during battle. There is *nothing* else! I didn't have it clear at first, but I have come to realize that I will never be able to lead a normal life. I will never marry. I will never have children." Her chest was heaving. "I will never have someone to love." She shot a quick glance at his lips.

Arthur listened intently. A burning sensation settled in his stomach.

"It angers me that we cannot disagree with anything the Order, the King or the Church say. It makes me furious to know that people are publicly tortured and executed for having a differing opinion. And now, we are the ones that have to defend and die for the King and the Church." Alice suddenly broke into a soft laughter. "If someone overhears what I am saying, I'm dead." She looked around.

Arthur's heart sank. He remembered. It was a painful and horrifying memory that he kept repressed at all times and hidden from her. *Alice would already be dead. I had to do it,* he thought, clenching his fist. *It was too dangerous… he would have accused her…*

"Arthur, are you listening to me?" Alice asked with a friendly frown.

"You have no idea what I would do to protect you," Arthur said, his voice aquiver. "You don't know…I won't let anything happen to you, ever. We will endure."

"We have fought against other men," Alice replied, heaving a sigh. "What lies inside Notre Dame is not human."

"No, we will endure, not only because there will be two Companies this time, but because we all are strong and unbreakable as a whole," said Arthur, looking her in the eye. "I believe our most important lifetime duty is to protect this land from the perils that loom over us. There will be sacrifices, but I swear to you that we will prevail. I will make sure that *you* prevail," he repeated in a lower voice, staring at Alice.

Arthur began to lean slowly toward Alice. She stared at him expectantly, but looked away reluctantly at the last second and whispered: "People are watching. You know that is strictly forbidden. This is one of the reasons why I am angry."

"I know. I let myself go too far. But you know I care for you too much. I'm afraid of what could happen to you," Arthur replied. "If anything happened, it would be excruciating for me to bear it for the rest of my life."

"Me too," Alice said in a choked up voice.

There came a wild neighing right outside the bar.

Alice whipped toward the doors, her eyes wide with astonishment. Alice and Arthur looked at one another, and, as if by unspoken consent, they bolted from their seats and rushed out of the pub. They ran toward their respective horses, which were neighing and prancing wildly, trying desperately to free themselves from the poles in the ground.

"Everything is okay! Hush, Bliss," whispered Alice beside her mare, gently stroking her muzzle as she struggled against the tether.

"Hush," said Arthur in a soft voice as the stallion continued to whinny frantically. "What is happening?" he asked aloud.

As they were tending their horses, a hooded man with a dark, long cape rippling over his heels, his face concealed, entered the tavern. A few seconds later, there came a succession of heart-rending screams.

Alice and Arthur burst inside the tavern and they did not believe their eyes. There was nobody inside. The room was somber, dark, deserted and quiet. The four men in the corner and the bartender had disappeared without a trace. The candles were unlit, as if a powerful gust had rushed into the place and snuffed out all lights. The chairs that once were occupied now were tipped over. There was not a single drop of blood, sweat, or even a sign that anybody had been there for a week. There was not even a back door through which an attacker could have left the place. Yet, Alice and Arthur's empty cups were still there.

It was yet another of the many inexplainable situations that had occurred in Paris. There were never clues to the attackers, witnesses were never found alive, and the attacks progressively spread, consuming the entire city, until everybody had either fled the capital, or had vanished, or was lying dead.

Alice and Arthur looked at each other for answers that neither would find, dumbfounded and profoundly shocked. They still did not believe what they clearly saw. Promptly, they took off to inform their superiors, already knowing how futile it would be...

¤¤¤

In great confusion and shock, Alice and Arthur left Paris heading toward the White Bastion, hurrying to arrive before nightfall. They traveled across green rolling hills, grasslands reaching waist-high and covering most of the land, spurring their horses into fast gallops across uneven terrain, sometimes rocky and sometimes slippery.

From afar they observed the only place in the land they could actually call home. There was a great round citadel encircled by an impenetrable crenellated wall, with a glimmering white castle in the middle supported by arched buttresses and thick pillars, its bristling spire like a torch when struck by the light of the setting sun. Close to the castle there was a huge stone coliseum. Several conical watchtowers stood along the wall that surrounded the mighty fortress spaced at similar intervals of distance from one another.

A few meters before reaching the main gate, Arthur hoisted up a white banner, which he retrieved from his pouch, and began to wave it at the watchtowers above. At the entrance, the ten-meter wide and tall gate rose as the guards behind the parapet pried it open with the metallic levers. As they entered the fortress, Alice and Arthur informed the heralds about the lurid incidents, mostly relating the facts with clear difficulty.

"Yet, more of the same," said one of the heralds, writing down the report on a scroll as Arthur and Alice told the facts. He proceeded to seal it with a red ribbon. "Comrades, you can forget about Paris. The King has already, a long time ago, issued that the city be evacuated."

The next morning, marking the beginning of July, though cold and bleary, turned bright after sunrise, coloring the grass a vivid emerald hue, sparkling with dew. The sky was azure, bereft of menacing clouds that were now so often seen in Paris. After a turbulent sleep and after having eaten a healthy breakfast made up of greens and grilled meat, Alice and Arthur stood upon the white marble atrium before the barracks, and in front of a maroon statue made of steel. The barracks was a high, large and wide building, spanning at least two hectares of the fields. Most of it was made of granite and other stone, while some other parts, like the entrance, were marble. It could hold a population of thousands of knights, within two wards, where men and women were segregated respectively.

The statue stood upon a pedestal upon which there was a bronze plaque with the following words inscribed in it:

'To honor and remember his name: Marshal Montague, our greatest leader.'

Arthur stared forlornly at the statue, for it was his greatest figure and idol; it was the only remaining vestige of his illustrious father. He was an idol to all knights, not only to his son. He was considered the greatest defender and leader of the Order. The statue was an enduring representation of the most clever and strongest figure of leadership and companionship. He was commended as the most skilled and adept knight of all the Order, as well as the one most admired and loved. The figure itself was a man clad in armor and riding a horse as it reared back.

"Not even Notre Dame would make him cringe back," said Alice, glancing at him. Both were wearing the institutional uniform of the Order, which was composed of a woolen fabric in a certain color. Red represented the soldier knights, while heralds and couriers wore a blue one, and the Viceroy was clad in his own gold-colored livery. The *Fleur de Lis* symbol was emblazoned on the front and back of the uniform, underneath an image of two white knights clashing with jousting spears. Besides the fabric, the knights wore plated gauntlets and boots, and their pauldrons were made of scale armor.

"Unlike me, yes, most likely," answered Arthur glancing back at her. "Courage in flesh and bone, they say. And I ask myself whether I could reach his high standards by defeating the dangers that lie in wait in Notre Dame."

"Sooner or later you'll have a chance to excel. You just have to believe in yourself and know that nothing is impossible. Even the most insignificant forces, if given the right chance, can bring down the monumental ones," replied Alice, looking at Arthur. "Makes me think, by the way, that you want one of these statues for yourself," she added with a giggle.

"That sounds great, however," he said chuckling, and nodding at the statue, "somebody once told me 'Never wish for your tomb, as magnificent or honorable as it may come to be, for it is an omen that could bring you to an early demise.'"

"You better follow that advice to the letter," said Alice with a grin.

"Don't you worry," replied Arthur, smiling back. "I will."

A knight wearing the royal blue livery approached Arthur and Alice swiftly, the hooves of the horse making the dust swirl up.

"Marshal Arthur, new mission. You depart tomorrow in the morning," the herald said. He took out a rolled scroll sealed with a blue ribbon from a leather pouch attached to the belt, and handed it to him.

"Thank you," said Arthur. The herald rode away.

A shiver ran down Alice's spine when she saw the new assigned mission. But still, she was not completely sure that was the task she feared. She looked down, seeking nonexistent comfort, her heart racing. Arthur noticed her inquietude. He knew what troubled her.

"They are sending our Company into Notre Dame, aren't they?" said Alice with a shaky voice.

"Remember, I will not let anything happen to you. I understand your fears. Any man or woman would retreat immediately. Nevertheless, retreating means immediate expulsion from the Order. You know you don't want that either."

"I understand the risks and so I will travel with you," Alice replied. Arthur noticed some reluctance still in her voice. "I'll go tell Sonja," said Alice, looking into the distance. "I'm certain she is in the coliseum."

"I'll gather and inform the others to be prepared for departure," replied Arthur. "You don't have to come to the gathering if you don't want to. I'll see you at the stables for departure tomorrow afternoon."

"All right, then. I'll see you tomorrow," she turned around and headed toward the coliseum, following a road paved with stone.

Arthur glanced back at her and watched as she disappeared into the coliseum.

¤¤¤

The coliseum resembled the *Colosseo Romano* greatly, though this version was much smaller. It was made of blocks of granite. Its shape was rounded and had four entrances around the circumference. The entrances were all ninety degrees apart, as though they were following the compass rose. After the gates, there were corridors that turned either left or right toward the seats in the stands, or went straight into the battle arena. The coliseum was four stories tall with viewpoints along the circumference where the spectators stood and watched.

Alice crossed the gateway straight into the arena, where two knights were battling each other, swords clanging as they clashed against one another, while a group of three knights watched the fight at the edge of the ring. Each one wielded a wooden sword for sparring along with a rounded steel shield, and was clad in silver armor.

Alice waited for the match to be over.

Sonja deflected her rival's blade and lunged forward with a stab. Her opponent backed up and slashed upward, his sword skating off Sonja's shield. Both stepped back and stood still, glaring at one another, panting and sweating. Then they clashed with a swing, swords dancing as they struck one another's blade. Sonja disengaged and sidestepped, scarcely evading a thrust from her opponent and hitting him on the side of the face with her sword's hilt, knocking his helmet off his head and onto the ground. She proudly pointed her sword's tip at the loser's throat, and he, embarrassed, let his weapon drop. She withdrew her sword and sheathed it back in its scabbard.

She bowed and said: "Well done. Sorry for the blow on the head."

"At least I'm alive," replied the man while picking up his weapons, somewhat upset.

She smiled as the man turned around and trudged toward his teammates.

"I think you just humiliated him," said Alice at the edge of the arena.

"Not only him," replied Sonja as she turned around chuckling. "But them too, three times each." She approached Alice swiftly. Sonja was athletic-toned, but a few centimeters shorter than Alice. She had short straight auburn hair, silver-colored eyes and a straight nose. She noticed Alice's anxiety as soon as she stepped closer. "Alice…is everything all right?"

"I'll get straight to the point," said Alice. "Taurus Company is going into Notre Dame, and we depart tomorrow."

Sonja's jovial smile faded away completely. "All right, then I'll be prepared." She gripped her family heirloom, which was a golden medallion, hanging down from her sweaty neck.

Alice could not stand seeing herself reflected in Sonja.

"We are going in together and I will stand and fight by your side the whole time," promised Alice. "It's time for us to prove the meaning of our swordplay."

"Scorpio was crushed," muttered Sonja. "Why would we fare better than them?"

"Unlike them, we will have extra assistance; Capricorn Company will come along. It's a matter of perseverance and purpose. It's our strong will to survive that makes the difference between life and death. There will be sacrifices, for sure, but I promise you that we will prevail," said Alice, not only to reassure her friend but herself, too, by repeating and somewhat altering Arthur's words. It was an encouraging thought, and yet she knew that their chances of survival were slim.

"I've heard that what lies in there is not human," said Sonja. "And even so, the enemy must have outnumbered Scorpio; otherwise they couldn't have all been eliminated."

"That's what everybody believes, and certainly that is why we are two Companies together now," replied Alice, knowing that the truth about their foes was more than disheartening.

Sonja was uneasy. "It's like a death sentence," she said under her breath, not intending to have Alice hear her.

"I believe the same thing," said Alice, gesturing at Sonja's family heirloom. "Your father would be proud of you, of what you have come to achieve all this time."

Sonja nodded. "Our purpose is what matters, one worth dying for. We'll fight…to the last breath."

Alice looked into the distance. Her last day turned out to be like every other day…

Corvus

Alice mounted Bliss, her chestnut mare. She wore a chainmail coat, the livery of the Order, and silver plated armor. She put on her helmet and gripped the reins. Knights favored plated armor, even if it meant a reduction in speed and agility. Every knight received his or her plated armor according to their own size so that their movements were never hampered.

Alice slipped her steel broadsword into the scabbard, producing a steely rasp. The rounded shield had a special set of shackles that attached it to the wrist for better handling and movement. Then she hooked bow and quiver with a dozen white-feathered arrows to her back. Every knight had a leather pouch hanging by their belts where they stored medicinal herbs, fruit and bread, and an auxiliary, bigger pouch where they could stash away flint, tinder, and a little flask of oil. Some of the knights had horns hanging round their necks to call for aid. Their loud alarm calls could be heard within a long-range radius.

She and the other forty-nine knights were in the stables, getting ready for departure to Paris. Sonja was beside her, and Arthur stood at the head of the Company, observing his troops with brotherly pride.

Sonja climbed onto Syria, her white mare, who had been the closest thing she had had to a friend before she arrived at the White Bastion; the one with whom she had shared a sorrowful past and who remained loyal to the present. She gripped and secured her family heirloom under the cuirass: a very valued medallion gifted by her deceased father that depicted a shield crossed diagonally by two swords.

Arthur mounted his black stallion, and spurred the horse into a trot toward the end of the wooden building, the hooves of the horse thudding over the straw covered ground. Arthur came to a stop next to Antoine, Capricorn's Marshal.

Antoine was slender and of average height, jet black and trimmed short hair, dark eyes and several minor scars scattered over his face. He also appeared to be younger than Arthur. He was mounted on a dark brown horse and was clad in the silver armor. The gates creaked open and a refreshing breeze blew inside. Arthur faced his Company, his expression grave, and announced:

"A pleasure to fight alongside all of you!"

The Company lined up in rows and waited for the command of the Marshal. "We'll be right behind you. There will be a lag of about an hour while we haul the battering rams toward Notre Dame," said Antoine, beside Arthur.

Arthur nodded and raised his longsword skyward: "For the Viceroy! For the King! For France!" His Company rushed out of the stables and followed the dirt-track road toward the gates of the citadel, and out of the White Bastion…

¤¤¤

The setting sunlight was subjugated by the enormity of the menacing cloud. There were sudden violent gusts of biting wind that lashed at the knights and hindered their progress. Nobody had even conceived the idea that the weather would be altered. Not one of the fifty knights was wearing any fur to protect themselves from the bitter cold that rent through their armor. Alice quickly felt a series of shivers assailing her, her warm breath wafting away in small clouds white that were quickly dissipated.

When they saw the capital just a few kilometers away, Alice advanced toward Arthur and rode by his side.

"Look at that!" She pointed toward the city, trembling. "Where did that come from?" There, gigantic and looming upon the capital, was a dark and grim funnel-shaped cloud.

"It would be safe advice to stay away from it," Arthur replied, controlling his shivering. "Unfortunately, that's our mission, to disregard such warning signs. I would not be surprised if it became worse."

Upon reaching the gates in the walls, they noticed numerous caravans, crowded with people and littered with their belongings, leaving the city to move on to another. The citizens were now fleeing for good. It had all turned into an exodus.

Inside the capital, there was an odd sensation of sorrow, and, at the same time, the atmosphere felt heavy and compressed. There were strange currents of swirling wind, picking up dust and pieces of wood and carrying them aloft. The place was in much worse a state than it had been the day Arthur and Alice had been patrolling, just two days ago. Some buildings were completely demolished, while some others were crumbling almost to pieces: windows shattered and doors battered down, roofs blown off, or huge holes opened up in parts of the walls.

As they advanced further into the heart of the capital, the damage increased progressively. Up ahead, the dreaded Notre Dame cast its sinister shadow over the murky Seine. It was a high and rectangular structure with two towers and a round stained-glass window high in the middle of the façade, and it had three entrances: the portal of the Virgin, the portal of the Last Judgment and the portal of Saint Anne. At the top of the towers numerous gargoyles, poised upon eaves in a watchful position, leered down upon the Company as if waiting for the right moment to swoop down at them. All around, the trees were uprooted and plants were beginning to shrivel. With every gust of swirling wind, the ghost city howled in agony.

Duty and commitment to guard the kingdom from the rising dangers kept every knight determined to continue moving, even against the most adverse situation. All of the fifty knights were bound by honor and a moral code not to retreat, even if they were given the chance. The threshold into death was just ahead, across the fragile wooden bridge and through the three black iron-bound gates.

As the bridge began to creak noisily, each knight shared the same fear – that it would not hold long enough to hold the weight of fifty horses and riders. They crossed the bridge toward the Cradle of Paris, the hooves of fifty horses hammering on the rotting wood.

Arthur dismounted in front of the cathedral's atrium and announced: "Set the horses free! Keep in mind that we may not see the light again. I don't want them to follow our fate. Take the armor off them as well."

Alice had a hard time saying goodbye to her mare. She was bound to Bliss as her rider ever since being first assigned to her five years ago, and since then they had been an inseparable pair. They had been together so long that both seemed to understand one another and feel each other's sentiments of joy, distress and weariness. Alice's ordeal had come to this climax in which she would have to sever that long-forged, beloved link, given that chances of seeing Bliss again were almost nonexistent. As Alice struggled to contain her tears, she noticed that Sonja and many others were going through the same grief. She removed swiftly the silver armor that protected the mare's legs, head and back, and heaped it over the stony ground.

"Don't wait for me," Alice whispered, caressing the mare's muzzle. "Go back to the fields. Be free."Then she kissed Bliss' head and intimated freedom with a hesitant gesture. "Go."

"Let's go!" Arthur rallied his troops. They crossed the atrium, their armor creaking as they hurried forward. There were three sets of arches profusely carved with Christian figures above each pair of black metallic doors. Two knights filed out of the group and started unbarring the doors in the portal of the Last Judgment. Alice looked up and shuddered at the sight of the soaring building that harbored so many dark secrets yet to be discovered, stark and dark against the gray, troubled sky. She felt her limbs stiff, because of both the cold and the pain that fear had drowned out. Alice recoiled slightly as Sonja grabbed her gloved hand to give her a reassuring squeeze. Alice glanced at her and she saw that familiar look in Sonja's eyes that she frequently used to lift Alice's spirits.

Archers strung their bows and nocked arrows in the taut bowstrings, while infantry knights unsheathed broadswords, or readied their spears and halberds. The knights pushed the doors, which turned screeching upon their hinges, revealing nothing but wailing darkness, wind rushing in and out as if the knights were walking into the jaws of a gigantic beast.

"Leave them open," said Arthur as they entered the most feared place in France.

The Company lined up in five rows of ten, Arthur at the head of the group. Alice and Sonja blended in halfway along the fifth row. The stained glass windows up at the top of the building were shattered, and the broken glass inevitably made cracking noises as the knights stepped over it. Inside was darker, and yet the piercing wind entered freely. Alice and Sonja could feel the shivering of every knight around them: shaky and rapid breathing like theirs. Their echoes bounced off the walls, making them flinch at the noise.

They went through a wide and straight corridor into the main vaulted hall, flanked by columns. The great, extensive hall howled dismally as currents of wind rushed in through the shattered stained-glass windows, like the distant wail of the tormented. The baleful darkness consumed every part of the cathedral, and the lack of good visibility promoted ambush. Unlit torches were attached to the walls and pillars, but since they were all burned out, they were nearly useless. There were two rows of thirty wooden pews, all scratched and torn apart, and an enormous gilded altar far at the end of the hall. There were at least a dozen granite pillars at each side extending toward the end of the hall. The knights of the outer rows inspected the pillars, as in the dark anybody could be hiding behind them.

"Lieutenants Felix, Basil, Gerhard, Laz and Lucie", said Arthur, as they marched down the aisle in between the rows of torn pews. "Each of you will light and bear torches."

The five lieutenants knelt down, and as they extracted the flint and tinder from their auxiliary pouches, some other knights handed them a torch from the pillars. They coiled the tinder around the unused end of the wooden pole and produced sparks with the flint stones, immediately setting the torches ablaze. As they crackled into life the flames cast distorted shadows of the knights against the pillars and walls.

Lieutenant Lucie looked up from the torch and her gaze was

transfixed on the ceiling. "Look out!" she warned, pointing upwards.

All members of the Company looked up in unison and caught sight of the giant hole in the ceiling that loomed above them, where they could behold the terrifying funnel cloud. The mouth of the funnel was exactly above the altar.

Arthur walked over to it, onto the steps and looked skyward for a few seconds before turning around to face his troops, beads of sweat settling on his brow and neck. A lump had formed in his throat and he took a few seconds to swallow before speaking: "Lieutenants…split up into five groups of ten! One group for the second floor, another for the bell towers, another for the crypt, another for the churchyard, and the last group will stay right in this hall," he ordered. He paused and stood upright. "Blow the horns if anything happens. We meet again in one hour, right…"

"No, wait," Sonja interrupted suddenly, "there is no need to split up." She had moved outside the group and was squatting down, examining a trace of blood on the floor. The tiles were sprinkled crimson, dry, along with a couple of dark red hands smudged along as if someone had been crawling for dear life. Sonja sidled up, following the blood. Further into the shadows of the pillars, the shapes of the hands turned into deformed elongated stripes, as if that person had been dragged against their will. "It comes all the way from here," she pointed behind the columns. "Toward the crypt."

"The crypt?" echoed Arthur. "Sounds like the perfect place for an ambush. We need to send a reconnaissance team. Scouts Renée, Jackson, Christophe, Adrien and Charlotte. Blow the horns at the slightest sign of hostility."

The five scouts, wearing a lighter gear with a bow hooked to their backs, carrying horns and weapons ready, filed out of the group and strode toward the columns, turned and followed the blood traces, their steps fading in silence.

Arthur turned around to stare at the gilded altar, scanning its carefully decorated emblazonment, its flawlessly delineated lines that gave shape to its depictions. The golden cross, made with a material that was as luxurious as it was coveted, stood yet undefiled beneath the shroud of darkness. There was something that certainly disturbed Arthur. He looked up, troubled, finding no logical correlation to the positioning of the cloud over the altar. He could not determine what was making him so uneasy, whether it was something beneath the cathedral or the feeling that everything was going too quiet and smoothly, perhaps…too easy.

The knights scrambled around the hall in search of more clues. Alice sheathed her broadsword and approached Arthur.

"What if there isn't anything here?" she asked. Arthur flinched slightly because he did not hear her coming.

"There *is* something. I can feel it, as if we were being stalked."

Alice walked along the altar, gazing at the broken windows, the scratched pews and the stained columns and walls, as if she were recalling something.

"I've been here several times," she finally said, quietly. "All of which were a great waste of time…and energy."

"Why?" Arthur asked, as he turned to face her.

"It was a complete waste of time coming here to ask for help. I've already told you why. Foolish of me to think I'd receive any."

"Marshal Montague found you, did he not?"

"That was supposed to happen," replied Alice, raising her voice. Some knights glanced at them, troubled. She softened her voice, yet it was still with an angry tone. "And I stopped coming here years before he found me. It would've been better if it had been earlier."

"That doesn't mean someone couldn't have heard your prayers."

Alice caught a fleeting movement off the corner of her eye, right behind the pillars. She held her breath in a pause before replying to Arthur, her heart racing.

"You…may have sworn to me never to tell anyone about my disbelief. But I still don't understand why you want to force me to believe."

"It's not only because everybody thinks it's the right thing to believe, but because it's for your own sake. If they find out, you risk being executed," Arthur replied firmly. Someone had already found out; he had had to find a way to keep him quiet.

Alice twitched her head slightly to the side, letting her eyes flash almost undetectably toward the columns.

Arthur dimly perceived a flitting shadow slipping into a pillar as he followed Alice's eyes' pattern. Now both knights had their hands over their swords' hilts, their fingers flexing and curling over them, ready to clutch and draw them out.

"The right thing to believe?" scoffed Alice. "Do you know that those who claim to 'defend' Christianity, Templars, killed Sonja's father ten years ago? Just because they were 'defending' a belief."

"Well, we certainly need more heathens like you," called out a hoarse voice from behind the columns. A hooded man wearing dark robes appeared from out of the shadows. He had a crimson crow with its wings outstretched woven on his chest. His face was concealed. "You did well in refuting your unreal deity, for only one you shall serve and revere."

At the sound of the voice, Alice and Arthur unsheathed their swords. They pointed them toward the priest. In a matter of seconds, many knights realized what was happening, and quickly spread the word among them to aid their Marshal. Arthur held up his fist and the knights remained still.

"Those who dare trespass upon Antares' worship will burn in Tartarus, for eternity," the priest declared. He hurled at them a stained and broken horn. Alice and Arthur winced in disbelief. "You have just condemned yourselves by entering this sacred place. Although, not sacred to you."

"We are no Templars to judge you in that matter, but certainly you shall pay for all the lives your rites have taken away. You are under arrest by the Order of the Knights. May you be cleansed in Hell," said Arthur, loud enough to echo throughout the hall. "What kind of demonic powers have been bestowed on you to alter the will of Nature?" He pointed upward at the funnel cloud.

"Not demonic, but holy," the priest retorted. "Who else but Antares, the real god; the only god? Whoever stands between Him and His objectives shall be cast to the Tartarus, and face the Corvus!" He pointed at his chest; at the woven crow. "The Death embodied; a dark shadow upon the Void that sees everything and hears everything, the greatest Nemesis of every being; the force that controls the cycle of Life, creator of the Overworld and the Underworld, the scourge of Men and Dwellers, the bane of the Dark Lord: Corvus, shape of death."

"You have killed," Alice intervened, boiling with anger. "And you will pay dearly for it. You are the miserable reason we are here." She quickly sheathed her sword and drew her bow, pulled an arrow and set her aim on the priest. Arthur tried to block her, but Alice jerked back with the bow drawn and fired. The arrow met the priest at the chest.

"You know that is disrespectful?" he inquired as he beheld the moment Alice's arrow bounced off his chest, as if there had been an invisible barrier. "You should already know what a Harbinger is, since, I think, we are becoming famous. My name is Percival, Head Harbinger, and we have a message to deliver, straight from his lips, His Majesty, Antares: 'Rob the powerful of their wealth and dethrone them. Reap the souls of the innocent, the sheep, and give them eternal rest. Goeth forth, and bindeth the world in darkness,'" Percival recited solemnly. "And bound in darkness... it shall be." Alice realized that Percival's voice struck her as eerily familiar as he uttered his name.

"*We*?" snapped Arthur. At that moment, a thunderous boom made them all jump. The echo gradually began to die down in softer reverberations, and by and by, Percival replied:

"Indeed. Brethren, the time is ripe! The moon awakes now!" Hovering dauntingly over the cathedral, the funnel cloud opened up, revealing a nascent crescent moon, thin as a white thread and rounded as a perfect semicircle.

Four more men, hooded and wearing robes the same as Percival's, came out of the darkness into the dim light along the great pillars: two men at each side of the Company and there was fifth right behind them. And as they appeared, an invisible force began to compress the knights very tightly into a compact pack within the area of the pews. They were being pushed back against one another. There were five Harbingers: Percival to the northwest and another Harbinger to the northeast of the gilded altar behind the pillars; two more Harbingers stood at either side of the Company by the columns; and the last one right behind the knights, blocking the way toward the exit.

"The doors are shut. There is no getaway. You came too far, to no avail," announced the hooded figure right behind the Company, whose voice gave the impression that he actually was a young one.

"Cornered like the prey you are," said Percival with clear contempt.

There was a deafening wolf howl that boomed throughout the hall.

"William, first the rituals," said Percival with absolute calm. "Then you can have the leftovers." The man at the right side of the hall next to the knights began to pant like a dog. Fortunately, his face and muzzle were covered in darkness. "Also, remember that you need human form to work the summoning."

"Not if we arrest you first. We are forty-five against five," replied Alice unsheathing her broadsword and standing in combat position.

"You are under arrest," announced Arthur as he drew out his steel longsword. "By the Order of the Knights. There is no forgiveness for you. You may be judged in heaven, but not here."

"No, no, *you* are the ones who are outnumbered," replied Percival in the most solemn but gallant way. He bared his hands out of the darkness. His hood was pulled away by a strong howling wind. His eyes were wild. "In Antares' name, whose will be done, I invoke His vassals, in flesh and bone!"

The other four Harbingers did the same in unison. They spoke and chanted in an unearthly yet beguiling language, their bass voices deep and grave as their intonations echoed throughout the hall of Notre Dame: "*Vŏd dan eísod; braák da Mund aansund.*"

The ground below Alice and Arthur's feet began to change, too, with an intense white glow as they looked down with astonishment. A broad pentagram shimmered into existence. Arthur and Alice jumped off the platform and landed among the other forty-three knights in front of the altar. A dark, enthralling and spiraling vortex with fluctuating waves replaced the pentagram. It was a portal opened into another world, rupturing the space and time continuum to give way to Antares' vassals.

"Stop them!" yelled Arthur. Archers shot arrows at the Harbingers, which broke and shattered in contact with the invisible barriers. Therefore, they were forced to switch to swords or spears. The swordsmen tried to lunge at the priests, but every slash and thrust was in vain. Their swords only stopped short near contact, as if time itself slowed down, until they pulled them back.

"Too late," said Percival.

The vortex flashed in the knights' eyes with a sudden illumination, blinding them momentarily, as a powerful wind rushed into it, roaring vehemently, as if sucking in the air to compensate a vacuum. Screeching and shrieking, a swarm of giant bats crossed the threshold of the otherworldly portal into the Overworld. They rose up and soared over the halls, fluttering and flapping their leathery wings. With beady eyes they locked on their targets and hurtled down headlong toward the knights, going in for the kill. Their body size was similar to a big dog's and their unfurled wings were each one meter long.

To counter, the knights who wielded swords fixed their shields up over their heads and those who wielded a spear or a halberd pointed the weapons upward for the vampires to pierce themselves on the tips. After the first wave of attack, some vampires had died skewered, and those that were still alive learned the strategy the knights were using to counter them. During the second wave, the vampires hurtled down and lunged at the knights, and just before touching the tips the vampires spun and evaded the weapons, biting and tearing out their victims' throats.

They, as well, had to switch strategy and they then swung their swords at the vampires. Meanwhile, some of the Harbingers laughed and beheld the scene with joy. There were screams of pain, war and fear echoing throughout the halls.

In the end, when all the vampires had died and their corpses lay around, there were forty knights in total. The few that had fallen were lying among the crowd and were being mourned by their comrades.

"Stop this now!" shouted Alice in the middle of the crowd. "You gain nothing by killing us!"

"Oh yes, we gain A LOT!" exclaimed Percival. "Your bodies may be expendable, but your souls are…rather essential. The souls are for curing a god and summoning his vassals and servants! Let us see what you do against a horde of *reptilians*!"

"You are nobody's servants! Just bloody puppets being pulled by a string!" shouted Alice.

"Speaking of which, isn't this is one of those places where the puppets are made?" mocked the Harbinger at her right side, who had been watching silently the whole time. "Your society is nothing else but primal under the rule of a tyrant."

"An Englishman!" exclaimed Arthur, as he held down his stained longsword. "No doubt this is one of Edward's schemes."

"Edward?" the Harbinger sneered as the marks on his body began to glow red and white again. "That bloody Monarch? No, he's just a bloody puppet, like you, lad!"

"Be quiet, Siegfried!" snapped Percival, the runes glowing more and more. "The reptilians await their summoning!"

"This could last forever!" announced Arthur to his Company. "They are immune to our attacks. Pull back! To the exit!"

The Harbinger right behind the Company blocked their way with an invisible barrier. The Company split in half to the sides, racing toward the lateral exits, their hearts pounding heavily. All of a sudden, there was a strident roar behind: the roar of a monster.

Alice desperately looked for either Sonja or Arthur. She screamed their names several times in the hope that they would hear her. Finally, while running, a female voice answered her.

"I'm right here, Alice," called out Sonja at her side. "Keep running!" there was not any trace of Arthur.

The knights at the head of the group started trying to pry the doors of the western façade open. However, they would not budge. Then they tried pounding on the doors. Again, they did not budge.

"The doors are barred from the outside!" shouted one of the knights at the front.

Sonja tapped Alice's shoulder. "Alice, brace for combat!"

Behind, from out of the veil of darkness, five lizard-men appeared. The reptilians were burly, heavy and twice as tall as an average man, their scales ranging from green or golden to blue or red. They were clad in a murky bronze armor that consisted of a cuirass for their voluminous chests, a pair of pauldrons for their strong arms and shoulders, greaves for their shins, and a helmet that fitted their roughly triangular heads, all the while each brandishing two long scimitars and two lead shields that were hooked onto their scaly wrists, just the same as those of the knights. A dorsal crest of spikes jutting out of their backs ran all the way from their heads to the tips of their tails.

With their golden viper eyes, they beheld with greed their cornered prey, their forked tongues slithering out of their long narrow snouts.

The crowd of knights stared in fear at their deadly enemies, not willing to attack. Twenty knights, of the highest ranks and most arduous training in Europe, subjugated and intimidated by five hellish beasts.

Both groups kept on glaring at each other, as if the reptilians were waiting for any sudden or aggressive movements. One reptilian tilted its head and bared its long and sharp fangs, releasing a violent and prolonged hiss. As this happened, they could hear at the other side of the cathedral the beginning of battle of the other half of the Company: swords clashing and clanging, knights' screams and reptilians' roars.

The five knights at the front of the group decided to attack first. Without mercy, the reptilians countered their swords with bestial ferocity and inhuman celerity, cleaving armors, denting weapons and slicing bodies without any difficulty.

Alice and her comrades watched and winced in horror as their fellow knights slumped lifeless to the ground. With war screams, the fifteen knights now were aroused and eager to kill their enemies. They darted forth and attacked in unison the feral reptiles.

The reptilians held their ground tight, countering slashes and thrusts with their scimitars, blocking with their lead shields and swirling around at high speed, whipping with their pointy tails.

Among the uproar, Alice barely managed to dodge a slash and sink her broadsword into a reptilian torso. It was only for a split second, which for Alice seemed like an eternity. The monster glared at her with its golden slit-eyes as the blade went straight through its hulking chest. It was a piercing gaze of hatred and incredulity; a gaze that hypnotized its prey. The trance was broken as soon as the reptilian freed a deafening roar thirty centimeters away from Alice's face, releasing putrid breaths of rotten meat, its crocodile fangs and its slimy maw dangerously close to her head.

By acting instinctively against the roar, to back off, Alice let go of the sword's hilt, staring aghast at her agonized enemy. The reptilian bent its knees, panting heavily, gripped the sword's hilt, as if trying to withdraw the blade, which was already in vain, its forked tongue slithering out. It slumped with a thump to the stone floor and lay motionless.

At least ten more knights fell, and those who had survived the skirmish now were too exhausted for another battle. The five reptilians had been overwhelmed and lay among the dead knights.

With huge loathing and great struggle, Alice managed to move the dead reptilian onto its flanks to remove her tainted broadsword. The other three knights blessed and mourned their fallen comrades as quickly as they could because the battle at the other side of the cathedral was still raging on.

But right before getting into action, with horror, Alice and Sonja made out a familiar and painful scream: Arthur's scream. Alice took off in a race against the clock before her Marshal and lifetime friend could die, Sonja and the other three knights behind her, their hearts pounding heavily in their ears, hoping half-heartedly to find anyone alive, but Alice mostly hoping for Arthur to be.

When the massacre came into sight, all their gaze met with was a graveyard, all nineteen warriors and reptilians lying on the ground. Then, Alice and Sonja locked eyes with Arthur: a kneeling knight with the tip of a reptile's tail stuck into his right arm. Alice watched horrified as her friend withdrew his sword from a reptilian torso, his right arm stinging in pain as the tail tip's needle retracted from his skin. Then they noticed that the beast did not have legs at all, but a huge serpent trunk ending in a poisonous tail tip.

The dead reptile fell to the ground with a thud, and Alice ran over to Arthur and hugged him as if she had not seen him in a long time. She took her helmet off, tears streaking her grimy face, tears of joy, pain, loss and hopelessness in a hectic combination of feelings.

"Reptilian poison," the voice laughed. The six remaining knights were startled and turned back to face the Harbinger. "A shame it won't kill you before the next new moon. You have at least a month. Well, that's if you survive the troops of Antares rising upon your world, mortal."

The knights recognized the Englishman's voice.

Siegfried came out of the darkness, behind the group of knights, grinning.

"Don't, Alice!" Arthur tried to stop her by holding her back, but she released herself in no time. Alice bolted up and rushed toward the Harbinger, wrath flowing freely through her veins.

She raised her sword and thrust it forward.

Her broadsword stopped short near contact; she was paralyzed, as if time itself had frozen, right before Siegfried's face.

With a wave of his hand, Alice was repelled, thrown back like a puppet, and went skidding on her back down the hall, coming to a halt against a pillar.

"All mortals are always the same, thinking they can beat anything that stands on their way," commented Siegfried with contempt in his voice.

The other four Harbingers appeared behind him, their hoods hanging over their necks, their hands hidden beneath their long and black sleeves.

"William Bloodthorn, all yours," said Percival. "This number of souls should be enough." He raised his scarred right hand. A ripple of murmurs broke the sepulchral silence as a thread of faint white light ran all the way from his palm to the fingertips and faded into darkness: the souls. "No Asphodel or Elysium for them, not even Tartarus," he said as he hid his hand again.

The Harbinger at the left side began to transform. A painful procedure of becoming a lycanthrope, as his reactions proved. His mouth and nose started to transform into a wolf snout, his ears elongated into a tip, his eyes became gold and they grew, and his head and body began to grow gray fur. Claws and fangs gave the final twist to the transformation.

"What is that noise?" mumbled William as his wolf ears fluttered and traced the sound, searching for its emitter. Alice had not heard anything, but because of the werewolf's reaction, she knew backup had arrived.

The five knights were too stunned and terrified to speak. And yet, Alice steeled herself and stood up again.

"You look defenseless enough without your sorcery," she declared defiantly.

"You certainly should be grateful, for you will be sent to Tartarus for sure. It's better than fading into nothing," said the fifth Harbinger, with a sudden flash in his eyes.

Alice looked down at Arthur, who was bent on his knees. Her hope that there was still a minimal chance to survive the ordeal rekindled inside her. Nevertheless, Arthur was poisoned, and getting away alive was not that much of a relief for him anymore. "What is the cure for the poison?" demanded Alice.

"Why would you want it when you are so close to death?" Percival inquired disdainfully.

"Because we still have a chance to survive," replied Alice at the time battering rams broke through all three entrances of Notre Dame.

Alice helped Arthur stand up, curling his left arm above her neck. Sonja and the other three knights raced toward the exit as a volley of arrows whistled past their heads, bouncing off the barriers of the Harbingers. Ahead, an entire Company was waiting for them, above an utterly black sky and a haunting crescent moon. Before exiting the building, Sonja turned to check on Alice, who was struggling to save Arthur's life and hers. She sprinted back toward them.

Alice tried to run, while at the same time help Arthur reach safety. William, the werewolf, growled and leaped forward. Alice could not advance more than two meters before William pounced on her, sending Arthur to the ground, rolling to the side like a ragdoll.

Alice, face up and back against the stone floor, gasped and struggled to keep William's muzzle away from her face by holding his snout back with her forearms and kicking his stomach, the stench of death filling her nose. His fur was filthy and stained with dried blood. Small dreadful glimpses of his brow revealed two bloodshot and fiery eyes, and several scars covering his face. William managed to twist his muzzle and break through Alice's defenses and bite her wrist. His sharp fangs immediately went through her silver gauntlet and she cried out in agony.

Seconds later, there was a howl of pain: Sonja arrived with her sword ready and slashed the lycanthrope's back. William rolled to the side, giving Alice enough time to back up. Feeling dizzy and losing balance, as swiftly as she could, she picked Arthur up again and went limping toward the exit where the Company was waiting for them. William turned enraged to face Sonja and then Alice with blood dripping down his fangs. Before he could attack again, Sonja stood between him and Alice. He focused his golden slit-eyes on Sonja and howled with vigor.

"None will intervene in this battle," Siegfried chuckled behind the combatants, hidden in the darkness. "This looks interesting. None had ever challenged William in such a fight."

A halo of faint light materialized around Sonja and William Bloodthorn, locking them in a ring for a death match.

"Retreat!" Alice and Arthur shouted in unison just before exiting the cathedral, freedom and life within their reach. Alice released Arthur, ran over to the boundaries of the ring and tried with all her willpower to get into the ring, pounding on the invisible barrier pushing her back as tears streamed down her face. Despair overwhelmed her as, trembling sickeningly, she realized it would be impossible to intervene.

"To the last breath, remember?" said Sonja, oddly, with an aura of tranquility shining around her, glancing back at Alice. "I'll give this scoundrel what he deserves. Go now. I am giving you enough time for your retreat," she tore her most valued family heirloom from her neck, the Krauss medallion, and hurled it to Alice. She nearly dropped it to the ground out of shock and confusion, her hands shaking.

"No…why…you…?" she faltered. Her heart thumped wildly. It was that moment when she realized there was nothing that could be done to avoid losing the one she loved.

"Farewell, Alice. I told you to go now."

"Have a good night!" exclaimed Percival as Alice was shot by an invisible force out of the cathedral and landed on the dirt and among the Company, her world turning upside down, her life shattering, powerless to save Sonja, and at the same time, the gates of Notre Dame reformed and closed in a crash…

The Fall

"Where did you get that medallion?" asked a little girl of about thirteen years old. She had wavy brown hair, green eyes and an upturned nose. She was wearing red livery, an emblem painted on her chest and back which showed a confrontation between two white knights, both with a jousting spear and, beneath, *La Fleur de Lis*. Another little girl of about the same age stood in front of Alice. She had straight auburn hair, silver-colored eyes and a straight nose. She was wearing the same livery.

Sonja Krauss looked troubled and uneasy. "Do you mean my family heirloom?" she asked, unconsciously touching the amulet where it hung down her neck: a glittering golden medallion depicting a shield crossed by two swords.

Alice Houdin nodded. "It's beautiful! I like it a lot!"

"It's a gift from my father. He gave it to me just before I came here."

"Have you seen him lately?"

"No…I haven't, not in a long time…" Her eyes started to well up with tears, but she turned her head a little to prevent Alice from noticing.

"What happened to him?" Alice felt a twinge in her heart. She thought she knew what had happened to him. Alice could feel her pain. She had never met her own father, or at least, she did not remember, and her mother had been murdered a long time ago. "I understand, don't tell me if you don't want to."

"No, I do want to tell you. I have to tell someone," Sonja

steeled herself. "I trust you, I do. You won't tell anybody about it. Promise me!"

"I promise. You can trust me," Alice smiled sympathetically. It was a smile that made Sonja feel confident.

"I never knew much about what he usually did. Sometimes, he would call himself an inventor and a discoverer of new... things," she swallowed and paused a moment. "Sometimes, he didn't come home; I think he was hiding from the city guards. I never knew whether he was doing anything wrong. I now know that he never did anything wrong. He was a man who had great ideas that would benefit everyone." She paused again. "One day, he arrived, shaking from head to toes, stuttering when he tried to speak. He told me I would have to leave home; he would not be coming with me. Viceroy Nicholas was a great friend of his, and he made the difficult decision of sending me to the Order of the Knights." She blinked a tear off. "He gave me this medallion, which is the symbol of our family. That's when I left with my mare, Syria, toward the White Bastion." With trembling hands, she touched and glanced at the golden medallion.

"What about your other relatives?" Alice asked.

"My mother died during my birth. My other relatives are either dead or far from here, maybe in the Holy Roman Empire," Sonja answered, gazing at her heirloom.

"What happened to your father?" Alice asked in a soft voice.

"Templars," said Sonja with distaste. "They killed him because he did not believe. They had already blackmailed him since he had tried to claim that the teachings of the Church were not real. He had discovered new perspectives in the world that could have improved our society, he used to say. A new way of life: easier, richer and better. When you prove them wrong, you're just looking into the maw of death."

"I'm sorry about that," Alice muttered, thinking that maybe Sonja was feeling the same way she was. Then she asked: "Do you not believe?"

Sonja looked nervously around her to see if anyone were eavesdropping on their conversation. She shook her head. "And you?"

"There are many reasons why I do not..." In the blink of an eye, Sonja had faded away, and Alice was back in the real world...

¤¤¤

Alice awoke coughing hard. Her head was resting upon Arthur's lap as he knelt down, staring at her glumly. The other men of the Company were smashing the gates of Notre Dame with the battering ram. There were at least thirty knights, some of whom were holding torches. Arthur helped her stand up; due to her concussion it was difficult for her to do it alone. Alice's vision was somewhat blurry, since she could only make out the blazes of fire as fuzzy yellow sparks under an utterly black sky.

"Are you all right?" Arthur asked with concern, though Alice could barely see his face. "I thought you had fainted."

"I'm fine," she said curtly, and then as though she had just released herself from a drowsy trance she asked. "Where is Sonja?" Then the devastating memory struck her like lightning.

She saw how useless it was for the battering rams to smash the doors that way. They had not even scratched the surface. There must have been some kind of invisible barrier protecting the gates.

Then a frightening wolf howl boomed from the inside of Notre Dame and it kept echoing through the night. It was a howl of satisfaction and victory. Sonja had been defeated in battle.

Alice understood. She felt the same way as when her mother was murdered—as if her sister had just been killed. The pain was so intense that her knees buckled and she knelt down on the dirt.

"Sonja, humble and courageous, rest in peace, outstanding soldier. You have won the right to be called a hero," recited Arthur as tears streaked down Alice's grimy face.

The fact that they were allowed to leave Notre Dame unharmed disturbed Arthur. Those five vicious men alone had the capacity to eliminate thirty more knights, and yet they had been set free.

"Marshal Antoine, tell your men to stop smashing the gates!" Arthur ordered. "We have to retreat! Not even the entire kingdom will be able to defeat these threats. Let Paris fall into oblivion. It cannot be recovered."

Alice felt something in her fingers. She looked down and her grief increased when she realized that Sonja's family heirloom was still with her, in her trembling hand. She clenched her fist over the amulet and then left it hanging around her neck and hidden beneath her cuirass. For her, the medallion represented the only tangible remnant of her friend.

"Come, Alice. We have to go. Things can turn worse than they already are," said Arthur.

Alice nodded feebly, not wanting to go. Her legs trembled weakly and her vision was spinning slightly. She was extremely pale, but darkness would prevent the others noticing.

"Capricorn Company will, hopefully, lend us a horse to ride back to the White Bastion along with them," commented Arthur. Alice was staring blankly at the ground. The intense sorrow caused her to tremble strongly, and a feeling of nausea formed in her throat. "Come on, not everything is lost yet. There is still a purpose in our lives worth fighting for." Arthur stepped in front of Alice, holding her shoulders and looking her straight in the eyes. "We have to keep on living. You have to, even after all your losses, our losses. I know you, Alice. You are strong and have a heart of gold. Don't *ever* let anyone make you feel less than you are. Don't lose your faith just yet. We will prevail. We still have a commitment to fulfill, and that is to rid the kingdom of men like them. France needs you; *I* need you, please. You have to overcome your grief and put it away for now!"

As he talked to Alice, the knights stopped smashing the gates. The battering ram had four free-spinning wheels. It had a platform for the ram's operator to stand on. And the end was a silver ram's head. A knight bound two horses to the ram's handle and made them pull it from the cathedral toward the bridge.

Marshal Antoine rode over to Alice and Arthur, his helmet upon his lap. With one hand he was maneuvering the reins of the bridle and with the other holding up a torch.

"We barely made it on time," he said with a brooding voice. "A few moments later and you wouldn't be alive."

"It's not your fault," Arthur sighed and then replied. "We didn't act fast enough. I underestimated them. But for now we should leave as soon as possible; they might change their minds and come back for us."

"I've already ordered my men to retreat," Antoine answered

pointing at the battering ram that was being pulled down to the bridge. His thirty troops were now mounting their horses and crossing the Seine.

"Sir Christophe!" Antoine called out. One of the knights made his way toward them, riding a bay. "Marshal Arthur and Lady Alice need a horse. Find somebody else to share with."

"Indeed, Marshal." The knight complied and headed back on foot toward the whole of the Company.

Arthur chuckled. "That was a little harsh."

He turned to face Alice, who continued to stare blankly ahead. She was, as well, kneading her right wrist, her wounded wrist. The stinging pain no longer bothered her. It was dripping blood.

"Let me see your wound," Arthur said, taking hold gently of her arm without waiting for her to offer it herself. Antoine held the bay by the reins as he waited for Arthur.

"Marshal, with all due respect, I think we've lingered here long enough. Can you finish checking on her injury when we've crossed the bridge?" he asked with a beseeching grimace.

Arthur nodded slightly, staring at Alice with genuine concern. He pulled her after him to cross the bridge, while Antoine rode closely behind them, shooting quick glances at the haunted cathedral.

The crescent moon gleamed white as a thread of faint light above the undisturbed Seine. The pitch-dark along with the flicker of the numerous torches caused the buildings and structures around to cast frightening shapes. The howling gusts had stopped and there was a soft breeze.

Arthur stopped short in the middle of the avenue. He stretched out Alice's arm and scrutinized it in the little light that his eyes could catch. The other thirty knights were crowded behind them on the sidewalks, either on foot or horseback, waiting for their commander's signal.

"Marshal, I could use some light over here," said Arthur without taking his sight off Alice's arm. Antoine dismounted his horse and pulled both it and the bay after him by the reins, and held up the torch next to Alice's arm. Arthur glanced at her and noticed that her eyes were distant, still with a blank gaze.

Gently, Arthur unstrapped the silver gauntlet, slipping it off.

Alice finally reacted to the pain and groaned. She glanced at her arm and then locked eyes with Arthur. He knew that gaze well: a gaze of despair and distress. Concealing his horror, Arthur examined the wound closely.

"This injury is grave. I am certain his fangs were filthy. You'll get ill if we don't treat it now. I have some medicine down here in my pouch."

"What the hell happened to her?!" Antoine exclaimed, aghast. "Did a giant wolf bite her?"

"Well, as a matter of fact, it was a *werewolf*," Arthur replied while fumbling in his leather pouch for herbs.

Arthur took out a handful of dried green herbs and crumbled them to tiny bits, then placed them all over Alice's forearm and began to pat them to cover the holes made by William's fangs.

Alice grimaced in pain. She tried with all her will to shut down all of her emotions. She wanted to remain stoical. When Arthur looked up at her, she could but smile weakly, a smile that barely overcame all grief.

Suddenly, Antoine's horse went mad, struggling to be released of the reins. And he was not the only one having trouble. Soon, all the horses began to stamp their hooves on the cobbled ground, clacking noisily in unison, jerking their heads from side to side to loose themselves from the riders' grip. They neighed wildly, rearing back on their hind legs to throw the knights off the saddles and then rushed off.

"Troy, calm down!" shouted Antoine, pulling back on the reins. The horses began to gallop down the street; Antoine was thrown to the scabrous ground and dragged along as they tried to flee the place. He released the reins after three meters of being scraped all over his body, realizing how his efforts to calm down the steeds were useless. Astonished, he staggered onto his feet and went back to retrieve the torch from the ground.

"By experience, I can tell you horses sense trouble beforehand," said Arthur.

"It would be more useful if I weren't on the ground...," Antoine replied. "So what's happening?"

"Unfortunately, I think we're still in the frying pan," replied Arthur. "And ready to go out into the fire..."

Arthur and Alice looked around. They did not see anything. All Capricorn Company drew weapons, including Alice and both Marshals.

Suddenly, the land rumbled, then again and over and over again at intervals of five seconds every time, each stronger than the one before.

"This is not an earthquake," Antoine gasped, terrified.

What then boomed throughout the city was something far from their expectations. It was the roar of a legendary creature, one that they knew only too well from their own myths: a monster feared by many and known as the maximum predator and the lord of the skies.

Immediately after the roar, Notre Dame's ceiling exploded and went soaring through the skies. A monumental head burst through the remains of the cathedral. It was the head of a mighty dragon, its entire body as large and tall as the cathedral itself. It raised its head and turned to face the sky, and contracting its hulking chest, it shot a gigantic blaze that momentarily illuminated the skyline. Its scales glittered black against the flames. It had a long pointed snout under which its long fangs and forked tongue were concealed. Its golden slit-eyes gazed around the ruins of Paris. It lifted up its soaring scaly wings, and unfurled and shook them vehemently, creating a furious gale. The beast stood completely still, grappling its massive claws into the ground and folding its large wings behind its back.

Progressively, all around the atrium of the cathedral and farther away, crossing the bridge into the streets, several spots of stone began to shimmer white and curse marks appeared upon them. Alice and Arthur perfectly recalled what those things were. A chill went down their spines.

"We cannot deal with this!" Arthur yelled at Capricorn Company, whose leader was so dumbfounded that he was unable to give any orders. "Go now!"

Instinctively, he grabbed Alice's hand and she let him lead the way. But before they could move, Alice gasped and tripped over. With her heart pounding heavily in her ears, she looked down to see a huge, misshapen and purple hand holding her tightly by the ankle. The hand was poking out from a swirling vortex perilously close to her.

"No!" Arthur shouted as the hand began to drag Alice down into the vortex with incredible strength.

Alice was clinging with all her willpower to the surface, grasping Arthur's arms and clawing the ground.

"Go to the White Bastion! Tell the Viceroy everything!" Antoine yelled at his troops. He turned back to aid in Alice's rescue. He rushed toward the vortex, unsheathed his longsword and stabbed the back of the disfigured hand, black goo splattering the blade. The monster seemed immune to pain and just intensified the grip on Alice's ankle, pulling her down even harder. Antoine lunged again and just before making contact with the hand, a thick brownish layer covered it. The sword clanged back, releasing sparks. A powerful shell was draped over the hand.

All around them, hellish hordes emerged from the deeps of the Earth. At that moment, the Earth itself was starting to turn inside out. As paws, claws, talons, hooves and hands poked out onto the Overworld, monsters and demons began to drag themselves out onto the surface. As the monster pulled Alice even harder to raise itself up and out of the vortex, its head became visible. Its eye sockets were empty and spilling the same black goo. Its cheekbones were high and protruding. Its putrid skin was dark purple, but the most terrifying aspect to its appearance was its jaws: a huge pit crowned by ridged fangs. While emerging itself, it was dragging Alice and both Marshals down into the Underworld, the ghoul releasing reeking breaths and disturbing wails. Despite all its deformities, the thing gave the certain impression that it had been human once.

Antoine struck the ghoul's head with a thrust, sinking the sword all the way through its face, goo splattering on the blade and the ground. He withdrew and struck again, but this time the head was draped with the same shell. He stamped the ghoul's face and pushed it downward into the void. Still with a hole through its face, the ghoul was willing to fight its way up, struggling against Antoine's armored boot and thrashing with its second hand.

Suddenly, Alice noticed how all the troops of the Underworld had begun to unearth and populate the land. Soon enough, the three of them would be overrun and killed. Her mind raced back to her earliest memories, ranging from her childhood, her arduous experience that had hardened her to become a warrior, the moment her mother was murdered before her eyes, the day she was dubbed a knight, until this actual day, seconds before her untimely death. Her own life depended on whether both Marshals lived or died. Alice was not willing to let them get killed as well. She realized it was vital she was left behind. As Sonja's time had arrived, hers had too.

"Arthur, let go of me," she groaned, and then louder, "now!"

"Never," he managed to say. "Over my dead body," he replied while hardening the grip on her wrist, while Antoine shoved away the ghoul's jaws.

"That's what you're going to be if you don't release me now!"

Arthur shook his head, his eyes sparkling.

"Just look around you! There's no more time left!" Alice began to struggle her wrist against Arthur's grip. "There is still a reason to keep on living, a purpose worth fighting for, and that is to rid France of men like them. You have to overcome your grief and put it away for now!"

Behind, ten meters away from their location, another ghoul was emerging, with its misshapen hand gripping the surface. Before them, more reptilians and ghouls were rising. Farther away on Notre Dame's atrium and on the avenue next to the Seine, an army was being born.

"No, I can't let you go," he implored. "I don't want to, even if it means to risk my life. Even if it means to get myself killed as well! You are all I have left now! Come on, you can still survive!" His despairing voice softened. "Just, don't give up."

"Rid France of its ailments. Forgive me, Arthur, farewell..." She gave Arthur one last dismayed glance; one of sorrow, but at the same time, of grace and gratitude. Alice yanked her arm down, and that is how she released herself from Arthur's grip and was immersed into the abyss. With one last muffled scream from Arthur, she finally let her destiny carry her away in the cradle of death and plunged into the depths of the Earth. The vicious ghoul was still holding her tight by the ankle as she was submerged in the blackness of the Underworld...

Dawn and Dusk

Everything seemed to happen in slow motion after Alice's submersion in the vortex, through the emerging demons. At the moment she had fallen, Arthur screamed in disbelief.

Something must have changed drastically because of Alice's death.

Nothing had changed.

She was gone forever, and yet nothing had changed.

Everything was the same as ever.

Alice had only been another hindrance of whom the Harbingers had disposed successfully. Arthur knew who the perpetrators of her death were. An unfathomable anger flowed through his being. He was not bothered about the incredible amount of wrath he felt. Arthur felt the urgent need to make things even. For the first time in his life he desired revenge.

"Marshal…," Antoine gasped, "the monster followed her down the hole…"

Arthur was so dismayed and furious he had not noticed. Immediately, that matter was erased from his memory as he glanced back at the multiple vortexes rupturing open around them. He was not frightened of being overrun anymore. He rose from the floor and gripped tight the sword's hilt, scraping the scabbard's leather as the sword slid out.

After realizing what Arthur was thinking, Antoine finally reacted: "No, Marshal! We are leaving now, while we still have a chance!"

Arthur went on regardless. "Not before I am finished with this filth!"

"Wait, Marshal, don't!" Antoine tried to seize hold of his arm when he took off. Arthur sprinted toward the nearest vortex and pointed the tip of the blade above a reptilian that was still rising up from the portal. It peered up and saw Arthur's sword hanging above its head. Before it could react, startled as it was by the towering figure of the silver knight, the blade went through its head.

Restless and swift as the wind, Arthur went from vortex to vortex plowing his sword into them to kill whatever creature was climbing up. Despite the large amount of enemies that were climbing onto the surface, he was not daunted and kept on slaughtering them, all of them, except for the ghouls. Every time he stabbed one, it rapidly cowered into its protective shell.

Arthur had only killed a dozen enemies when he realized it was going to be impossible to stop them all. Around the cathedral's atrium, hundreds of Dwellers had already risen. Closer to them on the avenue, there were still several vortexes and more of them started to open. If they did not leave soon they would be surrounded.

"Get over it!" Antoine raised his voice at Arthur as he looked at the oncoming horde. He lowered his voice. "You can't face them. Think about it carefully, my friend: Alice, she didn't give her life away to save *us* so then you could go on a massive onslaught that will get us both killed. I beg you…she begged you!"

While huffing and puffing, Arthur managed to nod as he glared at the army, his eyes brimming with tears. He made a great effort to calm down while reflecting on what Antoine had told him. He felt a rush of guilt because he had ignored Alice's final wishes.

Antoine had his sword unsheathed and now was standing against Arthur's back: "We are being surrounded." Toward the avenues more Dwellers were climbing up.

The mighty dragon stood completely still, its keen gaze peering around the world that was new to it, waiting for orders from the Harbingers of its lord, Antares. It noticed the commotion down in the avenues of the ruined city. It watched how Arthur skewered the lesser fiends as they emerged on the avenue, as though it was watching how ants fight each other for territory. It just ignored the mayhem.

In front of Arthur and Antoine, a whole demonic army sprawled over the heart of the once graceful city. Arthur watched how a serpent reptilian crept above a portal, the kind of beast that had marked his destiny. The one characteristic that made it different from the others was the sturdy serpent trunk ending in a poisonous tail tip, a needle thin and small as the sting of a bee. They coiled up and stood upon their tails to intimidate their prey. Arthur had already experienced how deceptive their movements could be.

Vampires flapped their large leathery wings upon the troops as they tried to find their targets, otherwise they would have been the first creatures to attack, since they were the fastest.

For the first time, the knights saw the complete physique of the ghouls, since now they were standing up. They looked mostly like zombies, but the most characteristic aspect of their body was their legs. Besides the fact that their entire body was misshapen and scabby and purple, and their faces gaunt and missing the eyes, their legs resembled trunks of oaks, the toes branching into what seemed to be the roots; twisted, twirled and gnarled brownish toes.

The ghouls Arthur had wounded were behind him and Antoine, blocking the way and lumbering toward them, though now their protective shell was gone, and more enemies were still emerging. They could still make it through the city alive if they managed to pass through the gaps the ghouls and portals left between them.

"We are running out of time, thanks to you, by the way," Antoine mumbled.

Right there and then is when Arthur finally made his move: "Let's fly," he said as both knights, weapons ready, raced into the streets, zipping through the gaps their enemies made, as the ghouls sluggishly swung their long and burly arms at them as they passed, missing by a few centimeters.

The dragon watched everything, how the knights outwitted the undead and made their way out of the city. It made a growling noise within its throat, a noise at a frequency so low nobody could have heard it. And soon it got its response.

"Not to worry, your Majesty," Percival answered. "Engulfed in your mighty blazes they shall be, but there is no need to hasten, not quite yet. Their world will burn soon enough, all still according to plan…"

"And the woman? She entered Antares' domain unscathed," the dragon replied.

"A vile human will do no harm, Kronnix, "Percival answered. "Lord Hades will deal with Alice, and I, personally, will make sure she becomes a new resident of the Tartarus…"

¤¤¤

As she dashed her way down into the abode of the dead at suffocating speeds, Alice unsheathed her broadsword and turned backward to face the enemy that had dragged her into Hell. She could not make out anything around her, only that the background was blurry and grayish.

While falling, Alice jabbed the ghoul once more, and before she could hit twice, it was already under its shell, still trying to bite her. The massive figure held on to Alice by her ankle, and it was her leg the ghoul was anchoring to. Half-blindly, because of the speed and the whipping air, the wind thundering in her ears, she slashed the monster multiple times, the weapon clanging and sparking. To release herself from the beast's grasp, she also tried to kick the ghoul away. But its grip was still as firm and tight as a giant rock's against the ground.

Alice grew weary swinging the sword nonstop, to the point that she felt her arms leaden and she unable to defend herself any longer. And the powerful wind did not make matters any easier.

It was until then when Alice saw the light. She was heading straight toward the light at the end of the tunnel, the threshold that gave way into the abode of the dead. It was the entrance only humans could go through, and monsters could not.

The ghoul's wailing increased its intensity, and just when the monster itself disintegrated, it was then its wailing reverberated in Alice's ears. Astonished, she wondered what had happened, but before she could guess anything, she was inside…

¤¤¤

Arthur and Antoine traveled through the streets and avenues in almost pitch-dark, wary of the slightest movement or noise. Moving as stealthily as they could, they went from corner to corner, peeking around each before emerging into sight on the other side. They were aware that their armor gave them a minus point in the stealth stakes, in that they creaked with every step. It also occurred to them that the Dwellers might also be able to see in the pitch-dark. They kept on running for an hour before reaching the boundaries of the city. Now, kilometers away from the heart of the city where all chaos reigned, they could still hear the rumbling, the bellows and the havoc.

Antoine had made the hard choice of dropping the torch for safety's sake. They needed to travel light, quickly, silently and unnoticed. Antoine was still trying to figure out how they would get to the White Bastion fast and without any transport. They would usually travel one hour from the White Bastion toward Paris. Now there were no horses available, walking would take them around four hours.

Arthur, on the other hand, was thinking about other matters. He was concerned neither about the current situation in the city nor about theirs. As he remembered all the good moments he had had with Alice, he began to feel even worse, as though he was consuming a drug: the more he remembered, the worse he felt, the more he wanted.

It was then they exited through the enormous city gates and stepped out onto the grasslands. Without a horse, it was going to be a hard journey back. Without resting, they could be there in four hours.

There was only one thing that brought Arthur out of his mirthless thoughts: the break of dawn, a new hope. Arthur tried his best to bury his hatred and fury, feeling determined to fulfill Alice's wish to rid France of its ailments.

The nascent sun's attempts to breach through the baneful thundercloud were feeble. But only then did the knights realize how their armor began to gleam silver as the sunlight barely brushed the boundaries of Paris, keeping itself at bay before the Harbingers' territory.

"Paris will never know the sun anytime soon…," Arthur muttered to himself, loud enough for Antoine to hear him. And running, they set out on their journey toward their only safe haven…

¤¤¤

Bleakness and oblivion, shrouds of fog, breezes of spine-chilling cold rustling in the withered grassland, a penumbra where sight was slightly useful, the smell of dampness filling the nose, the howls of the tormented filtering in the wind and the distance. The lonely girl opened her eyes, all hope long gone from her heart, and as she peered around at the surrounding landscape and swept her stained hair back, she lacked the words to describe her whereabouts. Alice knew, and remembered, her free-fall through the void. What she remembered only since the moment she entered the light was that she had not impacted on the ground, but felt as though she had been gently placed on the harsh bedrock of the Inner World. She thought she had reached a divine realm.

As the haze began to dissipate, she could hear a slight rippling of water. In front of her, down a slope of mud, a wide blue river drifted as far as the eye could see in both directions, a small wooden quay going all the way toward the middle of the river. She was startled when the fog completely vanished and realized she was surrounded by scores of strangers, all covered in frayed rags, their gazes blank and unfocused: every kind and size of men, women and children. But some people were wounded, either slightly or severely. Some of them were covered in bruises, cuts and scrapes. Others were missing limbs and some of them had their head hanging by a thread. Others had their deathly wounds completely concealed. However, all outward signs of injury vanished when they crossed the river.

Alarmed, Alice gazed at her own body, and with incredible relief, she found that she did not have any wound, other than William's bite; otherwise she was still untouched. She also noticed that she was not wearing rags, but the now dull silver armor, and her broadsword was still hanging from her waist. She sighed with relief just as something caught her eye down at the river.

Within five seconds, she heard a low and dismal humming down at the riverbed. A vessel hovered upon the bluish waters, and it stopped next to the old quay. As if by instinct, the people began to advance sluggishly into the dock and onto the ship, as though they were spellbound and were being beckoned upon duty.

The boat resembled an ancient Greek ship. A single wide unfurled sail was tied to the mast, which was located in the middle of the ship, among numerous rows of long benches; except that the oars were missing. And at the bow of the ship a squalid, gaunt and bald man was standing still, at least that was what Alice thought she saw. As she neared the boat by sliding down the slope and onto the quay, she was finally able to describe the man.

"Are you boarding the ferry?" he asked in a coarse and grave voice. He did not move from the spot and did not even turn his head to face Alice.

"Quite extraordinary," the man continued as Alice looked at him with apprehension. "Not even a being like me could have ever imagined a situation like this."

Alice was still perplexed.

"Who are you?" she asked. "Where am I?"

"Because of some disruption to the Universal Law of Nature, you, a living being, have entered, without any permission, the abode of the dead."

"I'm still alive?" Alice shook her head. "That is impossible!"

"I have seen every age and aeon come and go, since the time of the Ancients and their heyday, and Antares' ascent to godliness, to this actual day of gloom and sorrow," he replied. "Thus I can tell you that nothing is impossible. Climb onboard, and don't keep us waiting."

Alice hesitated; she looked behind her, seeing nothing but water and rock with fog settled close to the ground.

"You can't stay here forever, or else you will die," said the man, turning only his waist forty-degrees to face her. Now she saw with clarity his deformities. He was gaunt-faced and squalid, and now that Alice could see him well, she realized he was not even a man, but a living skeleton with rotten flesh still stuck in his ribcage and skull. His sockets were empty and for so long he had been coerced to carry out such a task that his feet had merged completely into the vessel. He could not move from that spot unless he had his limbs cut off. "I will answer your questions, but right now I am running short on time."

Still with mistrust, Alice steeled herself and climbed onboard, the old ferry creaking under her feet, dreading that the boat would wreck under her weight.

"You need not worry," the skeleton said. "My ferry is completely unsinkable and safe from all hazards that would sink a regular boat," he told her as though he had read her thoughts. "Please, have a seat."

Alice trod down the aisle while glancing suspiciously at the many dead people seated on the long benches. She decided to sit down close to the skeleton, on the first row to the left of the boat. Her spot was next to an old man with a sullen expression, whose throat was slit and still dripping blood.

The vessel continued its voyage down the river, without the skeleton moving a finger.

"What is this place? And who are you?" Alice asked, still frightened by the captain's appearance.

"My name is Charon, ferryman of the dead. I transport the demised to the Tribunal of the Dead, across the River Styx," he said. "Behind is Erebus, the dark lands we just left. It's the first place the newly dead arrive just before their judgment."

"I've heard those names before. I've read about you. I thought you were all part of a mythology," Alice remarked incredulously.

"They have taught you wrong, then. I am tangible, and so is the Underworld and beyond. You, humans, are always so certain of everything, even when you are downright wrong. Your kind thinks they know everything, even though they have just scratched the surface. When something is shown to them, anything at all that cannot be explained in a way they understand, the first thing they do is make something up to explain it."

"Okay, so now I understand all that nonsense about Tartarus and Elysium. I was confused when I first heard about it a few hours ago."

"Have you heard about it recently? From whom did you hear it?" Charon asked eagerly.

"From some madmen who claim some Antares entity as their and our god: Harbingers," Alice replied with disdain.

"Be careful with all the information you, mortal, bear. If any wraith or usher, or any Dweller at all overheard you, you would be in serious trouble. And, this might sound terrible to you, but Antares *is* a god, named after the sun."

"What do we, or anyone else, need him for?" Alice asked. "What has he done to deserve any praise? All gods I know always require a sanguinary ritual. They are cruel and cold-blooded killers."

"He is mostly acknowledged as Hellgod. And the reason he is called by that title is because he is almighty, immortal, covetous and a tyrant whose power is higher than any other being's. And nevertheless, he is dying," Charon replied in a low voice.

"Why?" Alice asked, straightening up and leaning closer.

"Years ago, he was cursed by Death, the *Corvus*. When Death takes form and shape, it is the figure of a crow. She was revered and respected by the Ancients, the first Dwellers of the Underworld, since the first time they met her: when life was no more. Antares is the only Ancient Dweller still alive," Charon explained in a soft voice. The environment around them was shifting. It became a little darker and the grasslands transformed into a vast and harsh plain, stalagmites bristling up from the ground and stalactites hanging down from the faraway vault. To Alice's right side, there was a dim red illumination brushing the massive stalactites, as though there were great amounts of lava. "Antares taunted Death. He ignored her admonishments about staying away from the Overworld," he continued in a lower voice as they approached the Tribunal of the Dead.

"But if he's immortal, he can't die."

"Exactly," replied Charon. "He could not die, but now he is dying. Death is not only a symbol, but also a force, a Universal Law of Nature. Death is Nature itself. Death is Life. Death is the continuous cycle of Life that Antares is threatening to disrupt."

"If he dies, there won't be any more gods, right?" Alice asked.

"No, I'm afraid he can easily be replaced. Only Death grants might and immortality, and in all likelihood, she will have an heir to be bestowed by this power to keep on ruling the Underworld. It was because of his greed that he lies in his deathbed."

Alice fell silent, wondering what was next. She started to feel a comforting heat, and then she realized the red illumination now was brighter and closer to her right side, across the stalagmites' cemetery.

"Where's all that warmth coming from?" she asked, staring at the bristling stalactites, which hung far above the ground.

"You need not worry," replied Charon. "That is the River Phlegethon, river of fire. It disgorges all the lava down the titanic void of the Tartarus."

"Isn't the Tartarus where all those who deserve punishment are sent to atone for eternity?"

"Quite right. I've never been there myself, but I've overheard rumors and conversations about it that described it as a terrible place; a place of unimaginable pain, where victims are burned alive, stung with swords and red-hot steel rods. But you don't have to worry about that. You haven't done anything bad, I suppose," said Charon as though it was a casual and unimportant matter.

"But if I'm alive, they will just let me go back to my world, right?" Alice asked with a slight fear growing up inside her; a fear that yelled at her that all was about to go very, very wrong.

"I must say, I can't possibly imagine what will happen to you, being alive. Where will they assign you? I wonder," Charon reflected as he began humming softly again.

"Assign…me, what?" Alice asked, placing her hand slowly upon the leather hilt. "They can pull me up again. It shouldn't be too difficult. Those bloody Harbingers brought all that filth to my world!"

"As I said before, you entered the abode of the dead because of some sort of disruption to the Universal Laws of Nature. 'Neither living nor dead shall trespass upon the threshold of each one's world,'" he recited solemnly.

"Curious, then again, we all trespassed somehow." Alice stood up from her seat.

"It is unfortunate that I don't have the ability to take you back. To break the Laws is to defy the Corvus and, thus, face the grave consequences. Believe me, you don't want her as your enemy, and because of that, even if I were capable of opening the portals for you, I would not do it," Charon replied, deadpan.

Alice looked up at the horizon and saw, not far away, where they were heading. A huge Parthenon-like building loomed in the distance. Her heart thumped wildly.

"Turn back the ship," she ordered firmly.

"Or what? You're going to cut me into pieces? I noticed your apprehension since the moment you climbed onboard. That's why I like them dead. They are more malleable than you, mortals," Charon groaned aggressively. "Your fate is nigh, and you cannot avoid what the Corvus has laid ahead for you to stumble upon."

"Do my bidding, or else I'll make sure you are not ever merged again into your ferry." She unsheathed her stained broadsword and pointed the sharp tip at Charon, who was not making any effort to defend himself. The dead barely glanced at Alice, quickly losing attention.

"Do you know what happens to dead people who are not malleable, or, in this case, alive?" He did not wait for Alice to answer. "The *aurelians* seize them, and take them to the Tribunal of the Dead."

Now that the island was quite close, Alice perceived the beating of large wings in front of them. She realized there were two creatures heading straight toward the ferry, speeding through the air.

"Oh, you better behave yourself and not cause any more trouble for your own sake. If I were you, I would not try to fight them off," Charon said, staring at her with an empty gaze. "I decided I would help you. But first of all, hide your weapon before they see it."

Alice sheathed her sword and crossed her arms. She glared at Charon, alternately glancing at the winged creatures that were heading at high speed toward the vessel.

"Most likely, you are going straight to the Tribunal of the Dead to determine your destination, but if they cannot decide where to send you, they will probably make you pay a visit to Hades himself, Lord of the Underworld. I recommend you to treat him with respect and dignity. Don't shout, don't run, and don't draw out any weapons and talk as if you were asking for a formal request. If you're sent to Asphodel, just don't drink from the Lethe, whatever it takes! If it's Elysium, then I don't think you're going to have anything to complain about; but if you're heading toward Tartarus, then, by any means, you have to escape. And if you are to atone for your sins, you will be sent to the Purging Trials, and by completing all of them, you shall be rewarded with a higher prize. But the only question remains: how will you leave the Underworld? That's still a mystery you have to figure out by yourself."

The beating of wings got even stronger and now Alice could see what those creatures were. They looked exactly like men, except for the fact that they had a pair of large white-feathered wings; their eyes were completely white, missing the pupils and irises, their skin had a pale gold hue, and they were wearing what looked like white Roman togas. Hanging on their belts were their weapons. They landed swiftly behind Alice's seat and held her by her shoulders. Without moving, she glowered at Charon, who turned his empty gaze toward the aurelians.

He uttered a few words in an ancient language and the aurelians nodded, holding Alice even tighter.

"They are going to drop you off at the Tribunal of the Dead. Just queue up and wait for your turn." He ignored Alice's look of anger. "I bid you farewell…mortal." He turned to face the horizon, the dark island looming ahead.

As the aurelians swung their powerful wings, mighty gusts of wind were shot out, raising themselves and Alice from the old ship and into the compressed air of the Underworld; and getting far ahead of the ship at high speed, they headed toward the crossroads that would make the difference between liberty and seclusion, mirth and bane, and life and death…

Crossroads

The guards in the watchtowers caught sight of them from afar.

Limping and trudging over the grasslands, weary from arduous hours of running under the blistering sun, bathed in dirt and sweat, growing hungrier and dizzier, on the verge of fainting, the agonized knights strove toward their only home. After four hours of running, stopping briefly to rest, without water, having depleted their scanty rations of bread, the knights made it alive to the White Bastion after the expedition to Notre Dame.

Arthur had removed his right gauntlet and examined his wound where the serpent reptilian had stung him and cursed him for life. The needle had made a wart-like mark upon his flesh and it was oozing pus. He recalled the Harbinger's words: "A shame it won't kill you until the next new moon." If all said was true, he had little less than a month to live. However, he was not afraid; worse than that, he was completely numb, indifferent to his surroundings. "We made it, Marshal!" Antoine said in between gasps, his face trickling with sweat. Arthur merely nodded.

The heavy wooden gates creaked open, revealing the citadel of the Order of the Knights. At both sides of the gates were two small stables with a pair of horses hitched to poles. The parapet and the towers gleamed white against the full sunlight. Inside, the green plains extended far away across rolling hills, traced by the artificial roads dotted with trees and bushes, and in the midst of all, a mighty castle stood erect, with numerous buttresses and watchtowers, the main spire bristling high. The coliseum and the barracks could be observed in the distance, a few kilometers away, at the other side of the citadel.

"The Marshals are alive!" a guard called out next to the open gate. As Arthur and Antoine trudged toward the entrance, a pair of knights riding horses exited the citadel and trotted toward them. They pulled by their reins two other horses behind them.

"The Viceroy wishes to talk to you, Marshal Arthur," the officer said, handing him the reins. "He said it's an emergency."

Arthur nodded.

"How does he know we are still alive?" Antoine cut in, panting. He reached out for the reins.

"It was the first thing Capricorn told us when they arrived, horseless, one hour before you did."

"Where are they now?" inquired Antoine, trying to keep his eyes open as weariness threatened to make him collapse, while taking the reins and mounting his new horse, dreading that another hellish outbreak could occur at any moment.

"They are safe and sound, waiting in the barracks for their commander."

"You better go check on them," said Arthur. He mounted and raced off toward the castle. The crushing agony of losing Alice, a pang even stronger than that of losing his fellow soldiers, broke him down in a way that made him wish he himself had died in her stead. He saw himself as a total failure, as someone who should not have been the leader of the Company. Although he wanted to arrive early, he felt as though looking the Viceroy in the eyes would be one of the most shameful and humiliating punishments he could receive for being the only survivor in the Company.

He dismounted, almost stumbling on the floor, and went walking awkwardly across the atrium and into the main hall; he climbed up the staircase and went down a long corridor. He did not wait for the ushers to grant him permission to enter the Viceroy's hall, and as he did, with his head down out of shame, he decided it was not time to give in yet.

"I'm glad you're back, young lad," the Viceroy remarked. The old man was across the large oval assembly table, looking through the window next to his throne at the beautiful sight of France's grasslands. A gold crown rested upon his head, around curls of wispy gray hair. "We need to talk." He turned to face Arthur with his piercing gaze; Arthur felt as though his feelings were being read by those unfathomable eyes.

"I'm sorry," Arthur burst out. He stood still, trying hard not to remove his gaze from the Viceroy's. "I'm the only survivor, and as the leader, I should have been the first one to die. I overestimated myself."

"Or perhaps you were the fittest of all. Let us rejoice that you are still standing, strong...and thirsty, I see..." He asked one of the ushers to bring him a jar of water.

"I wasn't the fittest, nor was I the strongest," he replied. "It is Alice to whom I owe everything. She is the reason why I'm still standing." His gaze strayed from the Viceroy's, fearing he might notice the tears that were welling up in his eyes, his fists clenching and his tightly pressed jaw. "Now, she is gone, along with my whole Company. Who will you assign as my leader now?"

"I'm sorry for your losses." He looked away. "That was one of the several issues I wanted to talk to you about." The Viceroy approached his throne and placed a hand over its armrest. He faced Arthur with a grim look. "I want you to be my successor to the throne."

Arthur remained silent, completely astonished, lacking words at first.

"With all due respect, I should not be a Marshal anymore, let alone Viceroy."

"I'm an old man and I do not have an heir," the Viceroy countered. "You're the fittest for this responsibility. Didn't you say, countless times, how you wanted to be greatest Marshal of all time, a man who leads all brethren to battle, to conquer the highest peak, to defeat the rising threats? You wanted to prove you could be better than your own father! Now you retract?"

"I don't feel capable anymore of such a task. Much blood has been spilled on my hands." He glanced down at his arm.

"Listen to me carefully, my lad," the Viceroy said. "Everybody makes mistakes...grave mistakes. You are not perfect, though you are not entirely flawed. People will always die under your command. But something I'm well aware of is that you *are* capable of such a task, and you have been a first class leader since you were just a squire. I'm offering you a chance to become much more than what your father became, and I'm also heightening your chances to do much more. You will be powerful, fully able to take every decision concerning the Order, and even some of the entire kingdom, along with King Philippe!"

The thought of power crossed Arthur's mind as the doors creaked open and the usher entered with a jug full of water, which he handed to Arthur and went back out. He quickly drank half its contents and laid the jug upon the fine wooden table.

"So, what do you say?" the Viceroy asked, rather impatiently.

"When does my mandate take effect?" Arthur asked.

"That's how I like it, quick and well-taken decisions! You will be a great Viceroy, I assure you. But it's not going to take effect as soon as you might think. First of all, you must tell me everything that has happened these two days you've been gone, as detailed as you can. I need to know what's happening in Paris. It has been bothering me for quite a long time."

Arthur nodded. Both of them took seats and he told the Viceroy everything, from the weather when they arrived at Paris, all the way through to when he came back to the White Bastion.

"There was a dragon. Not even I can believe it. But they do exist after all," Arthur commented, still somewhat disheartened.

"As told in legends, they have always been formidable enemies, fire-breathing, insensitive and savage monsters of yore," the Viceroy replied. "I find it difficult to believe it as well, but now, given the circumstances, I think I will have to do so. Nevertheless, right now, I am concerned about the five men you mentioned earlier."

"The Harbingers?" Arthur queried, hesitantly.

"Did you, by any chance, hear any of their names?" the Viceroy inquired with a frown.

"Just once, and maybe I could be getting them wrong. I recall Percival, Siegfried; I think there were two more that were never mentioned. However, the name that keeps bouncing wildly in my head is William Bloodthorn. He transformed into a werewolf in front of us."

The Viceroy flinched. His eyes widened.

"What's wrong?" Arthur asked unsteadily.

"Something, let's say, out of place: bizarre, strange, uncommon; and now that you tell me, it sounds extremely dangerous. Are you sure it is *William Bloodthorn*?" the Viceroy repeated, emphasizing the name. Arthur nodded. "Arthur…that monster…he is the new Duke of Normandy!"

"What? How do you know that?" Arthur exclaimed, standing up abruptly.

"Remember that news flies. Bad news is like shooting stars. John II, son of Philippe the Fortunate, abdicated yesterday without prior warning, leaving the throne to William Bloodthorn. Both Philippe and John agreed that it was the right thing to do. William's rising to power was immediate. It may sound like a coincidence, but I don't like believing in coincidences," he sighed. "That's only the half of our problems. You said something about Siegfried yelling out loud that they were manipulating Edward, right?" Arthur nodded and took his seat again. "France's relationship with England is tensing to the verge of breaking. Philippe and Edward, as well, are taunting each other. Diplomacy between them is offensive and insulting. It is as though both of them wanted bloodshed!"

"What can we do about that?" Arthur inquired.

"I've already tried to reason with the King. I've sent him a couple of letters. He answered, telling me to stay out of the way. I'm afraid I doubt there is a way to talk him out of it. In fact, I'm sure Philippe is being manipulated as well. He moved out of Paris a long time ago, before the killings began."

"We could intervene and see for ourselves what is actually happening," Arthur suggested.

"No," the Viceroy shook his head decidedly. "That would taint our image. Anything the King might take as offensive would be a huge hazard against us. Nobody seems to know what is happening. Remember, all the streets of every city are teeming with ignorance. I'm sorry, but so far there is nothing we can do about it. We are powerless, as of right now."

"What about overthrowing William?" Arthur insisted, clenching his fists tightly.

The Viceroy shook his head.

"When is my mandate taking effect?" Arthur asked again.

"You said you believed that cursed mark of yours is going

to kill you quite soon," the Viceroy pointed a slim finger at his wounded arm.

"I don't know if that information is reliable, but recalling what those Harbingers were capable of, there is a chance it could occur," replied Arthur.

"In that case, we're in for even more trouble," said the Viceroy, rubbing his brow.

Arthur looked perplexed and opened his mouth to speak, but no words came out.

"It would be highly reckless to leave you my inheritance now, knowing that you are going to die soon. In that case, I should bequeath it to someone else."

Arthur tried to speak again, but he found himself again lacking words.

"The reason I wanted this information is for us to remain wary at all times. They might come here to sow their own seeds and destroy us from within." The Viceroy looked up, straight into Arthur's eyes. "This information is gold. I owe you the Order, which I must abstain myself from yielding now. You can go."

Arthur let out a sigh and stood up. He gave his back to the Viceroy, and just as he took the cold doorknob in his furious fist, the Viceroy spoke again.

"I'm sorry about your Company," he mumbled. "I know how it pains. But know well: your expedition has benefited us greatly."

Before exiting, Arthur glanced back, smiling coldly, already planning his next move…

¤¤¤

As soon as Alice was placed on the harsh and withered ground of the gigantic island, the aurelians launched themselves into the sky with a single and vehement swing of their wings. The gusts of dead air struck Alice's face, sweeping her hair back. A thick cloud of dust rose from the ground, wispy dark ribbons whirling about her feet. While airborne, Alice had beheld the baneful and twisted island in amazement and apprehension. The place where she was left was next to a steep, rocky cliff overlooking the vast and faraway horizon, dismal and cavernous. And below, the Styx stirred its murky waters, its waves crashing violently against the bedrock, at least one hundred meters down.

Alice backed off, vertigo beginning to take effect on her.

Behind her, down the slope of the mountain, she saw what she thought were trees: gaunt, shriveled and their boughs hanging low. Great but bald oaks towered over her, their bark gray and lifeless, and among them were weeping willows, which veiled the path with their rippling long curtains of leaves.

The path among the dead oaks and willows came into sight as the wind moaned, clearing the way of the cracked leaves that concealed it. The road down the mountain became steeper, to the point that Alice had to grab low tree branches and stop repeatedly to find her step. Loose and treacherous rocks were scattered along the downward slope. She climbed down cautiously, rocks dislodging and rolling headlong down the slope, swirls of gray dust rising up whenever she placed a foot in a wrong spot, immediately retreating and looking for a more stable place to step onto.

After an hour of climbing down, the ground became flatter. Still surrounded by trees, Alice noticed the raging Styx to her right side. She reached the gray shores; rocky and ominous. There it was, the River Styx lashing against the high promontories. Then something caught her eye. She thought she had seen something walking on the gray sand. She saw it again. Paying closer attention, she realized she was looking at a ghost: a translucent black shadow, hooded and legless, hovering upon the watery shore. No sound came from it. The specter was carrying two black-iron cutlasses. Alarmed, she noticed there was not only one, but scores of them guarding the lakeshore.

As she watched with apprehension and began to edge toward cover, a nasal voice nearly made her jump out of her skin. She had to stop herself from shrieking.

"Beware of the Stygian wraiths."

Alice turned around, unsheathing her sword and ready to attack. Swiftly and with great dexterity, the reptilian snatched the weapon from her by grabbing the cutting edges of the blade and, with a single upward spin, caught the hilt. He pointed the tip at her chest.

"What language do you speak?" the reptilian asked. He was

taller and stronger than Alice, and was wearing a gray toga, which made him harder to make out against the monotonous landscape. His scales were dull and his piercing serpent eyes stabbed fear into Alice. She wanted to kill that demon. Her fingers twitched. "White skin, green eyes, brown hair; your overall features tell me you come from somewhere called Europe, maybe France, more specifically."

"I speak French," she answered curtly and with anger.

"And once more, my senses have not failed me. You seem lost." The reptilian made a gesture with his head toward the beach. "The Stygian wraiths represent a perilous threat against you. They are ruthless against any dead…"—he stared at Alice in disbelief—"or living being who stumbles into their sight. If they catch you trying to avoid judgment you are in serious trouble."

"Why should I trust you?" Alice asked in a soft voice, clenching her fingers into a fist.

"I thought you were a logical being," the reptilian replied. Alice noticed he had a peculiar accent, as though he had a hard time pronouncing the words, perhaps because of his lack of lips and human tongue, along with hissing. "I am not a threat, starting off with the fact that I don't have a weapon, except for the one I took from you. I have no intention of using it against you. But you did."

"I have my own reasons. Harbingers summoned demons of your kind and they killed my Company."

The reptilian took hold of Alice's wrist, pulling her back toward the withered forest. She struggled while she was dragged several meters until he released her back into the forest, covered by the sparse foliage of the trees and undergrowth.

"You better watch what you say. Presuming you don't know, 'demon' is a pejorative term around here. Try to guess who uses it all the time," he hissed impatiently. "Humans; I'm sure it occurred to you. I just saved you from a wraith's gaze, by the way."

Alice nodded slightly, feeling rather remorseful. She still did not trust him and tried to keep at least a meter away from him.

"I don't have anything to do with anything that happened to you. Those reptilians that attacked you were most likely primal."

Alice frowned with confusion. "It means that they were either primitive beasts, or indoctrinated to become cannon fodder."

"So how shall I call you instead?" Alice asked.

"Generically, all inhabitants of the Underworld are called Dwellers. But you can also call any other specific group by their race's name."

"And more personally?" Alice asked.

"I am Khan, an usher in Hades' palace. I also guide any stray wanderer to their destination. But this was an exception. I had to confirm whether what Charon said was true. Yes, he informed me about you. He said something about a living woman who had mistakenly entered the abode of the dead. I saw a pair of aurelians transporting you across the Styx. That told me you weren't behaving yourself." He handed her the broadsword, holding it by the blade. "Now, will you?"

"Are you going to hand me over to Hades?" Alice asked, grabbing the leather-bound hilt cautiously.

"That might be necessary, but only if the Judge cannot determine a place for you to stay. According to me and Charon, it is going to be impossible to get you back up there. If you ask Hades, do not expect an agreeable answer. We better go now. Follow me."

Alice nodded resignedly. She sheathed her sword and followed Khan through the dead forest, keeping her distance, watching her surroundings warily. She could not help but wonder: What's worse, *being dead or alive*?

¤¤¤

After twenty minutes of walking silently, Alice and Khan arrived at their destination: the center of the Tribunal of the Dead. They exited the forest and arrived at an atrium made of stone, outside a large Corinthian building resembling the Greek Parthenon, twenty meters high. A long line composed of hundreds of men, women and children, from every race, all wearing brown and threadbare rags, stretched out all the way from the entrance toward the huge quayside, in which Charon's ferry usually docked to disembark the dead passengers. Alice turned to face the obscure horizon and could just make out Charon's ferry through the mist, going toward Erebus again.

They walked into the structure among thick pillars, advancing along the line of people, getting ahead of them. As they entered deeper, golden torches crackled along the walls, and the waiting line still went on. There were guards posted on both sides of the line, standing away from each other at intervals of ten meters. They were Stygian wraiths.

They entered through a wide gateway which led into an enormous courtroom. As Alice's eyes adapted to the penumbra, she made out a figure that scared all courage out of her: the Judge. It was the shape of a huge man, made of bronze and with a long arm outstretched toward the first defendant in the line, its stout fingers splayed downward upon the dead's head. The line of the dead ended in front of the dais of the Judge. Behind it, there were three metallic gates, each with a different word carved above, and each word Latin. The sign on the left said '*Asphodelus*,' the sign on the right said '*Elysium*,' and the one in the middle, just behind the dais, said '*Tartarus*.' The Judge was completely still, standing upon a huge white marble pedestal.

"It may look like a lifeless, dull and mindless statue to you," Khan said. "But just by placing its hand upon your head, it can see all your past life, all your actions, feelings and thoughts. And it can be inexorable against troublemakers. Hades' help is almost never required, but the fact that you are alive is surely going to leave the Judge confused."

"Why is everybody afraid of the Judge?" Alice dared to ask in a low voice, moving closer toward the reptilian, with whom she felt safer now.

"Simple enough, because they don't know what fate has in store for them," he answered with a serpent hiss. "And not only that, but also because those completely oblivious to our existence are in crushing awe when they realize what actually happens in the afterlife. Humans are creatures commonly afraid of unexplored environments. Your kind is *always* afraid of the unknown, all because of pure instinct. And thus it can be a difficult task trying to socialize with you. Yet, you in particular seem to be somewhat different from the others."

The line of the dead kept on advancing as they talked. Every day, hour and minute people died. Alice was aware that the line could be endless. And then, a thought swiftly crossed her mind and kept bouncing in her head. She was in the abode of the dead, where all her human ancestors resided. She could go meet anyone dead. But what actually mattered to her was to see Sonja again.

"How long have these people been dead?" she asked eagerly.

"I would say…a little more than a day." Alice's eyes widened and her heart pounded frantically. She knew it had barely been a day since Sonja's death. She began scrutinizing every face in the line, but she could not find her. "You stay right here!" the reptilian hissed, seizing Alice's right shoulder when she tried to move from his side. "It's your turn."

Against her will, the reptilian dragged her forward, shoving her just above the Judge's hand. She closed her eyes.

No gate opened.

"You are going to pay a visit to Lord Hades." Khan took hold of her right wrist and just before he could drag her out, Alice heard the voice she desired the most.

"What are you doing here?" Sonja stepped out of the line, twenty meters away. Alice yanked her arm from the reptilian's grip and turned around, a broad smile widening in her face, tears beginning to well up in her eyes. She raced toward her, ignoring all the threats that began to unwind around her with every step she took. The first thing she noticed about Sonja was that she was wearing the same tattered clothes as everyone else, and second, which shocked her deeply, she noticed her lethal wound: the bite of William, the werewolf. She had her neck severely bitten and it had stopped bleeding already, but it was still a painful thing to see on someone who is very much beloved.

Right after she noticed the wound, Alice slowed down, her eyes wide open with dismay. She shook her head almost imperceptibly, but still embraced Sonja, being grateful that she was not just a ghost. Sonja, on the other hand, was confused about her whereabouts and the turn of events that had been triggered so recently, but she still returned to Alice the pleasure of hugging her too.

It was only then that Alice noticed the real danger enclosing them, as a pack of wolves surrounding their prey.

Utterly silent and sepulchral, the Stygian wraiths, cutlasses ready, had been approaching the troublemakers without notice, phantasmagorical breaths casting out from their transparent maws. Looking at their faces caused Alice to cringe and shiver, and still she clung to Sonja. She was prepared to embrace death when she saw the wraiths raise their sabers, ready to thrust them forward.

"Halt!" Khan intervened with a hiss, stepping in between the girls and the wraiths, before they could move any further. "She is coming with me!" When he saw Alice's beseeching eyes, he added, "I want no harm against any of them." Indifferently, the wraiths returned to their respective positions. All the people in the line were glaring at Alice and Sonja.

"What is this place?" Sonja asked with a hopeless look.

"The Underworld, land of the dead," Alice replied, heartbroken.

"You have caused enough trouble already," Khan hissed at her side, placing a scaly claw on her left shoulder. "Know this: you tread a hostile land. Abide by its rules and maybe your punishment can be lessened."

Before walking away, Alice hugged Sonja one last time, nearing her mouth toward her ear and muttering low enough to avoid being heard: "Do not drink from the Lethe river…"

Her last words reverberated in Sonja's head as Alice was forced to walk through the open gate that read '*Tartarus*'…

Hades and the Harbinger

As the metallic gates ground shut behind Alice, she contemplated a rather odd but beautifully twisted world. Behind the Courtroom, there was an entirely different and astonishing land of diverse views. To her left side were the Asphodel Fields, the utterly gray, monotonous and never-changing realm of neutrality, encircled by a long, five-meter tall fence, its lands stretching as far as the eye could see. The fence was something that seemed easy to climb and escape through; however, not one of the residents tried to flee the place. The Fields were mostly rolling hills, dotted with little white specks, which were in fact, thousands of Asphodel flowers. The hills were, as well, spotted with darker and bigger figures, whose unmistakable shapes indicated that they were humans. She caught a glimpse of the Lethe as a gray and long string crossing a part of the Fields and disgorging farther away into the Styx.

To her right, the earth became more beautiful and less twisted, more colorful and alive; for what she beheld was Elysium, the paradisiacal region of the Underworld reserved for the righteous. It had tall trees with heavy green foliage, peaceful blue lakes and numerous small houses scattered around the region.

Nevertheless, the threshold she had crossed led toward two places: Hades' palace and the chasm of Tartarus, which lay at the end of the other path.

Grudgingly, Alice allowed Khan to lead her to the palace. It was a Corinthian building about the same height as the Courtroom, with the exception that Hades' palace was made out of dark bronze. They trudged uphill, climbed the wide three-tread staircase and crossed the hall among the thick dark pillars. Lit torches crackled inside, giving the building a haunted appearance, along with the dim walls and the amphorae posted on marble pedestals.

"Isn't there any other option for my judgment?" Alice managed to ask. "Charon mentioned something called the Purging Trials."

"Those are offered to the souls who want a second chance to redeem themselves by completing a series of trials that test your courage and worthiness." Khan came to a sudden halt and turned around to face Alice. "Now that I come to think about it, it is possible that you could be given a chance to face the Trials...if nothing went amiss, of course."

"How do I finish the Trials?" Alice asked, eager for a good answer.

"Know this: over the millennia, few humans have survived all Trials. That's only to warn you that it is not going to be easy. The first Trial you would face is the realm of Arcadia, and its master is Geister, lord of madness. Arcadia always has turbulent skies and is shrouded in eternal night. The forest outside the tower is probably the most dangerous place you can be in. It's full of creatures that could easily kill you. Geister will set challenges ahead of you through enigmas that you will have to solve to progress to the second Trial. In his realm resides a kind of ghost Dweller. Geister is a tyrant, and he turned every single inhabitant of Arcadia into a specter. He considers them his puppets and tools for his entertainment. His tower has dozens of floors with dozens of closed doors that contain different rooms, so that he can have a seemingly endless arsenal of riddles. Probably, your cunning will be your strongest weapon during his Trial. Be wary at all times and never, *ever* trust Geister."

"And what happens if I don't succeed?" Alice asked.

"Why, you head back straight to Tartarus." Khan turned around and kept on walking.

They reached a tightly shut wooden gate with a pair of bronze door knockers in the shape of a dragon.

Khan knocked on the doors.

The reptilian backed off one step as the doors flung open, as if he had predicted that would happen. The wind produced by the momentum hit Alice in the face, her expression hopeless now she was ready to confront her ultimate judge. As they stepped onto a dark velvet carpet, she noticed how Hades, from his throne, his right arm outstretched, slowly began to clench his fingers into a fist, and at the same time, the doors began to close.

"Time to tie up some loose ends, Alice," a hoarse and eerily familiar, yet dismaying, voice called from one of the dark corners of the chamber, next to a big window displaying the titanic chasm of Tartarus and the line of the dead queuing up in front of it. "I'll make sure Hades gives you what you deserve," he threatened.

Alice remained silent, her heart racing.

"Quite a warm welcome," Hades commented from his throne in the middle of the room, his brow concealed in shadow. "Or at least warmer than mine. Now, Harbinger, mind your own business..."

¤¤¤

As the wraiths pulled Alice out of the Courtroom, Sonja remained in shock, staring blankly into the distance before a wraith shoved her back into the waiting line for judgment.

Whenever a soul wanted to skip its turn or avoid it entirely, the wraiths, in the roughest of ways, forced them to face their fate. When Sonja's turn came, she walked forward, swallowing all her dreads. She stood upright, the sturdy fingers of the Judge hovering upon her head. Fearing neither the worst nor hoping for the best she already knew her destiny belonged to the utter neutrality of the Asphodel Fields.

"You have killed, executed your enemies in battle, disarmed and subjugated, and all their lives taken away by your firm grasp of the blade. Yet, they were justified actions, for you were born and trained to kill, ordered by a supreme being and an entity for you to craft the rest of your life, if you were not to fail. You never wished misfortune against those whom you disliked and you were the best among true friends." The Judge's grave voice rumbled inside her head. "You belong neither to Tartarus nor do you belong to Elysium. Hereby, I grant you eternal neutrality, for your actions are balanced in the scales of good and evil."

With that said, the gates at the left side of the courtroom screeched open. And they screeched shut after she had passed through.

Once outside, Sonja felt a stinging pain in her neck where the werewolf had bitten it. She remained motionless, gasping as the burning pain pulsed, gingerly holding up a hand as if to touch her wound. After a few seconds, the pain began to subside and she touched her neck slowly and with care. To her surprise, the gaping flesh and the blood were gone, and her skin was once again smooth as silk. She let out a sigh and continued moving.

At her right side were the two trails leading toward Hades' palace and Elysium respectively. In front of her, she saw the gray and rueful hills of Asphodel, enclosed by the tall fence. The gate was wide open, two reptilian ushers standing on either side of it.

"Afraid of lizards?" the reptilian on the right teased her scornfully when he caught her watching them with apprehension. "Aren't all humans the same?" he said under his breath.

She remained quiet, quickening her pace when crossing the threshold into Asphodel. The reptilian on the left slithered out his forked tongue with a snake hiss, brushing Sonja's ears. When she had passed through completely, both of them grunted and continued to guard the entrance.

As soon as she was inside, everything, even her skin and hair, turned to a phantasmagorical and sad gray. She could not smell or taste anything anymore; neither could she feel with the tip of her fingers the prickling of the drab grass.

Close to the entrance, the River Lethe made its way quietly across Asphodel. Several people, who had recently entered the realm, were kneeling on the sides of the riverbank, bent over and drinking from the murky waters of the Lethe by cupping their hands and sipping from them. At least a dozen wraiths guarded the river, watching them with their ghostly eyes that were concealed under their black hoods.

When she got closer, a pair of wraiths began spying on her. She was supposed to drink from the Lethe as well.

Sonja snuck past the river without any pause by passing

through the strait that led uphill, unwilling to do what everyone else did, but also hoping to get through unnoticed.

Suddenly, a slender hand, cold as ice and hard as iron, wrapped around her wrist, freezing her blood. Looking down, she saw five translucent bone fingers, slim and long, searing her wrist with a powerful glacial cold. The wraith pulled her back with ludicrous strength. She had not even heard it coming.

"Do you wish to be punished?" the wraith threatened her in a sepulchral whisper, and a soft and faraway wail cast cold breaths rife with sorrow.

Sonja shook her head frantically, peering under the hood, which kept the wraith's brow hidden for a reason. It dragged her back to the banks of the Lethe, where it forced her to bend to her knees, and then pushed her head down into the river.

She still refused to drink a single drop, and as she was forced to look upon the water, she noticed a faint ripple of light upon the dark-bluish waters. She knew that the Lethe would steal anybody's memory as they drank from it. To lose all her memories was one of the greatest punishments she could receive.

Unyielding, she fought against the wraith's pressure on her neck, while its claws seared her skin. The dead people at her side watched in bewilderment as she struggled, seemingly getting infected with the same rebellious sentiment. However, the wraiths quickly subjugated everyone else.

"Bane it is then...," the wraith whispered in her ear, a glacial and faraway voice, and then a dissonant and unnerving shriek followed. "Troublemaker!"

A reptilian was assigned to Sonja to guide her toward her ultimate judge...

¤¤¤

"Curse you, bloody bastard!" Alice yelled back at Percival, drawing out her sword. She darted forward, but a pair of sturdy scaly arms wrapped around her shoulders, disabling any further movements. Alice continued to struggle against Khan's grip, venting all the anger she had stored against Percival. "This is your fault!"

"I warned you to behave, especially before Lord Hades," Khan whispered almost imperceptibly into Alice's ear as he held her tight.

"Would you keep her quiet? We cannot proceed with the trial unless she is quiet," Hades complained.

"That's not a problem." Percival stretched out his arm, pointing at Alice's head and clenching his first. Alice was then unable to produce any sounds other than muffled ones from her clamped mouth. "You can proceed now. See? That was easy."

"You keep quiet too." Hades shifted on his throne, stood up sluggishly and came closer to scrutinize Alice's face as Khan backed off a step. Above them, there was a chandelier lit with dim torches. Now Hades' brow was revealed as the light hit his face. He looked more like an old and cynical man, taciturn and sullen, bitter of life, and yet, there was something in his face that made him look inhuman. He was dressed in a black toga, and the upper part of his head was crowned with wreaths. He had a short but thick, white and scruffy beard. His unfathomable black eyes had Alice hypnotized. "Well, a living human down here, first time through."

"I praise your keen sight," Percival replied with a chuckle.

"And why should I be concerned about that?" Hades snapped, exasperated, turning to face Percival. He glanced at Khan. "Off you go!"

Khan bowed and turned back, glancing only momentarily at Alice before closing the doors behind him.

"You have to get me back to the surface!" Alice blurted out when she released herself from the silencing spell. "This is a terrible mistake!"

"Oh, stay quiet! And stop squeaking like a rat," Hades exclaimed. He returned his gaze to Percival, who was glaring both at Alice and him, his eyes glinting under his hood. "Why did you bring that thing in here?"

"To make sure you were doing the right thing," Percival said with a hint of contempt. "Now, will you proceed? Or are you just too senile to remember what your task here is?"

"Well, under Antares' protection, anyone can gather the courage to be insolent to me," Hades mumbled and faced Alice, who was staring at him in despair.

"I can't send it back," he said, destroying Alice's shred of hope.

"Now, the only alternative is to euthanize it and send it back to the Judge, simple as that. Or you can just shove it into the Purging Trials." He pointed with a slim and cracked finger at a shrine at his left side, attached to the wall. There was a portal with fluctuating waves depicting a dark image barely visible to Alice. "That way there is good chance that she will die there."

"No, I know there is a way!" She pointed a tremulous finger at Percival. "He opened portals up on the surface and summoned all the Dwellers he could muster…!" Her mouth clamped shut again under Percival's will.

"Clearly, a violation of the Universal Laws of Nature," Hades said under his breath. "It seems as though you wish the Corvus against you, Harbinger."

"A danger that is evened when sided with Antares," Percival replied, and even though he was shorter than Hades, he seemed to get taller at the moment of intimidating the Lord of the Dead. "Whose side will you choose? Do you remember what happened to the Lord of Oblivion? Do you wish the same fate? Antares may be ill to the verge of death, but he is still able to crumple you to your knees and have you dance like a girl."

"All right. Just kill it and send it back to the Judge," Hades said, concealing his embarrassment. "But don't do it on my carpet. Blood stains are hard to clean up."

"No need to do so," replied Percival slyly. "Why kill her when she could atone for her whole life in Tartarus?"

"That's not the way we follow the rules down here, Harbinger," said Hades, sitting on his black bronze throne. When he saw Percival's eyes glint under his hood, he added: "Just do whatever you want."

"No wonder you are so bitter, coward," Alice blurted out, free from the silencing curse once again. She did not know whether she was planning on making Hades angry or inciting him to stand against Percival.

Hades remained stiff on his throne and cleared his throat, unwilling to talk anymore. Percival raised his arm and tried another silencing curse on Alice.

"Are you out of power, or just tired?" Alice teased the Harbinger, who then checked on his hands.

"Just out of souls," he replied curtly.

Right then, there was another knock on the door. Hades slapped the air with his hand and almost immediately, the doors flung open outward.

"Now what?" Hades complained in exasperation.

A reptilian came into the chamber.

"We have another troublemaker," he hissed as he pulled a woman in rags into the hall. "She refuses to drink from the River Lethe."

"Can I be left alone for just *one* minute?" Hades exclaimed. "Just force its head into the water even if you have to break it!"

"But you said you wanted to punish them when they caused trouble."

Hades was thoughtful for a moment. "Hmm…just send it to Tartarus," he replied lazily, sitting back against his throne. "I'm tired of trials for today."

Percival chuckled, unsheathing a menacing and wicked dark dagger which was concealed beneath his robes, the Corvus wrought on his cloak shimmering in light of the dim fire of the chandelier above. "Now there are two for Tartarus." He lifted the dagger toward Alice, still several steps away from her.

Alice was running out of time. She was not willing to go to Tartarus for any reason. Her mind raced at high speed, her thoughts speeding away. Then a crazy idea popped into her head, which no sane person would conceive without the given circumstances. It was a hard decision, but she had nothing else to lose.

As Percival stepped forward, Alice glanced back at Sonja, seized her right wrist and, along with her, rushed toward the shrine on the left. With a glimpse, she sensed how Percival stirred behind, running toward her, ready to wound her.

In a desperate attempt, she hurled Sonja and herself into the vortex, holding hands as they were plunged into the blurry image of an undesired place. Before the familiar lashing wind was in her ears as they went free-fall, she swore she could hear Percival shouting from behind, dangerously close to her…

The Heir of the Sun

During the past two days, Arthur had been either lethargic or uneasy most of the time, doubts and questions clouding his mind. The question that perturbed him the most was whether he should proceed with his distraught plan, which was as demented as it was dangerous. It was a last chance to prove that his short life was worth its existence.

He had told Antoine about it. Antoine replied, "It's nothing but suicide." *Well then, there is nothing else to lose*, Arthur thought. He also considered telling the Viceroy, but he decided to keep it a secret after he guessed the Viceroy would only be another obstacle, if not the only one who could stop him completely.

Unable to bear the thought of spending his last month cowering behind a parapet and doing nothing while Europe crumbled to pieces, Arthur finally made up his mind to proceed with his plan. But to control that great anxiety, he kept on training in swordplay, horsemanship, and archery and gaining all the strengths he could, while trying to keep Alice's memories out of his mind, oftentimes in vain. He could vividly remember Alice's plunge into the Underworld, his heart twisting with grief at the mere recollections of her.

If something else was out of place, he could certainly feel it, not as a concrete fact, but more as a bad omen. Gray ragged clouds hung in the sky, dimming the fields' beauty. Throughout the day, there were sporadic rains, after which the sun emerged gloomily and the grasslands sparkled with raindrops.

Finally, on the third morning after the expedition to Notre Dame, Arthur clad himself in the complete set of plated silver armor. He organized all his equipment for departure: sufficient water and food for the road, stored in waterskins and leather pouches respectively; his longsword hung from his belt and the shield hooked to his left wrist.

Down in the stables, he was just saddling up his newly assigned horse when Antoine intercepted him.

"Going alone to Normandy won't make a difference," Antoine stated firmly. "You'll just die a little earlier than predicted."

Arthur tried to remain patient while buckling up the last leather straps. "I am willing to do anything within my reach to damage the enemy. It is time for Taurus' leader to join his fallen comrades. No matter how adverse the situation is, I will fight my way through, as far as I may reach."

"No, I'm sure the Viceroy will do something about the Harbingers, soon enough, I hope," Antoine countered. "And we will need you there."

"Do you know how my father died?" Arthur inquired, looking at Antoine, who shook his head. "During the Battle of Cassel, eight years ago, after Philippe the Fortunate had hired the Order to help him through the fight, my father was killed by a peasant. The greatest leader and fighter of the Order killed by a mere farmer with no training whatsoever," Arthur said. "That's what will happen to William: a small and insignificant force will bring him down." Alice came back to his mind. He shut his eyes, trying to push the thought aside.

"Then there is no way to dissuade you, is there?" Antoine asked resignedly.

"Thus one more question remains: Will you ride out with me?" Arthur asked as he mounted his steed and gripped the reins. "To overthrow William and free Normandy from his tyrannical jaws, and to make a difference in this unjust match between good and evil?"

Arthur's words sounded tempting to Antoine, but his ultimate response was negative.

"I'm sorry, but not this time. We are a team, not lone wolves;

therefore I *will* contribute as part of a whole Company, not as a clandestine duo."

Arthur nodded. "Tell the Viceroy he was a father to me when my real one was away. I might not see him again."

"He will not tolerate that you taint the Order's image," Antoine replied.

A wry smile formed on Arthur's lips. "Not if they don't recognize my armor." He showed Antoine his cuirass: the symbol (*La Fleur de Lis* and the jousting knights) was scratched off the armor and smeared in soot.

"Before you go," Antoine said, holding up a hand, "do you know what I have always admired about you?" Arthur stared at him intently. "Despite the fact that we are hired mercenaries, you still fight for what is right and do great deeds, instead of working for money and power. Being a part of the nobility as you are, anybody else would have gotten away with its benefits already. Knighthood has made you righteous, Marshal."

Antoine's words hit him unexpectedly. He had never thought about that. Surprised, he nodded and then added: "I guess this is farewell then." They clasped hands together and Arthur spurred his horse to trot along the road toward the main gate. Antoine sighed and returned to the barracks…

¤¤¤

Arthur left the White Bastion with a pang of longing, memories of his childhood, adolescence and early adulthood flashing through his mind: the rides through the fields of the Bastion with his father, the moment he met Alice, the old days of peace patrolling in Paris, along with Alice. There was no pain, no sorrow, and no despair during those harmonious years. Getting out of the White Bastion was a relief, though, because he felt free to proceed according to plan. Now that he was out he could do what he pleased, but it also pained him to leave his lifetime home for good. There were many people he would miss from then on. He decided he would not let his feelings sway him away from his goal; he would not let anyone make his plans go amiss. He alone would slay William Bloodthorn and return Jean II to his legitimate duchy.

Even though he tried hard to suppress his yearning, his feelings eventually overcame him. A crushing sorrow came upon him when he remembered all the people he had left behind: Sonja, Antoine, the Viceroy, his Company, and most importantly, Alice. Glumly, he gazed at the pink horizon, newborn sun, the clouds drifting away as the wind swept across the vast kingdom. A little more than a hundred kilometers of green grasslands and small rolling hills sprawled across the land he was about to travel. To reach Normandy's capital, Rouen, it would take him at least a day on horseback.

Shortly after snapping out of his absentmindedness, he spurred his horse into a gallop toward Normandy, heading northwest.

Occasionally, a courier at full gallop would pass by his side, bearing news for the Viceroy, merely glancing at Arthur, making the dust swirl up in his trail. Arthur had been riding for an hour when, after getting to the top of a hill, he spotted an odd and suspicious traveler, just in front of him, his horse treading slowly toward the White Bastion. The uncanny rider was slouched upon the saddle, his head sagging over his chest, as if he were passed out. He seemed to be unarmed. He had a red slovenly mane of hair and was wearing a dark traveling cloak, the hood hanging over his shoulders. It took Arthur a couple of seconds to realize that the rider's horse was actually his former jet-black stallion. Arthur was dumbstruck and speechless. As he passed by the traveler's side he decided to address him.

Just when Arthur turned to face him, the traveler was already staring at him completely awake. He had a young but worn-out countenance. Arthur made out his inhuman red eyes, full of malicious shrewdness that presaged a baneful fate for the White Bastion. As Arthur drew his sword out, the Harbinger made his move, launching Arthur off the horse with an unseen force. Before he could do anything else, he felt his entire body as heavy as lead and he lay motionless on the dirt. He was unable to move at all. The Harbinger dismounted and crouched beside Arthur, contemplating his face with contempt.

"Where do you think you are going?" Arthur remained silent,

his own chest crushing his lungs. "I remember you from Notre Dame. You are heading down to Rouen, aren't you? My name is Viktor Berlinghoff, Fifth Harbinger. You seem strong and young. What a shame it would be to waste your precious body. You are cursed to die later this month. Let's set a challenge ahead of you, shall we? Soon you will know what it is. You can either head off to Rouen, or come back to the White Bastion. What do you say?"

Viktor stood erect, looking down at Arthur, with a devious smile on his face. The last thing Arthur heard before his mind clouded was: "Don't look back..."

¤¤¤

It was midday when Arthur awoke, releasing a gasp. He looked around frenziedly, immediately recalling the lurid incident with the Harbinger, and his former steed.

Clambering onto his feet unsteadily and standing upright, he noticed that his new horse was still by his side. It had been grazing while he had been out.

It was then that the ominous words struck him again: "Don't look back..."

Quickly, Arthur mounted the horse, prodding it into a race against time by stinging it with both spurs without respite. He had a terrible foreboding forming in his mind.

As Arthur sped his way back to the stronghold of the Order, he frowned at the intense sunlight that now hit his face, beads of sweat forming on his brow. He knew that at least two hours had passed since he had fainted.

Arthur did not think about Rouen anymore and immediately decided to head back to the White Bastion. He forced the horse to gallop even faster. He had to be there no matter what.

After retracing all his steps, Arthur sighed in relief when he saw the place exactly the way it was before his departure. However, he would not allow appearances to deceive him.

Arthur passed through the main gates and raced toward the Viceroy's castle, the bristling spire towering over the citadel. As he dismounted in the marble atrium and hurried into the main halls and rushed up the stairs, he noticed there were too few guards.

Most noticeably, he saw there were none guarding the Viceroy's chamber. His heart beating fast, Arthur burst into the throne room, hoping desperately to find the Viceroy unharmed, or at least alive.

Alarmed, Viceroy Nicholas looked up from the manuscript he was reading at the table, as if he had been nervous beforehand. "Marshal Arthur…what's going on?"

"Why is no one guarding your chambers?" Arthur inquired, upset, immediately shutting the doors behind him. "Not the best moment to shirk one's responsibilities," said Arthur under his breath.

"Maybe they are…I didn't realize they were gone until now. But why are you so anxious? What's troubling you?" the Viceroy asked, standing up.

"I don't think you're safe anymore, not even in the White Bastion. I believe a Harbinger is heading this way, as you said, to sow his own seeds and destroy us from within," Arthur answered, and at once, he grabbed a chair from the assembly table and set it down against the doorway, locking the handles of the doors with the chair's backrest, creating a makeshift barricade.

"How can you know that?"

"I'll tell you when we have plenty of time, but not now," said Arthur, unsheathing his longsword and facing the doors.

"But aren't you exaggerating a bit?" the Viceroy demanded.

"There *is* a Harbinger in the vicinity," replied Arthur, still facing the doorway. "There was something already distressing you before I came in."

"Remember that I told you bad news was like shooting stars?" Arthur nodded, glancing back. "Well, they are now raining on me. The King is not himself. I can tell by his words on this scroll he sent me. It is as though he wants war with England to break out already. And when war comes raging upon France, he is going to force us to fight by his side. Not only are we nearly at war, but strange things are happening in Rouen, too: it's like Paris all over again. It happens that the same week William rises to power, Rouen begins to suffer the same ailments Paris did before its demise."

"With war comes carnage," said Arthur, turning to face the

Viceroy. "What those Harbingers want is to start a huge massacre, and push us toward the brink of annihilation. What can we do against them, to thwart their plans, to save our kind from extinction? We have to fight back."

"Don't you realize that's what they want?" Nicholas snapped. "You said it yourself! They want massacre. There will be worse carnages if we send our troops, and that will only make them stronger. They have their own army where they can be safe and watch the bloodshed from a secure place."

"Then what do we do? Sit down and watch the world burn?" Arthur retorted. "Maybe, all we need is the will of a man to slay the Harbingers, hunt them down one by one. I will do it."

"So you wish to leave your only safe haven and set out to vanquish the evils that threaten our existence? Your plan is to become a lone wolf who will rout the evils and restore peace to our turbulent land, all by yourself?" The Viceroy emphasized Arthur's plan to actually make him conscious of the task at hand. "You know the will of a single man is enough to change the world, but you will inevitably need the support of your friends, the loyalty and truth of your allies, resources to survive, and, of course, a safe haven. But then again, what you seem to ignore is the fact that you already have all of that right here, in the White Bastion."

"Will you help me?" Arthur asked, beseechingly.

"I don't see brightness ahead of us; nothing but death and destruction. The odds are stacked against us. If there is one small chance to change the outcome of this crisis, and you are that chance, I want to make it count. You shall have my full support, but only as long as you keep your word," the Viceroy warned with a frown. "You will not use our troops to make war with the Harbingers. However, I will do my best to help you get to them," he added. "If there is one man willing to complete this death-defying quest, then that is you. You are our best chance."

"I am ready. We have to hurry," said Arthur, looking down at his right arm. "I don't think I have much time left."

"You're right." The young redheaded Harbinger went through the barricade Arthur had set against the chamber doors, physically traversing them like an evil spirit. "You don't have much time left."

Arthur whirled upon his heels, pointing the tip of his longsword at the Harbinger. "You have made a serious mistake by coming here."

"Why? Because a brave rogue hunter wants to destroy us?" the Harbinger mockingly inquired. "You take a task with such confidence that you could be mistaken for a fool. We are not just men, but something else you cannot even begin to comprehend."

"Then what are you?" demanded Arthur.

"We are legion." The Harbinger's red eyes began to glow white-hot, red marks covering his body. "We bear revolution. A whole new order is forming, and your hierarchy will drop to the lowest levels. I am Viktor Berlinghoff, Fifth Harbinger, and I have a message to deliver: 'Rob the powerful of their wealth and dethrone them. Reap the souls of the innocent, the sheep, and give them eternal rest. Goeth forth, and bindeth the world in darkness.'"

"You have nowhere to go. You're surrounded…by the entire Order," Arthur replied.

"So you believe we cower behind our troops?" the Harbinger asked with a note of irony. Then his voice shifted, mimicking the Viceroy's. "'They have their own army where they can be safe and watch the bloodshed from a secure place.' See who is talking, old man," Viktor chuckled. "We are Commanders, Marshals and Warlords who come to conquer your last defenses. You shall succumb in ashes. Fire shall consume you."

Arthur lunged forward, and as his blade drew near the Harbinger, time itself seemed to slow down. Viktor sent Arthur backward onto the assembly table, skidding down its surface toward the other end and coming to a halt only as he met the marble floor. He stood up with difficulty, and as he did, Viktor was already by his side. Even with the plated armor protecting his body, Viktor's kick to his stomach was enough to force the wind out of his lungs. And as he lay upon the floor, gasping for air, he saw the Harbinger's demonic dagger appear from out of his dark cloak, ready to plunge into his body.

The Harbinger whipped around, stopping cold the Viceroy's blade, sparks shooting off as both contenders clashed in a fight to the death. After a few seconds, it was clear the Viceroy could not withstand the fight against the Harbinger. Both blades danced, locked in frenetic combat as they clanged against one another. However, Nicholas' swings quickly began to falter, his arms turning to lead, and his old age unable to compete with Viktor's youth. The weapon went flying off Nicholas' hands, skidding down the hall, leaving him completely defenseless.

Arthur stabbed Viktor's back, but he whirled around in a flash, parrying Arthur's attack. And his Stygium dagger went straight through Arthur's plated armor, piercing his side.

Time froze. Arthur remained a few seconds staring numbly at the dagger's hilt protruding from his side, before slumping to the floor on his back as Viktor removed the knife, a burning pain lancing up his body. He tried to contain his breath, carefully taking in the air, his hip burning, and blood dripping down the silver armor. Viceroy Nicholas stared incredulously at Arthur, horrified, as one of his greatest soldiers, one of his best friends, and the one he considered a son, lay defeated.

As Viktor backed off a few steps and stood staring out the window, the Viceroy knelt beside Arthur, swiftly unstrapping his cuirass and sliding it off his body, leaving him under the lesser protection of the livery and chainmail coat beneath it. Nicholas, with his fingers trembling, extracted a couple of herbs from Arthur's pouch, crumbled them to bits and rubbed them on his wound.

"Why do you fight an already lost battle?" Viktor asked with contempt, not caring to look at his adversaries behind him. "Why do you keep on fighting if you are already dead? Wouldn't everything be easier if you just surrendered?"

"It's called…human spirit…," Arthur drawled. "It's something you may never come to understand…"

"Your wound is shallow," said Viktor, glancing back at them. "Nonetheless, your time has come to an end. I came here with a task to fulfill, and you will be no more hindrance." His voice shifted again and was now the Viceroy's voice. "'You know the will of a single man is enough to change the world, but you'll inevitably need the support of your friends, the loyalty and truth of your allies, resources to survive, and, of course, a safe haven.' What would you do if everything aforementioned just…disappeared, vanished from your world?" Arthur's eyes widened with shock. He struggled to sit up. "Let us make your quest a little more challenging…" and just before he could step in the way to take the blow himself, the flying dagger went through the Viceroy's heart.

"No!" Arthur shouted, catching Viceroy Nicholas as he went limp, the knife's hilt protruding from his heart. He carefully placed him on the ground, unable to do anything other than watch his second father slowly perish. The Viceroy could do nothing other than gasp like a fish and painfully stare at the ceiling above, with no hope of survival.

Wrath shot up through Arthur's body, restoring his vigor and drowning out the wound's pain. Arthur ran toward the Harbinger, sword in hand, and lunged at the young man, who made no effort to evade the attack or counter. He was protected by an invisible barrier once again.

"Why aren't you defending yourself?" Arthur blurted out as Viktor imperturbably stared at him. Arthur's eyes were wild and sparkling as he gazed savagely at the Harbinger. He would never forget that scarred young face.

"That was only step one," Viktor replied. "Let us proceed with step two."

"You know…one day…I will kill you…," Arthur growled, gritting his teeth.

"Loathe me and your fatal flaw shall bring your downfall upon you. Seek me out and you shall shorten your abject life." The Harbinger's eyes seemed blind, as if he were in a trance. "Don't look back…the Sun will not relent." His palms began to glow white as a sepulchral whisper came out of his hands. The souls had begun to fulfill his summoning. The chamber became chilly and the sky darkened to a pitch-black thundercloud. Swirling gusts of wind twisted around the White Bastion. Glancing outside the big windows, Arthur thought he saw a dark and gigantic cloud in the form of a hand looming upon the citadel.

"What have you done?" Arthur gasped, stunned, staring at the black ominous cloud.

"Your 'safe haven' is now marked with the Claws of Antares," said Viktor. "You can consider this place now taken by the enemy."

"Over my dead body!" Arthur struck at him again, an invisible force pushing him away, making him stagger to the ground.

"One last warning," said Viktor, his face deadpan. "Never

underestimate the devotion of a dragon, *especially* when his lord is at risk. Your world will be subdued in three…two…one!" The Earth shook violently, steadying during intervals of three seconds each time, the same way it had happened in Paris. "The Heir of the Sun is a matter not to be taken lightly. The Nemesis of the Knight, father of all reptiles, he will be the one to finally tame your feeble defenses and terminate your Order once and for all…"

From the Ashes...

Arthur watched with rapt attention through the windows, his blood freezing as a gargantuan black mass clawed its way out through a monumental vortex: a vast, beguiling and fluctuating hole that had opened amid the plains inside the citadel.

With a massive talon gouging the earth beneath, Kronnix the Sovereign emerged onto the surface, his black scales glittering majestically, even though the light of the sun was gloomy. Standing upright upon his strong hind legs, he unfurled his immensely large wings and shook them with vigor, his ridged backbone standing out. He gazed with his gilded eyes at the castle of the Order. Crawling four-legged toward the building, he moved without any difficulty despite his size, his arrowhead tail waving behind. He settled himself next to the castle, taller than the highest tower.

With horror, Arthur distinguished hundreds of dots and specks gushing out of the barracks, and in all likelihood, getting ready to fight off the dragon, even if chances of survival were nonexistent. The dragon began spitting pellets of fire, apparently amused by the spectacle, as if trying his accuracy. He stopped and began making a growling noise within his throat, with a frequency so low no human could hear.

"Shall I proceed now?" Kronnix rumbled.

At Arthur's side, he saw how the Harbinger closed his eyes. He was still unable to do him any harm: "I sense something troubling you, milord," said Viktor without opening his mouth. "And, certainly, that must be something I should worry about as well."

"Antares' condition is weakening fast. My concern is the rate at which his health is quickly deteriorating. I feel the moment we dread is close."

Arthur turned back to Nicholas, and as he leaned over him, holding his hand and suppressing his own tears, he noticed the Viceroy was trying to tell him something. He stooped over the Viceroy's mouth, and in between gasps, he scarcely made out three words: "Heir…stop…them."

"The more you kill, the better for him. Hunt down all these men and destroy their refuge. This is the quickest way to gather Antares' cure," replied Viktor, his eyes still closed. "I will gather all the souls while you kill off all these vermin, that way sending the cure to Antares immediately. There is one more thing I will ask you to do beforehand, though. Clothe us in fire, light us like a torch!"

Kronnix craned his neck to his side, glaring at the castle of the Order. "Are you certain?" the dragon asked.

"There is one reason why they call me Fireclad," Viktor replied soundlessly.

Kronnix's massive chest expanded as he inhaled the air that would help fuel and expel the long flame he was charging. An inferno erupted from Kronnix's maw, spraying and engulfing the entire castle. At once, Arthur began to feel the scorching heat within the Viceroy's chamber, tongues of fire breaking in through the windows and licking their frames. Arthur felt the oxygen quickly begin to get sucked out of the hall, smoke blocking out the view, the surroundings taking on a red-orange color as flames overwhelmed the castle.

Arthur struggled to his feet, and as he stood upright, feeling much pain on his hip, the effects of blood loss began to take him over. Dizziness and nausea shot through his body as he tried to lift the Viceroy. Nicholas forced two more words out of his bleeding mouth: "Leave…me."

Deep inside, Arthur knew the Viceroy was right, that he had to be left behind. Viceroy Nicholas did not stand a chance, and Arthur was appointed an important quest. As blazes of fire and heavy clouds of smoke began to surround him, his eyes watering, Arthur seized Nicholas' shortsword and when he turned his eyes back to meet the Viceroy's, found them already blank and lifeless. And yet, Arthur crossed the Viceroy's arms over his chest, slipped the shortsword's hilt into his left hand, the tip pointing at his feet, and brushed the palm of his hand over his visage, closing his inert eyes.

"Even when Death is calling you to embrace her in her arms, nothing seems to daunt you," Viktor observed as he cut his conversation with the dragon, and even with the flames brushing his dark cloak, he was still unaffected. "But I see it in the forthcoming future: you are not unbreakable as you think you are. If you survive the impending ordeals, by the end you will be broken. Think twice before challenging a Harbinger. *We will break you*!" And with that said, he made the floor under his feet shimmer and he dissolved into thin air.

Arthur's sight went a little off balance as he shuffled his way toward the exit of the chamber, retrieving his helmet to protect his face and pressing his hand on his hip; and as he reached the great doors, he could not help but linger there and turn back to look upon the Viceroy once more, large tongues of flame closing in on him and gradually overwhelming him.

The entire tower was actually a fiery torch as its insides were consumed in fire. Showers of sparks began to rain down as parts of the ceiling gave in to the heat as Arthur arrived at the main staircase, his gloved hand heavily clamped over his nose and mouth, his eyes watering due to the deep shroud of smoke and sheer grief. The stylishly woven tapestries on the walls were charred and were gradually burnt away, their ashes billowing up to the ceiling. The marble floor reflected the illumination from the flames as they played up and down, dancing around and spreading their tendrils to turn everything into cinders.

As Arthur reached the last step of the staircase, disorientation, lightheadedness, grief, despair and pain finally overcame him, and he tripped and tumbled to the glowing scarlet floor, his helmet flying from his head as he touched ground.

Viceroy Nicholas was dead, his entire Taurus Company was dead, *Alice* was dead, his only home was burning and turning to ashes, he was wounded, his fellow knights were being decimated, and the Harbingers were just too strong, too mighty for him to deal with. The castle was about to collapse over him as he lay defeated on the floor, carrying the weight of the world.

Smoke quickly swathed him in a cloak of darkness, poisonous fumes killing his lungs, the blistering heat making his face burn. His body quickly began to heat up under the armor. The exit was just ahead, down the corridor.

"Arthur!" His name was called out, but he was not sure whether he had even heard it. Yet he heard it again, clearer this time as he raised his head from the floor, his eyes half-shut. There was no one in the world that called him by his name without first addressing his rank, other than someone who was already dead. "This is your time to prove them wrong."

Alice offered her hand to Arthur as he looked up astounded. She was clad in plated armor, her eyes tear-filled and her other hand covering her nose and mouth.

"Not everything is lost yet," she continued as Arthur rose with her help. "We are still fighting, and that's what matters. You have to keep on living, even when the world turns your life upside down. Believe and don't give up!"

Alice turned around toward the exit and Arthur limped down the hall after her and along the corridor, traversing capes of smoke as blazing debris began to fall behind them, blocking the entrance into the hall. As both knights struck open the castle doors with their shoulders, the dull gray light of the sun flashed before Arthur's eyes, and Alice was gone, vanished from the world and back in the darkest corners of his mind.

Somehow Alice's unreal and sudden appearance had compelled Arthur to go on, even when all his odds of survival and success were null.

The first thing Arthur noticed when he came out into the open was the gigantic dark claw about to swallow the sun, looming overhead, and the chaotic turmoil that was taking place in the plains.

His horse was still hitched to the pole in the atrium of the raging castle, desperately struggling to free itself from the bonds that held it prisoner. The dragon's head and wings were prominently visible to the left side of the building. The troops of knights had Kronnix the Sovereign's full and undivided attention trained on them. Before mounting the horse, Arthur stroked its muzzle to calm it down and whispered: "Time to interfere…"

¤¤¤

"Give them death from above," said Viktor, standing upright upon the dragon's broad and strong shoulders, overlooking the vast citadel of the Order and beyond, his eyes closed as he concentrated on gathering the souls of the fallen and sending them to Antares, while, at the same time, communicating with Kronnix by infrasound.

"Antares' death is nigh; I can feel his pain and agony growing greatly every moment," said Kronnix, scrutinizing the fields ahead to get a closer look at his targets. "They brought archers and catapults…just as Dwellers, they never learn." He peered upward and shot out a ball of fire. After it had gained enough height, it began to angle down in a steep dive, crashing down on and enveloping a wooden catapult in fire, showering the close surroundings with sparks. "Our attempts to keep Antares alive are feeble. For every single soul we give him, his life is prolonged only for a minute. Nevertheless, his life is decaying twice as fast as that," he replied.

"Then what do you suggest, milord?" Viktor asked as Kronnix continued to shoot down more catapults.

"Nothing, actually. Nothing can be done except prolong his life until we are unable to do so anymore, and that moment is about to occur," replied the dragon, jerking his head to the side to evade a flying boulder that was about to strike him. "Eliminating every single man I see before us, I reckon, it would extend Antares' life at least eight days, and if we halve that total, he will only live four more days. Keeping in mind that if we do not let this species of men reproduce, they will go extinct, and we will have depleted our source of souls."

"We are the next step in evolution. We will dominate both worlds as their species passes away. It is natural selection, and by far, we are the strongest race," Viktor replied, his voice imperative. "And if we run out of souls, we can always resort to the depths of Tartarus, Asphodel's vast rolling hills, and Elysium's peaceful fields, since they are teeming with them. And remember that these men are not the only ones who bear souls, but Dwellers and dragons do as well."

"Be careful with what you say. Your beliefs are warped, Harbinger," Kronnix warned while spraying long flames over the army before them, the troops scattering like ants as the flare grazed them. "You should already know that life must be preserved. You can sow a thousand sprouting seeds, and after a while, reap most of them. However, a certain number must be allowed to live so they reproduce again. By exterminating every human, you would be committing an unforgivable sin; you would be breaking the cycle of life and death." Kronnix craned his huge head toward Viktor on his shoulder, his snake eyes drilling into his. "If I ever hear you threatening my race again," he snapped his jaws, "I shall make sure you cease to exist." He snorted angrily, standing erect upon his strong hind legs as a stone boulder soared the skies toward his head. With a claw, he caught the rock in mid-air, and with a powerful swing, he hurled it back. As it hit the ground, the crag went rolling with enough inertia to mash the sender catapult to pieces…

¤¤¤

Arthur headed for the raging battle, making his way toward his allies, trying as much as he could to avoid the dragon's piercing glare across the open fields.

As Arthur raced toward the parapet, he saw from the corner of his eye how fire-mortars the size of horses glided to the citadel before crashing down. The fire spread as it touched ground, immediately clinging mercilessly to the knights who were close to impact. They threw themselves to the ground and rolled from side to side to put it out, often to no avail. Arthur watched completely appalled by how they were being slaughtered as he tried to cross unnoticed. He saw how archers neared the dragon and began shooting volleys of white-feathered arrows, all bouncing off his glittering armor. The few heavy boulders that struck him would only shatter on contact, causing him to stagger back a little while continuing to fire fireballs.

When Arthur arrived in the knights' midst, he observed how a large number of them were panicking, and many lay on the ground, either hyperventilating or retching. Weeping men dragged their fellow burnt comrades to a temporary shelter that they knew soon would fall. As knights fell, either wounded or dead, and their defenses diminished, they were promptly replaced by those still untouched. The knights formed several lines of defense, layers the dragon would have to breach. Among them, the catapults were lined up together in several rows, either destroyed or flaring with furious fire. As Arthur retreated further toward the parapet, the number of wounded knights increased, some of which were being treated by healers. There were screams of pain, despair and grief all around and they never ceased. Arthur headed all the way down toward the walls of the parapet where he knew the highest ranking knights would be, planning their next strategy.

Antoine had been commanding Capricorn Company, staying as far as he could from the fiery dragon, just as every other Marshal did. "How did that beast get in here without anyone noticing?" he demanded when he saw Arthur approaching. "Where is the Viceroy?" he asked, a little more softly.

"The Harbinger killed him," said Arthur in a rush as he dismounted tiredly, nearly missing his footing because of the pain in his side. "I tried to save him, but I wasn't quick enough. It doesn't matter anymore. Just focus on the present!"

"Both arrows and catapults seem to be useless," Antoine replied.

"How many knights have fallen so far?" Arthur asked, already worrying about what he would hear.

"The casualties have not been too great, as I would expect," he replied, crossing his arms. "Either that beast is not as mighty as we think, or something is wrong with it."

The other Marshals were beside them, trying to come up with a good idea, but none was clever or efficient enough. They only favored fleeing, so far, but the exit was not as close to them as they would like.

Arthur descried a miniature figure upon Kronnix's mighty shoulders, his own fists clenching involuntarily. From that distance, it was a mere brownish spot, a smaller faint spark glistening on its middle. Arthur knew that was the Harbinger, already absorbing all the souls he could gather from his fellow fallen comrades.

Kronnix stood upright upon his hind legs, catching a flying boulder with his claw and sending it back against its own catapult.

"Great!" Antoine exclaimed with a tone of sarcasm, watching with awe how the boulder went rolling over the sender catapult. "Now it's using our own weapons against us!"

"What's the ultimate plan?" Arthur asked, his breathing agitated, beads of sweat forming on his brow, his hand keeping pressure on his wound. "One does not simply kill a dragon! We have to leave, now!"

"I agree with fleeing…as long as that beast lets us go through the exit," Antoine replied, pointing at the far end of the citadel.

That is when Arthur realized what the solution was: to switch the dragon's attention to another target. "I will rally the knights. Make them all follow you to the exit," said Arthur, dabbing the sweat off his forehead as he awkwardly mounted his horse, his wound stinging. He remembered his former steed, and he realized he had not seen him again. His hopes of reuniting with him had been extinguished. "You will leave, and I will stay," he told Antoine.

"There is never a way to dissuade you, is there?" Antoine asked, his face grim with sheer anguish.

"Never. You know me," Arthur replied, with a faint smile. "Tell the other Marshals to be prepared."

"Aye, Marshal," Antoine replied, and as he mounted his horse and began to ride, he caught a glimpse off to the left of something glowing like a furnace. Antoine winced when he saw the bright glow inside Kronnix's throat as he opened wide his maw. "Look…" His voice was cut off as a gigantic long blaze flared at his side, twenty meters away. He could feel his skin peeling and hair singeing as the blistering heat blasted past before him. The horse snorted and reared back wildly, turning around looking for coolness. Screams of pain resounded across the immense fields as multiple knights were burned alive, their plated armors gleaming white-hot against the obscurity of the sky. As the fire cleared, a long and broad trail of scorched grass with smoldering catapults and corpses was revealed, now a deep scar on the White Bastion. The smoke became profuse, even where Antoine's horse had stopped, farther away alongside Arthur, who was watching completely stunned. Thick smoke and ashes clogged the atmosphere around them and a cape of blackness was draped over them and the surroundings.

"Run!" yelped Arthur, coughing violently, his eyes watering and lungs straining as they were infected with foul and venomous fumes. He covered his lower face with one hand while deftly maneuvering the horse out of the smoke.

"Where are the other Marshals?" Antoine shouted over the din of screams and destruction. "I cannot see them!"

"They are gone!" Arthur replied, sorely dismayed. "I saw how the fire swept over them; we were lucky, by a hair's breadth." Terror sparkled in his eyes as he caught Kronnix's glowing throat once again. "This is the end," he muttered to himself. "From the ashes...," he mumbled, as if in a prayer, "...unto salvation..."

A gigantic spellbinding fireball was shot up into the air, and as it hung low under the baneful skies, hovering still upon the land as it shone on the landscape as if it were *the* sun, it began its downfall like an asteroid about to strike the Earth. Crashing against the once pacific land, it exploded, sending a massive blast of fire as well as a thundering sonic boom within a lethal circumference. Flames showered and teemed on the earth around the impact zone, leaving a huge concave crater. Spiraling pitch-black smoke hung low over the land, gradually blotting out the sun completely. Numerous knights' and horses' carcasses lay within the impact zone, charred and smoldering. Those few left untouched began their belated and frenzied retreat toward the exit, which the dragon would surely blast to kill them off.

Arthur and Antoine watched in despairing stupor how they were being exterminated. In an adrenaline rush, Arthur reacted and spurred the steed into a fast gallop toward the fleeing knights and thus the dragon. The knights were quickly moving toward Arthur as he sped toward them. He himself already knew that rallying the knights for departure was completely hopeless, unless he managed to take the dragon's attention.

Arthur dismounted, letting the horse gallop away, and seized an archer's bow and quiver from the ground. His dwarfed stature let him go unnoticed as he quickly approached the towering dragon, who was already taking aim to fire at the fleeing knights, the flaming castle collapsing at his side. Arthur's heart sank when he saw, spellbound, how Kronnix's throat began to glow red-hot once again.

Arthur knelt on one knee, nocked an arrow to the bowstring and took aim. He set his aim on the dragon's head and let it drift slowly toward a more vulnerable point: the unwary Harbinger. He inhaled deeply and held his breath, time running slow as he marked his target, letting wrath and serenity balance out to achieve maximum concentration. He released the white-fletched arrow, the string grazing past his cheek as its tension loosened, returning shuddering to a standstill.

The whizzing arrow pierced the Harbinger's lower torso, sending him off the dragon's shoulder and into the air, headlong toward the earth. With clear disbelief, Viktor reacted while in mid-air and materialized himself back on Kronnix's shoulder and landed squatting, the shaft protruding from his body as he groaned with pain.

Kronnix the Sovereign jolted as he sensed what was happening, and suppressed the flames that he was charging. He lowered his monumental head and turned it sideways so his huge gilt eyes could behold Arthur closely. Arthur stared captivated into those fear-inducing orbs, both nearly as big as his entire body. Adrenaline lanced up his being, and yet, he was unable to move. When the dragon looked back at the multitude of fleeing knights, most of them had already crossed the exit.

"Our attempts are nothing but futile," Kronnix remarked with infrasound. "Even if we killed every one of these men, Antares would still die within a few days. We have to give him a bigger and dearer soul than these for him to last more than months."

"Kill that bloody bastard!" Viktor barked aloud as he lay kneeling on the dragon's shoulder, his hands bloodstained from keeping pressure on the wound.

Arthur had already scurried off behind a wall of the smoldering ruins, close to Kronnix, and remained there hidden.

"You will heal," said the dragon, getting more and more impatient. "We have to go back to Antares, now!"

"To do what, exactly?!" Viktor retorted.

"You shall focus on the task at hand, Harbinger! Antares has been like a father to me," replied Kronnix, letting out a clamorous aggressive growl. Suddenly, Arthur began to feel groggy and dizzy, and still he leaned his head out of the wall to get a small peek of what was happening.

"But what do you mean by 'dearer'?"

"I will return him the favor. Give him *my* soul and he shall live longer," Kronnix said.

The gigantic vortex opened at his feet in front of him, and right before the Harbinger dissolved into thin air and the dragon leaped into the ravenous darkness, Viktor groaned: "So be it…"

The last thing Arthur saw before passing out was how Kronnix leaped into the immense vortex, giving the knights a certain chance of survival. However, he felt his head feverish, as if it were about to explode, his perspiration increasing profusely, bathing him in sweat under the ash-blackened armor as the castle beside him turned completely to fiery ruins. His breathing became hard and came in shallow and rapid bursts. His skin itched without respite, making him wish to be able to scratch all his body, but all he could do was remain quiet and immobile, agony eating away at his life and consciousness as he finally fell into a turbulent slumber…

...Unto Salvation

Alice awoke with a start.

She bolted upright, bewildered, and completely oblivious to her whereabouts. She peered around her surroundings, eyeing every detail minutely. Alice caught a dim light glimmering upon her; it was the light of the moon filtering through dense boughs of trees in faint arrows of silver. For a brief moment, she thought she was back on Earth. Remembering recent events told her otherwise. It dawned on her that she was now stranded in the Purging Trials. Upon that realization, her senses heightened, her eyes flashing everywhere, sharp ears attentive toward any sound. She fumbled around in the darkness, looking desperately for the weapons that had detached from her belt during the free-fall. She snatched her sword, feeling the comfortable balance of its weight under her clenched fingers, and yet, having such a weapon in her possession did not diminish her fear.

There was a sudden rustle at her side. Alice gasped and clamped her mouth shut; to survive she would have to be extra careful and quiet. After her eyes had accustomed to the penumbra, she gazed around, noticing gnarled and knobbly roots of trees protruding out of the ground, large and thick. The dark forest sprawled across kilometers in all directions, covering the land in seas of dark trees of different kinds and sizes. Her eyes followed the way upward, scarcely noticing the voluminous tree trunks, their gaunt and dense branches blocking out most of the starlight overhead. Her heart skipped a beat when she noticed a dull glint upon the boughs just above her, ominous and black. A loud caw startled her, yet she remained motionless, dreading the presence of predators. The crow, perched high above her on an oak's branch, beheld her with little beady eyes glinting under the starlight. Alice tried to ignore it, but she could still feel its gaze piercing the back of her neck as she turned around. Then it flew away, the beating of wings sounding rather odd, giving her a sense of longing, reminding her of the surface, of her life.

After several minutes of careful and quiet observation, she steeled herself to stand up and take a look around. She was in a glade, surrounded by immense oaks, leafy weeping willows, high firs, gaunt larches, twisted elms, and dense prickling underbrush. Then she distinguished a shape lying on the ground motionless.

"Sonja!" Alice gasped, relieved to see her. She crouched beside her and shook her shoulders. "Wake up, please," Alice begged, but she got no response. Sonja lay curled up on her side, barely breathing. The sense that they were being spied upon from among the pines and oaks froze her on the spot. She could hardly move as she sharpened her ears and listened raptly, her heart gradually pumping harder and faster until it hurt.

Alice slowly glanced back at the gaps among the trees, still unwilling to lower her guard. She whipped around as something crunched behind them, sending a chill down her spine.

Sonja stirred upon the grass, her rags rustling as she stretched. Alice shook her shoulders slightly and stooped down to whisper in her ear, barely audibly:

"Quiet." She paused for a second. "We are not alone."

Sonja acknowledged the message and sat up as slowly as she could. Still crouched, Alice found her steel dagger near her, and gave it to Sonja, hilt first, and both remained frozen, feeling each other's breaths as they formed into small white clouds, wafting away as the cold air rushed throughout the woods, both under the dominion of fear. Alice was starting to feel cold, despite her livery and plated armor, but then she guessed Sonja must have been freezing to death because she was in mere tatters. However, as much as she wanted to, she could not give Sonja anything else to protect herself from the relentless cold.

"Welcome to my realm," a grave and mischievous voice

boomed throughout the world. "My name is Geister, Lord of Madness." Alice and Sonja stood quickly, weapons ready and in a back-against-back position. They ran their eyes through the gaps of the trees and beyond the gloom, searching for the emitter of the voice. Alice happened to look at the star above. The bright side of it had been darkened and only two openings were left lit, resembling a pair of slit slanted eyes gazing at the vast land below. "My realm is the first stage of the Purging Trials. You are supposed to solve all my enigmas, should you want to reach salvation. Only the most cunning, strong-hearted and iron-willed souls are able to perform such quests."

"Show yourself!" Alice shouted, despairing, her back against Sonja's, while both whirled around periodically to check all sides for enemies.

"You do not need to shout, for I am able to read your thoughts whenever I will," the voice replied. "I am watching you, the whole time. My gaze is unavoidable. Complete my enigmas and you shall be redeemed."

"He is not lying, Alice," Sonja muttered. "He is within our minds." Alice nodded in agreement and waited for their host to proceed with his introduction.

"What do you expect us to do?" Alice asked within her mind, reaching out for Geister's mental link. Even when he was not speaking, Alice could still feel his presence.

"'From afar I shall be seen, towering and mysterious,'" the voice recited. "'Seek me out and you shall be sheltered. Make no heed to my riddle and you shall perish.'" Geister finished the riddle and rumbled inside the knights' heads. "An enigma awaits you, and you should hurry, for all that is dear to you." With that said, Alice and Sonja felt the mental contact broken and all fell silent once again. The star brightened wholly once again and so it remained, undisturbed. Unearthly wind roared throughout the dark forest, brushing violently the tree branches, plucking numerous leaves off them, carrying them aloft, swirling in mid-air and flying away.

Sonja smiled weakly, offering her hand. "Come on, Alice. We can do it."

Alice nodded, reaching out and holding her hand.

They moved onward, huddled together, blades ready and stepping onto massive roots that crept out of the floor, many times almost stumbling over them as they made their way to the innermost part of the woods. There was not a clear path to follow, and all they could do was weave in and out among the pines. The earth where they stood was invisible to their eyes chiefly due to the darkness and the dense scrub. Alice and Sonja often got their feet stuck in roots. Every now and then, bushes close to them shook as something hurried off when they came nearby. The thick underbrush made the journey harder for Sonja, because she only wore rags. Her legs were often scratched and scraped against thorns and spines, but she tried her best not to complain. Alice passed untouched due to her silver greaves and boots. As they moved through the forest, Alice was not sure whether it was only a bad feeling that she had, or whether the trees around them were actually moving. She could not see any movement; however, she was sure that something unnatural was at work. While carefully trudging upon the roots, she felt as though the branches of the trees above curved down like demonic claws seeking their prey, reaching for her. The faint whispers of the wind gradually shifted as she listened closely. She was sure she could hear voices, all blended in together and murmuring at the same time what she could discern as nonsense. They seemed to have no end, and after a few seconds she just about detected an intelligible word: *Alice*. Her heart thumped frantically; she thought she was going mad, and yet, she forced herself not to say a word to Sonja about it.

After a few moments of warily moving through the trees, they arrived at another glade further in the forest where they decided to stop and rest. Alice's chest was heavy and she was making an effort to keep her sanity. The voices stopped, but even then, she remained restless.

Alice sat down beside Sonja on a protruding root, their backs against the trunk. Her distress was downright noticeable, and yet darkness concealed it, but not her trembling voice. "I still can't believe the mess we are stuck in. It feels more like a nightmare, and yet, I can't seem to wake up."

"Regrettably, it is all real," Sonja replied. "I feel it too. I didn't believe what people said of the afterlife, and even if I did believe,

I never would've thought it would be so horrifying and gloomy. I didn't believe what the Church said. I thought that maybe, if I did what was right in the world, I would die in peace. Even after all my actions, I was punished. Was it because I didn't believe in their teachings?"

"That would be a simple explanation. We are stuck in this world, and our only exit is to finish all the Trials ahead of us. Why must we do this? I don't know the reasons behind it yet. But what I do know is that the Church's teachings are not related." Again, Alice could not shake off the feeling that she was going mad, after reflecting upon what she had just said. She could only define that as absurd and illogical. "Yet I can't get things straight," Alice said, her fingers rubbing her temples, her voice rife with anguish. "Ever since we went into Notre Dame everything went off course. Everybody died, even you, and still, you are here with me. Arthur believes I died, and he only has a month or so left to live. Paris is in ruins and France is in grave danger. How did any of this happen?"

"As you said, our only exit comes with finishing these trials. I don't know what they are, but I'm sure that the only way to succeed is to never give up and continue living, as long as you can. We lost our lives, our homes, and yet we stand, so that means we're still fighting, because we have a purpose worth dying for, and that is what matters now. If there is a way to stop the Harbingers, this is it," Sonja remarked. "The first step is that we solve the enigma."

"You're right," Alice sighed. "We have to keep moving."

"'From afar I shall be seen, towering and mysterious. Seek me out and you shall be sheltered. Make no heed to my riddle and you shall perish,'" Sonja recalled.

"That's easy to guess," said Alice, pointing toward the sky, just above the canopy of the trees. A tall, rounded and ominous tower loomed high, peering all around the extensive land, its bristling spire nearly touching the dark clouds. "The answer is right there in the stanza. It is seen from afar, towering and mysterious. We'll find shelter in there. However, we can be killed outside."

"It's still far away," Sonja replied in a low voice. "Around three kilometers from here, perhaps."

There was a sudden rustle, just ahead, behind the weeping willow in front of them. Both bolted upright, drawing their weapons. A black silhouette stepped into view, a man, seemingly wearing armor.

"Arthur?" Alice gasped as the man removed his helmet. The skin on his face was pale, his eyes empty, but darkness concealed those facts. Alice approached the figure with caution, resisting the urge to embrace him, warily looking into his eyes.

"Don't, it's just a decoy!" Sonja yelled as Arthur's eyes began to glow red, a wide wicked grin forming on his face.

Alarmed, Alice shoved him off when he lurched forward to grab her. He began to melt and turn into strips of shadow, swirling around and producing perturbing wails. A black goo of darkness, formless and squirming, was all that remained, wringing and twisting about, taking on several different shapes and sizes, and constantly turning into something else. All of a sudden, the shapeless goo expanded and burst into shreds of shadow, hitting Alice and Sonja, and immediately afterward, disappearing altogether. The first thing that Alice noticed was that the whispers had returned, more agitated and furious than ever and repeating *Alice* incessantly. Alice clamped her ears with her hands, shutting away every noise and subjecting herself to a perilous world where the sense of hearing was of vital importance. She gritted her teeth. The whispers were still there, stronger than ever. It was her mother's voice, and sometimes it switched to Arthur's. Alice could hear them, calling her to help them because they would die if she did not.

Sonja was trying to get a word out of Alice as she knelt down on the earth, gripping her head and moaning silently, tears streaming down her face. All of a sudden, the tree branches above them began to actually curve down, reaching out for them with their shriveled leaves, creaking as their rough bark gave way to their unnatural movements.

Sonja backed off, nearly stumbling over the bloated roots of an oak.

Out of the bark of a tree, a cloud of darkness formed, taking the shape of a winged and leathery creature, eyeless, with a broad pit crowned with fangs, displaying them as it clung to the branch like a bat, just above the knights. However, it did not produce a single noise as it opened wide its maw, leaning menacingly toward Sonja.

Neither of them knew whether those figures were real or just a part of their imaginations, but all the same, they did not care about that. All they wanted was to disappear from that place, or even forget anything that had happened. Out of the gloom came the creature that Sonja abhorred the most. A huge spider, the size of a warhorse, came crawling toward them as its leg joints snapped and cracked noisily. Ever since she was little, Sonja had had a phobia toward spiders. She would recoil with immense disgust whenever she happened to get her hand tangled in a cobweb. The mere sight of the giant arachnid froze her blood as nothing had done before. Neither the reptilians nor William as a werewolf had frightened her as much.

Alice was unaware of her surroundings. Her entire attention was trained on the unfaltering voices that threatened to steer her toward madness. Sonja backed off a few steps as the black spider advanced, towering over them, its jaws twitching and snapping. Sonja was hyperventilating, sweat streaming down her neck. Sonja could not help but shriek as fear and impotence over took her once she realized she was unable to help Alice.

Alice's eyes flicked open. Without hesitation, she stood up and unsheathed her broadsword, hacking away mercilessly at the spider's legs as it cowered back, wailing in pain.

Alice whirled around and gripped Sonja's hand and both took off in a rush as a black hooded figure began to dig itself out and rise upon the ground. Her one constantly active sense was that of survival and a gradually expanding need to protect Sonja at all cost. Sonja's helplessness served as a cue that somehow triggered something inside Alice, prompting her to overcome her own fears.

Besides darkness, their blinding race through uneven terrain caused Alice to trip over, dragging Sonja down with her. At once, black energetic snakes dug their way up onto the surface and wrapped around Alice's wrists, chest and neck, constraining all the oxygen that went into her lungs. Not even her plated armor could stop the relentless constrictor attacks. She floundered on the ground, trying to break free and reach her sword, but in vain. Lightheadedness was her first sign of air deprivation. Shallow gasps of air were all she could muster, only to let them go unused once again. She could feel herself drifting away into unconsciousness.

Sonja managed to seize her dagger and slide it between her chest and the snake. With one quick, strong swipe, she severed the snake and it faded away. Immediately, she turned to help Alice, who tried to remain still as Sonja stood over her. Alice stopped thrashing, resisting the sudden spasms to fight back. Sonja promptly gripped the serpent at Alice's chest and pulled it back, sliding the dagger in between and rending it in two; it quickly dissolved into strips of shadow.

Coughing, Alice quickly sat up and took out of her auxiliary pouch a handful of tinder, a pair of flint stones, and her small oil flask. Sonja immediately knew what she was thinking and fetched a sturdy stick from the ground, giving it to Alice. Deftly, Alice coiled the tinder around the end of the stick, unscrewed the oil flask and poured all its content onto the tinder.

All around them, scores of formless shadows, constantly taking on different shapes and sizes, slowly began to close in on the knights, ghostly silent and heart-rendingly terrifying: winged otherworldly creatures fluttering in mid-air, hooded and faceless men, giant arachnids, voluminous and large snakes, hunched beasts with long arms and misshapen faces.

As Alice worked the flint stones with her freezing hands by scraping them against one another, struggling to ignite one spark, the silent clouds of darkness slowly drifted toward them. She knew they were all behind them and she still continued to work frenziedly, confident that she would create a blaze before it was too late. Just as a hooded faceless figure laid a hand on her shoulder, a spark sprang from the stones and landed on the tinder, the oil immediately catching fire and spreading, creating a blazing torch.

Alice spun around in a squat, defensively waving the torch from side to side. The intensity of the fire quickly caused the shadows to dissolve. And for the first time they felt a little safe, but only under the protection of light.

"We'll have to keep it lit for now." Alice heaved a sigh of relief and slumped against a trunk.

"I'm sorry. I feel useless," whispered Sonja at her side. "I couldn't move…that thing…the spider…I'm sorry. I was too scared."

"You don't have to apologize," Alice remarked firmly, curling her arm around Sonja and holding her close. "I will always protect you." Her voice took a more grim tone. "I'm afraid this is only the beginning. We haven't even solved the first riddle."

"We'll get there, eventually," Sonja replied, pointing at the tower.

"We're closer now," said Alice. "We should rest a few minutes. At least under the light feels safer."

Sonja nodded.

After the minutes had gone slowly by, Alice decided to continue.

"Come on, we should keep moving," Alice said. "How are you feeling now?"

"I just hope I don't get to see any more spiders," Sonja said.

"They are all like everything else. They eat, sleep, breed and bleed. You can kill them as easily as you would halve a snake or bring down a knight in battle. Don't let them daunt you," Alice responded.

Sonja let Alice help her to her feet. They set out once again. As they cautiously trod through the woods, Alice's torchlight inevitably cast frightening shadows of the trees.

Only a few minutes after they had resumed their trek, they heard a rustle in the undergrowth just like they had done only a few minutes ago, but this time it intensified. Alice and Sonja were startled, fixing their eyes on the vibrating bushes. The torch could not cast light at a long range, so they were unable to tell whether the creature was small or big. They heard a strange squeak, followed by a shrill screech, as if bones were being scraped heavily together. Remaining motionless, Alice and Sonja stared fixedly, their armed hands trembling with fear, trying their best not to move.

The rattling quieted. Alice was not sure whether they were being watched. The screeching began once more, now louder and nearer. Alice glanced at the castle ahead; she realized they were close to their goal. Within seconds, a human-sized and roughly triangular head poked out of the thorns and leaves. Under the blaze of the torch and the little starlight that was able to filter into the clearing, they noticed two pairs of holes in the head. Soon afterward, they realized they were empty eye sockets and nostrils. The head had a yellowish hue, intensified by the lunar light. With a chill, it dawned on them that it was an animal skull. It had a long canine snout, its long and sharp fangs bared due to the lack of skin and fur.

A living jackal-sized skeleton leaped out of the darkness into the clearing, the empty sockets glaring at the frightened knights. The entire body was shuddering, perhaps because of its soundless growls. It made no single sound except for those unnerving screeches, which came from the constant joint motions as it moved its limbs. It had an elegantly formed spinal column, its ribs curving down accordingly. It glowered at Alice and Sonja avidly, arching its spine as if it were ready to pounce over them.

Alice stepped in front of Sonja, in a protective position, broadsword ready, and in the act, she snapped a twig. With only that sudden movement, the skeleton made its attack. With a flick of her wrist, Alice slashed the skeleton, sidestepping right afterward as it flew past them.

Contrary to their expectations, the animal rose again from the ground, staggering a bit before recovering itself completely. Right behind it, the undergrowth shuddered once again, revealing another skeleton of the same kin. Both glared at the knights, ready to attack together.

Alice and Sonja looked at each other. Without spoken consent, both turned back toward the castle and rushed through the woods, the hounds pursuing them, their bony joints screeching as they scurried under the low-hung branches and the undergrowth. The thick roots made their escape even more difficult, proving to be highly obtrusive, making it harder to step or hurdle completely over them. They ran, colliding with low hanging boughs that materialized from the darkness, the twigs whipping and lashing at their faces.

"You go ahead," Alice shouted at Sonja's side, not stopping from their headlong race. "I'll be fine. Just head toward the castle and meet me there." She tried to protest, but Alice stopped her short before she could utter a word. "Don't try talking me out of it."

Still while running at Sonja's side, Alice looked back, glancing at her small but nasty enemies. They had almost caught up with them, their knife-like teeth sparkling under the starlight, anxious to get a bite off her. Reluctantly, she slowed down a little, sword ready. One of the hounds pounced over her, bones screeching, and she sidestepped at the right time, the hound falling on her previous position. She sliced it sideways right afterward.

The second hound did not miss its target, causing Alice to stumble and fall down, rolling and, fortunately, barely evading the blade of her own sword during the roll, but dropping the torch to the ground at the same time. The hound landed next to her left leg, clenching its fangs upon her armor, piercing it as if it were a thin metallic sheet. Alice cried out in agony, shoving the hound off her legs with a swift kick in the snout; just releasing herself from its teeth made her flinch painfully. The first hound caught up with them and vaulted onto Alice, landing upon her cuirass. She glimpsed inside its empty throat as it lunged its teeth against her face in a flash. In a split second, she struck the hound with her sword's hilt right before its fangs could bore into her face.

Panting and sweating, she managed to stand up and continue her frenzied rush. Due to the heavy amounts of adrenaline, she was able to continue without respite while ignoring the pain. The stark citadel came wholly into view. It had a bridge which crossed the murky sea onto a gigantic promontory. The bridge was as broad as it was long, and it was made of granite and other stone. Her armor steps hammered upon the cobbled ground as she sped down toward the great castle. Now that the tower was closer, she realized just how high it was, nearly one hundred meters tall, a balcony standing out with several rectangular windows carved into the brick walls. Beneath it, there were various narrower and shorter towers that branched out and were supported by buttresses. Both fierce and mischievous-looking gargoyles with bestial faces were threateningly poised upon eaves and pedestals, up on the towers and on the ground, guarding the entrance. The citadel was encircled protectively by a tall rampart and a crenellated parapet. An imposing tall wooden gate, operated by a lever on the other side, loomed over the entrance.

Fortunately, the gate was already halfway open. She slipped

inside, and while doing so, she glanced at both sides, looking desperately for the lever, since she already was experienced with strongholds. It was at her left side and she jumped toward it, skidding to a halt as she rammed the lever downward, chains rattling as the gate groaned, making its vertiginous descent, crushing both hounds as it slammed shut, broken bones, ribs and skulls flying away and clacking on the pavement to lie motionless.

Alice sighed, relieved, and turned back to the main door of the castle. She had to walk through a long corridor, which was flanked by green thorny bushes that acted as walls that led to the entrance of the castle. The door in front of her was iron-black and had a door knocker in the form of a dragon's head. Two gargoyles guarded the entrance at its sides, sternly watching any visitors from their marble pedestals, their heads and eyes strategically placed to look Alice in the eye the whole time. One had a fierce look, glowering and hissing. The other had a rather mischievous face, leering at Alice as she crossed the threshold, but she gave no heed to its stalking eyes.

The door groaned open as she, warily, pushed it in, revealing a dark and gloomy but extensive lobby of a once ostentatious castle. A creaking old spider chandelier hung low right above her, its few candles lighting the room dimly. There were several wooden doors at both ends of the lobby. A broad staircase rose upward in front of her; two pedestals carried a porcelain statue, each depicting different images. The one on the right represented a man being tortured with knives being stabbed into him, while the second showed another man, about to hang himself with a noose, his eyes demented.

There was one door, peculiarly wider than the others, that was open. Instinctively, Alice entered through that door, looking eagerly for Sonja. As the door turned upon its creaking hinges, a voice boomed inside Alice's head, making her jump. It was Geister.

"You have solved your first *easy* riddle," said Geister in a rumbling voice. "'Life lends and life withdraws; poisonous to the fire and delightful to you; source of existence and scourge of humanity; across the twisted realm you shall tread, into the elixir's haven you shall venture, and recover your greatest treasure.'"

Now Alice found that difficult to guess. She quickly made a mental list of all that occurred to her, but was not sure of anything yet. All of a sudden, she was interrupted by strange noises, whose origin she sought right away, sharpening her ears and looking around on the threshold where she was standing. The sounds intensified. They were like whispers, funereal and almost inaudible, and utterly unintelligible. At the same time, she began to shudder even more, goose bumps forming on her arms and shoulders, her neck tingling. She caught a faint noise in her right ear and immediately turned her head that way, seeking for the source, but there was no one. Her heart pumped faster and she tried to pay more attention.

Alice walked forward, determined to ignore them. She stepped into a gigantic hall, almost one hundred meters tall. A broad circular stairwell went up right in the middle of the hall, running all the way up the dazzling height. Looking up, Alice could barely make out the outlines of the floors that stretched from one side to the other as bridges. There were dozens of them, although she was unable to see them all. A red velvet rug was placed upon the floor, spanning the entire hall. There were more doors at the sides and several dimly lit torches hung next to them upon corbels, crackling against the moldy walls. Casually, another door was open further down the hall.

As Alice walked toward it, she could not help but keep listening, astounded, to the faint susurrations. She broke out in a cold sweat when she heard a feeble *Alice*. She thought her torment was just about to begin all over again.

She quickened her pace, her steps thudding on the velvety floor.

Alice.

Shuddering, sickened, she reached the slightly open door and placed her gloved hand upon the icy doorknob.

Alice.

Sweat streamed down her forehead and her eyes were dilated. She flung the wooden door open, making it creak loudly and unnervingly.

Alice.

"Alice, I can't find your dear friend. She has been running away from me." Her heart skipped a beat. It was a rough and hoarse voice, although the emitter was still unseen. "Or maybe I don't need her anymore, since you are here."

"Stay away from us, Percival!" Alice shouted into the room. Suddenly, a silhouette's outline came into sight, as if a man had just stood up from a chair against a window, through which the starlight lit a poor part of the extensive room. "What do you want us for?"

"Why, I want your souls, of course!" he replied, still unseen. "There is no way out of this hellhole, not even for me, and it's your fault I am stuck here with you. If you just had given up, everything would have been simpler. Now you will not even atone in Tartarus, but you shall vanish into nothing when I dispose of you. There is no crueler fate I could give you." All of a sudden, Alice heard a slight moan coming from inside the room, but she dared not enter. There was another groan, but louder and more disturbing. Then there was a noisy snapping echoing through the hall as a pair of fiery eyes glinted in the swallowing darkness.

And all Alice could hear was Percival panting like a dog before howling like the wolves do moonward…

¤¤¤

Arthur awoke from his sleep, and still drowsy, he gazed around finding only utter darkness, through which not even the keenest eye would pierce. With a gasp, he realized that he was standing in absolute darkness as well. Despair and fear gripped him when he thought he had died and had gone astray from the path of souls. Yet he was conscious and even more anguished because of what might have happened after he passed out. Most of the knights had been killed and he feared for those few who were still alive.

He tried to remember what had happened before his fainting. He recalled how the Heir of the Sun had retreated into the Underworld. His eyes still stung because of the intense heat they had been exposed to. Then he remembered how terrible he felt before slipping away from consciousness: his head feverish and ready to explode, while he had remained quiet and paralyzed, and his skin itching and his breath labored.

Arthur sought for a logical explanation to his whereabouts, but none came to his mind. He began pacing back and forth. He told himself reassuringly that it was only a dream and soon enough he would wake up. He felt quite awake. That is what unsettled him mostly, because it seemed so fantastic.

After a moment, he perceived a soft cry, as if uttered from afar, kilometers away. He stopped short to listen. Judging by the sound of it, he thought it was his own imagination. Then a disturbing and strident caw resounded from somewhere nearby, sending a sudden jolt down Arthur's spine.

Arthur stared, afraid, at the darkness about him, and he noticed, with his keen hearing, a powerful beating of wings getting nearer and nearer to him. His mind became blurry, unable to think clearly, while all his thoughts scattered away in a hurry. He did not even think of running. And as he lingered on the spot, a faint silhouette appeared in front of him, as if it were a dark aura surrounding a great winged beast.

The murky wings were outstretched and the head was looking down directly at his unbelieving eyes as a massive black bird emerged from the gloom, its talons reaching out for him, ready to grasp Arthur and drag him down into the deepest bowels of the Underworld…

¤¤¤

"Marshal, wake up!" Antoine said in a rather imperative voice while shaking Arthur's shoulders. At their side were the smoldering ruins of the former castle of the White Bastion, now charred debris amassed in a single sizzling pile.

Arthur gasped for air and sat up on the grass, coughing roughly. Sweat streamed down his forehead and his eyes were bloodshot. "What's happening?" he managed to ask between coughs.

"It seemed as though you were in a semi-delirium. Your forehead burned as you uttered unintelligible cries," Antoine answered, clearly relieved. "I thought we were losing you. But you actually did it, Marshal! You actually warded off the dragon!"

Arthur heaved a sigh and nodded slightly, looking down at his ash-blackened armor."What I saw in that dream was nothing I could have ever dreamed of. It was an immense crow, and just before it seized me, it faded away into nothing as I awoke. It felt like death."

"There is no point in worrying about a dream," said Antoine, offering a hand to help him up. "They are completely unreal and unreliable. By the way, look who found you."

Antoine gestured at a magnificent jet-black stallion, which was five meters away from them, grazing on the little pasture that remained pure and free from ashes. They clasped hands and Antoine helped Arthur to his feet.

"I found you, because of him," Antoine said, as Arthur stroked the steed's nose, greatly thankful. "He was prodding you to rise with his muzzle, but in vain."

"I missed you," whispered Arthur as he continued to stroke the horse's nose. He glanced back at Antoine. "Why did you come back for me?" Arthur asked, still perplexed and not sure whether his reunion with his horse was actually real.

"When I saw the beast disappear, I thought it was our time to retrieve you. We had to be sure you were alive."

Arthur nodded distractedly and replied: "Now that I come to think about it, I think I know what it was, what I saw," Arthur mumbled. "It could have been a message from beyond, or that's the way I interpret it. It could even mean that my time is nigh and cannot be stopped; death will drag me down."

"Why?" Antoine asked, and immediately answered his own question. "It was an early stage of the venom, right?" Arthur nodded downcast.

"Why do you think it was triggered earlier, even before it was predicted?" Antoine asked.

"I cannot tell, but if I seek through all the possibilities behind the new moon, it could have been the lack of light. We were draped under an absolutely black cape of smoke, blotting out the sunlight entirely. That must be the reason. I will die when there is no light," Arthur finished, explaining his surmise, and heaved a sigh, since it was still difficult to breathe due to the reptilian poison, which was slowly wearing off. Streams of gold sunlight streaked the dark clouds in the form of a hand; as Viktor had called it, the Claws of Antares.

"Why do you think that, Marshal?" Antoine asked, glancing down at the spot of the cursed mark, which was covered by the gauntlets.

"Simply because I can't think of any other reason," he answered curtly. "When sunlight is gone, there is moonlight, and when the moon wanes into a new moon, there won't be any light at all."

"There is another problem," said Antoine, looking back at the men that were reassembling and rummaging through the aftermath of the battle. Some were mourning their fallen fellows. "There are less than a thousand knights left, whereas we had two thousand before the attack. Also, there are only two Marshals left, and no Viceroy. We need someone to guide us now; someone who is actually reliable for the task, and that's you, Marshal. The remaining White Bastions have to choose the next ruler, unless Viceroy Nicholas had an heir, which I doubt."

"As Viceroy Nicholas lay at the verge of death and I mourned his demise, he said to me, in a barely audible voice: 'Heir… stop…them,' meaning the five Harbingers," Arthur said in a soft voice, then louder as he retold the Viceroy's death. "And so will I. I will not stop until I have found them all and…killed them," he said softly, gritting his teeth.

"We'll take care of that when we reach Rouen. We should not linger here anymore," Antoine replied. He immediately realized that something was wrong with him. "After Paris' Bastion, the closest and most important one is that of Rouen. We need to leave immediately and take refuge there for the time being."

"All right. Muster the knights. We take off now," Arthur replied coldly as he mounted his horse.

"Can I call you Dragonslayer?" Antoine said.

"Beg your pardon?" Arthur replied bemusedly.

"I know you didn't kill that beast, but what you did was downright incredible! I still find it hard to actually swallow what you did," Antoine exclaimed, chuckling, truly enthusiastic.

"You should've seen my face when it turned its attention to me," Arthur replied, his expression significantly softening. "Had not been the circumstance, it could have been comical. But I'm glad we are alive, though I'm still uncertain why it left."

"It's not just the act of you facing off such a legendary beast that I admire, but that you actually had the audacity to do it. You defied it without hesitation and still came back alive," said Antoine with a grin.

"Not even do *I* know why I came to do such a thing," said Arthur, smiling faintly. "Maybe a little bit of madness is all you need to act." He heaved a sigh and added. "All right, let's go. How many horses are there left?"

"Many horses either fled or died. Many of us will have to share the same horse, and some others will have to make the journey on foot." Antoine swallowed. "My entire Company…most of them died," he said in a softer voice.

"Come," Arthur said firmly, clasping his hand. "They shall be avenged. The Harbingers will all die by my hand." And so they went.

After a few minutes of hustle, collecting armament and supplies from the crumbling barracks, and mustering all the knights for departure, they finally rode northwest, toward Rouen's White Bastion, the red sun sinking on the horizon while beaming coppery streaks of light.

Once and for all, they left behind the place that they had once called home, now polluted and dilapidated. The Claws of Antares loomed upon the once white citadel, now a Harbingers' territory…

Beloved Paradise

Alice barely managed to slam the door shut before Percival slipped his lunging paws through the gap. The door rumbled against the werewolf's raging pounding, as she pressed herself against it to serve as a blockade. Alice desperately looked for a quick escape route as the door shuddered. The closest doorway was a few meters away from her.

Right at the moment she moved, the door was flung open, causing her to stagger backward. As she raised her gaze, Percival walked into the extensive hall, with a peculiar canine gait, his hind legs askew and his long tail rustling upon the velvet rug. His body was bare and the Corvus' cloak was gone. His voluminous torso contracted and expanded massively with each calm breath. He was completely covered in grayish-black fur and his slit-eyes sparkled in the dark. Each of his four limbs ended in razor-sharp claws. He bared his dagger-like fangs from under his long snout and howled.

Alice unsheathed her sword with a steely rasp and stepped back slowly, without losing sight of her mighty opponent. Percival studied her movements and demeanor with ardent eyes before swiping at her sword intending to send it flying.

Alice saw it coming and swiftly flicked the sword against his paws. Percival withdrew and growled, his lips quivering. His next movement was more unpredictable, pouncing brutally onto Alice and knocking her down to the floor. She raised her shield over her face, blocking the lunge that had been directed at her bare throat. The strike was so hard that the shield bounded against her face, disorienting her and leaving her completely vulnerable for a couple of seconds.

There was a sudden war cry right before Percival could take advantage of Alice's confusion. Sonja moved in from behind and leaped onto him, sinking her dagger into his furry back.

Percival howled, backed away from Alice and thrashed around with his front legs, trying to get Sonja off him and smash her down in the act. She withdrew her dagger and backed away a few steps. Percival panted and shot quick and fierce glances at both knights; now they were behind and before him, respectively.

Alice quickly moved up in to a crouch, and then onto her feet. Sonja glared defiantly at Percival, who was undecided about whom to attack first.

"Get away from her!" Sonja growled, directing Percival's attention at her.

"Or what? You'll kill me?" Percival replied in a heavy grunt. "You will vanish before you even cripple me. One swipe of my claws at your throat and you are gone, forever."

"I am willing to take the risk, again," Sonja answered without wavering.

"If you get any closer we will kill you," Alice threatened from behind. Both Alice and Sonja knew that bluffing would only keep Percival away from them temporarily; they knew it would take much more to take him down.

Sonja began to circle slowly around Percival toward Alice, who stood on her guard while waiting for Sonja to reach her.

Alice.

Alice shuddered and her gaze strayed from Percival to her right, toward the middle of the hall and the stairwell. All of a sudden, a shadow in the form of a little girl appeared and slowly began to take color and definition, walking calmly across the hall and up the stairwell without regarding them. Her attire suggested that she might be of a wealthy family. She carried a woolen doll in her fingers as she swung her arms back and forth, humming a merry tune that seemed distant and otherworldly.

Noticing their distraction, Percival leaped at them and landed between Sonja, who reacted with a missed swing, and Alice, who took longer to respond. Percival swung both of his claws sideways, slashing Alice's cuirass. Sonja tried to evade the blow and she only caught a claw that barely cut her unarmored hip. Percival's strike roused Alice from her involuntary absentmindedness and she back stepped before he could swipe at her again.

Percival distinguished Alice as the greater threat, since she was almost completely armored, and armed with a long broadsword and a broad shield, therefore turning his back to Sonja. Unlike Alice, Sonja was only wearing rags and wielding a dagger.

Percival swiped at Alice and she countered with a swift jab at his paw; but this time he did not retreat and attacked again, slashing quickly with both claws alternately. Alice countered with celerity and struck with her own jabs, missing every weak point as her opponent parried her attacks. Percival did not care about the deep gash Sonja had made on his back. Sonja tried to stab him again, but every time she got near, he would kick her back with his hind legs.

Alice's blows began to falter and she could feel her arms quickly becoming leaden, making her attacks slower and weaker. Shortly after that, she realized that Percival had been toying with her; she could even see a glow of satisfaction in his eyes. In a desperate attempt, Alice mustered all her remaining strength and condensed it into one quick and devastating slash.

The werewolf did not anticipate Alice's move being so fast and took long enough before leaning back, evading part of the slice. Alice left a long and shallow furrow upon the werewolf's torso, crimson blood trickling out of the wound. He looked down and growled wrathfully. Now he was going straight for the kill. He dashed against her, knocking her to the ground and relentlessly lunged at her throat.

Percival stopped short, his long fangs already boring into Alice's neck, but only slightly before he could tear it out. Sonja clutched Percival's enormous head with one arm while sinking her dagger into his upper back with the other. All had happened in less than a second. Percival was seized by both the knife's grip and the excruciating pain in his back. He knew that killing Alice would get him killed as well.

"Let go of her!" Sonja snarled with ferocity, pulling down

the knife as a lever, intensifying Percival's pain and making him grunt. Alice remained flabbergasted, her eyes wide with disbelief while panting rapidly, staring blankly at the face of death. "Draw back, slowly and with care. I swear to you that if she dies, I'll make sure you suffer a long and painful death."

Distrustfully, Percival retracted his fangs slowly while shooting quick glances at Sonja. When he had removed his teeth from Alice's neck, with great exertion Sonja pulled back Percival's outstandingly heavy head, while, at the same time, dislodging the dagger from his back as she shoved him behind with all her might. Percival lurched back, lightheaded and weak, nearly stumbling to the floor, while Sonja hurried to help Alice up, who at first took seconds to react from the shock, curling her left arm around Sonja's neck. Alice's perception of reality was blurry as Sonja and she shuffled their way toward the nearest door and slammed it shut behind them.

Sonja was crying with fear for her friend as she half-carried, half-walked Alice across the labyrinthine kitchen. As soon as they crossed into the dimly lit room, Sonja noticed the large number of tall shelves containing many different cooking ingredients, spices and kitchenware. Coarsely hewn meats hung under hooks against the dingy walls. Seared stoves and ovens stood everywhere. Apparently, there was enough food to feed a small village for weeks.

Together, they took various bends and twists around corners around the shelves in an effort to elude Percival. Sonja had heard the door groan open only moments after she had closed it.

Sonja arrived at a door with a small window displaying the citadel's garden. At the end of the courtyard stood a tall fountain attached to the rampart gurgling smooth jets of water. To the sides were the thorny grass walls that were twice the height of an average man. She hesitated and out of the corner of her eye spotted a closet at the end of the room, near the garden's door. Thinking about Percival's likely attributes as a werewolf, she deduced that he might be tracking them from afar through their scent. Then it occurred to her that he could get confused as their essence mixed up with the stench of the meat and the odor of the spices.

Sonja opened the garden's door and instead of going out, she rapidly carried her friend to the closet, opened it wide, cramming Alice and herself inside and closed the door again as carefully and quickly as she could.

Keenly alert, Sonja held her breath and listened with caution while covering Alice's mouth to keep her from making any noise. Alice was still panting and sweating; in dismay Sonja could even hear her heart beating. Gradually, she began to make out Percival's muffled footsteps and his pained grunts. Warily, he began to sniff the air loudly, his eyes darting everywhere. Percival approached the open door and stepped out, at first with some hesitation, and then entered the garden maze decidedly.

After making sure that he was gone, waiting for eternal minutes in that enclosed space, Sonja stepped out of their hiding place, inhaling fresh air, and proceeded to close the garden door. She grabbed a long rough key from the keychain next to the door and locked it. Immediately afterward, she turned to check on Alice, who had leaned against the wall, slid down it and was now hugging her legs, shaking from the shock.

"He is gone. We are safe now," said Sonja, deeply concerned and approaching her.

She sat beside Alice and curled her right arm around her tenderly. She saw Alice's expression of profound trauma and how she stared blankly ahead, tears in her eyes. Her neck was bleeding from several puncture wounds. Absent-mindedly, Alice leaned her head upon Sonja's shoulders and remained there, just looking ahead in the distance.

"I will look after you…," Sonja murmured. After minutes of pondering and comforting Alice, Sonja stood up and said. "I will get you something to eat. Get some sleep while I look for something decent enough in here."

Alice nodded slightly. She groped blindly on the floor beside her, where she laid herself down, and within seconds, she was deeply asleep...

¤¤¤

As soon as Alice opened her eyes, she felt free from all anguish and pain that she had ever sensed. Forsaking the world and plunging into dreams, she could embrace total freedom and do all she willed. Her mind was clear and without doubts. She felt no danger but sheer peace. She brushed the spot where her wound was supposed to be, but there was none, only fresh and rejuvenated skin.

The sky was heavenly azure and sparsely smudged with white clouds. The soothing sun shone streaks of gilded light across the leafy green rolling hills, as cool breezes of wind occasionally rustled the thin blades of grass. Every knoll was mottled with diverse flowers of different colors and kinds, as well as many types of tall tree standing irregularly across the vast fields.

After contemplating such a fantastic view for several minutes, she stopped to ponder the possibility of her whereabouts. She thought about death, but then said to herself that it was implausible: she would be again in Erebus, the dark lands where Charon's ferry picked up the dead. Then it seemed logical to her that it was a dream. She realized she had never, ever had so much peace in a dream, or until that moment.

"Dream or nightmare, reality or fantasy, that is for you to decide," a grave, deep voice boomed across the world. Alice cringed back with fear, her head whipping around in bewilderment. "Nightmare it is, then."

Immediately afterward, the firmament was clogged in a thick cape of stormy clouds and the wind began to roar vehemently as a gale. Thunderclaps split the air and lightning lanced across the obscure land. Alice looked down in amazement and marveled in fright at how the flowers and stalks of grass, that were once full of life, began to shrivel and lose beauty as they bent down upon the darkened and sterile land. The trees were grayish, the corrugated bark slowly peeling off their trunks, bereft of hydration.

Alice felt her knees incapable of sustaining her weight anymore and they buckled, causing her to kneel down on the wilted pasture. Then she was assaulted by dizziness and a headache so strong that she tumbled backward upon the ground. She closed her eyes unwillingly.

"Eden, beloved paradise...," said the voice again. Alice flicked her eyes open again and her heart jolted at the sight of the Lord of Nightmares. "Becomes your worst nightmare!"

The wolf-headed beast stood astride her, glaring at her with his ghoulish, yellow eyes. His long muzzle had his canine teeth exposed, sharp as daggers. He had a hulking furry human-like chest, rough paws instead of feet, and long and pointed ears capable of detecting the slightest of noises. He was tall and strong, with enough muscle to brandish a heavy war ax.

"Welcome to my realm, mortal." His deep, rumbling voice seemed to come from the depths of the Earth and the infinity of the sky, making the land shudder. "Those who seek redemption submit themselves to the Purging Trials. My realm is one of those, and it can only be accessed through one's slumber, at any time and without exception." All of a sudden, the werewolf vanished into strips of shadow and seconds later reappeared again, but in another shape. The hooded man resembled Percival in voice, wearing the Corvus robe. "But come to think of this: during the ordeal of the Trials, all souls suffer greatly, and naïvely think they will ease the pain in their dreams. That is where I, Zartha, Lord of Nightmares, take action and bring a punishment to them."

Alice remained speechless and began to fumble blindly around, looking for her sword, and realized she did not have it.

"Do not even think about it," Zartha remarked. "Why would I let you bring any means to harm me? You cannot hurt me, but you do not need to worry, for I do not intend to kill you, only to accomplish my task," Zartha moved a few paces away from Alice as she stared at him warily.

"What sins?" Alice asked more in anger than in fear or doubt as she staggered to her feet. "Are you…my punisher? What did I do?"

"My eternal task is to accomplish the suffering and purging of those who chose the Purging Trials as their way to redemption. I will fulfill my task, regardless of what you say," Zartha replied, the storm howling above them. "Let us proceed, shall we?" Zartha chuckled and faded once again in shadows. "What are your greatest dreads?" Alice remained silent and Zartha answered himself, his voice resounding in Alice's mind, bringing her most feared dreads back to life. "Death…pain…loss: what every living being fears." A black shroud of darkness materialized before Alice, murky and turbulent, swirling and taking on the shape of a caped phantom, its skull face, greatly resembling a Stygian wraith, leaning down on Alice and glaring at her face a few centimeters away.

Alice kept her composure steady, her hair undulating against the twisting gusts of the ferocious wind.

"I will let you choose what punishment to receive first, but only for now," said Zartha. "Choose: omen or a flashback; a look into the impending and threatening future, or a harrowing reminiscence of the past."

"I choose the omen," she said, her voice wavering with a hint of doubt.

"Then let the nightmare begin!" Zartha exclaimed, Alice's surroundings fading away and clouding the environment, engulfing her in utter and unreal darkness…

¤¤¤

Alice examined the place where she materialized, seeing only more darkness.

The image of the landscape changed abruptly and the first thing she felt was loneliness, as if she had been isolated for months, or even years. But the strangest fact was that the isolation gripped her without prior warning or reason. A storm of hatred, disgust and ache enveloped her heart, yet such ailments were repressed, almost as if she were numb. Her mind and judgment were clouded in a haze of recklessness and resentment, but the heaviest sentiment she felt at that moment was anger.

"What happened?" Alice asked, heartbroken, but got no response.

Something must have gone awfully wrong before that point in her future that she was now seeing. Alice found herself trudging upon a world with neither sun nor moon, a barren wasteland full of foul quagmires, wild and threatening alien plants draping the entire land. There were several ponds and large murky lakes with mysterious waters everywhere she looked. Even though there was neither sunlight nor moonlight, there still was some illumination, apparently coming from the clouds that emitted a green glow, brightening the land in a grim manner.

The feeling of isolation and sorrow was excruciatingly strong, and what unnerved Alice even more was the fact that she did not know the reason why. Alice could not bear anymore that feeling and wanted to wake up right away; it was as though she steadfastly regretted the past and wished it was just a nightmare and had never happened. Her chest burned from sheer grief and remorse.

What can I do to prevent this? She thought, however, she could not help but feel absolutely powerless. Then she realized. *Where... is Sonja?*

After what seemed hours of trudging and plodding across the vast marshland, the image shifted suddenly and now she was staring at herself. Everything around her looked blurry, and she could not make out anything even a meter away from her. At first Alice was unable to tell what she was looking at until she realized that she was not looking into her reflection, but that there actually was a person who looked exactly the same as her: her *Doppelgänger*. They were facing each other five meters apart. Alice felt overwhelmed with confusion and dread. She stared at her double with a sense of wonder mixed with some sort of warning that ticked her off from within, while the other returned her look nonchalantly, with a hint of arrogance and superiority, her irises looking scarlet.

Alice could not move a single muscle. She felt as if she were a mere spectator just watching the events unfold, having nothing to do with the action that was taking place.

What can I do to prevent this from happening? The same answer came rushing to her mind: nothing, most likely.

Alice could not understand how such encounter would ever occur. Not only was she afraid and without hope for the future, but she could also feel anger surging through her body. She had no clue why such fury suddenly gripped her, but she certainly knew that there was a cause still unknown to her.

Her hand on the broadsword's hilt ready to draw, Alice surveyed that calm countenance of her double, noticing a sparkle of sly malice and wickedness in her eyes, that scarlet hue which made her own skin crawl. All of a sudden, Alice herself spoke, without actually intending to, as if the dialogue were already scripted. "Who are you?" Alice demanded.

"Who am I, if you are me? Who are you, if I am you?" the twin replied cunningly. "There is only one Alice Houdin, and that is me. Try to replace me, and I will not hesitate before killing you, even if you possess the same appearance as me. That is hardly going to stop me." Alice held her gaze steady, looking into those baleful eyes that portended nothing but chaos and destruction. The venomous tone in her double's voice felt so much in discord that Alice could hardly believe it was coming out of what would be her own mouth. "I hold an advantage over you because I know everything about you: your strengths and your weaknesses. Yet, you know nothing about me. Why do you oppose us? Why do you bother to sacrifice your own life for a world ruled by tyrants, whose greed and envy is unmatched? Why do you care about a world where only a handful of people control everything while the rest is subject to pain and misery? They make you feel like you matter, when you are just another piece in their game, a tool. Why do you fight for such people, who shun you, who only use you as a means to fulfill their own whims while the rest remains enslaved? You are a *slave*," the *Doppelgänger* said, emphasizing her disgust with a grimace. She paused, clenching her fist. "I bear the Fate of the world. Upon virtue, ill and chaos I shall walk, and thus my message deliver. Neither death, nor shame, nor pain shall daunt me from fulfilling my destiny. I am the herald of the End, the voice of the Sun, and the sword of the Crossbred. Hardship makes me tougher, defeat makes me stronger, and failure makes me wiser. No one can stop me...no one can stop my destiny from becoming true. The world shall be scourged and blighted. And then, when all is ashes and all is cleansed...the world shall be reborn."

"I'm not doing this for them; not for the King, not for the Church, not for the nobility. I seek to protect and save those whom I love," Alice replied, gazing into those ominous scarlet eyes.

"You and I know that you have already failed," the twin said.

As soon as she uttered those words, Alice felt an intense twinge in her chest, and her gaze drifted into the distance. After a few seconds, she said: "No, Tartarus will not stop me. I haven't failed... not yet. If it takes a journey through Hell to prove so, then Tartarus I shall travel. But not now, not until I see your kin destroyed."

"Then this is it...this is the moment where you die with dignity," the twin remarked. As soon as both drew their weapons, everything faded away in strips of mist and Alice was back on Arcadia, regaining consciousness. The moment Alice saw Sonja, her eyes welled up with tears of both joy and deep grief, and her first impulse was to embrace her, to cling to her as though she felt Sonja was going to slip from her grip and she would lose her forever…

Moving On

After four hours of riding nonstop, the knights of the Order reached Rouen's outskirts just before midnight. Unfortunately, a fair number of knights had to take the journey on foot and were still on their way. The crescent moon above released soothing glimmers of light that revealed the trail toward both Rouen's White Bastion and Normandy's capital, the city of Rouen, whose outline was perfectly visible from the stronghold a few kilometers away.

The survivors of the attack of Paris' White Bastion still grieved the events that had so miserably hit them just hours ago. They still mourned the Viceroy and the countless knights that fought for an uncertain victory. The worry regarding who would be chosen as Viceroy Nicholas' successor was great as well. Arthur continuously glanced up to find the moon in its same position, crescent and mysterious; the clock that timed his life. He rode at the head of the group alongside Antoine, around six hundred knights following behind, dust swirling up as the tide of knights crossed the land.

Rouen's White Bastion castle towered up ahead, its spire greatly resembling the former Paris' Bastion. Arthur commanded an officer to hoist up a white banner to alert the watchtowers' guards to their urgency. They swiftly approached the crenellated parapet as the metallic gate rose up, its chains rattling loudly.

Right in front of the entrance was a circular junction, in its center a majestic tall fountain sprinkling water. The guards of the Bastion began to call for assistance as the entrance atrium began to flood with people. The knights' frail and damaged appearance was distinctly noticeable. After a long while and much bustle, every single rider was inside the White Bastion, lining up in rows as orderly as they could manage.

Unlike Paris' Bastion, Rouen's did not have those extensive fields that had to be crossed to get from one facility to another; there was no Royal Chamber, but an Assembly Chamber in its stead. Most of the roads and streets across the stronghold were cobbled and the buildings made of fine granite and whitish stone.

Arthur sent an officer for the Regent: every White Bastion but that of Paris was ruled by a Regent, a rank that rose higher than Marshal, and they tended as well to become Viceroy after the latter had chosen his successor.

"What do you think the Regent will think of you becoming Viceroy? Nicholas never announced you officially as his heir," Antoine said under his breath.

"There will be a clash. There always is," Arthur replied as some guards approached them for questioning.

Both made an effort to tell the officers what had happened before the Regent arrived. They were clearly incredulous. They obeyed Arthur instantly when he ordered them that his knights were to be settled in, even if they had to be crammed together. Around six hundred knights dismounted and followed the guards who would show them to their abode while their horses were sent to the large stables. The remaining two hundred knights were to be expected the following day. Arthur motioned for Antoine to stay at his side.

"Marshal Montague!" a man called out, riding his way through the crowd upon a roan. He was clad in the lavish platinum-colored livery of the Order. He had black hair cropped especially short so that not a strand fell over his forehead, thin black eyebrows upon his strict and stern eyes that evidently showed the experience of battle of a middle-aged man. He had an aquiline straight nose and a slim black mustache right under it. An elegant rapier clipped to his belt hung down from his waist.

"Regent Blanc," said Arthur, saluting his superior, Vincent Blanc.

Blanc bowed and looked over Arthur's shoulder, watching

as rows of knights advanced toward the barracks. He frowned slightly. "Marshal, I welcome every man that belongs in the Order or simply desires to join it; however, it intrigues me why an army just poured through my doors."

"Viceroy Nicholas is dead…and Paris' Bastion is nothing more than charred stone." Arthur wavered for a split second. "And our beautiful city has been lost to infernal beasts emerging from Hell itself. Paris has plunged into darkness and oblivion."

"I knew about Paris' disaster because all Regents received the news on a daily basis, but not about the Viceroy's passing," Regent Blanc replied, and he pressed the bridge of his nose, frowning, but did not pursue the topic any further. "And what happened to you? You look rather battered and exhausted."

"The same thing that happened to Paris: it's happened to us now." Arthur made a gesture to his blackened armor in a tone of distress.

"It was a dragon," Antoine chimed in. "Bigger than the castle itself, spewing flames over us, destroying our catapults and lighting the Viceroy's tower like a torch."

"A dragon?" Regent Blanc asked, casting unbelieving glances at both Arthur and Antoine. "That's hardly convincing. Dragons only exist in fantasy tales and the like. But then again, there would be no reason for you to be here otherwise. How many of you made it alive?"

"Roughly eight hundred, whereas we were around two thousand at the beginning of the attack. Also, several dozen knights lost their steeds and had to make the journey on foot," Arthur replied.

"And *how* did you make it alive?" Blanc inquired, with much more noticeable curiosity.

"Marshal Arthur took care of that. He scared it off," Antoine said. Arthur realized that Antoine did not know what had actually happened, that he had shot the Harbinger off the dragon's shoulders.

"Not exactly," he broke in before Antoine could say another word. "I pierced a soft spot with an arrow, but it doesn't quite explain why it left. We cannot know for sure."

"I'm sorry for all your losses," said Blanc. "But I do assure you that nothing like that will ever happen under my watch." Arthur thought that the way the Regent was trying to reassure them about something that clearly was beyond his power seemed childish, and they were not such fools as to believe such a comforting lie. "But tonight you may rest, gentlemen," said the Regent solemnly. Arthur and Antoine bowed simultaneously. "I'll call for someone to show you to your rooms in the castle." With that said, he rode away. When he was out of earshot, Arthur spoke to Antoine.

"I will be visiting Rouen every once in a while. I have an old friend living there I made on one of my missions. He is a blacksmith, Jacques Bettencourt."

"What are you going to do there?" Antoine asked. "Are you still planning on overthrowing the Duke?"

"Still etched in my mind…"

¤¤¤

When the first rays of dawn poked over the horizon, Arthur awoke with a beam of light across his face that was seeping through the interstices of the window of his room. He rested upon a pretty decent bed that was made of wood and had a thin mattress. He sat on the side of his bed against the warmth of the newborn light and propped up his head on his hands, a feeling of nausea in his throat. He could almost feel the reptilian poison traveling through his veins.

Arthur dressed in the livery of the Order and went over to the corner of his room where he had placed his blackened armor overnight. He had been offered brand new polished armor, but he had requested it to be darkened. The armor looked the way it was after he was engulfed in the smoke of the dragon's fires.

Now armored, he left his room and trod down the lengthy corridor where people were already in an everyday hustle. He descended the stairs in quick strides and, after reaching the main vaulted hall through which the Assembly Chamber could be seen, he headed toward the exit. Right before he could step outside, the familiar voice of a man stopped him short.

"Good to see you again, Marshal," Vincent Blanc, Regent of the Bastion, greeted him in a friendly tone. He wore the usual platinum livery. "Marshal Montague, I thought that you should be reminded about the assembly that will be held today in the evening." He smiled with a hint of superiority. "Be on time."

"Aye, sir!" Arthur saluted his superior, and after he was gone, he exited the castle and went toward the stables.

After mounting his horse, Arthur had an eerie sensation, as if he were being watched from afar, as he rode away toward the city of Rouen, Normandy's capital…

¤¤¤

After riding under Rouen's gateway and having traveled across the busy streets full of carriages and riders going about their ways, Arthur noticed a dark aura upon the city, one of insecurity and fear. He could feel it in the worried eyes of the people that passed around him. Guards and sentries were rarely seen doing their duties and a curfew had been set in place to get all people to refuge themselves right after sunset. Recently, attacks similar to those of Paris had broken out: limp carcasses were found lying in the middle of the streets, cases of murder abounded everywhere and every day. And still, the market was teeming with people. It was alive with the racket of hundreds of people talking at the same time.

It reminded him of the time when he met Jacques, three years ago, when he was sent to escort a herald to Rouen to look for an arms provider for Paris' Bastion. There were frequent bandit attacks on the road and the herald would not run the risk of getting assailed. It was later considered a waste of time since there was not the slightest possibility that the Order could obtain enough resources from a couple of blacksmiths at least five hours away.

For five hours or more they had ridden across the rugged grasslands, under intense sunlight, without shade, and at the mercy of dry, searing winds. Once they had made it to Rouen and found out all the information they needed, they faced the daunting challenge of going back across the same unpleasant terrain.

Once they had finished negotiating with the last blacksmith, Jacques, he happened to overhear the herald's grumble about going back. He could see that both Arthur and the herald were worn-out. He offered them shelter under his roof and ale from his barrels.

Arthur remembered with pleasure how they had spent the night talking and joking. Jacques inspired a certain trust toward him. Arthur somehow knew that Jacques could be relied upon, that he might have been a peerless friend, if given the time. However, early at dawn they had to leave and rarely had they seen each other since.

As he turned a corner, Arthur reined in his steed next to a rather humble house with a thatched roof, a smoking chimney jutting out from the middle. He dismounted and hitched his horse to the closest pole and went toward the wooden door to knock, his excitement almost palpable.

He turned to face Rouen's Castle as he waited, located outside the town to the north and in a dominant position, where Duke William would probably be at that moment plotting his devious schemes. It was a large, irregularly squared fortress with several conical towers and a tall rampart, its entrance accessed only via a bridge at the front. The fortress had its own numerous guards posted at the front gate and walking watchfully upon the parapet.

"Jacques, are you there?" Arthur shouted impatiently after several minutes of waiting and peering down the streets and glancing eagerly at the looming fortress. "It's Arthur Montague and this matter is quite urgent!"

After five more minutes there was still no response. He crossed the yard and peeked in through a tarnished window, missing most details of the interior and failing to grasp what was inside. Jacques' horse was inside its stall, poking its large head over the door.

Arthur, seeing no other option and getting increasingly worried, forced the lock open and carefully broke into the blacksmith's workshop, making sure no one was watching him.

The first thing he noticed right after taking his first steps across the threshold of the house was an obnoxious stench combined with the smell of red-hot coal burning at the hearth of the workshop. At his left side there were two large bellows close to the forge, next to which rested a black chest-high anvil with a disfigured sword carefully placed on the tip waiting to be shaped with hammer blows. The stone walls were covered with steel racks holding varied and numerous quantities of blacksmith's tools—hammers of different sizes and weights, tongs, pliers, chisels, shears, picks and shovels.

Arthur could not help but cover his nose, frowning at the foul smell. The place was rather dark and somber, the forge being the only source of illumination in the smithy. The sunlight that crossed the darkened windows did not help much; it even accentuated the gloomy appearance of the place. Looking down at the dirt, he noticed a small leather-bound hammer lying casually on the floor. He picked it up gingerly and examined it for a brief time and then placed it on the anvil. He followed his way up the stairs that were at his right.

Warily, Arthur entered Jacques' room, from where the stench was coming. He looked around hesitantly for the source of the foul odor, noticing a pair of motionless feet peeking out from behind the humble bed. He had already imagined the worst since the moment he stepped into the house, at the instant the stench of death crawled up like demonic tendrils into his nose. The corpse of a dear friend well advanced in putrefaction was one of the most horrific things Arthur had witnessed. It was against his will that he approached to get a better look at the corpse's face.

Arthur clamped his mouth and nose with both hands at the sight of Jacques Bettencourt's pale and cadaverous countenance. His sockets were sunk and his blank eyes were drying up. Jacques was a broad-shouldered man, strong and stalwart as a blacksmith's tasks demand. His skin was tanned, although his skin was paling more and more as time passed. His chiseled jaw was covered in a rough black beard that had been stained with his own blood, judging by the red pool that surrounded him.

Breathing deep, Arthur squatted next to an inert Jacques and began to inspect his body, to determine the way he was killed. Arthur easily found out what his friend had gone through. He had been stabbed in the back with a sword, but his left hand was outstretched as if to pick something up. Arthur recalled that Jacques was left-handed when it came to hammers at the forge and swordplay. And indeed, a short blade was lying untouched upon the nightstand. The hammer Arthur had seen at the entrance quickly came to his mind and he guessed that Jacques had been threatened as he worked on the forge. Right before he could grab the sword to defend himself, the killer stabbed him in the back. Arthur brushed his fingers poignantly across his friend's back and the bloody floor, noticing that the blood was just drying up, and he deduced it must have been approximately a day since the crime was committed. He placed a hand upon Jacques' forehead, sliding it down to close his glazed eyes.

Arthur stood up, unbelieving. *What did this man have that was so important to kill him?* Arthur thought, clamping his nostrils shut with his thumb and index fingers. He reckoned the murderer was still incognito and the crime not yet reported to the authorities. Someone obviously wanted him dead, but there was yet no telling why.

Arthur stood next to the wooden shelf where he spotted a couple of sealed letters. One had *Jacques Bettencourt* written on the front of the envelope in a rough handwriting. Next to the name was a quick scrawl that resembled an eagle written with coal, and which had begun to get smudged. The scribble of the eagle attracted his attention and he removed the seal of the letter. Without hesitation he opened it and began to read, each word surprising him more and more; he even had to read it twice to fully grasp the grave and mesmerizing situation that had been unfolding around him.

The letter read as follows:

Jacques Bettencourt:

We have been warned, my friend. If we keep protesting as we have done in the past days we might end up in jail or on the gallows. We ought to be more careful. It is at once clear that our protest will not change the new regime of the Duke.

My men on the nest have been informing me well about the events that take place there, and I have recently been informed that the Duke has obscure dealings. But that does not quite guarantee our victory since our militia is just forming, and we need more men, more professional soldiers, and all the resources we can get. It is good to have you as the second in command. Before we start the raid, we will need to get everyone organized and well-armed. You can supply us with weapons and armor.

From now on we have to be wary, before we are hunted down one by one. One of my men, a spy, was found murdered a few days ago. I suggest you keep your eyes open and not mention anything about the militia to anyone.

Best regards.

A.B.

Arthur rolled up the letter and put it inside one of the pouches that hung from his belt, telling himself to find the author of the letter at once: A.B.

Before leaving, Arthur pulled the blanket off the bed and draped it over Jacques. He gave him one last blessing and left the workshop.

Once outside, Arthur questioned the nearest guard about the events that had occurred within the last week.

"Sir?" Arthur asked. The guard turned and looked at Arthur's armor with curiosity, though he still regarded him as a high-ranked knight.

"I'm all ears, Marshal."

"I need a brief report of the city status."

"The city has been rather turbulent these last weeks. We are seeing too much violence."

"Is it true there have been protests ever since the new Duke rose to power?"

"Aye, sir, ever since the new Duke rose to power. The rules have changed around here. Our ways of dealing with felonies were more lenient before his ascension. Not only that, but sometimes he sends guards to arrest people for no apparent reason. I believe they are trying to rebel because they are afraid they might become slaves. The people have become hostile and aggressive. I would expect riots soon, and we have to respond reciprocally."

"Understood," said Arthur. "What about former Duke Jean? Where has he gone?"

"He is still in the castle. Nobody knows why, but he's been there the entire week."

"Do you happen to know who the head of the marchers is?" Arthur asked. "Do you happen to know who gives the cue to march?"

"I'm sorry, sir, I have no idea, but I think one of these farmers or merchants around must know. They march at his signal. We had to suppress the last march a day ago."

"Understood. And one last thing," Arthur said, raising his finger. "I have been informed of recent murders happening in the city," he lied. "Do you have any idea about the perpetrators yet?"

"We know about an assassin on the loose, but we haven't caught him yet. Though, strange thing, many of the victims seem to have been murdered by a beast instead of a blade. They often have deadly marks on their necks, such as claw marks. The number of killings has climbed sharply since last week. We don't know why any of this is happening, but we'll find out soon, I hope."

Arthur frowned. Jacques was not murdered by claws. "Well, I've found out there has been another murder." He wavered for a split second. "In the blacksmith's workshop. It already stinks." Itching to leave the place at once, he ordered the guard to carry out his duties of disposing of the body and trying to catch the assassin as well. And, shortly afterward, a group of guards was already transporting Jacques' corpse for its burial.

Although Arthur was unaware of the figure observing him from the next block as he rode away to the Bastion, he could still feel an uncanny presence, but remained oblivious to its intentions or whereabouts. The slim figure left the mug of ale on the table and went outside the pub to mount its horse, following him far behind. Arthur felt like someone already wanted him dead, just like Jacques...

Crisis

Alice awoke with a jolt. She had to stop herself from screaming Sonja's name. The moment she saw Sonja, her eyes welled up with tears of both joy and deep grief, and her first impulse was to embrace her, afraid that she might never see her again. "It's all right," Sonja said in a hushed voice. "I brought you something to eat."

Alice sat up and leaned against the wall with Sonja's help. Sonja was on her knees in front of Alice. She had brought a porcelain platter containing a steaming steak that had been grilled on coals and spiced with pepper and salt, and accompanied by an apple, cabbage leaves, a carrot and a loaf of bread. Standing on the grainy floor beside the platter was a silver goblet full of water.

Alice had eagerly hoped to awaken in the barracks of the White Bastion instead of that gloomy and dank kitchen. Instead, she was back just where her nightmares had begun. Now that they were allegedly safe, Alice remained limp, her head sagging feebly against the wall. She still felt blood on her neck. Alice desired to get back home and a painful longing assaulted her, reminding her of life above and the few people that she cared about: Viceroy Nicholas, Arthur Montague, and Sonja Krauss. But she was already with her at that moment, with the ghostly image of her friend. Battle to the death with another human within a code of honor was one thing, but confronting hellish monsters, having mighty beings toying with her mind, and treading an infernal land without any hope of return to the Overworld was quite crushing. All her feelings condensed into despair. Demoralization, famine and pain mixed up to create one single tear.

"We'll make it out of here," said Sonja gently, although she knew those were weak words. She moved beside Alice and leaned against her cold armored shoulder.

"We should have never left for Notre Dame. That was our doom," Alice muttered, her eyes sparkling under the dim torchlight.

"Probably not," Sonja replied. "Not going would have just extended our lifetime for a few months. There would've been more demonic outbreaks anyhow."

An excruciating thought struck Alice as she tried to calm down, only making her despair even more overwhelming. "Are you alive?" That was one of the most painful questions she had ever asked. Knowing the answer with certainty made her choke up. "Sometimes…I just feel like I'm alone."

Sonja took her time to answer carefully. "Yes, I'm alive." She raised her finger and pointed at her heart. "Right here."

"No, I cannot accept that," Alice replied, stifling a sob. "You look alive, but you're still dead. So long together, I never thought I would ever lose you or Arthur. Now I have lost you, and he has lost me, but he doesn't know that I'm still alive," Alice sniffled and asked. "Sonja, am I dead, too?"

Sonja curled her arm around her shoulders. "Your wound is shallow, unlike mine," she said, deeply moved. "I would bet all France's wealth that you are still alive and *still* going to make it out of here."

Her words comforted Alice somewhat. She turned to face Sonja with a feeble smile of hopelessness and sorrow.

"Why did you do it?" Alice asked in a low voice. "You wouldn't have died. You shouldn't have saved me. You did not have to."

"It was my duty," Sonja replied. "I had to. Even if it wasn't entirely my responsibility, I would do it again, and again, and as many times as it is possible. That's what true friends do. I played my part accordingly."

Alice shook her head weakly, her gaze blank.

"Just remember: you are not alone in this. I have faith in you; I am most certain that you will overcome this ordeal, that you will defeat Percival and find the way back home," Sonja dabbed away Alice's tear with her thumb. She smiled faintly. "Alice, you are the most precious thing that has ever happened to me," Sonja said, holding her closer. Alice rested her head on Sonja's shoulder, suddenly feeling peaceful at last. "I do not regret what I did," Sonja whispered. Then she began to sing softly:

Push aside your woes
Soak in the light
Safe from your foes
Be free, it's your right

Look to the stars
Forget the pain
Despite the wars
We still remain

Extend your wings
Take flight, fly away
We'll find meaning
Along the way

Look to the sun
For warmth and care
I am undone
Without you there

Never forget
Here you are safe
Never regret
That you were brave

I am undone
Without you there

Alice welled up with tears. They both kept quiet for several minutes, holding each other close. Alice did not want to break apart.

She could not let her go. There was nothing else to care about in that world.

At last, Sonja spoke up. "You should eat. How long has it been since the last time you did?"

Alice realized that the gnawing in her stomach had become painful and she imperatively needed both water and solid food after lacking them for approximately two days. She did not even know, but the passage of time elapsed a little faster in the Underworld.

Alice took the porcelain dish from the floor where Sonja had set it down. After gorging down every crumb of bread, piece of meat, and leaf of cabbage, she drank the water, savoring every drop as though it were the last.

"Don't you think it's strange to find these rare and expensive delicacies in this place?" Alice asked, contemplating the silver goblet.

"Yes, that's what I was wondering about," Sonja replied in a whisper. "Maybe there are people living here…"

Alice was not sure what to say. Khan had explained her that Geister turned the inhabitants of Arcadia into specters. "I think they are all ghosts."

"I hope we go unnoticed," Sonja replied, peering down the dark corridor flanked by a shelf and the moldy stone wall.

"Did you eat?" Alice asked.

Sonja glanced back at her and nodded. "Yes, I did, but now all the food and drink tastes dull and insipid to me, regardless of how seasoned they are." She leaned forward to examine Alice's neck wound. "We better patch that up. A wound that serious might make you ill. Do you have any medical supplies?"

"Not much, just a couple of bandages and a few medicinal herbs," Alice admitted. Her injury stung her painfully, as if she still had a blade inserted. Her head lolled back against the wall when she tried to move, and she heaved a sigh.

"Don't," Sonja ordered. "Just tell me where they are and rest, while I get to work."

"They are in my pouch, right here." She handed the pouch to Sonja.

Sonja carefully eyed each item. She took out a handful of herbs and kneaded them in her palms to crumbs and applied them to Alice's bare wound, finally swathing her entire neck three times and attaching the bandage's end over it.

"How's that? Are you feeling better?" Sonja asked.

"It's still painful, but I am much more relieved knowing that at least it's going to heal," Alice answered. "Thank you," she whispered.

"My mind's a little fuzzy. I feel as though I'm starting to forget some things," said Sonja, her voice a little delicate, as she sat beside Alice, shivering from the cold. Alice struggled to unstrap her cuirass and slip it from her body, leaving her under the protection of the red livery and chainmail coat underneath it, and then she removed her gauntlets, her hands moist with sweat. Gently, Alice curled her left arm around Sonja's neck and let her snuggle up to her side, sharing heat. "I want to remember. There are things about you that I think I starting to forget. How did you arrive at the White Bastion? How did we meet?" Sonja said.

"Do you still remember that I lost both of my parents?" Sonja nodded. "After my mother's death, I had to live alone, trying to convince myself that nothing was real, praying that something or someone would come to my aid, but nothing came at all." Alice paused, glancing at Sonja. "A few days after my mother died, my house was struck by lightning during a deluge. It was set ablaze and there was nothing that I or anyone could have done. I spent every day and night in fear living alone in the streets, snatching anything I could just to stay alive, although, for a moment, I had lost the will to live. I became a thief. The only things I aimed to steal were purses, coins and food. I got caught several times and always got beaten up by either guards or the owners. And thus I always learned from my mistakes, minimizing the amount of times I got caught as years slowly went by.

"I remember *one* time that I got caught, the kind man seized my hand and placed a big loaf of bread on my palm. I stared at him completely astonished. He just smiled at me and went on his way. That loaf of bread was priceless; it tasted sweeter than anything I had stolen before, maybe because I was filled with hope, like I hadn't been in years. That day I learned that people can still be kind in desperate times; they may be rare, but that doesn't mean they don't exist.

"'I often traveled through the city, staring across the River Seine. Often, I would go into Notre Dame to pray, to ask for my mother to be sent back to me, to send me help in any way, but nothing came.

"Three eternal years went by, and by the time I was twelve years old, my long sought aid finally arrived. Marshal Arthur Montague's gold-packed purse caught my eye as he rode past me on his horse. As he turned his back to me, I deftly approached and claimed the treasure. 'That's too much gold for one girl, don't you think?' He had caught me as I tiptoed back to my place. I stopped short and turned to face him, but he wasn't angry…I remember I was blushing. I gave him his money back. 'So what's your story?'

"After I was finished telling him about my situation, the next thing he asked me was whether I would like to go with him to a place he called the White Bastion. A place where I would have free food, free water, free clothing, free shelter and the escape from that life that I had desired for years. He also promised me that, because my heightened senses and advanced skills should not be wasted, I would become his personal page, a knight's assistant, and learn the basics of combat to grow as a real knight. I was not allowed to live there like an idle guest, though; I had to do something. I agreed to become a knight.

"In the White Bastion, he introduced me to his son, a squire. His name was also Arthur Montague." Alice paused for a moment. "He was my only friend for a long time, before I met you. I was too shy, and I had difficulty meeting other people. Living alone, without friends for so long affected me badly. Arthur was the only one that ever put up with me. When I learned how to read and how to write, I realized that besides being with Arthur, reading and writing were the only ways I could cope with being alone most of the time." Alice looked at Sonja. "Do you not remember how we met?"

"I do, vaguely," Sonja replied, frowning slightly.

"Around two years after I came to the White Bastion, you arrived from Paris, and you were completely alone, except for the mare that carried you all the way there. Her name was Syria, remember?" Sonja nodded slightly. "You made friends quickly. You were dauntless, and always cheerful. The day we met, it was a hot day. I dropped from exertion after hours of training. I couldn't stand up, and nobody bothered to help me as people passed by my side. You were the only one that offered me a hand."

"How could I forget?" Sonja replied with a hearty smile.

"Back in Notre Dame, you tossed your family heirloom to me before you...you know..." Alice faltered. She did not want to break down again. She pulled the medallion out from beneath the livery and took it off to show it to Sonja. "I know it is one of your most valued items."

"Keep it. It is but an object," Sonja replied, enclosing the medallion in Alice's hands. "I realized, that in the end, the money in your pockets or your titles of nobility do not make a difference. There are more important things in life. You're going to make it back alive," Sonja said, resting her head on Alice's shoulder.

Alice nodded and put it back beneath her livery.

"Did you love him?" Sonja asked after a few seconds. Alice was taken aback by the suddenness of her question.

"I did," she answered, choosing carefully her words. "Just as I loved you."

"You know what I mean," Sonja replied, a little timidly. "In a more serious way?"

"I don't know...I'm not sure...," Alice said, hoping that darkness would conceal the blush in her cheeks. "Was it too apparent?"

"I'm certain many people knew it. You could just feel the aura of affection. Besides, you two were always together whenever you had the chance. Yes, it was evident."

"I miss those times, when we went on patrol; it was like a break from being bound to the wall. Even if the White Bastion was my home, I still felt imprisoned sometimes, repressed and unable to do any more than the tasks they demanded. In a way, this place gives me a sense of security that allows me to vent my discontent, to express what I believe, everything that was suppressed back in the surface, out loud and without fear of getting stoned or banished from the Order. Here, at least, you can love and be skeptical without someone forcing dogmas into your head," said Alice.

"There is no need to hide *anything* in this place," Sonja remarked. "We are not in the White Bastion anymore, and even there, I don't think Viceroy Nicholas would've given it much thought anyway, although the policies demanded not having any relationships with anyone."

"You're right. Not him, but many would have. Now I ask myself, for what reason do we fight for France? Or Europe? Or the world? Come to think about it, our creed that says that protecting France with our lives is our most important priority almost sounds like a method to make you feel like you matter. Why fight when only a handful of people control the world, over thousands who suffer day by day without hope? We are all slaves of 'nobles', clergy members and the Monarchy. Even if we stopped the Harbingers from taking over, where would we end up? Back where we started, poor and miserable, without liberties? Why fight to save those who submit us to fear, those who control our lives, those who shun us?"

"I understand what you feel, why you vent all your anger on them," Sonja whispered. "But think about the beauty our land has to offer, the joys you spent on the surface with the people you love. Are you going to yield such treasure to the Harbingers, just like that?"

"I've lost everybody already. I feel like I wasted my life," Alice said under her breath, shaking her head, almost breaking down again. "I wanted to live a normal life. I wanted to form a family… the White Bastion took all that away," Alice was quiet for a few seconds, breathing in, trying to calm down. "But you're right: *we* cannot allow the Harbingers to take what belongs to us, because if we do, nobody else will have a chance to live a normal life…I don't want to lose you, again."

"I'm not leaving you, I promise," Sonja took hold of Alice's hand.

"You are all I have left. If Percival dares lay a hand or claw upon you he will regret it." Then she took notice that everything was too quiet and remarked in a soft voice, looking down the dark aisle, "Why didn't he come back?"

"Don't ask me. No door has been opened since we settled in here. It's strange. I figured he would come back and break the door open," Sonja said. "I think we have lingered here long enough. We should get moving. What's next?"

"We finish this Trial," Alice replied. "I recall the last riddle perfectly; it's still bouncing in my head: 'Life lends and life withdraws; poisonous to the fire but delightful to you; source of existence and scourge of humanity; across the twisted realm you shall tread, into the elixir's haven you shall venture, and recover your greatest treasure.'"

"I don't know what could be my greatest treasure," Sonja commented. "Most of the things I value are rather intangible…or simply impossible to get back," she said sadly.

Alice nodded and began to ponder over the riddle: "I suppose the puzzle is all said in figurative language, possibly metaphors. What thing could possibly lend a life? A deity? I don't believe that. It could be birth, though, but I doubt it."

"Not only lend a life, but also destroy it, and at the same time, poison the fire and be a delight to me," said Sonja aloud. "Do you think it could be…?"

"Water? It extinguishes the fire and it is surely a delight. Without it we would cease to live, but an excess may be our demise as well. I can't think of anything related to the twisted realm it refers to. This place is twisted enough. Into the elixir's haven? What could possibly be a sanctuary for water?"

"I imagine it means a pipeline, sewers, dam or a cavern," Sonja replied. "We don't know whether there are any of those things around here. All four are possible. We don't even know yet whether any of those four things is the answer."

"And in the elixir's haven we are to retrieve our most beloved treasure," Alice muttered. "I can't imagine what could be there that I'd value so much."

"I would stop the garrulous chattering if I were in your stead, because someone else has taken the lead!" Geister boomed inside their heads with a mocking tone. "It looks like Percival is a quicker thinker because he just solved the riddle. Better hasten because what I have decided is to heat things up a little more. Since this is the first time I've received triple victims to purge at once, I have decided to add a little more competition. Now, if things continue to go this painstakingly slow, I shall be obliged to make drastic changes!"

"Sounds like he is quite bored," Alice commented, "and we are his entertainment."

"Yes, we better hurry," Sonja replied. "Do you know what this means?"

"I do. That Percival is not just a piece in this game, but our greatest threat," said Alice. "He was before, I know, but now it is imperative that we defeat him to overcome the Trial…"

The Point of No Return

"Where is your helmet? Didn't you have one?" Sonja asked as she helped Alice strap the cuirass back to her body, getting ready to leave their refuge.

"I lost it at the battle of Notre Dame," Alice replied, picking up her broadsword and sheathing it into the scabbard on her belt. "As a matter of fact, I already need to change my armor altogether. I don't think it would last another round against Percival. Though I haven't unslung my bow more than once, I'm already running low on arrows; most of them have been falling out of my quiver without me noticing."

"As long as we don't encounter Percival we'll do fine," said Sonja with a hint of optimism. "We have to avoid any fights, for as long as we can."

"Yes, and as long as we don't encounter any of the things that emerged in Notre Dame either," said Alice, countering Sonja's positive words. "Anything that may dwell in this land. Accept it: we are ruined already."

Alice had hardly finished the sentence when Sonja spoke up. "Alice, I think we are not alone." A shiver ran down their backs as they heard a low groan from the door at the other end of the kitchen.

Both crouched down against the wall and hid behind one of the shelves containing seasoning herbs and greens.

"I thought you had locked up all the doors," said Alice, her heart pounding hard.

"Yes, I did!" said Sonja in a soft voice.

They stayed quiet, hoping to remain unnoticed by anything that had stepped into their only refuge. But neither footsteps nor bursts of breath were heard, except for their own muffled breathing.

"Are you sure you heard something?" Alice asked in that brief lull, making her lose the constant attention to her dangerous environment, considering that at any moment it could become a deathtrap.

And unaware of the floating knife that had lifted over the counter beside them, they continued searching for the threat while lying low against the moldy walls. There came a clang on the counter and the knife was now lying still. As it rang out, Alice and Sonja were startled because it was right next to them, and both got to their feet in an instant.

Sonja clutched her dagger as Alice unsheathed her broadsword and brought her shield up to her chest. All of a sudden, one of the giant steaks hanging from a hook against the wall rose into midair and made its way toward the counter, which it squelched onto. They watched with rapt attention as the cleaver lifted again and began mechanically to cut the meat.

Now Alice could see it: a shadowy man, haggard and emaciated, as if he had suffered from a dearth of food, despite the fact that there was plenty of it in that kitchen. He was nearly transparent, almost utterly invisible, and yet he could hold solid things without any difficulty. He glanced at Alice and Sonja, who were still in their defensive position, staring at him with fear and distrust, and his eyes seemed to be somewhat sparkling. It was a look that caused them insecurity and melancholy.

Alice remembered Khan telling her about Geister's tyrannical reign: how he, in his lust for entertainment had built a stage for his victims and turned nearly every Dweller into a specter. They were all his tools and he was the puppeteer.

"Lord…Alænnor…," the specter whispered, almost unintelligibly; it sounded like those whispers Alice had heard after she had entered Geister's castle. He returned his attention to the meat and continued to chop it without any more words of acknowledgement. Shortly afterward, he carried the meat and put it into a coal stove.

"What?" Alice asked in a soft voice, but the specter ignored her, and then she thought it would be better to avoid it. Alice and Sonja walked stealthily across the kitchen through rows of shelves, noticing about another six ghosts going about their own work cooking fancy meals for their masters. She was rather thankful that they were apparently harmless, yet she was still disturbed by them, although she was slowly becoming accustomed to undead people.

"Where should we start looking?" Alice asked softly, sheathing her weapon.

"Percival already solved the riddle, and he never came back when I locked him out," Sonja answered. "Do you think we should head outside as well?"

"It's a good guess. I think we ought to give it a chance." Sonja used the same coarse key to unlock the backdoor and they went outside into the open. It was chilling as ever, wind blaring under the churning dark clouds that swallowed the sky in a pit of darkness.

Out there, Alice experienced the same feelings of sorrow and despair as when she had been in her nightmare hours ago, and when she had woken in that undesirable world, Eden. But, in an instant, all those feelings transformed into incredulity as she peered around the enormous garden that extended for hundreds of meters in a circumference around the crenellated parapet that encompassed the stronghold. High, thorny, green walls of spines stood to the sides, creating patterns and shapes, all together forming a treacherous maze. Before them, a tall ornamented fountain spurted water, and they approached quickly, glancing at both sides in search of any threat. Seeing no apparent danger, Alice crouched down in front of the fountain and began to examine its base, looking for any clue in the marble and under the shallow water, while Sonja covered her back.

"I can't find anything," Alice remarked, sidling over to the other side.

"Maybe we have to search for the pipeline," Sonja suggested.

Alice glanced back at the spiny walls of the labyrinth and remembered one of the lines she had not considered before. 'Across the twisted realm you shall tread.'

"That's the twisted realm." Alice pointed to the maze at her right side.

"There are two entrances," Sonja mumbled, glancing at both sides. "Should we split up?"

"No, I'd rather not," Alice replied, taking a look into the mouth of the maze. "Not with Percival or beasts lurking around."

"Understood. I'm right behind you," said Sonja, dagger ready, as they entered the maze.

They had turned just one bend when they realized that coming out of that labyrinth ever again was going to be no easy task. Every few meters there was a new entrance into another stretch of corridor, and in every new corridor there were at least two new bends. Sometimes the walls followed a strange pattern that was nearly random.

Not only was it hard to remain on track, but soon Alice noticed that she was now all alone. Sonja was gone without a word or a trace. When she looked back, her eyes widened and she felt as if her heart was going to bump out of her chest.

"Sonja," she choked out, and unable to get the word out of her throat, she shouted again, louder than intended. She clamped her mouth shut, regretting having uttered her name so loudly. But now it was too late, and she contemplated helplessly how the echo of her misery reverberated throughout the maze.

As paranoia overtook her, she glanced to both sides, up and down, every way. Alice felt like she was going to throw up just at the thought of what might have happened to her friend, to the only person in the Underworld with whom she had a connection. She could feel the terror churn in her stomach and the fear clog her throat with a lump. In the confusion, she had lost the way back, and she raced toward the nearest twist, after which she found more corners and corridors. The memory of the nightmare where she found herself stranded upon a marshland came rushing back to her mind almost as vividly as if she were actually there. She felt exactly the same way she had felt then, in her nightmare: forlorn and despairing. Alice could almost hear Geister laughing at her; they had fallen in the mousetrap, and the maze was the cage.

Without her knowing why, her sight got blurry and the sky darker as she glimpsed some movement in it: right above her, formed by the clouds' intricate shapes, a flock of dark and huge skulls floated aloft, being carried away by the howling wind as it moved, stirring the clouds. Her sight began to recover slowly, and, indeed, she saw them, mocking, laughing and crying, but silently. The thorny walls had faces carved in them, grinning and making gestures, almost speaking out; but all was quiet, except for the wind. She began to hear lamenting whispers, spine-chilling moans, bloodcurdling screams and a constant buzzing as if there were a nest of furious wasps surrounding her. But as she turned her head frantically to every side with every noise, there was nothing that could possibly be producing the sound. There were no people, no beasts, no Percival, no Sonja; only her alone.

Alice's knees buckled and she found herself kneeling down on the grass, feeling a stabbing sensation of pain in her chest, then in her hands and finally in her head. She looked down with an expression of horror, seeing how her hands had begun to sweat blood. Then she looked down at her chest, which began to burn within her. And all of a sudden, as she stared down at her legs, she felt a sticky fluid dripping down from her eyes and falling into the grass, turning the stalks into crimson blades. Too terrified to even move, she realized that she was crying blood from her eyes.

As sagacious as she had always been, she managed to regain control of her mind and fight back the madness. She tried to convince herself that none of this was happening. The maze was somehow poisoning her mind, and she had to get out as soon as possible. Alice staggered to her feet and laid her left hand against the wall for support and to bolster her wounded gait. Her legs were leaden as she slowly shambled across endless corridors and twists, with a single goal of success and survival, with an iron will, she was overcoming madness, as few men or women have succeeded to do. Every trip was meant for her to straighten up again and resume the arduous quest. Not a man or woman, not a demon, not Percival, and definitely not a god were going to stop her from surviving madness and finishing the ordeal. The heart of a warrior she had forged over the course of her life was going to fight and not surrender. Alice had to prove where she belonged: to Taurus Company, the indomitable. She felt almost as if as she were carrying the weight of the world.

Alice awoke, standing up solemnly onto her feet, her mind clear as a watery mirror, and all madness was gone; all venom had been purged from her head. Alice defeated dementia, and her Lord, Geister. Free and unburdened of all the weight of insanity, she felt changed, wiser and stronger than ever. No blood, no skulls, no faces and no noise remained. All was unchanged, as before the ordeal.

"You have proven yourself to be worthy," Geister muttered, inside her mind, not so blithely as usual. "But I promise you, that at the end of this conundrum, you shall not be so proud. It will be your end."

"What did you do to Sonja?" Alice snarled.

"Nothing…not just yet," Geister replied. "She is still in the Maze of Madness; she has not proven herself to be worthy of ascending the Trial. She is weaker than you."

Alice acknowledged, and felt the mental link break and she lost contact with Geister. Now she would wait for Sonja to finish her own ordeal. The worry she felt for fear that Sonja might not pass the test was drilling in her mind. Alice walked down the corridor in which she had arrived and came to a twist. After turning around that corner, she spotted an openwork gate, leading down another broader corridor.

Across the grille, she could see a great octagonal monument, ornamented with alien, otherworldly runes, inlaid with lackluster gemstones the color of crimson, and damasked with glistening jet-black thread that ran across its sides. The gate groaned open as Alice pushed it aside lightly and approached the rough granite structure, noticing that it was fenced by tall walls of thorny bushes, and that its only entrance was the gate she had entered through. It was as tall and wide as a two-story manor. The only entrance into the structure lay in front of Alice: a huge rounded, black iron-bound door.

Alice pried the heavy, leaden handle down just to make sure the door was open. It was open, but predictably heavy and it required a great effort. Her intuition told her that the elixir's haven was right inside that structure, but she could not just go in by herself and leave Sonja behind. While she was absent, Alice began to wander around the structure, ever warily, noticing that there were small openings into the structure on the lowest parts of the walls. Through every one of them, water from an artificial narrow canal was running into the edifice.

All of a sudden, there was a mighty roar that thundered across the murky sky. Alice's blood chilled. She did not know where to go, where to hide, or what to do, other than remain still as the bellow swept across Arcadia. She made out a dark outline stirring far away along the skyline, as though it were a beating of wings.

After another clamorous bellow, Alice recalled her memories from Notre Dame: the Underworld was swallowing the Overworld outside the cathedral, the infernal troops emerging onto the surface. There came the first time she heard the raucous and thunderous roar of a dragon.

The contour of the dragon came closer to the citadel. Jet-black, big as a house, yet slender and elegantly poised, Alænnor, vassal of Dementia, peered down at the world of his master, Geister, and continued his flight without minding Alice, whom he could easily spot from such height and in the dark as if it were just midday. Alice, expecting the dragon to plummet down and seize her with its razor-sharp claws at any moment, wondered why the mythical and vigorous predator would ignore her.

Alænnor headed toward the top of Geister's tower at a headlong speed, and right before crashing against it, he pulled up, outstretching his wings fully to the sides retaining the air like a pair of parachutes. He seized the walls with his claws and clung to the tower where he remained perched for a brief time before clawing his way into his lair at the top, through a big hole that was carved out of the walls.

With a mix of fear and admiration, Alice watched enthralled as the dragon entered the tower and left the world subdued in silence once again.

Still uneasy, Alice waited for several hours for Sonja to catch up with her, and with every minute that passed, she lost more and more hope. As she waited, seated on the grass and leaned against the green walls, the apprehension that Percival might appear any moment held her awake and with the sword in her hand. She shivered while the wind continued to blow harder and colder. A livery, chainmail and metal-cold armor was all she had against the inclement weather. Soon after the dragon encounter, she was able to see her own breath, due to the freezing temperature, drifting and wafting away as it dissolved into the distance. With every breath inhaled, she could sense her nostrils burning and mucus running down her nose nonstop. The only other times she had felt that way were during snowy days in Paris, but she was always prepared for those days. Her eyes were streaming and she tried covering her face with her gauntlets, but it was almost no use since those were too cold. Her throat was sore and her lips cracked, the skin on her bare face drying out.

Her hope that Sonja would be able to overcome madness deflated completely; she became engulfed in anguish and grappled with her own self, undecided about whether she should go back into the maze, even if it meant losing her mind, just to find her and bring her back unharmed. She had a lump in her throat, which she was unable to get rid of; all misery and distress located on that point. Dismay strove to get tears of sorrow from her eyes.

The promise they made to each other, not to leave the side of one another, gave her courage and strength enough to rise up to the fatal challenge and go back. As she approached the gate, it slammed shut, and, bewildered, Alice went to it and pulled it back, but it did not budge.

"She cannot be helped," Geister chuckled. "I know what you want. I can wholly fathom your mind; you cannot hide anything from me."

"Open the bloody gate!" Alice replied, making the gates rattle with a metallic noise. She could feel the anger burning in her body, the spark of fire in her eyes; never in her entire life had she felt such exorbitant fury. From the outside, Alice looked calm and serious, but inside she was a raging sea, boiling hot. Her hatred of Geister and Percival was now inconceivable. She kicked the door once and recoiled, the armor on the sole of her boot clanging against the metal grille. She considered battering down the gate with the broadsword, but it was already too damaged, and, virtually, it was her only useful weapon against her formidable enemies. Gasping rapidly, Alice dropped to the ground, kneeling and feeling utterly impotent against the cruelty the Underworld brought upon her. Now, she thought, all she had to do was to act as commanded, like the puppet she was.

"How is she doing?" Alice asked jadedly, hoping that Geister might respond, in a brief respite.

"Most humans fail the Trial upon reaching this riddle. Almost none reach the third enigma, let alone the second Trial," Geister replied softly. "But I shall admit, she is a tough one. This long and she is still standing. Although, you are the one I am interested in; you are the only human that has ever overcome madness after a brief moment."

Now Alice's memory flew back into the past, clearly recalling how she was nearly every day trained against psychological breakdowns, to keep sanity in the midst of battle, back in the White Bastion. She knew that was one of the reasons she had defeated madness, and yet was uncertain why she had made it so quickly. Clear mind? Strong volition? Godlike powers? She could not guess.

When she looked up again, there, shuffling her feet across the broad corridor was Sonja, crumpled and exhausted, to the point of stumbling over. As she approached, Alice noticed a faint smile of pride and victory in her lips. Evidently, Sonja had suffered much more than her. Alice flung back the grille gate, and immediately raced toward Sonja, who fell into her arms completely worn out.

"I've got you," Alice whispered, shedding a tear.

"I didn't think…I would make it," Sonja mumbled, shuddering, straining to remain awake.

"You made it. It doesn't matter anymore. We're almost finished with this. Can you stand?" Alice asked, trying to encourage her. Sonja nodded. "I believe the elixir's haven is right there." She pointed at the dome. "Come on, let's get this over with!"

They stood before the iron-bound, three-meter-tall door, fearing what may be lying behind it. Alice pushed down the metallic handle and, with great effort, the huge door screeched open, metal rasping metal.

They stared wordlessly at the abyss that howled before their feet, a black hole that swallowed all the sound. The dome was eerily silent, and all that was in there was a pit, rounded and pitch-black, spanning thirty meters in circumference. The water-filled canals Alice had seen outside filtering into the structure were now barely visible, disgorging their contents into the deep well.

Alice looked back, at the entrance of the maze, and thinking about going through there ever again sent a chill down her spine. But jumping into the unfathomable abyss that howled before her was gut-wrenching.

"I think this is the point of no return," Sonja heaved a sigh, and began to doubt their sanity. She thought that maybe Geister was playing a ruse on them. "Wait, Alice. Think twice what we're about to do. What if it's just a trap to kill us? Percival might be involved in this!"

"I don't think it's a trap," Alice replied, calmly. "Percival wants our souls for his own ends. Geister is supposed to test our minds."

"But are you willing to jump into this hole?" Sonja asked. "There's no telling what might be at the bottom of it."

"It's only another test, and our minds are the experiment. If we are not up to the challenge, we will fail helplessly," Alice replied, glancing at her. "So, let's find out," Sonja shrieked in surprise. Without spoken consent, Alice leaped in, dragging Sonja down behind her. Holding hands together, they travelled kilometers free-fall, compressed and dank wind whipping on their faces, roaring thunderously. With a flash of complete awe, Alice spotted ground, oddly liquid and glowing, while the background was swollen in utter darkness. With a sign of regret, she sobbed for having acted so recklessly confident, and tightened her grip on Sonja's hand, bracing for impending doom.

As if all the free-fall had been a dream since the beginning, Alice could feel herself awakening. She awoke, standing on her feet, and her gaze immediately went astray in search for Sonja: everything was black, except for the ground beneath her boots, which was shallow water barely reaching her thighs, glowing with a mysterious alien gleam, as if the water had its own luminescence; but nothing else, and above, not even a glint. But there was no sign of Sonja.

"It is now your task to choose one of your greatest treasures to be cut out of the assortment," Geister said. "As I see into your mind, I bring into life and solidness what you yearn for the most. You shall choose what to take out so the two other choices remain. Choose wisely, for failure to know yourself will become damnation. And behind you, a mirror of your unconscious." He laughed cruelly and the mental link was broken.

Out of the water, three images shimmered into existence, five meters away from each other. The first to come into solidity was a big coffer with the lid open. Inside it, were copious amounts of rings, necklaces, amulets, gemstones and gold ingots, and on top of all the things, there was the diadem of a queen. For three years, Alice wandered the streets of Paris in search of a home, a family, but to no avail. For three years, all she knew was cruelty; for three years, she lived without love. Wealth, mostly, was what she unconsciously craved for a long time. Beside the coffer was a large and wide canvas of herself. She had a stern countenance, brave, and yet beautiful, wearing a fine silk dress, a gold crown resting upon her head.

She had hardly glanced over the treasures when she whirled toward the second image, breathless. It was a vivid image of Arthur wearing the livery of the Order, grinning like he always did when Alice showed up. He was sitting sideways on a wooden chair, next to a counter, looking at her expectantly. And even though he was just an image, it seemed to Alice that he could actually see her, beckoning her to approach him.

The third image was similar, but it was Sonja the one smiling and waving at her instead.

"Use the mirror," Geister whispered temptingly, and Alice felt as though he were right beside her. She jumped back confused, disturbing the shallow water, moving away from where she heard the voice.

"The mirror," Alice echoed with a soft voice, as if in trance. She turned back altogether and found a crystalline, barely visible barrier that cut across the path into the 'other room.' There she was, on the other side, staring at herself with gloomy eyes, in a fog of indecision. Suddenly, Alice caught movement across the mirror, even though she was not moving. Her reflection drew a devious smile. "What happens if I don't choose properly?"

"Profound regret is something not many humans are able to withstand," Geister hissed. "The consequences, should you fail, will have you stigmatized for eternity. There shall be no remedy for such scars."

Alice stared at her reflection in the mirror; it was still there, with that sly smile. All of a sudden, she began to move and Alice, motionless, surveyed her movements. The reflection went over to the coffer and pointed at it, grinning at Alice. She shook her head. The reflection dipped her fingers into the pit of gold and scooped up a fistful of golden sparkling coins. They tinkled in her fingers and began to shower back into the coffer in a mist of gilt. The reflection picked up the light diadem, with a diamond inlaid in the front, and placed it over her head, without straying her piercing gaze from Alice's.

"Get rid of the wealth and power," Alice said firmly.

"You are predictable, indeed," Geister observed. "It is time to make things more interesting." The coffer, along with all the gold and the painting, vanished into billows of watery mist and the other two images remained.

"Let us recapitulate. Sonja is dead, and Arthur has only one month left to live. It was your fault that both of them are gone, almost, and the damage is beyond repair."

"How can that be true? No…no, it wasn't my fault." A lump started to form in Alice's throat. She began to doubt the validity of her own words.

"Yes, it was, in a way. It was your whining at the altar what caused him to be unfocused. You two got caught unawares because you were complaining about 'the right thing to believe,' remember?" Alice's reflection in the mirror began to shake her head disapprovingly. Alice bit her lip.

"And Sonja—was her demise too early? Maybe it would not have been if you had not insisted so much on saving Arthur when his fate was already sealed. He was not going to live for long anymore, and yet, you insisted. And that is when Sonja got in the way to save you from the Harbinger."

Deep inside of her, Alice always knew she carried some of the blame for some of the events that had taken place at Notre Dame. When the truth came rushing out, it hit her more strongly than she could have foreseen.

"Your mother was murdered, your father went missing, and

your only real friends were scarce, and both are gone now, because of you. In short, your life was short-lived. When terrible things happen to a human, his mind begins to recreate the tragic events and it goes on to alter them into 'what if' situations, until all that remains is a perfect scenario of what the man wishes had happened instead, and along such recreations come the overpowering feelings of impotency and regret, when the man realizes that nothing can be done to change the past; he can only mold the future through his actions. Back to the riddle: you are to choose between Arthur and Sonja. Had you a second chance to replay the events at Notre Dame, whom would you save now? Would you risk your life by saving Sonja, knowing that Arthur would die in the act, or would you rather save Arthur and leave Sonja behind, like you did, without him getting poisoned?"

The images of Arthur and Sonja changed. He was not sitting on a wooden chair inside a pub anymore. The background in Arthur's image consisted of thick pillars and a dark vaulted ceiling. He was clad in his silver armor, kneeling on the bloodstained floor, despair ever present in his eyes and his pained expression. His right arm was extended upward, gripping the hilt of the longsword that went through the massive serpent reptilian that towered above him.

Sonja, on the other hand, stood her ground in combat position, her shield raised in front and her broadsword making contact with the werewolf's claws, sparks springing from their clash as she valiantly fought against William Bloodthorn to give Alice a chance to escape the deathtrap that Notre Dame had become.

Alice could almost hear the rage of battle on both images as all four opponents struggled to take the other one down, but they were simply frozen in time: a picture captured at those precise moments.

"What did you give Sonja to choose from?" Alice managed to ask.

"Similar to you," Geister replied.

"And Percival?"

"His daughter, his wife and Antares…"

Alice heaved a sigh.

If she had a second chance, who would she save from death?

Who does she actually love more? For her, it was an impossible question to answer. It was almost as if she had to choose between saving her mother, or her father…

Shooting quick glances at the two images, she realized she had not the strength necessary to choose between the two persons she cared the most about; the fact that she had to decide which of her only two friends got to live and who got to die swiftly overwhelmed her. Alice desired to save both, but only one was to be chosen, for good.

Seconds felt like minutes and minutes like hours as she debated with herself, unable to find an answer. Alice walked slowly over to the images and stood in the middle, between both, water rippling against her thighs and sending waves that expanded in big circles. Glancing at both sides, her mind was clouded with doubt, overcome by indecision. She felt her heart torn apart at the thought that she was to leave someone behind. She perfectly knew that whether she chose Sonja or Arthur, her conscience would never forgive her. Alice knew she had to make a sacrifice to continue the journey. It was then she found the answer.

"I'd rather die," Alice called out into the void.

"I have to admit that was rather unexpected," the reply came back through the void after a few seconds of unnerving silence. "Sacrifice yourself for both of them, is that what you wish?"

"I do."

"Realize that this riddle will not actually reverse what is done or what fate has in store for you," Geister stated.

"Then what was the purpose of this task? It was nothing but a waste of time," Alice said, containing the sorrow that threatened to surge out of her, the sorrow that came rushing back at the realization that nothing could be done to save her friends.

"It was not a waste of time. You have accomplished many feats. This riddle was to prove that you are worthy of advancing to the final riddle, which will ultimately allow you into the Second Trial. It was the illusion of hope; it was the illusion, or rather, the lie that they could be brought back which made your decision to sacrifice yourself worthy of ascension. It is quite possible that you have been the quickest ever to finish the Maze of Madness. You have proved yourself to be worthy, for it is no small deed to give up your own life to save another; it is admirable, of course, but mark my words: a time shall come when you will be faced with such a decision, carrying great consequences. But do not get too confident. Few have ever finished the final riddle, and I will make sure you are not one of them…"

Assembly

Still hurt because of Jacques' untimely death, Arthur went around the bustling marketplace asking merchants and peasants about the leader of the marchers. But they just shook their heads. The place was packed with people, from blacksmiths, butchers and tailors tending to their clients to beggars trying unsuccessfully to cope with their plights. Arthur never questioned society's hierarchy and followed the rules according to the creed of the Order, and that was to faithfully and blindly defend the Kingdom and Monarchy of France without a second of hesitation, without questioning the position of those at the top. Halfway through the afternoon, Arthur realized that his time was up and that he had to go back early to the White Bastion for the Assembly that was going to be held in the early evening. He bit his lip; his investigation had been less than productive.

He rode back to the outlying White Bastion and arrived just as dusk began to color the world a scarlet and golden hue. As the gate rose, his horse's hooves began a rhythmic and constant hammering on the cobbled road that would continue all the way to the castle. He went around the broad roundabout with the fountain and then passed next to the barracks, its masonry consisting of granite. Before the atrium of the castle, he hitched his horse back in the stable alongside and went into the tower. He strode across the marble halls, thick and imposing pillars looming about him, and went into the Assembly Hall.

There was a round great table made of finely carved white

marble in the middle of the hall. The walls were covered in excellently wrought silk tapestries, depicting ancient and victorious battles of the Order, embroidered with a gilt thread along the edges. The room was well lit by the long windows, through which the sunset could be contemplated with a magnificent view, but now that the sky was darkening, all around the circumference of the hall ten vivid torches were set ablaze, and the Assembly was ready to begin.

Arthur took his place, and more people began to arrive shortly afterward. Arthur did not know many of them, but among the new people, Antoine came over and took his seat on Arthur's right.

"How's Jacques?" he asked as he leaned against the back of the copper-bound chair, adjusting the black leather cushion beneath.

Arthur shot him a wary glance and slightly shook his head with a grim look. Antoine acknowledged and turned to the new guests, who sat on the remaining eight chairs, Regent Blanc taking the ninth.

"And who might these gentlemen be?" asked a fifty-year-old man, who had a disquieting resemblance to Viceroy Nicholas: trimmed gray beard and mustache, wispy hair streaked with gray, and a small diadem upon his head. All ten Regents wore the same diadem and the same platinum livery, with a magnificently wrought azure cape rippling down their back.

"Excuse me, Regent. These two gentlemen are Marshal Arthur Montague and Marshal Antoine Martineau: the last two Marshals from Paris' Bastion," Regent Blanc intervened.

The other eight Regents saluted them and Arthur and Antoine regarded them reciprocally.

"My name is Francisco Cortés, Regent de Perpignan," the old man continued, turning his attention to Arthur and Antoine. His French had a marked Spanish accent. "I've heard about your father several times, and unfortunately I never had the chance to meet him in person. Such a legend. Good that I finally have the pleasure of meeting his son."

"Of course, Regent, a pleasure to meet you too," Arthur replied with a smile.

"This man next to me is Jean-Pierre Marchand, Regent de Orléans," said Cortés, gesturing to the young man at his left side, who nodded in acknowledgement, and so on until the last man. "François Frey, Regent de Marseilles. Jacques Dumas, Regent de Valence. Markus Schlesinger, Regent de Strasbourg. Cédric Rousseau, Regent de Rennes. Charles Chaney, Regent de Brest. And Armand Renoir, Regent de Calais."

"Thank you, Regent Cortés," Vincent Blanc replied. "Now that the acquaintances have been made, let the Assembly begin!" He laced his fingers, leaning on the table. "First of all, and most importantly, we have to discuss Paris' most recent events. I am sure you all know about them."

"Of course," answered the young Regent, François. "The country's economy is in a critical situation. We heard of Viceroy Nicholas; it was mournful news. We also got news of your Company's losses, one of the finest," he said, turning to Arthur.

"There is also evidence of what we are up against," said Blanc, gesturing to Arthur and Antoine. "These gentlemen are that living evidence behind the mystery of Paris. Their men gave their lives defending Paris, because the enemy was ruthless; it was savage, and quickly obliterated one of our greatest Companies. Tell them, Marshal Arthur. Tell them exactly what happened."

Arthur inhaled deeply, preparing to share his life-breaking experiences. He tried not to think of Alice or anyone in his Company that had not made it alive; but it was nearly futile, which made him dither momentarily. He began by explaining first-hand Scorpio Company's mysterious disappearance, and made his way through the events with Alice that befell them during patrol in Paris. He had difficulty telling about Paris' strange situation, deserted and rather ghostly, and about the battle of Notre Dame. He felt that the men were not going to listen to him. From the mouth of a man, the telling of such an event happening on Earth seemed so ludicrous; dragons and undead monsters emerging from the bowels of the Earth, hooded priests worshipping demons and raising the troops of Hell with black magic. He saw that glint of disbelief in some of the Regents' eyes as he told about the Viceroy's death and the emergence of a monumental dragon within Paris' White Bastion, and how the few men alive rode tirelessly across the fields to reach their closest safe haven, Rouen's White Bastion.

As he did so, the door across the Assembly Hall opened soundlessly and a shade slid into the chamber. It was a slim woman covering her face and hair with a dark veil. She had a white corset tightly wrapped around her torso under a black laced-up V-necked silk tunic that ended in a knee-length half skirt toward her back. A pair of black leather gloves concealed her hands and wrists. Beneath the veil, Arthur could see a ghostly white traditional Venetian mask. With firm and resolute strides, she went directly toward Regent Blanc, her black leather boots rapping rhythmically on the marble tiled floor. He leaned back toward her as she stooped down slightly and the two exchanged whispers for a brief time. She straightened up and glanced at Arthur, who caught her glance from the corner of his eye, and without stopping the narration of his story, he went on. The woman walked out and Arthur finished telling the events.

"There's no way such a thing could have happened," Regent Jacques commented. "I just can't believe it. With all due respect, Marshal, I will not believe until I see it with my own eyes!"

"How can you be so skeptical?" the Regent of Calais, Armand said. "It is one of Satan's schemes. I advocate we all pray and render the Lord a tribute. Call him for help, for it is only the Lord that can defeat Satan!"

"I don't think He's going to help us," Arthur replied, recalling Alice's complaints, that no help came when she needed it most. "Not even I believe it is one of Satan's schemes. Those men said the name of the deity several times. I think it was Antares, as I recall."

"That's blasphemy, Marshal!" Armand countered. "You are not to deny the Lord's full potential! He is almighty and He will decide when to help us all. I know He will. It is better if we pray for salvation."

"I'm sorry, Regent," Arthur replied, getting impatient. "But I don't see any angelical troops being deployed across the vast blue firmament. We ourselves have to act now before this formidable threat! All fiefs must join together into one, united and together we shall fight until every one of those demons is dead. Nobody is coming to our aid. We must act by ourselves or else they are going to kill every one of us. I saw it with my own eyes, and I escaped

Paris by a hair's breadth and that with Marshal Antoine's help. My soldiers, all my comrades, fell in battle against those vicious men who are willing to exterminate their own race!"

"Are you suggesting that we should join…England?" Regent Blanc asked with surprise.

Arthur nodded steadfastly to make it clear.

"You do know the wick to spark a war with England is about to ignite, right?"

Arthur nodded again.

"Not only England, but the Spaniards and the Holy Roman Empire as well," Arthur replied. "It is imperative that we do it now. Does everyone remember the mythical and feared dragons, gigantic fire-breathing monsters?" he said aloud. Everyone nodded. "Then, us alone, how do you expect us to bring down such a beast?"

"It was one of those that nearly wiped us out," Antoine interjected. "The reason we survived is because Marshal Arthur gave us the chance to flee the Bastion as it turned to cinders."

"Then what do you propose, Marshal?" Regent Markus asked.

"Does anybody here find odd and strange the newly assigned Duke of Normandy, for instance?" Arthur asked. Everybody nodded. "How did the Duke ascend to power with Jean and Philippe's entire support, without any kind of procession or anticipated announcement? It was completely sudden! Duke William Bloodthorn is a Harbinger!" Arthur declared. "He, along with the other four men summoned the troops of Hell right in front of my eyes! And now he is a major political figure with influence over the people and the clergy! The Viceroy himself believed it!"

"How do you know that?" the Regent of Brest, Charles, snapped. "How do you know it was the same man with the same name?"

"The leader of the Harbingers said it aloud," Arthur retorted confidently. "But I admit William Bloodthorn is the only name I can recall, besides the one who killed the Viceroy. Let's say, both caused me the most shock. I might remember more if somebody happened to say them." He paused. "Now, referring to your question Regent Markus, what I propose is this: to put the Duke in his place, and restore Jean to his legitimate throne."

"Why do you insist the Duke must be dealt with?" the Regent of Rennes, Cédric, inquired. "Is it a personal vendetta for what he did to your Company?"

"I would say it's a spice you could add," Arthur replied. "But, overall, he controls a great part of the kingdom. And I believe more of these schemes are at work over Philippe as well. All these five men *must* perish for us to prosper and defeat these impending threats." Arthur paused and took a deep breath. "I walked around the city for a while. And as I did, I realized what the city had been struck with. I talked to many people, and they told me grievous things, about events unheard-of before the Paris attacks. Murders happen every night, assailants break into houses and manors. Guards and sentries are found butchered and mangled the next morning in the middle of the streets. And one coincidence is that it only began to happen the day William was named Duke of Normandy. Besides, he is an Englishman. How can an Englishman be Duke of Normandy?" he paused. "If we do not stop these five men, we are all doomed! Viceroy Nicholas himself appointed me for this mission. We all know he was an outstanding leader, much loved among us. Do you want to make his death be in vain, or do you want to help me make a difference in this world? United we stand; divided we fall." With that said he added, catching every eye in the chamber, "What say you?"

"I agree the Duke's ascension is a mystery, but it would be considered a crime to do anything to him without evidence of his crimes," said Regent Cortés. "It's possible what you say, Marshal, but it still would be treachery against King Philippe if he supports William. I agree with you. We just need concrete proof."

"I do not agree," said Regent Blanc. "You cannot attack an important political figure just because you believe he is the enemy behind the attacks on Paris. Even with proof, he has under influence many affairs regarding the kingdom. Everybody would turn against us in his defense, both the King and the Church!"

"Not everybody," Arthur replied. "The citizens of Rouen are, in fact, organizing a rebellion against the Duke. They have their own reasons, and I do, too. We all have a reason to overthrow William."

"That's of no concern to us," Vincent Blanc retorted. "The

King and the Duke will deal with the rebellions. We'll act only when they call us for help."

"What if the rebels call for our help?" Arthur inquired.

"Not to worry, Marshal. The King pays better," Blanc said with a wry smile of satisfaction.

"So what's your ultimate decision?" Arthur asked everybody, hoping that he had won their support.

Only Antoine, Regent Cortés, Regent Markus and Regent François agreed with Arthur. The other six Regents refuted him.

"Four against six. So be it," Regent Blanc announced. "We will not act against the Duke."

Arthur nodded resignedly and heaved a sigh.

"Now, we also need to discuss Viceroy Nicholas' successor," Blanc went on. "What do you say? Voting? Or is anyone planning to seize power by force?" he joked, and the Regents chuckled.

"I have something to say," Regent Cortés interjected, raising his voice above the casual laughs. "Possibly none of you knew, but Viceroy Nicholas once told me himself, in a letter, who would be his successor to the title of Viceroy. It wasn't official, but he told me he thought that Marshal Arthur Montague would be the wisest choice."

Arthur looked up to find everybody looking at him. All the Regents but Antoine and Cortés looked at him as if they resented him. There was no evidence about that feeling in the Regents' appearances, but he could feel it. He could even swear he saw some of the Regents' eyes twitching. He had not wanted to say anything about him being the Viceroy's favorite, but now that was not a problem anymore.

"Did the Viceroy ever speak to you about that, Marshal?" Regent Cortés asked, turning to Arthur.

"Yes, he did. Actually, before he died, he whispered to my ear 'Heir, stop them,' meaning the Harbingers." He remained silent then. He would not say anything else about it. His right arm tickled weirdly, in the spot he had been stung, the venom flowing in his veins, and as the feeling of close death came upon him, he realized what he was being tasked with: with the burden of leadership, and how he was jeopardizing the whole Order with his early demise. On the other hand, he felt the urge to become the Viceroy, thereby to attempt arresting Duke William and make his true identity public.

"The Viceroy never announced it officially to authorize the Marshal's ascension," Regent Blanc stated. "The Viceroy is gone, for good. We cannot ask him to sign any papers, can we? Now, let us proceed with the voting."

"Of course, Regent, go on," said Cortés, with a tone of disdain against the arrogant man.

"We all shall submit one vote," Vincent went on, looking at the impatient countenances of the Regents and the Marshals. "It can be anonymous if you will, and you can either vote for yourself or for anyone else. It can also be on any kind of paper or parchment you like. We will review the votes tomorrow evening."

Everyone nodded plainly, with a hint of anxiety in their expressions.

"Assembly adjourned," Regent Blanc finalized. "You can go rest now, gentlemen. Good evening."

The Regents rose from their seats and without regarding anyone, they left the Hall, and right outside, each one was assisted by his personal bodyguards. Cortés went over to Arthur to congratulate him on his efforts, praise him for his experiences in Paris and give him his condolences about the Viceroy. Finally they shook hands and Cortés departed.

After Cortés had exited the room and the torches had been snuffed out, Arthur and Antoine headed for the exit, and right before touching the doorknob, Arthur stopped short under the penumbra and blurted out in a soft voice: "Jacques was murdered," and with that he felt the relief of saying it to someone he could trust.

"What?" Antoine exclaimed, awe-stricken. "Have you any leads on the murderer?"

"Not one clue," Arthur sighed. "But I did find this letter." He took it out of his pouch and unrolled it. He let Antoine read it.

After he was finished reading, he looked up with a look of amazement: "So you weren't making it up! This is a great chance to take against the Duke!"

"That's exactly what I thought, but…" He pointed at the name of the author of the letter, whose initials A.B. were inscribed on it. "I still need to know the name of the author and where he is. The reason Jacques was killed is most likely because of what he's been playing with. He was warned, and...something came out wrong. This is my only lead toward both the Duke and the murderer."

"So you'll continue to ask around the town?" Antoine guessed, holding the doorknob.

"Of course. But I would also like to do some reconnaissance around the Duke's château," Arthur added. "I am more concerned about the city's situation than about becoming Viceroy. So, yes, I'll spend more time outdoors."

"Yes, I noticed," Antoine replied. "Unlike you, the Regents don't seem to care about anything else..."

Hecatomb

In the afternoon, the brown wooden gate rose upward by the pull of chains rattling in the struggle to get the gate fully open. A large group of guards armed with shields emblazoned with the coat of arms of the House of Valois—blue background dotted with small golden *Fleur de Lis*, wielding spears, bustled out of the stronghold, *Château de Rouen*. Their armored feet hammered on the narrow bridge that linked the stronghold to the mainland, as they trotted toward the menacingly big throng of denizens of Rouen's slums and farms. The mob flared and blazed with anger; a desperate, disorganized and futile upheaval hoping to bring about the Duke's overthrow.

Arthur peered down from an elevated position from afar at the unusual spectacle. He was overlooking the entire fortress and had ample sight of the city as he listened to the uproar of the mob in front of Rouen's Château. He was lying down on the grass of a knoll, partially hidden beneath bushes and the shadow of the arboreal canopy, close enough to hear the rumble, but far enough to avoid detection. He was still trying to figure out who the leader of the rebels was, but there were too many people in the tumult.

Rouen's guards began to fend them off with their shields, shoving them back. In any instant, the scene would become carnage, Arthur thought. The rebels had been hurling stones at the walls and yelling insults at the Duke. They were serious felonies, often punishable with slow torturous death.

Soon afterward, another phalanx of about ten knights came

marching down the bridge, carrying broader and heavier shields emblazoned with the same symbol, while brandishing long steel lances. Their armor was heavier and with a strange, darker material Arthur could not recognize. As soon as they reached the turbulent throng, they began to surround them threateningly, lances aiming high at the people on the edge of the multitude. Unlike the original guards, these heavy guards had their faces completely covered under their helms and they were taller.

The heavy knights quelled the uprising and very soon the people were silent. Those on the edge backed off, wincing with fear as they did. Arthur became tense as he watched. He expected the worst: an impending massacre.

Then a tall figure appeared at the gateway of the château. Duke William trod nonchalantly across the bridge, smiling deviously as he did so, his boyish lips curled with malice, eyeing carefully every countenance in the group, as though to memorize each one of them. His attire consisted of a mazarine, broad, high-necked outfit, the collar reaching high above his neck. The cuffs of his long sleeves were wide and they concealed his arms and hands completely. A long and wide cape bound to his shoulders by shackles rippled behind his feet as he approached the mob with satisfaction. His black leather boots rustled on the dirt as he stepped on the land. The quilted front of his livery was laced together, the corners of the ducal gown elegantly folded backward.

"What's all this fuss about?" he shouted, his smile contrasting remarkably against the hostile environment. "If you are hungry then go eat some grass, you sods!" he exclaimed in mockery, with a jovial smile.

The heavy knights kept the lances steadily aimed at the throats of the people closest to the edge. Nobody had the courage to reply. Their plated armors were inhumanely big and thick, so much that it seemed impossible for a common man to wear them.

"I've seen you before, your Highness," was the only reply from within the multitude. It was an old man who feared neither the guards nor the Duke. "I have seen you before, a decade ago." As he uttered these words, several lances flew toward him, stopping short before his face. The Duke whistled an order and the knights returned their weapons to their previous position. William listened intently. "Weren't you the wandering teenager that arrived from England ten years ago? I remember your face. I gave you bread once when you most needed it, I recall. Then one day you disappeared. Nobody knew what happened to young William."

"Bollocks!" exclaimed William with a sneer. "Say your petitions! What is it you want so eagerly? I have no food for you. You make the food. You *are* the food." The last phrase he said under his breath.

"We've lost our scant money," replied another man who had the courage to speak before the tips of the spears. "We hardly manage to survive with what little we have. You demand too much from us. We want to live as before."

"You are the fellows that have been causing trouble lately. Why would I be clement with you?" said William. "Who is your leader? Who is the fellow that feels so overly interested in your affairs?" he asked aggressively, with obvious sarcasm.

The crowd remained silent; some men were already cowering behind others or trembling to the point of buckling. Only one spoke:

"We decided to stand up for our rights. Nobody commanded us or roused us to rebel. All we want is to live as before, without fear."

"Do you think I'm bloody stupid? Who is A.B.?" the Duke yelled, drawing forth a dagger as his hand slithered out of the long sleeve. "My vassals have intercepted letters with those initials that give away information such as the time and place of your revolts."

"We cannot tell. We are forbidden to speak anything of him," a man answered, trembling, looking fragile and about to break down both physically and psychologically.

The number of guards almost equaled the number of rioters. But the heavy knights were insurmountable as they advanced mechanically further into the crowd, compressing them into a small area of space. The guards recoiled back, feeling uneasy as their heavy counterparts moved like automatons.

"And who is going to help you now?" William growled. "If he cares about you so much, why isn't he here? He has betrayed you. Would you not rather live than die for the fallacy of a man?"

Arthur stood up from the grass.

The crowd remained silent.

"No luck, eh?" said William. "It is death, then."

Arthur went toward his horse and unhitched it from the branch of a tree. Arthur clenched his fingers into a tight fist and struck the trunk of the tree, feeling utterly useless and impotent, and then he noticed his bow and quiver hanging from the harness of his steed.

"Wait, your Highness," a man stammered out. He was trembling and sweating streams. He shouted. "His name is Amos, Amos Baudelaire!"

Arthur mounted his horse, heard the name, and kept it in his head for further investigation. He knew, for certain, that all the people gathered before the *Château de Rouen* were in a crucible, having nowhere to run and nowhere to hide; they were already dead.

The other men in the crowd glared at the traitor.

"Very well, that's all I needed!" William exclaimed, jovially. "It wasn't too hard, was it, mate?" The poor man swallowed and nodded, intimidated by both the heavy knights and his fellow rioters. William hissed: "*An*..." but was interrupted as he tried to utter an order in an alien language. The whooshing arrow whistled right before his face, sticking shuddering into a wooden pole connected to the bridge.

Arthur's horse careered down the slope of the knoll where he had been hiding, drawing another arrow as he rode toward the mob. His face was concealed beneath the helmet and its visor to avoid having a reward put on his head, if he came out of this alive. Yet, his provenance could be recognized just by the sheer sight of his armor. The knights of the Order always wore silver plated armor and bore the official symbol of the Order, the jousting white knights and *La Fleur de Lis*. And to avoid such an inconvenience, Arthur had had to scratch the symbol off the armor, and along with the ashes that blackened it, its material could easily be deemed iron, rather than silver. Along with his jet-black horse, he looked like a black knight.

"Beware of what you're getting into, lad," William warned as he glanced at the arrow that had just grazed past his face. "Are you Amos Baudelaire?"

"Let them go!" shouted Arthur, his voice muffled in the helmet. "I'm the one you're looking for, Harbinger!"

The word 'Harbinger' tipped off the Duke. "Have we met before?" he shouted back. "Remove your helmet!"

"Joking, right?" Arthur retorted and launched the nocked arrow, missing William's body by a few centimeters as he moved nimbly aside. His reflexes were inhuman.

Infuriated, William Bloodthorn pointed at Arthur. "Kill him!" he yelled at his guards and knights.

Without hesitation, Arthur's steed took off in a full-speed gallop, several heavy lances spearing deep into the ground as he wove around their quivering shafts, trying to predict where they would fall to evade them. As he looked back, he saw how the mob began to scatter away like a panicked swarm of ants, while the guards and heavy knights hurled their spears at him. Eventually, Arthur was able to get out of the knights' throwing range. He flew through the streets, not daring to stop, and only hoping that his brief intervention and defiance had bought time for the rebels to flee the place. And with any luck, he would still be able to escape the city before word of his crime spread, that way closing the gates for him.

And, fortunately, the gates were still open. He rode straight toward the White Bastion after making sure he was not being followed, thenceforth to decide the fate of the Order by electing the new Viceroy…

¤¤¤

An hour later, Arthur hitched his horse back in the stables next to the castle of the White Bastion, and headed directly toward his room, where he discarded his armor and groomed himself to be presentable for the Viceroy election. As soon as he was finished, he went into the Assembly Hall and took a seat, where many of the Regents were already waiting for the Assembly to start again. The Regents greeted Arthur with a cold nod, which he reciprocated. Regent Cortés came over to him and they shook hands as if they were old friends.

"Today is the day," said Cortés with an amicable smile. "Godspeed, Marshal." The Regent returned to his seat on the opposite side of the large round table.

Antoine sat beside him. "Marshal," he said in salutation and placed a roughly folded piece of paper in the middle of the table.

Arthur grabbed a parchment, tore off a piece and quickly scribbled down his name with a quill and ink that were set on the table. He folded it neatly and piled it up with the other papers.

"Good afternoon, gentlemen," Blanc announced, standing up from his seat, looking everybody in the eyes. "Has everyone submitted their votes already?"

The candidates nodded.

"Then we shall begin the counting." Blanc bent over the stone table, curled his arm and swept all the pieces of paper toward him. Blanc gingerly unfolded every slip consecutively until they were all open. He looked up, with an indignant look in his black eyes and stammered out. "Armand de Calais, one vote. Jean-Pierre de Orléans, one vote. Jacques de Valence, one vote. Cédric de Rennes, one vote. Charles de Brest, one vote. Vincent de Rouen, one vote. Arthur de Paris, five votes..."

Every eye flicked toward Arthur. Eyes of arrogance and deep avarice were locked on him. Arthur was taken aback since he did not expect to be the one elected Viceroy. The Regents remained silent and looked at Arthur with cold eyes, then glanced briefly at Marshal Antoine, Regent Cortés, Regent Markus and Regent François; they had no votes whatsoever.

Yesterday was full moon, Arthur thought, *so that means I have little less than two weeks left to live. It's time to take action.*

"When is the coronation?" Arthur asked.

"Congratulations, Viceroy Arthur Montague," Blanc announced in general. "We shall prepare for your official coronation tomorrow..."

"This is outrageous!" Regent Armand de Calais blurted out, rising from his cushioned chair and pointing at Arthur accusingly. "All of this was staged! Those five men planned everything from the start!"

"Be tranquil, Regent." Vincent Blanc tried to reassure him. "None of this was staged, was it noble Regent?" he asked without expecting an answer. "Even if they planned it from the beginning, it doesn't matter. It's their choice who they will elect, isn't it?"

"This was not staged at all, Regent," Cortés retorted. "I believe

Viceroy Arthur had the legitimate right to become the successor for the reasons addressed before."

"This is not fair!" Armand de Calais went on, incensed, exhaling angrily. "This is unbelievable! I'm leaving to my Bastion."

"Calm down Regent, you are still rich and powerful," said Blanc sarcastically, with a hint of contempt toward the old man. "Besides, you are required by the Order to stay until the end of the coronation."

"Bah, that's nonsense!"

"We will be expecting you in the Viceroy's Hall, Mar...Viceroy Montague," Blanc corrected quickly before smiling. "This Assembly is adjourned."

Regent Armand de Calais was the first to leave the Hall, flinging the great doors open and striding resolutely toward his own quarters through the corridors. The other Regents went to theirs behind him.

Antoine turned to Arthur before leaving. "I wish you good luck, Viceroy. May your reign grow strong and prosperous."

"Thank you, Marshal," Arthur replied, and they shook hands warmly. "Your vote means much to me, I will remember it. I owe you much."

"No, noble Viceroy Dragonslayer," Antoine said, "I owe you my life. You were there at my side in the harshest of times."

"But if it were not for you," said Arthur. "I would have died in Paris as well, along with all my Company. Your celerity in taking action brought me home alive."

"And if it were not for you," said Antoine. "My actions would have been in vain. We wouldn't have made it back. I'll see you at your coronation, your Highness." Antoine bowed and went his way.

Taking advantage of his solitude, Arthur rolled his right livery's sleeve up to his elbow. He did not have to look any closer; the spot where he had been stung had become a hideous pustule tinged in blue, oozing pus. The bluish hue was slowly advancing further through his skin; in a matter of days, his arm would be completely swallowed by the blue color. Touching the spot produced no pain whatsoever; it was utterly numb. Instead of his mind clouding with despair at the thought of his life imminently coming to a terrible end, he remained serene, standing straight and solemn. The time had finally come. It was a new dawn, a new horizon to look at, for mankind's hope of survival against the impending strife for domination, a contention against a higher race of olden beings, was being rekindled. They have made the first strike, and now it was time to counter. Arthur knew what to do: assemble the squad of the White Bastion that would arrest Duke William, summon up all remaining strength to retaliate right in the weak point, even against Viceroy Nicholas' wishes, burst into the eye of the storm and subdue the dark cloud that had settled itself upon Europe, swallowing the world...

¤¤¤

Later that night, as the moon continued to wane ever undisturbed, Arthur felt tense around people. He could not help but constantly glance behind his back. During dinner, every single Regent and Marshal was dismissed earlier than usual by Vincent Blanc, claiming that everyone had to sleep well and be presentable for the Viceroy's coronation. Some of them took it naturally; a handful were hysterical, like Armand de Calais raving over his own issues, probably in part because he lost the election, but sooner or later they had to give in. Arthur, in fact, thought it was a little strange, though he went, along with everybody, to his own quarters.

Along the way, in one of the narrow corridors, lit by torches perched on brackets, he found Regent Armand de Calais about to enter his own room. "Good night, Regent," Arthur saluted.

"Keep your words to yourself," Armand grumbled. "I'm still in a higher position than you, Marshal."

"Sure I will, Regent," Arthur replied, staidly. He heard the Regent's door shutting close behind his back and he continued on his way a few more doors ahead, where he entered his room.

The first thing he did before crawling under the covers was to remove the upper part of the livery and set it over the backrest of a wooden chair. He snuffed out the candle that was already dripping wax down its stick. Having the window open, with a clear view of the starred sky and the waning moon, had a soothing effect on him as if he were unloaded of the day's burden; he was at peace. No worries came to disturb his mind as he drifted off into slumber, other than his daily mourning for Alice.

It was still a painful pang that shot through him every time he remembered her heartbroken face, her pleas to let her sacrifice herself to save his own life and Antoine's. Images and memories of the old times spent with her, since their childhood and into adulthood, flashbacked helplessly through his head as his grief loaded up to the point of becoming unbearable. The sorrow that burdened his being was as strong as when his mother and father died long ago. His nostalgic thoughts chased away his sleep, destroying all signs of drowsiness. Arthur remained under the blankets, fighting off the insomnia that had taken him over, as always, when he heard an unusual muffled noise. He thought he had heard something akin to a cry. How many hours had passed since he slumped onto the bed? He was sure it was the dead of the night already when the sudden noise made him jump.

And so the door of his own room began to creak slightly, almost soundlessly, as it slowly inched open inward, but Arthur had heard it. His heart skipped a beat as he turned his head imperceptibly to the right, just as much as he needed to catch a glimpse outside. The torches in the corridor had been snuffed out, contrary to other nights when they remained lit until dawn. His room was utterly dark, except for the faint light of the waning moon. Some deft and invisible hands pushed open the door as much as the figure needed to be able to squeeze through. Leather boots rustled upon the stone as a thin and dark silhouette slithered into the room. Arthur forced his vision through the darkness, desperately trying to catch the most insignificant glimpse of what lay ahead to ascertain what he feared. Whoever was there, Arthur assumed the intruder was taking long to step forward; the room was not large. He pushed back his blanket as carefully as he could, trying to avoid the slightest rustle, and then, he intentionally stirred in bed, grunting and shifting his position and curling up on his right side to appear to be asleep, and thus facing whoever was at his door more easily.

As soon as he felt the presence within his reach, he slowly managed to position himself, setting one bare foot upon the cold stone floor, and propping himself up with his right elbow he lunged forward. The first thing he felt was a short and thin, yet stout, blade ready to repel any attack. As unexpected as his attack was, the intruder was not holding the dagger tightly, and as soon as Arthur felt the metallic material with his fingers he swiped it away and seized the hand holding the weapon with his right. Before the attacker could struggle, Arthur pressed his hand upon the attacker's chest and rammed it against the hard wall.

Arthur heard the attacker grunt and he began to struggle against his grip. Then he noticed that the chest he was pressing was the bust of a woman. Startled, he removed his hand to push her upper shoulder against the wall.

"Drop the weapon," Arthur growled. The dagger immediately clanged on the floor and the echo reverberated in the room. "Who are you? I demand an answer!"

"I am Whisper," she whispered. "I am the last thing you hear."

"Not this time," Arthur replied, holding her pressed tight against the wall. "I demand your real name and your purpose."

"My name is Valerie Barbaroux," she answered softly, no longer struggling. "My purpose? Nothing important. I am just doing the rich man's dirty work, that's all."

"Who do you work for?" Arthur demanded.

Since there was no response, he pressed his elbow against the hollow of her neck and she choked for a few moments before he withdrew.

"I'm not letting you go until you tell me everything," Arthur snapped. "Who is this 'rich man'? Why?"

She chuckled. "I am a hired assassin. The Cult of Tiberius," she coughed. "Don't you know who hired me? I thought it was obvious."

"Enough," said Arthur. "I'm going to turn you in…"

"I wouldn't do that if I were you," she chuckled, letting herself be pulled by Arthur's grip toward the door.

"What do you mean?" he stopped abruptly, restraining her right hand.

"It's him that wants you dead," she retorted. "I'm only doing his dirty work."

"Who does? I am the Viceroy already," Arthur replied. "This means treason!"

"If you turn me in, either he or one of my brothers will end the work before you can utter your first word."

"What?" Arthur exclaimed. "There are more of you?"

She nodded nonchalantly.

"How many? Who are their targets?" Arthur urged. He quickly bent down to pick up the dagger at his feet. Arthur wielded the knife and pressed the sharp blade against her throat. "You answer every one of my questions at once. Who are they targeting?"

"You've got some skill with that," Arthur pressed tighter. "Okay, okay. It was Vincent, Vincent Blanc!"

Arthur had suspected Armand de Calais, since he seemed the one most resentful after Arthur won the Viceroy election. But when he realized how wrong he was his heart sank, and he heaved a sigh.

Ever since the Viceroy's election topic came under discussion, Blanc had always been anxious and acting strangely. But Arthur had never seen it coming, not at such scope. There was only one way to usurp power without an obstacle, without any kind of hindrance, and the infamous way was to eliminate competition.

"You know? I think you're the first to ever stop Whisper from doing her job," Valerie chuckled. "Are you still going to turn me in, or kill me, or run away, or let me do my work?"

Arthur was not listening to her. He knocked her out cold with a single punch to her face and let the assassin drop to the hard floor, her Venetian mask cracking. His only home had become dangerous for him. The only haven, sheltering from ill and chaos, giving refuge against inclement weather and raging wars, where his friends and fellow comrades resided and coexisted, the one valuable covert that was worth fighting and dying for, had turned against him. Arthur's heart sped up at one single thought. *Antoine!*

"No!" He burst out of the door into the dark corridor, dagger ready.

With a pang in his chest, Arthur went stumbling through the murk and across the narrow aisle, trying to calculate the distance at which Antoine's room was located. He arrived at the place he was sure was his door, fumbled blindly in search of the doorknob, and flung it open.

Already under the threshold, he sensed the emptiness of the

room, devoid of any life, as if all the air had been vacuumed out of the place. And strangely enough, the body was nowhere to be found. Many things could have happened, but he could not afford the time to guess; he had to flee, for good.

Back in his room, Arthur blindly put on his entire gear, being the blackened silver armor set, his longsword, his shield, and retrieved his leather pouches.

As Arthur came closer to the main hall, lit torches began to appear attached to the walls as he went deeper. Finally, when he had made it back to the staircase of the main hall, from which the Assembly Hall could be seen in front, he began to walk more furtively, making sure that he was completely alone. So far, he did not see anyone…until he was about to push the great doors open.

"Where are you going in the dead of the night, Marshal?" Arthur turned on his heels to find Blanc, in his livery, staring at him coldly, with an unfriendly scowl across his face. Vincent Blanc had called him *Marshal* and not *Viceroy*. That was the first thing Arthur noticed. Blanc came from the corridor at Arthur's right. Then he heard more steps echoing through the main hall, and as he lifted his eyes to the summit of the staircase, he spotted four men and one woman coming down.

He finally had a clear look at Valerie, who remained behind the convoy. All five of them wore ghostly white traditional Venetian masks. She was a slim woman covering her eyes, forehead and hair with a black veil. Valerie pulled back the veil, and gently slid open the cracked mask to reveal deep emerald eyes with an almond shape, a slightly upturned nose above crimson lips, and long jet black hair gathered in a carefully plaited braid. A purplish bruise gradually took color on her right cheek. Her countenance reflected a constant sly and mischievous, though not detectable, smile.

The group trod down the staircase, and in unison, as if by cue, they all halted ten meters away from Arthur, at the base of the steps.

"Shadowblade," Regent Blanc called out. The man at the head of the convoy turned to face him without moving from his spot. "Have you met my friend here, Marshal Arthur?" he said, gesturing toward Arthur with his hand, who looked surrounded like a rabbit before a pack of wolves, his back against the doors, his eyes flashing from each of the members and back to the Regent. He had his right hand ready on the sword's hilt and his left on the doors' handles, concealed by his body in front. "Why so tense, Marshal?"

Arthur's face burned red with wrath, but he did not show it, nor did he speak out. His first repressed impulse was to lunge at Blanc, but he had to restrain himself from making such a reckless move; it was not the right time, not just yet.

"Why don't you go back to sleep? Please, I insist," the Regent frowned. "Why are you speechless, Marshal? I'm asking you a question."

"No, you're asking too many questions. Wasn't I the Viceroy already?" Arthur replied with credible anger.

"Not until after the coronation, but yes, that's correct," answered Blanc straightforwardly.

"You forgot to add 'If I survive the night,' though." Blanc's expression turned hostile. "Yes, I know your plans. Kill off the competition, huh?" He held out Valerie's dagger.

"Whisper," said the veiled Shadowblade with an authoritative stern voice. "That is not your dagger, is it?"

"Yes, it is," Valerie admitted from behind. "I couldn't kill him. He disarmed me in a flash and kept my only weapon. I couldn't do anything then."

"Well, that can be resolved with a secondary weapon," said the leader, putting it simply.

"So what are you waiting for? I'm paying you to kill this bloody piece of cannon fodder!" Blanc blurted out, exasperated.

"And then what, Regent? Who will you blame for this unexpected and coincidental accident?" Arthur intervened. "Them?" he pointed his finger toward the hired assassins, hoping his accusation will make them feel uneasy. "In what reasonable way will you be able to hide such a mess before dawn breaks?"

With a glimpse he caught off to the right, Arthur hardly had any time to react against the flying knives that came whistling to find his shield lifted up to his face. The daggers clanged off the metal and their echoes heavily reverberated throughout the main hall, off the thick pillars and vaulted ceilings. Arthur turned toward the assassins. Valerie was only staring at him, with a look of curiosity, while Shadowblade began to unsheathe some more knives to cast at Arthur.

"Pay close attention, Whisper," he said, preparing another handful to throw. "This is how you do it!"

Arthur quickly sidestepped with his shield raised as the daggers stuck themselves into the wooden sections of the iron-bound doors. He knew he would fail to evade the next attack; he knew he had to act quickly.

Still looking at them, Arthur pulled the great doors open behind him, making a great struggle to get them as wide as he needed to to be able to squeeze out, while keeping his shield up.

"Heavencloak and Nocturnal, don't let him get away! Feathertread, you stay at my side!" barked Shadowblade as Arthur slipped out through the door. "Whisper, you stay here in case he should come back, which I doubt. Just do it!" He approached her and they kissed. "This is it! The bounty of our lives!" and he disappeared behind the door.

Valerie glanced at the impatient Regent, and rapidly after making eye contact, she removed her gaze, asking herself who would be the one considered guilty for the mayhem that took place in the White Bastion.

And she slid back the mask to cover her face…

Reminiscence

Atop the World,
Upon the summit of the Nether land,
Wherein Black Shadow-King of Arcadia, towering and baneful,
Upon you overlooks and stalks,
Gauzy eye of guile, greed of men, opulence of the proud,
For you to retrieve and thus into the socket of the Cyclops inlay,
For toward me you shall come and the Guardian defeat,
Thereby to claim worthiness, or lack thereof,
For your actions weigh the scales of liberty and bane…

Just seconds after she had lost mental contact with Geister, she regained consciousness and awoke on her feet, outside the green maze and in front of the fountain. The first thing she did when she opened her eyes was to look frantically around for Sonja, for she was all that mattered in the world to her. All of a sudden, Sonja appeared out of thin air at her left side. Alice threw herself into her arms with a sigh of relief and embraced her as though she had not seen her in years.

"Thank you, you're all right!" said Alice under her breath.

"Alice, this isn't over yet," Sonja replied as they let go of one another. "But we have nearly finished this Trial."

"This is your final enigma," Geister announced sonorously inside their minds. "Solve it and you shall be absolved. And for the third time, I remind you not to delay any further, for there shall be a drastic change if you do. Just to make things more fun."

Just then the dark sky began to churn restlessly, sending strong whirls of wind that howled through the tower.

"We should head back inside," said Alice. She forced the kitchen's door open and closed it behind them as the strong wind ruffled their hair and bustled inside.

"Alice, the first line of the enigma implies that now we have to go all the way up," said Sonja as Alice slid down the wall on the spot where they had rested hours ago. Sonja slid down by her side. "But I still can't figure out what the Black Shadow-King of Arcadia is."

"I think I know what that is," Alice replied, and her expression became grim. "I believe it's the dragon that flew over the place while you were still in the maze. I saw it cling to the highest point of the tower and crawl into it."

"Wait...what?" Sonja exclaimed, keeping her voice down. "You don't mean the giant fire-breathing lizards, do you?" Alice realized that Sonja had never had the chance to even know that they existed. She had already gone when the outbreak in Paris occurred.

"Oh yes, that's exactly what I mean," said Alice, noticing that she did not find the idea of the dragon too frightening, maybe because of the thought that she should be long dead. "In fact, I believe that's what Geister wants us to face."

"What I would give to see one. Of course, I wish we didn't have to face it," said Sonja.

"Lord Alænnor...that's what the ghost whispered. All those giant steaks that hang on the walls are to feed that beast, and those specters we saw before are its slaves," Alice thought aloud.

"So what could the 'Gauzy eye of guile' have to do with it?" Sonja asked, frowning.

"Maybe we'll find out later when we face it," said Alice, huddling at Sonja's side. "For now I feel worn-out. It's a long way up we must go," she said, her eyelids dropping. Then she forced herself to remain awake. "Where is Percival?" she said in a soft voice.

"I don't know, but there are no more ghosts either," Sonja replied, peering up and down the corridor between the shelf in front and the wall behind. "You should get some sleep; you'll need it. If I hear anything I'll wake you up."

Alice could not hold her eyes open any longer and she quickly drifted off. “Please, don’t leave…,” she whispered, almost gone into the world of dreams.

“No, I won’t. You are safe and sound,” Sonja answered softly.

Finally, out of the horrors of reality, Alice came to a lull where she felt neither sorrow nor despair. It was a brief moment of peace that she craved to retain forever, when all of sudden she found herself in a world of eternal nightmares.

Alice arrived at Eden…

¤¤¤

“Welcome, welcome back,” a heavy ghoulish voice boomed in the forsaken paradise, “to Eden, beloved paradise.”

Alice regretted having fallen asleep, but she was exhausted.

“Whatever you are going to do, do it now and get this over with!” Alice called back. The green rolling hills began to lose their color, turning dead gray. The fine delicate stalks of grass and colorful petals of flowers began to wither and die off, one by one, slowly turning to ashes in the most unnatural of ways. The sky was azure, sparsely smudged with clouds that hovered peacefully above the vast land. Then it began to turn slowly into a sky like that in Arcadia, swollen with anomalous darkness, overcast with turbulent clouds that blotted out the sun, distorting the sky with baneful images that only dreams are capable of producing. Macabre skulls loomed above, taking on the forms of the clouds, or, alternatively, shifting into dragons or ghouls.

Alice just stood there, watching as the world around her turned into what she feared the most, but no longer caring. She inspected her inventory and realized she was unarmed, like last time.

“Your fear in regard to nightmares has diminished, I see,” said the voice again, eerily close to Alice. She whipped around, recognizing it with a jolt.

“Percival!” she gasped, now yearning for something to defend herself with.

“No, just your tormentor” said the deity, his squalid face grim and threatening. “I take on the form of what you dread the most.”

Alice calmed down, but retained her wariness.

"I have learned to fear only what is tangible and that is ready to harm me or someone I care for in any way whatsoever. Percival is wounded, probably dying already. He is still a threat, I'll grant you that. But it looks like your powers of terrorizing me have subsided," Alice replied steadily, steeling herself, for it is no small feat to defy a deity.

Percival's deadpan countenance came to life with a grin. "We shall see about that. The last time we saw each other I told you that you would choose between two different tests: an ominous foreboding, and a reminiscence, a look into your appalling past." Alice's skin paled and her eyes dilated with fear. "This drug of fear I shall give you, one painful and long look into the past." Now it was not Percival's voice talking, but a grave, ancient and deep rumble that made the earth quake. "Let us reminisce!"

All went black...

¤¤¤

Where am I?

All I could think of was that I was having a nightmare.

What do I fear?

I fear the horrors of reality. My childhood was a nightmare after tragedy struck my home. Before that, I was happy. Rarely have I been happy after that tragic event.

My name is Alice Houdin. I am nine years old. I should be dead. Mother is gone. Father is long gone. They left me alone in an unknown world where threats stalk everywhere I step.

For a single moment of peace, I thought that my mother's murder had been just a nightmare...only an unreal event that took place in my head in the dead of the night. I wanted to believe it was all a bad dream. But it was not. Opening my eyes was like inducing me into the one real nightmare.

Who was my father? Constant fear and distress made me forget his name. I was only three when he vanished. What happened to him? As if I knew. One day he disappeared all of a sudden, without one clue of his whereabouts. But before disappearing, he managed to get us, Mother and me, to Paris with enough money to live well. But when he was gone and didn't come back, we struggled to maintain our accustomed way of life. A few years later we were next to broke.

The time came. I was awoken by a sudden noise downstairs. It was odd; it was midnight. My mother and I were cocooned together in bed. The sorrow was still too strong and hard to deal with for my mother. After six years without my father, the pain was still powerful, like a deep gash within her being. I often climbed up to sleep alongside my mother. It was a relief for her not to deal with the grief all by herself the entire time. She was worn out by the hardships of life, working her hands to the bone and her mind to despair. Sowing and harvesting in the fields barely earned her enough money for us to live off the scanty food we could afford during the week.It was barely enough for us to keep on living in our old house in Paris. On my ninth birthday, March 14th, now the year 1324 AD, all Mother was able to give me as a gift was a carefully crafted wooden doll. I always kept it by my side every night, including that one.

"Mom," I whispered, shaking her awake. "I think there's something downstairs."

"Don't, Alice," she said, still drowsy. "I'm tired right now. Can you wait until dawn?"

I shut up reluctantly and tried to fall asleep again. But I was still disturbed. Something was certainly out of place.

The next thing I remember was the crashing blast of an urn shattering to pieces right outside our bedroom. Mother and I bolted upright, both equally frightened. Since Father's disappearance, she had become somewhat paranoid and always kept a large knife close to her in case strange situations like this one ever happened. Mother tightened her grip on the knife's hilt and ordered me to bed.

I was reluctant to lie down, but she forced me with soothing words, reassuring me that 'everything is going to be okay, my princess.'

"I'll be back before you can say 'I love you,'" Mother said, straightening up and heading for the door.

"I love you," I called back in a soft voice. She only smiled faintly and disappeared behind the door.

¤

"No, stop it!" Alice moaned as she tried to grasp consciousness, writhing on the black floor. "Stop playing with my mind!"

"I told you it would be painful," Zartha replied in his ghoulish rumbling voice. "Maybe my powers over you have not yet subsided..."

¤

It was not long before a bloodcurdling shriek shattered all the silence that reigned over the dark room. I immediately bolted out of the door, heart racing, struggling to catch what lay ahead through the darkness.

As I reached the head of the staircase, I caught sight of a figure upon the ground, motionless. I knelt down before the inert body, my left hand running through the brown curled locks that framed Mother's face, my right hand pressing her blood-slicked hand to life, but in vain. Tears streamed down my face, droplets falling on Mother's cheeks. All I could think of was that I was simply having a bad dream. But it was real; it was tangible. All I could do was produce a low wailing with words like 'No' intertwined with the constant grief. It was the greatest pain of my life...

¤¤¤

"Mother?" Alice squinted open her eyes, propping herself up with a hand upon the pitch-black floor. Ahead, a few meters away, a female figure began to walk leisurely toward Alice.

"Everything is going to be okay, my princess. I'll be back before you can say 'I love you.'" It was her voice, exactly as Alice remembered it, but it had a subtly different tone; a different feeling.

"Mother?" Alice repeated, making an effort to discern her face. It was hers, the same face from thirteen years ago. It hadn't changed at all.

Her mother smiled slyly and raised her hand, clenching her fingers upon her skin, pressing tightly, right below the eyes and around the nose, and pulled back the skin, as if it were a mask. Her face began to detach, uprooting the skin from her head, the brown curled hair and the brown eyes and the upturned nose looking appallingly unnatural. Her hand ripped off her entire countenance, leaving a formless, shabby thing without any facial features.

Alice gasped, buried her head in her arms while lying on the abyss floor, and shut her eyes, crying her tears out in pain. Zartha's rumbling voice broke the uncanny silence. "Everything is going to be all right, my princess…" Zartha approached Alice and began caressing her hair as he stooped down. "Everything will be okay, my princess…"

"No, stop it!" Alice moaned beneath her arms, like a child innocently shielding herself from the inevitable. "Stop impersonating my mother, bloody demon!"

"Alice…" Zartha's voice suddenly changed to one familiarly spine-chilling, hoarse and rough. "So long since I vanished. Don't you remember me anymore? Don't you recognize my voice, my name, my *face*? You still have a father. Look at me!"

Alice's curiosity finally won out over her. She gingerly looked up, and her heart skipped a beat. Now not only did she remember her lost father's appearance, but she also confirmed her suspicions about his true name.

She was staring into the baneful dark eyes of Percival…

Filial Turmoil

"No!" Alice choked out as she jolted upright, trembling sickeningly and covered in cold sweat. Sonja was at her side when she awoke, staring at Alice awe-stricken.

"It's okay, I'm still here with you," said Sonja soothingly. "It was only a dream."

"No, it was not a dream...If you fall asleep, he'll torture you..." Alice trailed off. She sat up against the wall, trembling, her eyes teary, though she did not shed any. Her jaw was tightly clenched.

"Alice, what are you talking about?" Sonja asked, worried. She leaned in closer and looked Alice in the eyes. "Are you talking about Geister?"

"No...Zartha, and Eden...," Alice murmured. "There is no respite, not even in your sleep."

"So he gave you a nightmare...is that what you are trying to tell me?"

"No..." Alice looked up at her grimly. Her voice became firm and steady. "He provided me with a deeper understanding of my life; he provided me with a truth."

"What did he show you?"

"My past...I relived my worst fears...I felt the years passing once again, all condensed in a couple hours..."

"I understand...," Sonja began, but Alice blurted out in anguish:

"No, you don't!" She was now standing up. "You don't understand!" Sonja stood up too. "I got over it. I no longer cared about what happened in the past. It just happened. I grew, and I am what I am because of that, and in part I do not regret it. Somehow, it made me see things differently. I became a survivor, someone who can look after herself, but because of the past I feared…" Alice finally began to shed tears, although she retained the hardened expression. She avoided breaking down; her sorrow was in a muddle of grief, hatred and incredulity. "Sonja…Percival is my lost father…"

"How do you know that?" Sonja asked, in disbelief.

"Zartha was impersonating my mother," Alice replied, a pang shooting through her body. "Then he impersonated my father; it was Percival's face and voice. I know that is the truth, because those few blurry memories of my father became crystal-clear."

"And still, he is willing to kill you," Sonja said, nodding at Alice's red bandaged neck-wound, where Percival punctured her with his wolf fangs.

"You stabbed him, twice," Alice replied, unconsciously stroking her wound. "He might be running out of blood. Maybe that's why he went to solve the riddles: to make it out of this place alive."

"He is a threat to the world; the world where you belong," said Sonja somberly. "Consider the facts. He is still your father. Are you willing to end his life to prevent the Harbingers from taking over your world?"

"I will finish him off," Alice retorted ardently.

Sonja looked down, speechless. When she looked up, Alice's face had softened and tears were running down her cheeks, forming streaks of grime. However, Sonja smiled and held out her hand to Alice.

"Shall we go to the top of the world?" said Sonja.

"To the very top," replied Alice.

"But not together!" Geister boomed. Alice and Sonja reacted defensively, standing back to back against one another, holding up their blades in the air. "Your time is up. It is over. I warned you not to linger anymore. You did not listen. I am bored, and that is disastrous for you. The contest has been assembled. It shall be a competition between two for one prize. The first to solve the enigma shall be rewarded with the greatest of prizes."

"Competition for what? Against who?" Alice called out to the air.

"Why, Percival against you!" Geister returned with a heavy rumble. "What is Percival's most desired treasure? A soul to digest, of course; a soul to flee the world, of course. What is it that you so dreadfully want? Oh, yes, your invaluable precious friend, indeed."

Alice turned around desperately to find Sonja flashing her eyes wildly all around, as though she were surrounded by an unseen threat.

"The rules are set. The first one to solve the enigma shall have the rights over the prize. Let the race commence!"

Alice instantly thrust herself forward to seize Sonja's hands, to save the one thing she cared about and could not live without, from Geister's grip. Sonja faded into thin air right before Alice could lay a finger on her.

"Sonja!" Alice gasped, her heart racing. One single thought pervaded her mind: that Percival might already be halfway through the enigma. Without hesitation, she took off, speeding through the narrow passageways between the shelves and out of the kitchen into the main hall, where the gigantic stairwell made its way to the top of the tower.

The coast was clear.

Alice bolted onto the stone stairs, heading all the way up to the dazzling heights of the top of the world. She was weary, but neither the harshest of hungers nor thirsts would stop her. A powerful determination dominated her mind, with only one constant thought: that Percival would not win, not while she could still draw breath. Her armor was cumbersome, the metallic joints creaking with her every movement, her laden boots hammering vehemently upon the stone. And yet, she flew.

As she sped on, phantasmagorical black figures zipped past her side, faintly whispering alien words that she caught with a shiver. Suddenly, she just about heard the words 'Time is ticking, Alice.' Giving heed to the warning, Alice mustered all her strength, and with a groan, her speed augmented, her legs screamed in exertion, but she went on with one single goal, thinking that everything now depended on whether she gave up or risked everything to save what she cared for and loved most.

Just as Alice came onto the next floor, she heard a groan of pain. Right before bolting onto the next flight of stairs, she noticed the figure that leaned tiredly against the thick balustrade of the corridor. Percival looked up and smiled.

"How can you…still be standing?" he groaned. "I guess I won't get her soul after all." He chuckled with some difficulty. "These phantasms here got me pinned down after I tried to absorb theirs. They are bloody violent!" Just as Alice approached him, she subtly noticed from the corner of her eye a shadow steering clear of her.

Alice strode grimly toward Percival, clutched his robe at the neck and pounded him against the floor. Percival began to thrash before Alice seized his hand and slammed it hard against his back, then releasing all her weight upon him as she knelt down on his backbone, crushing it with her greave's kneecap. With her right hand she slithered her broadsword's blade below his chin, and with her left she held him imprisoned beneath her grip.

"Bloody hell!" Percival growled with pain, though with some insane amusement. "You are killing me, Alice!"

"What is your name?" Alice hissed into his ear with ferocity. "Your real name."

"Damn you, wench," he replied, gasping for breath. "And I thought I was mad!"

"Prepare to hurt!" Alice snarled. "Either you tell me, or I will turn your life into hell!"

"What is your problem? My name is Percival. I hope you are happy now. Now get off me." Percival struggled against her weight, trying to shake her off and get his hands released. "You are breaking my back!"

Alice pressed harder. "What else?!"

"…Houdin," Percival gasped.

"Why did you leave us?" Alice demanded, her voice breaking as she grappled with her feelings. "Where did you go? Mother and I never knew of you after that! We were desperate. You left us alone. What happened to you? Why do you worship such a deity like Antares?"

"It is all quite simple," he replied. "You should pay Him tribute as well, for your own sake and welfare. I am his Head Harbinger. I am the First Harbinger. I am the first to answer to his requests, demands, pleas and wishes. I relay his words to the other four.

His orders are to collect and send him the largest amount of souls we can gather. But souls are also our source of power. Extraordinary skills require an extraordinary price. One soul can be more valuable than all the wealth of the world. With souls, I can move across the land by just wishing it, I can rise into the air, I can cast the elements from my fingertips, and many other things that you cannot begin to fathom. I give you an offer, my daughter. Become the Sixth Harbinger and you shall overpower the king of France. You will subdue the world along with us. It is wise to join the winning team. What say you? Father and daughter, together, to take over the world..."

"You have lingered too much on that issue," Alice interrupted, pressing her knee against his back. "Why did you leave?"

"I did not leave," Percival replied. "Antares recruited me, as he did to the others. He was desperate for a cure. We've found his cure and are administrating it periodically."

"So you'd rather kill thousands of people than be with us?" Alice asked, unbelieving.

"I'd rather stay true to my sire," Percival replied. "When I was coming back from my trip to Marseilles, nineteen years ago, my vision blacked out and when I awoke, I was looking into those majestic and enigmatic eyes of Him to whom I owe everything," Percival explained, resting his head on the red velvet rug. "His voice was deep and piercing, his language enthralling. I was in a hot place, possibly a world of fire, where I could not see anything other than Antares the Sun. He performed an occult ritual for me, one he called the Kiss of the Fiend. From that moment thereafter, I became bound to him for ages to come. I could not go back to you. I had important things to do."

"I cannot believe the things you are saying," said Alice, her voice rising. "You feed and heal a being that is about to swallow the world...Where did you go afterwards? If you had stayed in Paris, either Mother or I would've seen you eventually."

"Antares sent me to gather souls in the Spanish kingdoms," Percival continued, clearing his throat and speaking with difficulty. "Small towns and faraway rural villages. You know, where the prey is easy to catch. For some time I traveled alone. It was in England where Antares introduced me to Siegfried Quinn the

Dragon-scaled. Then we met the young William Bloodthorn the Men-eater in Normandy, where Antares inferred that his hunger and violent mind would prove quite useful. During our pilgrimage in Rome, Antares recruited our fellow man, Salvatore Cavalieri the Snaketongue, a former skillful spokesman for the Holy Roman Emperor Louis IV. And finally, in one of our last trips within the Empire, before coming back to Paris, Antares gave the Kiss of the Fiend to the teen Viktor Berlinghoff, the Fireclad, an eager entrepreneur skilled in theft and deceit. All those years, we, together, collected massive amounts of souls. If we had not, Antares would have died a long time ago."

"Tell me your plans!" Alice demanded, pressing the blade against his bare throat. "What are the other four up to?"

"You can't do anything about them," Percival replied, defiantly. "They are far beyond your reach. And remember, Alice, that you and I are both stuck in this mire, at least until one of us solves the enigma."

"Do you want to live?" Alice inquired aggressively, pressing down on his back with her armor's kneecap. "Antares needs you, Father. Are you willing to die now, knowing that He desperately needs you?"

"I do not care whether I live or die," Percival replied earnestly. "As long as the job gets done."

"And it won't get done if I kill you now, will it?"

"Siegfried is manipulating Edward III; he is steering Europe into war, clashing with King Philippe VI. He is making sure every act of diplomacy is a certain failure. William is working on the largest massacre the world has ever seen, in Normandy; a feast for Antares and him. Salvatore is working on a plot of taking out a figure who has major influence over Europe that will ultimately influence the entire world. And young Viktor, he was supposed to lead the Heir of the Sun, Kronnix the Sovereign, into battle with our greatest threat so far, in the heart of France, the Order of the Knight. They are all supposed to be dead by now. But wait just a minute, aren't you one of them?" Percival mocked with a tired smile.

Alice, for a brief moment, lost her concentration on Percival and wandered off in her memories. A pang struck her squarely in her heart as she imagined smoldering carcasses lying in the aftermath of the battle against the colossal dragon, all the people she knew and lived with for most of her life now deemed dead. Viceroy Nicholas was dead, Arthur Montague was dead, and Antoine Martineau was dead. Everybody was dead. *How could they have survived?*

Alice did not notice the tufts of rough fur that quickly began to sprout from Percival's hands and arms and spread over his body until it was too late. His ears were sharply elongated and his snout was already in its full wolfish form. His entire body grew burly and the robe gave way to the sprouting heavy fur. Before Alice could slit Percival's throat, he quickly released his left hand from under his weight and swiped the blade away, pushing himself upward with great force, sending Alice off his back helplessly.

As Alice regained her footing and confronted Percival, he was already glaring at her, shooting daggers with his eyes. Hunched down by his wolf's skeletal structure, his hind legs ending in powerful paws with long claws, Percival faced Alice with a determination to end his own daughter's life in the name of Antares.

"I will give you one last chance, my daughter," said Percival. "Will you join the Harbingers, or will you die now?"

"Don't call me your *daughter*," Alice snarled, shifting her broadsword's hilt on her palm and tightening the grip. "I will not die at your hands, nor will I let you have Sonja's soul!"

"How's that bite healing up?" Percival asked, nodding at Alice's neck. "You know I worry about my daughter's welfare. But right now, you are only another hindrance that must be dealt with."

"I must say I don't feel quite the same about you," Alice replied, glaring at him unwaveringly. "You are a stranger to me, nothing more."

"I know that is not true. I can feel it," Percival retorted with a wolfish smile of satisfaction. Alice bit her lip slightly. "But if you say so, so be it."

Alice saw the next attack coming, just like the last time she fought against Percival. She stepped back, holding her shield high as Percival clawed its façade with a quick swipe. Alice countered with a horizontal wide slash that could have opened up Percival's torso as he leaned back with difficulty, the sword's tip whistling one centimeter away.

Percival's lower lip quivered as he let a growl escape his throat. His back stung him excruciatingly where Sonja had stabbed him with the dagger at the time of warding him off Alice. Percival's task of resurrecting Antares was not anywhere near completion and he knew that the Hellgod was in dire need of his powers. So immense was his zealous love for Antares that if He were to die because of his failure, Percival would find no more meaning in life.

At the moment, he was unable to counter with all his might. Alice could clearly see that Percival was weak and vulnerable, and the fact that he was seen like that infuriated him intensely. His every movement was cumbersome and it took him a long time to withdraw after each lunge.

For a moment, they glared at each other. What started as a hunt had become a game in which they were stuck, competing for what they treasured most: Sonja or Antares. They were locked in a rivalry that could potentially mean salvation for one, and damnation for the other. Alice would go as far as to kill her own next of kin for Sonja, and so Percival would for Antares.

Alice darted forward with a sword thrust, which Percival managed to avoid by sidestepping out of the way. She consequently slashed away at the Harbinger without mercy. Percival could barely keep up with Alice's pace as he blocked some of the attacks with his claws and arms, but failed to protect his chest from the rest. In the brief lull that followed Alice's onslaught, Percival took the chance to kick her away.

His chest was bleeding from several shallow cuts that had managed to go through his defense. Alice was sure he was finished, and Percival knew that he was not going to last long at this rate. But he could not stand the possibility of being defeated and Antares dying because of his failure. He could not fail, and he was not going to. Giving up was not an option. Percival summoned up all his strength to ignore the pain and entered a berserk state, thus heightening his speed and resistance to pain.

Alice noticed right away Percival's change from slow and burdensome to nimble and wild. Percival unleashed a frenzied series of slashes onto Alice's shield, as she struggled to keep it up and not yield to his ruthless attacks. There was a fleeting respite in his strikes...before he whirled around and shot a powerful kick with his hind leg, sending Alice into the air. She flew backward, two meters across the floor, before she landed upon the creaking ground.

Percival vaulted over her as she lithely rolled to her side and regained her footing, sending a powerful upward slash that hit Percival directly on his upper torso all the way to his lower jaw, leaving a long shallow furrow from which blood spurted freely.

Alice trusted she had the kill already, and to finish him off, she charged a bold thrust with the tip of her sword into Percival's abdomen. Percival caught the edges of the sword between his two paws, causing them to bleed, and yanked the weapon back, along with Alice holding on tightly. Using Alice's force against her, Percival whirled, released the weapon from his bleeding claws, and pounded Alice on her back as she passed his side, sending her into the balustrade.

With a brief stroke of vertigo as she looked from the height above at the depths below, Alice gasped, clinging to the balustrade, staring into a howling abyss that would surely mean her death. She turned around to see Percival approach and moved out of the way just in time as he landed a blow on the handrail that shattered the stone to smithereens. Percival shook his paw, grimacing in pain.

Alice realized she was unable to take on Percival by herself without dying in the act. Right there and then, she darted onto the next flights of stairs and climbed more floors, aware that Percival was still hot on her heels. She could hear his strong breathing and growling as she reached the final floor of the tower after climbing several stories up.

There was a giant gate before her, looming high and menacing. Alice did not hesitate to open it as far as she needed to to be able to slip in, even if it was incredibly heavy. Once inside, she pressed her back against the heavy gate and shoved it closed, which required all her strength. For a short time, Percival pounded on the gate. When it did not give way to him, he stopped and Alice remained there, panting for air, leaning tiredly against the giant door.

It was only a brief respite before it dawned on Alice where she had stumbled upon. She was within an extensive open chamber with a ceiling so high it could barely be seen. Without any explanation, every torch began to burn, a few meters between each, encompassing the entire area with light. Strewn all over the floor were masses of gold and gemstones, with skulls and skeletons scattered here and there. And below all the gold, marks of dark bold lines were imprinted in intricate patterns, lines turning in bends and twists, forming spirals and weird shapes. It resembled a drawn labyrinth on the stone floor.

Suddenly she heard a powerful thud behind the door, sending a shudder down her back. Then she was knocked down to the gold-littered floor as the gate was flung open. Percival stood there under the threshold, growling. As he stepped in, the gate swung back and he let it close with a screech.

The latch of the door snapped locked behind them. There was no way back.

As Alice looked behind her, turning her gaze away from Percival, a verse of the riddle came rushing back into her mind. *Black Shadow-King of Arcadia.*

Carved out of the wall of stone was an enormous rounded hole through which the twisted gusts of wind entered howling, the black sky churning in the distance above.

And upon the huge pedestal before Percival and her, elegant and dark, proud and sinister, the dragon Alænnor craned his long neck toward them, displaying his dagger-like fangs under his long and sharp snout.

Gauzy eye of guile, greed of men, opulence of the proud.

Encrusted onto the end of Alænnor's arrowhead tail was the eye…

Before the Storm

Wind whirled and buzzed, lashing eardrums and blinding eyes. Uneven and sometimes slippery terrain made the task of riding at high speeds a dangerous one.

Arthur spurred his horse into a full gallop, racing down the green fields of the Order and out of the gate in the middle of the night, running away for good from his only home. Four deadly figures were hunting him down due to unfinished business. The Cult of Tiberius would not let their prey escape while it was still within their range.

Arthur headed toward Rouen where he would try to hide. Out in the open it was impossible. He quickly glanced back and caught a glimpse of his attackers, all four assassins were closing in on him, hooded black figures under the faint moonlight like the heralds of Death, giving pursuit on their fierce speeding steeds. But still, Arthur had the lead by a few seconds, since he took off several moments before the assassins could climb onto their horses; they did not foresee someone escaping their clutches.

A few minutes later, as Arthur arrived at the gate of the city, a gatekeeper stepped out to block his way.

Arthur flew past him. After a few seconds, as the assassins drew nearer, the gatekeeper tried to raise the alarm. Before he could utter his first word, a flying knife came from the shadows to sink into his throat. He clutched his neck as the red substance began to seep between his fingers' gaps, gagging and drowning in his own blood, the four riders flying past his side, as the gatekeeper, clinging ever so dearly to life, slumped to the ground.

The city was silent and asleep. The clattering of the horseshoes echoed noisily on the cobbled streets, bouncing off the walls and buildings, as Arthur turned several corners to hide from his pursuers. He could hear the authoritative voice of Shadowblade, the leader of the Cult, barking orders at his fellow assassins to split up.

Right after turning a bend, under the protection of darkness, Arthur dismounted onto the sidewalk and headed into the first narrow alley he saw. One of the assassins was still following his trail, and as he slipped into the passageway, another clack of horseshoes echoed right behind him.

There was the steely rasp of a blade being unsheathed a few meters away from where Arthur stood, flattened against the moldy wall and concealed from any light that might glint against his plated blackened armor. His unsettled breathing inevitably disturbed the night's silence. He clamped shut his mouth with his gloved hand, in an attempt at muffling the noise. Arthur silently turned around the corner of the next intersection. For a moment, he thought his pursuer had already lost his track, since there was not the slightest sound. Arthur leaned his face into the alley whence he had come, with great care, trusting that he was already alone.

Out of the silence came an almost imperceptible rustle. Arthur strained his limited vision into the darkness before him, seeing nothing. There was a heavier rustle, but he could not decide where it came from. Arthur could swear there was something in front of him, inferring that any pursuer would follow him from where he had come into the alley, until he looked up to see the stark silhouette of the spiderlike figure creeping its way toward him, pushing itself in between the two walls.

Feathertread released himself from the walls and hurtled downward onto Arthur, dagger ready. Arthur quickly moved out of the way, parried a slash with his plated brace, evaded a second slice, and seized hold of his attacker's wrist as he withdrew from his third lunge. Arthur twisted Feathertread's forearm until he was obliged to drop the blade, and as it clanged on the stone floor, he deftly disengaged from Arthur's armlock, swirling around and elbowing his face, knocking the helmet off his head.

Arthur covered his face with his gauntlets to ward off the succeeding quick jabs and countered with a hook. Feathertread crouched immediately and retrieved his dagger. He stood up, swinging and slashing like a madman, as Arthur stepped back and tried to block with his braces.

After a reckless and miscalculated slash, Arthur kicked Feathertread back, who backed up a little, all the air sucked out from his lungs. Without mercy, Arthur released a powerful uppercut into his chin, breaking his jaw and knocking him unconscious.

Arthur gingerly stroked his right temple, where the helmet had struck against him, before putting it on again. He went staggering back along the alley, panting, pushing himself upright with the help of the walls. At the end, he saw the empty and quiet streets. Before going out, he leaned out, looking for any movement. When he saw there was none, he stepped out into the sidewalk, under the dim beams of the lamplights hanging above, and took hold of his black horse's reins. Some distance ahead, he could see the watchman keeping an eye on the streets, carrying his own dim lamplight.

Arthur walked his stallion along the sidewalk until he reached an obscurely lit tavern. He hitched the horse to a nearby pole just as a disturbing clattering of horseshoes came around the corner. He quickly entered the tavern. The only source of light available in that bleary place was the few sparse dying candles scattered along the occupied tables and the counter of the bar. A few people sat by it, drinking mead or ale from their tankard mugs. Others sat by the tables in the corner, speaking in soft voices and glancing furtively behind them.

But as soon as Arthur saw the eagle carving on the wall to his right side, the insurrectionist symbol, he knew that he was close to his target.

The bartender remained leaning over the counter, eyeing the drunkards nearby with suspicion as Arthur sat down on the stool to the right. He removed his helmet and cleared his throat.

"What can I give you, sir?" asked the bartender, hurrying to stand upright and show respect. "A pint of ale, or a cup of mead, or even a glassful of wine?"

"I didn't come for a drink," said Arthur, taking out Jacques' letter from his pouch and showing the scrawl on the envelope to the bartender. "I come on behalf of your movement," he muttered, leaning in a little closer. "We all share the same objective, and that is to see liberty restored in this city. I have urgent matters to discuss with your leader."

"Why would I trust you?" the bartender replied, frowning slightly. "How do we know you don't plan to apprehend him? He is well guarded and not many know of his location. And other than that, I don't think it would be wise to tell you anything else."

"I am your ally. I support your movement. I do not agree with the new Duke. I promise you, I am going to see him dead myself," Arthur said softly. "In fact, I have to confess, I nearly killed him a few hours ago when there was still daylight, with an arrow that flew right by him. It is because of me that many lives were saved, lives that were being put at risk by your so caring leader, so I believe it would be wise to tell me where he is. I do not seek him to bring him to justice, or to slap him across the face. I need your leader to help me get closer to the Duke, close enough to kill him."

"Rumors have been spreading about you, about a knight in dark armor that defied the Duke. I think I'll tell you, and even if you lie, there is no way you can arrest him without getting killed in the act. I don't know him personally," said the bartender in a soft voice. "Most places around here bear at least one eagle of liberty; a symbol of defiance to the regime. I can't tell you exactly where he is, but I do have a general idea of where he might be. It's not far, just head north from here, along the Seine, and near the coast. He resides in a tavern, if I recall correctly. You shouldn't have a problem finding it. If it's facing the ocean, and the street runs along the Seine, then you've found it. Just look for the symbol once you're inside."

"Your help is appreciated. I promise you, we'll make a difference," said Arthur as he rose from the stool. The bartender nodded coldly and sat down again.

Once outside, with his helmet on, Arthur mounted his horse and headed toward the river, taking paths in alleys and following the soft and chilling breeze. Concealed in the darkness as he was, he arrived at the edge of the street, overlooking the river, waves rippling across its murky surface. Even though the four assassins were carrying torches, Arthur managed to stay out of sight and under the shroud of darkness, staying quiet when they approached, hidden down alleys. After an hour of scurrying across streets and along narrow alleyways, all the while following the Seine, he came to a halt as he found the sea a few hundred meters away. Its waves crashed loudly against the sand, and beacons along the docks made the sea glitter as they were manned from left to right in search of vessels, to guide them safely into land.

Arthur dismounted.

The sight of the sea brought him many treasured memories from his childhood. He remembered the walks he used to take with his father along the docks and the scant precious moments that he spent watching sunsets with him, when he was not busy being a Marshal. His admiration for his father was so great that he gave up his dream of becoming a sailor to sail across the sea toward the world's end in exchange of becoming a Marshal like his father, a leader everyone would look up to, a beacon of hope ready to guide his comrades to victory and glory.

His father's untimely demise impacted Arthur deeply and reinforced his wishes to be like him. Arthur hoped he would inherit his father's legacy and continue to carry on with his duties. At certain points, Arthur even went as far as to envy his own father for all the accolades he had gathered, even posthumously, only to remind himself that he had the potential to achieve his father's greatness or even more. Alice's sudden abduction and his Company's utter destruction brought about a radical change in him, a change so great that it could be referred to as some sort of inner numbness, one that not even a dream or passion could reverse. The Viceroy's passing, the obliteration of the Order of Paris, and Blanc's betrayal had only made it worse. There was a special place for Viktor and Blanc in Arthur's slowly withering heart. He swore to everything he loved that there would be nothing that could get in his way to stop him from defeating both Viktor and Blanc, even kill them, savoring the satisfaction that he expected to come from such acts.

Arthur's knees buckled. He knelt on the dirt, crestfallen, clenching his fist. Then he looked up toward the sea and wondered: *Should I have followed in my father's footsteps? Should I have stayed here?* But he knew he had made the right choice. Having met Alice had been worth it. Deep inside he knew, if he had had the chance, he would have followed her right into Hell and to the end of the world. His mind then flew back to the moment he was betrayed by Blanc. He had been so close to gaining a huge advantage in his quest to destroy the Harbingers. With Antoine presumed dead, and the entire Order being on the lookout for his head, he had no safe haven or any allies to count on. His only friend left was his horse. Arthur had never felt so alone, weak and vulnerable in his whole life. His only chance now of defeating the Harbingers was to find the leader of the insurgents to lead him to Duke William.

Arthur stood up and grabbed his horse's reins. He would use any means necessary to destroy the Harbingers, no matter the cost. Before moving out of the alley and into the streets, Arthur peeked around the corner, and after making sure the coast was clear, he began to walk his horse by the reins while looking for the tavern that Amos, rebel leader, supposedly resided in. Silence reigned over the streets. Arthur could almost hear the Seine flowing. He could feel the breeze from the sea on his skin. It reminded him so much of his early childhood. So much hassle had made him forget momentarily about his time left alive. The waning moon rested upon the sky, ticking Arthur's last days away. He was sure his day could not get any worse.

The streets were hazily lit by lamplights hung along the sidewalks. Arthur walked slowly, his horse following close behind him. Even though he could not hear anyone closing in, he knew he was an easy target, and that he had to find the tavern fast. Arthur moved slowly and with care, trying to be silent as a cat, although to no avail. His armor made so much noise as the joints creaked and rasped past each other that he wondered why nobody had found him yet. Seeing that his horse made less noise than him actually irritated him somewhat.

As he passed by an alley, an overwhelming stench made him grimace, quickly clamping his mouth and nose. Curiosity overpowered him as he turned into the alley, along with the horse, not before detaching one of the streetlamps above him. It took no more than five strides to find the mangled corpse rotting away on the dirt, a pool of blood spread around it. An army of flies buzzed wildly over it.

Arthur immediately knew, to his mischance, that the events that had devastated Paris were starting to take place in Rouen, too. He crouched down to examine the body, all the while keeping his nose clamped shut and taking small breaths in through his mouth. The corpse's clothes were mostly torn and drenched in blood. Arthur knew by the bite marks on the man's throat that it had been the misdeed of a beast, of something out of this world.

Arthur was transfixed by the sight before his eyes. So much so that he at first did not heed the quickly approaching rattle of horseshoes until they were at most thirty meters away. Arthur wavered for a second, glimpsing only the distorted and frightening appearance of the corpse's face as he snuffed out the fire inside the lamp. He remained crouched, stooping down gently, nearly touching the body. He did not have to worry about his horse as long as it kept quiet, since it was camouflaged in the dark. The racket of horseshoes was heard closer, suddenly coming to a halt and resuming a slow walk.

The stench rent right into his innards. The horrendous smell actually bypassed his clamped nose, coiling around his fingers and into it. The nausea reflex kicked in, making Arthur heave and swallow. He could hear the rider, leisurely strolling down the street. The horse snorted. Arthur attempted to glance over his shoulder since the posture he had to hastily take left him in an extremely uncomfortable position, facing the opposite direction. With what little he was able to see, he did not see anyone behind him. Looking in front of him made him shudder, imagining the corpse's distorted face looking him right in the eyes.

Arthur could hear the rider approaching slowly. His heart beat frantically. He was desperate for fresh air. The retching sensation was becoming too strong for him to contain. One little noise and he was done for. He was not even sure the darkness would conceal him enough to drive off attention. The revulsion was too much to hold, the fear too persistent.

There was an abrupt commotion.

A drunken man burst out through the doors of the building next to where Arthur crouched hidden, hollering nonsense and throwing insults at imaginary things. Arthur glanced back, only to see the drunkard keel over the sidewalk, shattering the bottle of ale he was carrying into a thousand shards.

"Son of a…," the rider muttered, galloping off down the street, the hoofbeats dying away.

Arthur sprang back to his feet, grabbing his horse's reins as a burning sensation took hold of his legs, where he had blocked circulation for an extended period of time. He finally felt relief as he unclamped his nose, and the nausea reflex subsided the further he moved away from the body. As he passed by the passed-out drunken man, he crouched to check on his pulse. Seeing he was all right, Arthur stood back up and looked down at him with pity.

"Sir, you just saved my hide," Arthur said, chuckling. That man had also helped him find the tavern he was looking for, overlooking the distant sea. Arthur hitched his horse to a pole next to the drunkard and went into the tavern.

The place was similar to the one he had been to before. Right after coming in, Arthur found a comparable eagle carving on one of the walls, and he confirmed he had finally made it.

"What's your drink going to be?" the bartender asked as Arthur sat down before the counter.

"None," he replied, pulling out Jacques' letter and showing the eagle scrawl to the bartender. "I come on behalf of your movement. I have important matters to discuss with your leader."

"I understand," the bartender smiled. "He is right behind that door, in his humble quarters. See those men in the corner, all five men? If something should go amiss with Amos, you'll have to pay the consequences."

"I will not cause any problems at all," Arthur replied.

"You'd better not," the bartender raised his voice. "Hey, Bernard! This gentleman is looking for a meeting with Amos. He won't cause any trouble."

Bernard, a broad-shouldered man, his one eye covered by a black eye patch, wearing a turban over his head, and taller than Arthur, opened a door that led into a dark hall, right behind the counter. As Arthur tried to slip in, Bernard blocked his way with a stout hand.

"Your weapons," he said in a heavy voice. "Sword and shield."

Arthur complied and went into the dark room ahead that could only be the cellar. Immediately afterward, the door shut behind him. He headed up the narrow creaking staircase on the left side of the room. He came to a stop at the top, where another taciturn haggard man sat on a low stool by another wooden door. He looked up wearily.

"I'll sound the alarm if anything wrong happens," he croaked. "Don't cause any trouble."

"Yes," said Arthur dismissively. "No need to remind me three times." The gaunt man pushed the door open, staying seated.

There was a steady and bright glow inside. Arthur slipped in through the door, and as he let it close, it stopped short. The squalid man on the other side had placed his foot in the way, leaving a narrow opening for him to spy on Arthur. "Boss, someone came to see you," he called into the room.

The room was rectangular and it had a low ceiling. There was a bed in the far left corner and a rough wooden desk in the middle, where several candles provided the only light in the room. There was only one window, closed, high above and as small as a book. On the desk, a man with thick brown hair, neglected and disheveled to the sides, was just rousing from the dark wood grain, where he had lain sprawled before Arthur came in. The moment he saw Arthur, the man jolted from his seat, staggering back a few steps.

"Do I know you? Have you any business with me?" he questioned, his eyes dilating, his nostrils flaring.

"What's wrong with you? I came here to talk to you. I need your help," Arthur replied.

"It's all right, Boss, we are here keeping watch," the man outside called out.

Amos looked down at the table. The parchment on which he was writing had somewhat creased. He sat back down.

"I apologize. I cannot trust just anyone I bump into. I've seen the posters outside in the streets. I'm a wanted man. It's a little unnerving. At least they still don't know my face." He regained his composure, sitting upright. "How may I serve you?" Amos made a gesture toward Arthur. "Please, take a seat." As Arthur sat down across the table, Amos spoke up again. "My name is Amos Baudelaire."

"I know," Arthur retorted. He rubbed his forehead. "I'm sorry. These have been dire times." Someone outside started shouting a bunch of gibberish. The drunken man had resumed his foggy trek through the streets.

Amos began to tap his fingers rhythmically against the table. "So, are you from the Order? I thought they were all white."

Arthur nodded. "Look, I don't know how to ask you this. I need to find a way into the Duke's castle."

"And you came to ask me this because...," Amos said, frowning.

"I'm willing to kill the Duke for you," Arthur blurted out. "You just have to help me find a way in."

The shouting outside still went on. The man took an excruciatingly long time to move on.

Amos observed Arthur closely, pointing a finger at him. "You're the one everyone talked about. You are that black knight!"

"I believe that's right," Arthur said. "I also believe it was a stupid move on your part to send all those men to riot before the doors of one of the most vicious monsters in Europe."

"You cannot put the blame for that on me. All those men consented to do it. It's not like I brainwashed them and ordered them to do it. And besides, not one of us could have foreseen it would turn that ugly. However, we are all grateful it didn't lead to bloodshed. We all owe you."

"I disrupted what could have been a fun time for the Duke, one that you and your men voluntarily granted him. You don't have the least idea of what is going on here, the underlying reason why this Duke rose to power and why everything else is turning to dung. This is all a part of a plan designed to slaughter our entire race. Those men will not stop until we are all dead." Arthur clenched his fist under the table. The shouting outside continued. "The Viceroy of the Order assigned me to find and kill these five men. It is of crucial importance that I do. We have to do everything in our power to tip the scales to our favor."

"What are the five men you keep mentioning?" Amos asked with a frown.

"The Duke is one of them," Arthur replied. "For now, just help me get close enough to the Duke. I will kill him. I know that's what you want to do."

"How do you know all these things about me? My name, location, purpose…?" Amos could not help asking.

Arthur merely handed him the letter he had found in Jacques' workshop. The drunkard kept on making loud noises. At times, Arthur distinguished what could have been grating and discordant singing.

Amos looked up from the letter.

"How did you come to have this?"

"Jacques was a friend. I came to visit him. He had recently died when I found him," Arthur replied.

"As the letter states, I have spies infiltrated in the Duke's castle, pretending to be his servants. They just told me that he is planning to have a ball in two days, late at night. He has already sent out invitations to several other nobles. You can only wonder what he is planning to do with them. Of course, all those partygoers won't hesitate to accept his invitation." Arthur nodded. "What we can do to get you inside is this: shortly after the ball begins, my spies will take out the guards and dress in their liveries. As guests continue to arrive, they'll usher them in as they are supposed to," Amos explained.

"And how do *I* get in?"

"You'll wait right outside the Château and look for a man waving a torch out of a window. That's your signal that you can proceed inside. The guard will ask for your name. You will say 'Black Knight.'"

Arthur could not help scoffing at this, shaking his head. "That's truly a bad idea. Are your men that versed in the art of swordsmanship to handle all the guards? I think it's insane."

"Have you a better idea?"

Arthur pressed his lips and shook his head slightly. "Antoine would have one," he said under his breath.

"If you want a chance at taking on the Duke, this is probably your only one," Amos declared. But Arthur was not paying attention to him. Amos pretended to cough.

"Can you hear that?" Arthur asked him, looking at the small window above.

"It's just a boozer. You'd think they are common in a place like this. Those drinks only lead to debauchery and nothing else," Amos answered, brushing aside Arthur's comment.

"I drink with moderation," he stated firmly before turning back to the window above. "Listen to what he is saying."

"Oi, whatcha looking at?" the man outside croaked loudly. "Stand back! I have a weapon, and I ain't gonna hesitate to use it." He swung the broken ale bottle from side to side. "Sod off!"

What followed were his gut-wrenching screams. Arthur's horse began to neigh.

Amos jolted from his seat, his pupils dilating and his nostrils flaring. Arthur stood up, preparing to draw his longsword, when he realized it had been taken away, along with his shield. "Damn!" he exclaimed with anger.

"Adrien, go check downstairs!" Amos ordered, almost in a whisper. The gaunt man outside the room looked at Amos through the narrow gap in the doorway with a look of terror in his eyes. "Right away, off you go!"

Arthur was sure he had something to defend himself with. He fumbled around his belt, looking for a sidearm. Then he went on to rummage inside his pouch. He felt a surge of relief as he pulled out Valerie's dagger from the sack. He had just remembered that he had had to store it somewhere safe as he fled the Order in a hurry.

"Hide!" Arthur commanded. "Quick, under the bed!"

Amos complied without further ado.

For a moment everything was quiet. Arthur could just make out a few hushed voices downstairs as he approached to leave the room. Before leaving, he turned quickly to Amos and pressed a finger against his lips with a hush.

Suddenly there was a crash that made the walls shudder. And shouts of battle followed. Arthur could see the shadows of the men on the floor and walls moving in frenzied patterns as he made his way downstairs. Right before he entered the saloon, a man slumped to the floor in front of him, a pool of blood blooming around him.

Arthur burst into the tavern, right as the last man standing succumbed to the claws of a dark beast. A reptilian, taller than Arthur and clad in black robes, stood astride the corpse of the last man it had killed. Unlike the ones Arthur had battled in Notre Dame, this one was slender and black-scaled. The reptilian displayed a set of razor-sharp claws on one hand, and a long scimitar in the other, deftly brandishing it, the blade swinging around its arm, as if to show off its swordplay skills.

The moment Arthur looked it in the eye he realized he had forgotten how critical it was to avoid their gaze. He felt stiff, hardly able to move, unable to look away from those golden serpent eyes as they held him still. He could feel his heart pumping hard in his chest, his respiration accelerating.

"You are the one that has been causing trouble to Master Sirius," the reptilian declared, pointing accusingly at Arthur with one of his large claws. Arthur then noticed that its other hand, the one wielding the scimitar, was missing all five claws. "It is not you, the one I seek, nonetheless." Arthur managed to break free from the trance and rushed to retrieve his sword and shield from where Bernard had sequestered them, on one of the racks behind the counter.

The reptilian had not moved and remained still as a statue, watching Arthur closely. "What did you just say?" Arthur snapped, trying to look no higher than the neck. "What are you talking about?"

"Master Sirius, one of the Crossbred's agents. He is whom you might call William Bloodthorn. Due to respect, I call him by his true name. And due to disrespect, I'm taking you down," the reptilian hissed, its tail swaying from side to side.

"So you are the one that has been hunting down Amos and his spies!" Arthur exclaimed, keeping his gaze below neckline. He gritted his teeth. "You are the one that killed Jacques..."

"And many more will follow, including you," the reptilian replied coldly.

"I've killed several of your kin. I know your fighting style; I remember the ferocity and passion they fought with. But I shouldn't have any trouble dealing with you," Arthur replied.

"Allow me to tell you why you could not be more wrong," the reptilian hissed. "This blade,"—the beast held it up in the air—"I tempered it myself in the fires of Tartarus. A few days in that place are enough to turn anyone into a monster. Darkness reigns over it, fire and brimstone making up the land as far as the eye can see. Not only was this blade forged in the depths of Tartarus, but my soul and will were as well. An eternity I spent there, atoning for a crime I had not committed. Instead of suffering and bowing before anyone that trod over me, I decided to whet my skills, up my strength and test my courage. Ever since, many Tartarus warders have fallen at my hands. I was then confined to a pitch-black chamber, alone, where the ashes of those punished showered over me incessantly, destined to spend my time there until the end of it all. And it was then that Master Alchiba offered me salvation, by pledging allegiance and compliance to Antares."

"So you're an escaped inmate under pressure to fulfill some lunatic's orders?" Arthur replied disdainfully.

"No, I am Krov, shadow assassin," he countered, his robes coming off, revealing his branded chest from years spent being punished with fire. "I am the Night." The reptilian slashed the air with his claws. At his will, a gust of wind rushed into the tavern, snuffing out all the candles, embracing Arthur in darkness.

"I've had enough of today," Arthur declared, daring to look Krov in the eyes, which did not have the same paralyzing effect in the darkness. "The Harbingers are going down and you are not going to stop me. I will make sure you go back to the hellhole you came from."

Krov hunched down in all fours with a hiss, ready to pounce on Arthur. The knight ducked to the side as the reptilian rammed the wall with his flank, quickly recovering to vault again onto Arthur. He raised his shield and bashed Krov as he flew toward him. The shield gave way at once as the reptilian's heavy bulk crushed him, sending ripples of pain across his arms. Arthur kneed the reptilian right in his guts, shoving him off momentarily.

Arthur swung his longsword. Their blades met. Their clash resounded throughout the building. Krov alternated between scimitar and claws as he fended off Arthur's attacks. After a series of quick swings, Arthur struck Krov's scimitar so hard that he knocked it free from his hand and sent the blade across the other side of the saloon. As the reptilian registered what had happened with a gasp of surprise, Arthur lunged forward in no time, already savoring his victory, expecting his sword to find flesh. The reptilian skillfully somersaulted back, Arthur's sword whistling a centimeter away from his torso. Arthur took a lurching step forward with a sword's thrust, covering the distance between him and Krov. Right before the blade's tip could touch the reptilian, a black pall of clouds shrouded him in darkness for a second, vanishing right afterward into thin air.

Arthur whirled around to meet the scimitar with his sword, just a couple centimeters from his face. He shoved it back, responding with a slash, which Krov easily deflected and countered with his claws. Right at that moment, Arthur dropped his sword as a stinging pain surged in his hand. Krov shot a sword thrust into Arthur, who blocked it with his shield, the scimitar skating off with a spark. Arthur started to back up, trying not to lose his opponent from sight, while at the same time stepping carefully over the bodies of the rebels scattered around and blocking the reptilian's attacks.

Suddenly, another black cloud wrapped Krov in darkness and faded into thin air. Arthur swung around and blocked the reptilian as he hacked away at his shield. A third cloud shrouded him and Arthur turned to block more attacks. The reptilian repeated this process several times, until he finally managed to jostle Arthur's shield aside, leaving him completely vulnerable for a second.

Arthur had pulled out Valerie's dagger without the reptilian noticing. He parried the scimitar as it went toward his chest, locking the curved blade in the dagger's cross-guard, snatching it away from Krov's hand, and swiftly plunging the knife into his abdomen.

For a brief moment, Krov stood incredulous, unable to take in what happened, when a black cloak swathed him in darkness and faded away. Immediately, Arthur readied his shield in advance, expecting the reptilian to reappear. After ten seconds of silence, he knew Krov was not coming back.

Weariness overcame Arthur as he fell to his knees, huffing and puffing, sweat trickling down his grimy face. He checked on his hand to find it was bleeding from four different cuts on its back. They were not deep, but not shallow either. It amazed him that Krov's claws had eaten through the gauntlet so easily.

"What was that?!" Amos exclaimed from the threshold, after peeking out to make sure it was safe. "Is it gone?"

"That, my friend, is the reason why I seek to destroy Duke William," Arthur replied, rising to his feet. "I don't think it's coming back in a long while. So, how do we proceed?"

"I'll have a coach arranged to take us to the Duke's château the day of the ball...," Amos said, his voice trailing off as he made out the eight corpses in the dark.

"This is the deed of a true assassin, one that I truthfully fear," Arthur said in a soft voice. "Not even the Cult of Tiberius is match enough for this assassin. And, I'm afraid, I'm sure it's still alive..."

¤¤¤

Valerie Barbaroux sat upon the wide windowsill, cross-legged and leaning against the frame of the window, scouring the green fields and stone buildings of the Order with her restless gaze, taking all the sunlight into her, wondering what had happened to her fellow assassins. Her cracked Venetian mask rested on her lap.

Behind her was one of the many thick pillars that kept the ceiling from crumbling down, and behind it, a team of guards was carrying eight stretchers down the stairs. The bodies were covered by white shrouds, their pained faces completely concealed.

Regent Blanc went down the stairs alongside the team, with a grieved look on his face. One officer spoke: "You are not safe here, Regent. The killers are still on the loose. We must stop them from striking again."

"Marshal Arthur Montague attempted to usurp Viceroyalty," said Blanc. "Order your men to keep a lookout on him. He should be hanged by the neck if caught."

"Aye, sir." The officer saluted and walked away. The moment he turned away, Blanc's sorrowful expression became smug.

Blanc noticed Valerie looking at him from the window and he approached.

"Should Arthur not be found, I will have to withhold your payment," he said in a soft voice, glancing around.

"That's understandable," Valerie replied. "It shouldn't be too hard to find him. But I have to admit, in all my years of service, nobody has ever given us this much trouble."

"No, you just mucked it up," Blanc retorted.

Valerie remained silent and looked away, almost feeling Blanc's harsh gaze resting on her. She began to rapidly click her fingers upon the sill while looking out the window, hoping to a great extent that her fellow assassins would return soon. Valerie looked down at her Venetian mask. It showed a simple design. It was mostly white, except for the coat of gold around the openings for the eyes. She held it close, caressing the mask on its sides with her thumbs, staring at it. She genuinely lamented over the fragment that had broken off the mask's lower part, when Arthur knocked her out. Now when she wore it, one half of her mouth was exposed. At that moment, she had forgotten about everything, about Blanc glaring at her, about the tasks they were hired to perform, about the worry that sickened her soul. She heard voices, but they were muffled by her thoughts. She was so immersed in her imagination and her memory that she did not notice that Shadowblade had returned, along with the others, until they were standing by her side.

"Whisper," Shadowblade said in a soft voice. "Is everything all right?"

"No, it is not," Regent Blanc burst in, struggling to keep his voice low. "I couldn't believe what I discovered a few minutes ago." His voice was tense and shuddering with anger. "Not one, but two escaped from you."

"I apologize," Nocturnal murmured. "He discovered me entering the room. He leapt at me with a knife. I countered and knocked the dagger out of his hand. As soon as he could, he jumped out of the window before I could stop him. Again, my most humble apologies."

"Why didn't you jump after him?" Blanc inquired, his scowl deep and his intimidating eyes burning with fire.

"I tried. The fall was too high. I didn't think he would survive. When I went down to check on him, to my surprise, he was already gone."

"And what about Montague?" Blanc asked, turning to Shadowblade.

"Nothing…we couldn't find him. We combed the entire city, but there wasn't any trace of him left. The only time one of us caught up with him, he gave Feathertread a good beating," Shadowblade replied. He patted Feathertread on the back, as he leaned tiredly against the pillar, groaning and holding tight his broken jaw. "We looked in every street and every corner. We went into public taverns and shops. There was nothing else we could do but come back to regain our strength. We promise we will leave no stone unturned."

"Um…I see…" Vincent nodded. "Maybe that's all you need, a break; after all, you have been up all night. I wouldn't want you to become useless," Blanc remarked, his lips tightly pursed. He turned around and left with no more to say.

Shadowblade nodded slightly, looking down at the floor.

"We have to leave, now," Valerie whispered as soon as he was gone, looking up from her mask. "Blanc cannot be trusted anymore. I could feel it in his voice; I could see it in his eyes. He will have to blame somebody, sooner or later, and it won't be just anyone. Blaming Montague for these crimes is not going to be enough evidence. He has had enough of us."

"He wouldn't dare," Nocturnal mumbled with contempt. "He would have to face the wrath of the Cult. *Illuminat viam, ensis in tenebris.*"

"He ignores what is in store for him should he betray us," Heavencloak said, frowning. "If what Whisper says is true, then we should prepare an escape plan."

"I just hope, Val, that you are wrong," said Shadowblade.

"I am not. We need to vanish, now," she urged, bolting from the sill. "By the time we finish devising a plan, we'll be either dead or apprehended…"

Right as she uttered those words the great doors opened and armored boots hammered on the marble floor as a squad of guards burst inside. All of them were wielding two-handed spears and quickly closed in around the assassins, enclosing them within a circle. They could only unsheathe their daggers and turn their backs against the pillar.

"In the name of the mighty Regent, you are under arrest!" the officer announced. "Drop your weapons, assassins!"

"You are making a serious mistake," Valerie mumbled, making her daggers dance and rotate deftly around her fingers.

"Drop the weapons. This is your last chance!" the officer ordered. "You are charged with multiple murders. You shall be hanged by the neck."

With a flick of her two hands, the two knives flew, rotated once in the air, and their sharp tips sunk into the throats of two guards. Shadowblade swiftly drew a long curved sickle and flung aside the incoming spear directed at his abdomen, leaving his opponent defenseless, and lashing the sickle upward against the guard's throat. He began to drown in his own blood and collapsed backward. Valerie flung aside the spear's tip from her with the dagger, whirled around into the guard and slit his throat, and immediately continued for a second kill.

They heard a cry, a groan, and finally Feathertread slumped to the ground lifeless. Enraged, Shadowblade pulled out his second sickle from his belt and parried another thrust, swirled upon his heels and stabbed the first sickle into the last guard's throat.

They only had a moment of relief. Shadowblade knelt down, panting, and closed Feathertread's empty eyes.

"You know what this means, right?" said Shadowblade, his eyes dejected. Valerie nodded, spotted with blood. "Go now and spread the word of this treachery. Let our brothers and sisters know what happened on this day. Be swift, be strong. Do not let anyone step in your way. The Cult of Tiberius will prevail!"

Valerie stared at him in disbelief. He was not joking.

"I want to stay with you…" Shadowblade pulled her in and kissed her.

"We'll buy you time. Go now, before they see where you go!" Valerie said nothing, slid her mask back to her face and climbed lithely onto the windowsill behind the pillar. Covered from sight, she heard the doors swing open and more boots drum on the floor uniformly. Sooner or later, Shadowblade and the other two would fall, too, overwhelmed by guards. She threw herself down two meters and skillfully rolled on the grass, quickly clambered onto her feet and sprinted toward her horse right outside the stables. It was not there. She stole one of the other horses and made her way out, ignoring shouts from guards and steering the horse out of blockades. The word about the assassins had apparently not yet been spread through the entire fortress. The gates outside were open. As she came near, the gate began to rise upward. She forced the horse to leap over it and tirelessly headed toward Rouen, where she hoped she would be safe from her pursuers. All with one thought in her mind: Vincent Blanc would pay dearly…

Eye of the Storm

What is it that drives me to do this? Why do I feel so much anger that I can barely control? Arthur thought as the coach started toward the Château of Rouen, *William Bloodthorn is a monster. He killed Sonja. I've heard enough of him to know perfectly what he is capable of doing. Shedding his blood will free Rouen of tyranny. Shedding his blood will free Europe from his demonic clutch. He deserves to be executed. But a prosecution must be held, in the name of justice. Yet, to keep him alive until that moment is highly dangerous. What if he breaks out of prison? It's too dangerous to keep him alive. A stab in the back would be against knighthood's principles; my own moral principles. I must face him and challenge him to a duel. He will fall at my hands, regardless of the cost.*

From Amos' quarters before the sea, the coach took Arthur through several twists and finally came into an avenue next to the Seine, still deep and murky. The waning moonlight glimmered off the broad river and shone back at Arthur's window. It was always there, constantly reminding him that his life's end was nigh. His final task would be to free Rouen from the clutches of Duke William, before he ran out of time.

The coach headed north of the city, jostling its passengers from side to side. As Arthur tried to reflect on his future actions, the bumpy road made the coach clatter as it wheeled through cobbled streets and struggled uphill, nearing the Duke's fortress. Beside him was Amos, dressed in leather armor and staring blankly at his lap. Across were another two men staring out the window, clad in the same armor.

The Château's conical towers and great walls gradually came into view as the coach came closer, growing in size, along with the men's fear. The coach stopped a hundred meters away from the Château's entrance, far from the walls to avoid attracting unwanted attention. Arthur, Amos and the other two rebels got off and trotted stealthily toward a low knoll, situated around thirty meters away from the château. They lay down and watched. Sure enough most of the guests had already arrived. At that moment, one man along with his mistress was just descending from the plush coach before the bridge, and it departed immediately, leaving the couple to be escorted by a guard across the bridge and into the castle.

Two more coaches arrived at the spot where Arthur and his men had been dropped off, and four more men alighted from each one. They lay down next to Arthur's partners.

"We'll wait now," Amos whispered to Arthur and the men beside him. They listened intently. "The time to move comes when you see a man waving a torch out of any of those windows in the castle's façade."

They nodded and waited, remaining still, shifting periodically to more comfortable positions. Arthur continued to muse:

A new hatred is driving me into reckless actions. What has happened to me? I'm not a monster; I do what's right, that's it. Vengeance is unacceptable. The way of the knight is through honor and pride, not ambition, greed or hate. Blanc…I can't believe what he did… and I would be the one called a monster? After I'm done with William, I'm coming after you, Blanc…

The waving red glow from the higher window of the main tower snapped Arthur back to his bearings. It was time.

"Move," Amos commanded. "You know what to do," he whispered, glancing back at Arthur.

The twelve warriors slid down the slope and trotted across the bridge after making sure no coaches were coming. The guard behind it handled the lever and opened the gate. Another guard with a torch in his hand appeared gradually as the gate rose, staring at Arthur, the crackling torch making his armor glisten dark red. He simply asked his name.

"The black knight," Arthur answered right away.

"I know." The guard smiled and moved out of the way to let the twelve men in. "We are counting on you. Try not to cause any other casualties, though. Head straight into the dining hall; the Duke should be there around the guests."

"You've done a great job. Well done!" Amos said to the spies. "Now stay alert, in case we run into trouble."

The team walked into the main compound right outside the castle but within the crenellated walls. On both sides there were narrow staircases that led upward onto the parapets ten meters above the ground. The fortress was almost square, with at least six conical towers around the wall that encompassed the main building in the middle. The barracks of the guards were in those towers and in the side-buildings of the wall; most of the guards were in there, already asleep. Those guards still on duty were inside the castle, and they were all already taken care of. They stood outside the hall where the ball would be held, and they were easy targets for Amos' spies as they knocked them out cold from behind.

Without hesitation, Arthur pushed the great doors open wide, letting them creak upon their hinges; as the twelve rebels stepped into the castle, the doors swung back shut. The noise would not alert anyone. With no guards and all the guests in the midst of entertainment no one would notice their presence. The only guards there were more spies, playing their part accordingly. They walked together in a compact group, their weapons concealed in their scabbards by their belts, across a rectangular hallway lined with pillars. As soon as they reached the main hall further into the castle, Arthur pushed the great doors with care and shut them gently.

To both sides there was a broad staircase that came to a landing, and turned to the side onto the second story. The stone floor was covered by a red velvet carpet. The pillars that supported the second floor had crackling torches on their sides. In the middle, there was a circular chandelier with intricate designs hanging from the ceiling, holding eight lit candles. The dark walls, parts of them covered by finely embroidered draperies, had more torches hanging by corbels as well, all placed in intervals between the high black-tinted windows.

There were noises of chattering, laughs and shouts of joy coming from the dining hall just a few meters away from Arthur and his team.

"Is there a view of the dining hall from the second floor?" Arthur asked one of the spies posted beside the pillar.

The guard nodded.

"I want four of you to overlook the hall from the left side, and four from the right," Arthur ordered the men, pointing to both staircases. Amos nodded in approval. "Amos and you two will stay at my side. Now, always keep in mind what he is capable of doing. You have to prevent his summonings at all costs."

Arthur inhaled deeply and held his breath for a short period of time, then exhaled and placed both of his hands on the brass doorknobs with some hesitation. More chattering and more laughs: that is all he heard through the doors. He closed his eyes briefly and then swung the doors open.

Nobody noticed him at first. He looked up to his right and then his left at the second floor; the rebels were already in position with their bows, unnoticed. There was a long rectangular dining table on the right side of the hall full of plates with first-class food and goblets of fine wine. Some people sat along the sides of the table, chattering with the people beside them or eating from their dishes with silverware. On the left side there was another long rectangular table filled with different types of delicacies: chicken breasts, grilled steaks, pork meat and greens, as well as bottles of wine and ale from which the guests served themselves. The middle of the room was reserved for the young mistresses and gentlemen who wanted to dance. Hanging from the ceiling was another chandelier. More torches hung by the walls. And an intense bright hearth lit most of the hall at the back.

Arthur noticed Jean, King Philippe's son, sitting at the head of the table on the right side of the hall. His gaze was vacant and distant, but that did not stop him from talking with people. The Duke was still out of sight, maybe mingled with the guests. Still, nobody noticed the new armed guests.

Arthur glanced at Amos, who was nervous as well, and he turned to give him a quizzical look. Arthur and the three rebels stood there and nobody even glanced at them. They walked in cautiously and among the guests, everyone dressed in luxurious liveries and apparels, in fur coats, silken dresses and velvet attires. Some had rings around their fingers, or jewels embedded in their costumes, or lavish necklaces hanging round their necks.

As Arthur passed among the crowd, he could hear them talking, chit-chatting or chattering about their dresses, jewels or hairstyles. Frivolous and shallow topics seemed more important to them than the actual imminent danger in the world. They were oblivious to the happenings of the time. And even as he and the rebels passed among the guests, none of them revealed a hint of suspicion at all. They kept looking for the Duke.

And find him they did.

"How's the party? Are you enjoying it?" William Bloodthorn snapped.

Arthur turned to his right, drawing his longsword. "We still have a score to settle, Bloodthorn. This time you are not getting away."

"Not bloody likely." He was leaning against the pillar beside the dance zone of the hall at the upper left side of the hall. He was still dressed in the mazarine high-collared ducal gown. His lips were curled with malice and his sly eyes drilled into Arthur. "I thought I'd have no more problems with you. I made it clear to that bloody idiot that no White Knight would interfere."

"Blanc?" Arthur inquired. "That explains his refusal after all."

"Ha, surprise, surprise!" William exclaimed. "Most importantly, I didn't even have to brainwash him. All you have to do is extend your arm with a fistful of coins to dominate some men. You care for some, too?"

"I hope you are joking," Arthur growled, tightening his grip.

"Not likely, right?" William replied with a grin. "So, tin man, what's the news? You were kicked out of home, weren't you? In case you didn't know, the entire Order is looking for you. There are posters asking for your head, offering a slew of money that the Viceroy himself will pay."

Arthur frowned and bit his lip.

"Ha, surprised?" William said derisively. "Your new Viceroy wants you dead! How ironic is that? Tell you what: I can get the job done, quickly and painless, lest you die with shame and a tainted name, and that way not dying on the gallows while being humiliated to death. Sound like a deal?"

"William Bloodthorn, you have caused the deaths of many. I will not die without you coming to hell with me. I will not allow the fate of Europe to rest in your hands any longer. Duke of Normandy, I hereby challenge you to a duel to the death. You cannot retreat. The doors are sealed behind me. There is no getaway. If you decline my offer I'll have my rebels do what they please to you," said Arthur solemnly, deflecting all mockery.

"How does the poison feel? Doesn't it tingle?"

"By the time its effects kill me, you will already be dead." Arthur raised the tip of his sword and pointed at William. All the people around were completely oblivious to their surroundings. "I challenged you to a fair duel. Will you comply, or will you decline?"

"Why the hell would I decline?" the Duke snapped. A blade slithered down his hand and out of the long and wide sleeve. The material was unknown to Arthur. It was neither wood nor steel nor iron. The sword had a tint of red along its curved blade, and the material resembled hard rock. The hilt was leather-bound, with a small rounded stone below it as a pommel. Above the grip was the guard of the sword: a wicked figure that looked like a demonic hand, with its long and sharp claws protecting the hand of the wielder. "Stygium," added William, smiling at his weapon with pride. "The material with which Antares' sword was made; the same that vanquished the dragons eons ago. Its ore is recovered from the shores of the River Styx and is then forged in the fire. It can be made thin and sharp, yet stout and overpowering; it hardly ever breaks. It can cut through the hardest of materials. With one strong blow I can cut your breastplate as if it were a thin sheet of foil," William raised his gaze from the sword. "*En garde!*"

Arthur glanced back at Amos and the other two rebels. "I want you to evacuate the guests, quickly! Duke Jean is the priority!" They immediately took off to finish their task. As soon as they touched them, the people seemed to wake from their deception, but only briefly. They did not understand why they were being pulled out and sometimes struggled against the rebels' grip.

"This is between you and me, William," Arthur declared. William kept his eyes on Arthur, but as the rebels began to evacuate his victims, he moved...

Arthur dashed forward with a thrust, and with a flick of his hand, William diverted the tip of his blade. Arthur regained his aim and riposted with a horizontal slash, which William easily blocked. The Duke stepped back without any further attacks and lifted up his blade chest-high, the tip of the sword high above his head, thereupon lowering it to his right side, his silhouette dark and red against the blaze of the hearth behind. Arthur moved in an attempt to block William from harming the guests and the rebels.

"Have some manners, mate," he said with an acerbic smile. William let his cape fall from his shoulders and to the floor.

"As if you had any," Arthur snapped. He looked up at the rebels on the second floor, who had now their bows trained on William. He still did not give the order.

Instead, Arthur lunged forward. The Duke caught Arthur's blade with the flat of his sword, sparks shooting off as his sword glanced off William's. Arthur released a series of slashes, which the Duke parried and blocked skillfully without faltering. Arthur realized he was toying with him, waiting for him to tire and lose his strength in his failed attempts. As Arthur recovered, William shot a quick jab at him, puncturing his armor and stinging his right arm.

The wound began to burn as though he had been branded with a red-hot rod. Arthur could not help but yield to the pain and cover the injury with his left hand, groaning and wincing.

William finally saw the opportunity and did not hesitate to take it. He darted to the side and wrapped his arms around an entranced man from the dining table before he could be evacuated.

"Shoot now!" Arthur shouted at the rebels on the second floor. The fletched arrows hissed in the air, and before they could hit their target, William spun behind the pillar beside him for cover, away from the archers' sight, still with his arms around the man.

The Duke slit the man's throat and sucked the soul out of his body, a thread of white faint light rippling across his palm, ghostly whispers emanating from the soul. Satisfied, William flung the body, no more than a shell, to the side and out of his cover.

Arthur had just realized what he had done when the Duke sprang out from behind the pillar and hurled his sword at Arthur, a rotating gleaming blade that severed the air and ended up quivering against the wooden wall, missing Arthur's cheek by a hair's breadth.

William smiled at Arthur with arrogance, weaponless and defenseless. Arthur was just moving forward, to take advantage of his odds, when he heard the wood crunch behind him.

Impossible! he thought as the Stygium sword withdrew itself from the wall and retraced its previous trajectory. Arthur ducked to evade the flying weapon, which William caught in his hand.

"One soul," he said. "Enough to cause mayhem."

There were still two people left in the hall, hypnotized and oblivious to the conflict around, when William pointed his forefinger at the great doors, just as the rebels were dragging out another three guests, to shut them and lock them out without even touching them. Without delay, Amos and the rebels were shouting and pounding on the doors to get them open, though to no avail.

"Leave them out of it!" Arthur demanded as William eyed the remaining guests with hunger. The Duke ignored him and had hardly made any movement when Arthur ordered: "Take him out!" The rebels on the second floor fired another round of arrows. This time William reacted, spinning on his heels and putting out his hand to stop them. The arrows stopped short in mid-air and remained there, floating for a brief moment, before flying back at their senders at the Duke's will.

As soon as the arrows struck down the rebels, William retracted his hand before Arthur's sword could cut it off, the blade descending in a gray blur. Arthur recovered from the swing just as William countered with an upward slash, more sparks shooting out from their weapons. To maintain the flow of the battle, Arthur continued to clash swords with William, constantly raising his shield to block his attacks. Just as Arthur began to tire again, and seeing no weariness whatsoever in William's movements, their weapons clashed faster than ever, swords dancing and striking each other in quick succession without faltering, sparks igniting, clangs echoing through the hall. In a whirling blur of gray, Arthur could sense his own sword giving way to the damage, its edges denting and losing their original fearful sharpness. At any moment his weapon would yield and break into pieces.

Arthur raised his shield to bash, but as he rammed against the Duke, William evaded and slashed Arthur's back. The weapon cut flawlessly, soundlessly and without any difficulty through a cuirass made up of an alloy of steel and silver, guaranteeing maximum protection against sharp weapons and blunt objects. In this case, his armor proved to be futile.

The gash on Arthur's back turned out to be shallow, but that did not mean there was no pain. He groaned as he turned around just in time to deflect William's thrust. Now that Arthur was back against the hearth and William against the doors, the Duke took the chance to quickly annihilate the hypnotized man that sat on the chair before the dining table, staring blankly ahead, before Arthur could even react. He watched helplessly as the thread of light rippled its way into William's palms, as he sucked in yet another soul, making him even stronger.

"You have thwarted my plans, lad," said William, no sweat pouring down his brow and no panting warping his voice. "And that I do not forgive. Lord Antares needs his souls, yet I'm spending his entire cure on you. All my prey has escaped!" he snarled, striking the pillar beside him with his fist, knocking out a chunk of marble with his bare hand. "I am hungry now. I haven't eaten in a while. Hell, I could just eat the whole city! Of course, after I'm done with you!"

"You'll have to take me down first," said Arthur, blood trickling down his back.

William sniffed the air, the blood's odor galvanizing his nose. "You'll make a hell of a feast! Roasted, even better!" His palms began to glow red-hot, gradually turning from a dull crimson to a bright scarlet.

Arthur only realized what was going on when a large fireball sprang from William's fingertips. Because of the encumbering weight of his armor, Arthur dove clumsily to the side, the fire orb grazing by. Shielded by a strong metal armor, he still felt the intense blistering heat as the fire flew closely past him. He took cover behind the pillar at the other end of the hall and listened to William laugh with amusement.

"Hey, look what I found over here!" the Duke called out jovially.

Arthur leaned his head out from behind the pillar to spot William, at the other end of the hall, sucking out the soul of a dame at the dining table. Arthur clenched his fist with anger and smacked the floor; the remaining guests had died, and William was only getting stronger.

He quickly began to analyze William, sorting out his strengths, and what he thought were his weaknesses and flaws: they were almost nonexistent. The Duke did not have any armor or shield, but his sword was unbeatable. He did not tire and his speed was insurmountable. His strength reached inhuman capacities. Somehow, he would have to breach his defenses and get the kill without mercy, before the Duke could regain himself. He would have to somehow sink the blade into his body.

As he mused, shrill screeches, low at first, began to intensify gradually to the point that Arthur had to cover his ears. He winced as his eardrums throbbed with pain, the screech still resonating through his skull and the hall. He had no idea what was happening. He leaned out his head once again to find the Duke levitating a few meters above the ground, his face expressionless and a dark aura emanating from his body's outline. Just as Arthur could not bear the noise anymore, it stopped abruptly and, at the same time, William landed on his feet with a thump.

Outside the dining hall, a ceaseless and rumbling sequence of heavy thumps began to resonate. As if in unison, a cohort of giant men started to march down the second-story floor and down the staircases rhythmically, making the place shudder with every step of their armored, pounding feet. The chandelier swayed with metallic jingles. Dust sprang from the ceiling and floated down. Arthur heard Amos call out to his rebels through the doors to retreat as the noise began to feel closer.

"Call of the Harbinger," William said. "Nothing to worry about. I'm just mustering my troops. My long planned massacre will not stop. It shall be carried out according to plan…now. Not only will you and your rebels die, but also the city's entire population. Let it fall on your conscience that this is your fault," William grinned. "This night was supposed to be bloody fun. This was my especial night, when William Bloodthorn ended the infamous nobility!" He lifted a hand to his chest and closed his eyes. Ancient runes and alien markings suddenly imprinted themselves onto his skin as if they were tattoos, glowing fierily. William's eyes blazed scarlet, his inner demon releasing all of its fury. Now Arthur realized what he was doing. He rose from the column and rushed toward William. As he tried to thrust his sword into William's immobile body, an invisible barrier launched Arthur into the air, blowing the air out of his lungs as he crashed heavily against the stone floor, the armor intensifying the impact rather than softening it. He momentarily writhed on the ground with pain and then rose up.

A large-scale pentagram shimmered out of the ground. It was as if he were reliving Notre Dame all over again, alongside Alice and his Company, only now he was all alone. Out of the pentagram an enthralling and fluctuating vortex opened up, rupturing the Universal Law of Nature, unlocking the portal into another dimension: the Underworld.

Arthur was completely transfixed, staring with consternation, unable to move anymore. He saw a familiar creature clawing its way out of the vortex, hissing and snarling. The dragon stood upright before William, as if paying reverence, completely ignoring Arthur, who staggered back on his feet and was now leaning out from behind a column.

"*Vonix dan Alonduur*," hissed William. "*Anlix dolvaara!*"

The dragon, as big as a house, crouched down in readiness on its hind legs and bolted forward, bursting through the great doors and tearing them off their hinges, immediately going out of the fortress, taking flight high in the air. Soaring through the skies of the night, it glided toward the unsuspecting city of Rouen.

"Want to see the fireworks?" William called out as Arthur stepped out of cover. "It is something fantastic to behold. I shan't miss it," William rose from the floor a few centimeters and kept still in the air. In a flash, he flew out of the fortress, his shape blurred as he sped down both hallways and across the wooden bridge of the stronghold, leaving Arthur exhausted before a crackling dying hearth, with a nicked sword and dented armor.

Arthur still had his only and final wish firm in his mind. The Duke would die before he himself did. Arthur tried to hurry, shuffling his feet and lumbering through the hallways, huffing and puffing, and finally he crossed the bridge, seeking support from the railings. He spotted William, standing upright and beholding the cataclysm that was taking place in Rouen's most populated areas. Fires rose and heavy dense smoke billowed up to the skies, darkening the newborn dawn. Hundreds of houses, big and small, wrecked and stable, miserable and wealthy, they all burned in the blaze. The dragon glided and drifted overhead, extending and beating its long membranous wings as it devastated the city. Thousands of people cowered in terror, their disheartening screams drowned out by the dragon's deafening bellows.

As Arthur approached the Duke with apprehension, he could hear William hissing and mumbling alien words, a dark radiance shimmering dimly out of his body. Paying more attention, Arthur realized that William was already casting the Claw of Antares over the city, the same one that took over Paris' White Bastion. The column of evil nimbus hovered overhead, gradually forming the gigantic dark shape of a hand with long claws, as if about to seize the world below it.

Arthur drew out his longsword, tightening the grip and feeling the reassuring weight in his clenched hand. A nicked sword and a hidden dagger were all he had left to defend himself with and accomplish his final goal. Now all he felt for William was an unrelenting hatred, a strong desire to terminate his enemy without mercy. It was a new hate that drove him to actions that he would not normally have even considered carrying out. As he watched his city being burned down to ashes, his patriotic sentiment took over, the fire and smoke only fueling his determination and hatred. His honor had vanished.

Arthur drew out Valerie's dagger as well and silently crept over to William, who was still watching everything from atop the knoll. Inevitably, he still made the grass rustle and his armor creak. He increased his speed almost to a sprint. He readied the dagger and thrust forward into William's back.

In a heartbeat, the Duke was already facing Arthur, his eyes wild and blazing, the Stygium sword colliding with the edge of the dagger. Arthur stepped back, dropping the dagger to the ground to quickly replace it with his longsword. William darted forward, with a vertical slash, and with a quick succession of multiple attacks, their blades danced, parrying and countering one another, sparks twinkling in the breaking dawn as the swords struck and glanced off one another.

William crouched down as Arthur shot a horizontal slash, and as Arthur recovered from the lunge, William charged a massive counter. He shot a powerful upward slash, and as Arthur blocked it with his blade, the sword finally reached its breaking point, shards of steel gleaming as they sped through the air.

For Arthur, it was a moment of defeat and disillusionment as William's blade went straight across his, the strength of his enemy's blow so strong that he felt his fingertips tingle at the hilt of the broken sword. And before Arthur could either block the attack entirely or dodge to the side, the Stygium blade cut through his gauntlet as he began to raise his shield, diverting the Stygium sword from his abdomen.

Arthur fell hard on the ground, the air blown out of his lungs, the same burning sensation firing up in the whole of his right arm as blood poured out of the gash in his gauntlet, but still holding tight to the broken sword, which still had a sharp end though it was less than half its former length. William stood over Arthur, the tip of his sword hovering over Arthur's abdomen. Arthur stabbed the fractured sword into William's ankle, but it only bounced back.

"See you in hell, mate," said William with a wicked smile.

As he lifted the sword above his head to execute Arthur, a disturbance in the air made him react, releasing the hand from the hilt and putting it out to his side. An arrow whistled out of the darkness and stopped cold before William's raised palm. Instead of sending it back, the Duke let it drop to the grass, seeing nobody he could shoot it back at. Another pair of arrows whizzed into his palm. From afar, a small red glint glowed into existence, and suddenly it was already flying through the air. The flaming arrow stopped against the Duke's palm, but this time the fire from the tip made his hand burn. He cursed and in a succession, many more arrows were shot at him, one after another.

In the midst of the confusion, Arthur began to inch his way up without making noise or touching the Duke's legs. He thrust his broken sword into the Duke's right hand, the uneven tip slithering in between the gaps of the sword's intricate guard. With one bellow of pain, the Duke jerked back his hand, releasing the hilt and letting the Stygium sword imbed itself into the grass. Arthur kicked William in his stomach, launching him off his feet and into the air. As the Duke nimbly rose, swearing like a fiend, his face red with anger, his veins about to burst open, Arthur staggered back up and withdrew the Stygium sword.

"Bloody hell!" William shouted, examining the severe gash on his right fingers. "Damn you…this hurts like hell! Look, you almost cut them off!" he complained, lifting up his hand for Arthur to see. Another arrow stopped short before his palm, this time shooting back at Arthur, who raised his shield immediately with his right hand, pain lancing up through his arm. "Who's the sod bugging me?"

Arthur heard steps rustling on the grass behind him, expecting Amos to speak up at any moment. "You don't give up, do you, Marshal?"

Arthur felt the hair on his neck stand on end as he heard the voice. He knew it was reckless, but he could not help turning back, completely astonished. The voice's emitter had just disappeared the day of the massacre. Antoine emerged from the murk, pulling back the hood from over his head.

"Seems like a good moment to show up," he said, nocking another arrow into the bowstring.

"Marshal?" Arthur gasped.

"I knew this was the place where I'd find you."

"Did you finally accept my offer to join me?" Arthur asked, immensely relieved.

"Take it for granted," Antoine replied, aiming his bow at William, who now had his eyes closed. "This is it, Duke! End of the line! Give up and you shall not be harmed."

"It's too dangerous to keep him alive," Arthur interjected with determination in his voice. "Just look around," he added, tipping his head at the city, where the fire burned and the dragon roared, roasting everything in its path.

"Agreed," said Antoine.

"*Vorka anligár!*" William hissed under his breath. The Duke grimaced as his bones and muscles snapped sickeningly, groaning and moaning, as his face and body contorted and transformed into a new being. His ears elongated into sharp tips. All his skin was replaced by dark brownish fur, rough and stained with blood. His teeth and fangs grew, standing out of his mouth, which quivered and lengthened out as he growled like a beast. His eyes took on a golden hue, the dark pupils turning into serpentine slits. And his majestic ducal gown stretched out beyond its normal size, threads yielding to the expansion, the gown shredding to strips of fabric, all as William's torso broadened, the shoulders and muscles increasing in mass and size.

Antoine released the arrow, shattering it to pieces the moment it bounced off William. The werewolf pounced at supernatural speed, landing before Antoine and slashing his chest, throwing him off his feet as his leather armor was torn according to the shape of the claws, blood spurting out. Antoine yelped, desperately unsheathing the sword from his belt to stab the werewolf.

However, instead of killing off Antoine right there, William whirled around, countering Arthur's attack. He was now wielding the Stygium sword. The Duke was enraged as he saw his own weapon in the enemy's hands. He swiped again at Arthur, confident that the knight would drop it eventually. Arthur easily countered and lunged forward as William evaded, but the Duke shot another claw at him, rending the right side of his face, flesh opening and blood pouring out of the four gashes, ranging from the corner of his lips to the corner of his right eye, barely missing the eyeball.

Arthur slumped to the ground, tasting the iron flavor in the blood that dripped into his gaping mouth. His face burned. Arthur could hear Antoine clashing with William; he could hear his cries as he countered and received minor injuries, but still fighting back. The dragon roaring and scorching the city, the screams of thousands of people, the heavy stench of the smoke filling his nostrils like venomous fumes, and Antoine about to be killed by one of the most vicious men he had ever met; all these elements together filled him with a new energy he had never felt, a new hatred that began to take him over, powerful and overpowering.

Antoine finally gave in to the limits of his strength, William viciously knocking him down to the soft green grass. And right before William could finish him off with a bite, a thick spike went through his back, emerging out through his gut. Antoine watched senselessly as William looked down with bewilderment at his own blade as it slid back out of his body, all as Antoine began to lose consciousness.

The Duke began to lose his wolfish form, pressing his now human hand against the big hole in his abdomen, blood seeping between his fingers. His size decreased back to normal and his skin turned to a peach color. Out of thin air, the dark Corvus robe materialized like a shadow and automatically enveloped itself around William's naked body. He fell on his side, blood gushing out of his mouth as he tried to formulate words, staring blankly at the pink sky overhead. Arthur stood beside him, pointing the curved sword's tip at him, not with dread but contempt.

A dark aura began to emanate from his robe, this time forming a misshapen cloud hovering above William's body. Arthur raised the sword and pointed it against the ball of black haze. There was an unrecognizable sound at first, but then it formed into a guttural voice with understandable words.

"Murderer…," it rumbled, almost forming the shape of a person, still without any definite facial features. "Heretic…deicidal; know this, *dæmon*, that I am unbeaten. Antares shall live forever…"

The dark spirit vanished from the world. Out of its hazy remains, a vortex opened up, splitting the air. Arthur crouched down, fearing that another demonic outbreak would occur. Suddenly, the same screeching noise that Arthur had heard from William, the Call of the Harbinger, began to reverberate across all of flaming Rouen and its outskirts. In the distance, Arthur saw the dragon take a sharp turn and fly toward the Château, beating its wings, calm and serene, drifting along with the gusts of the morning wind. Taking no heed of the three men on the ground, it dove into the vortex. Arthur knew there were more hellish troops in the city, but he assumed that they would retreat as well. The vortex remained open above them, although the Claw of Antares was already fading away.

He heard a cough and looked down. William was regaining his senses. William squinted, glancing at Arthur and groaning as he tried to sit up. Nonetheless, his lethal wound refused him any further movement.

"What is…going on?" he stuttered with pain in his voice.

Arthur eyed him warily, thinking that it was only a final dirty ruse. "You know what happened, Duke."

"I don't remember…anything…where am I?" he mumbled in a despairing, strained voice. "Why am I bleeding?" he asked, horrified, as he brushed his fingers over the hole in his stomach, coughing blood out of his mouth.

Arthur knelt down beside the man, losing all mistrust of him. "Somebody…something was manipulating your body…something you would not comprehend. I had to destroy it."

"I remember seeing a pair of…serpentine yellow eyes…I heard a piercing voice…I don't know how it happened…I don't remember…," he faltered, his eyes brimming with tears. "What year is this?" he asked with a despairing look.

Antoine came back to his senses and stood beside Arthur, listening respectfully to William.

"It's 1337," Arthur answered, a lump in his throat choking his voice, formed out of remorse, guilt and hate against himself.

"Twenty years of my life gone…" He stopped himself, feeling his wounds. "I remember the horrible things I did…b-but I was against them…I couldn't help it…," he sobbed, gasping for air. "I'm sorry…"

Arthur looked down at his hands, the Stygium sword sliding from his palm onto the earth, perfectly knowing that he was accountable for his death, his hate against William melting away completely. He wondered whether there could have been any other way to purge the dark spirit out of William, any other way in which he could have spared his life, whether any other way could have avoided so much death and destruction. He began to form a dreadful image of himself. *I'm not a monster. I'm a knight, bred to protect the helpless and the weak, to put order in the world in a righteous manner. I am supposed to have honor; has that faded away?*

"You did what you had to…," William muttered in his final moments of agony, his voice feeble and dying, his eyes hardly moving. "Please…don't leave…not yet…"

The vortex was still open. Down the road that led to the castle, the phalanx of heavy knights lumbered up the hill, making the earth shudder with every step. They ignored the men as well and entered into the portal. It vanished the moment the last automaton stepped into it.

And yet, Arthur never removed his gaze from William's inert eyes as the hellish troops passed beside him. He brushed his fingers over William's face, closing his eyes. Antoine placed his weary hand on Arthur's left shoulder, as a sign of sympathy and solace, guessing at the internal struggle Arthur was going through.

And Arthur thought with heavy remorse, *Am I a murderer? An assassin? What I do know is that I don't deserve the title of knight anymore…My final task here is done.* He gingerly brushed the gaping flesh on his face and his dying arm, *I must go now…*

As the sun rose to give way to a new day, subduing the efforts of the smoke to blot it out, a big black crow perched high on the branch of a tree atop a cliff facing the city, cawing loudly and glaring at Arthur and Antoine. *The Corvus…*

Bedlam Stories

Alice and Percival shrunk back, intimidated, as the Black Shadow-King, Alænnor, towered over the platform twenty meters away, tilting his head to the side as he inspected the new intruders in his chamber. As he lashed his spearhead tail from side to side, Alice and Percival spotted their objective: the eye, a glinting huge diamond, the light of the torches refracting into its transparency, embedded in the tip of his tail. He stood upright in readiness, four meters tall, unfurling his long black wings from his back and shaking them awake. Alænnor slithered down from the pedestal in a serpentine way, approaching Alice and Percival at high speed, rattling coins and lifting whirling billows of dust from the floor, stopping cold a couple of meters before them, his black scales scintillating against the blaze of the torches. As he snapped his jaws with sudden aggressiveness, a prolonged hissing came out of his quivering snout, and at the same time he craned his huge head toward Alice, and then toward Percival.

"*Raukuur, vud une Fortuudal*(Harbinger, what a fortuity)." The barely distinguishable words came out of Alænnor's half-closed lips, addressing Percival.

"*Dumil-Im dan Vos, Alænnor* (Give me the eye, Alænnor)," Percival demanded. Alice switched glances from one to another in bemusement. Percival pointed at Alice with one of his claws. "*Un lix dem an!* (And kill her!)"

"*Na, kunra une Frauduum, Raukuur* (No, you are a fraud, Harbinger)," Alænnor replied with what sounded like a disdainful snarl.

The moment Alice tried to move from her spot, the dragon was already snaking his head toward her, displaying his dagger-like fangs, glaring at her with his crimson serpent eyes. His piercing gaze drilled into Alice, imbuing her with fear as the predator closed in on his prey. Alænnor spoke to her in the same language, forming a loop with his tail so he could show his tail's tip to her as if in a tease, shaking it like a rattle, the diamond glittering against the scarlet blazing light.

Behind, Percival moved in a blur, heading for the dragon's backside. Alænnor bellowed, taken off guard, causing Alice to stagger back, raising her shield to prevent damage; however, Alænnor twisted his long neck enough to bash Percival from his back with his head. Almost immediately, he turned back to Alice and slammed his tail against her shield, knocking her to the ground, the armor providing little protection against the strike that knocked the wind out of her lungs. As she struggled to sit up, gasping for breath, she watched how Percival nimbly evaded Alænnor's head lunges, clawing the dragon's snout as he dodged. They faced one another with snarls and growls, circling around in the middle of the arena. Alænnor had his head lowered almost to the ground, equating Percival's height, who was completely dwarfed next to the dragon.

Alice regained her footing. The werewolf pounced toward Alænnor's head, and before he could land on it to claw his eyes out, the dragon cast him back against the nearest wall with his stout arm, leaving him dazed and near unconsciousness. Immediately afterward, the dragon returned his gaze and locked his eyes on Alice, who reacted defensively by raising her shield. One second later, Alice glimpsed Alænnor's jaws descending on her, a pit crowned with deathly fangs, resilient threads of slime crossing his maw, a long forked tongue about to drag her down his pitch-black throat.

Instinctively, Alice raised her broadsword up above her head, jabbing Alænnor's palate with the sharp tip. He reared back with a bellow and pounded her off her feet with his long, strong foreleg before she could get away. Alænnor lunged at her with his head, baring his bristling fangs as she fell on her back to the ground.

She rolled once to the side and onto her feet as the dragon struck the gold littered ground, knocking loose a slab of the hard floor, billows of dust rising up.

Without hesitation, Alænnor charged again, this time crashing his fangs precisely against Alice's shield as she raised it over her body. Her arms gave way to the overpowering strength of the dragon as she received the brunt of the impact, letting the shield pound against her chest and knocking her to the ground, spraining her arms, leaving her limbs painfully tingling from the vibration of the force that struck her. With a groan, she forced her hurt right arm out of the shield to defend herself with her broadsword.

Alænnor pressed his huge talons on her body, disabling any defensive action altogether, crushing her against the ground with enough strength to keep her still, towering over her. Alice stared at her monumental predator, who was imposingly lowering his snout and leaving it to hover over her terrified face, the black scales glittering, his nostrils flaring and releasing powerful puffs of air.

"*Galæ, fortuúm Valakiir* (Farewell, brave warrior)." The dissonant hissing came out of his large snout as he prepared to dispose of his prey, when he realized with alarm that something was going amiss. Just then Alænnor turned his head back to his tail to find that the large diamond was missing. Alice recovered her weapon and sunk it into the claw that held her captive. Alænnor jerked his arm back. Alice stood up swiftly, but before she could brace herself, Alænnor flung her back with his other arm, slamming her against the wall. Percival hurried toward the middle of the arena. Quietly, Alænnor slithered toward the werewolf, furling his extensive wings on his back to improve his silent speed; four meters of stature and at least ten tons of mass were nimbly gliding across the arena.

As he caught up with Percival, it was too late for the werewolf to react in his defense. Alænnor rammed against Percival, sending him off his feet and to the ground, causing him to drop the diamond.

While lying on the line-painted floor, watching the fight from the corner of her eye, Alice caught sight of the diamond hitting the ground and skidding to a halt. The reverberation snapped her back to her senses. It was her personal and most important goal.

She imperatively needed the 'eye' to save Sonja from a horrible fate. The next step was to locate the Cyclops. *For you to retrieve and thus into the socket of the Cyclops inlay*, the verse of the riddle bounced back into her mind. Alice had already pinpointed the location of the Cyclops: the middle of the room, where Percival was heading as Alænnor stopped him, and right where they were still clashing against one another. In between them, there was an octagonal concave aperture that took a conical shape to make the diamond's pointed end fit perfectly.

Alice felt her fortitude and courage fly back into her as she rose from the floor and rushed toward the fight, her vision focused solely on the object that represented her friend's salvation. She headed toward the eye, which was still lying on the ground, close to the adversaries.

Before she could reach it, Alænnor's tail accidentally sent it flying against the wall on the edge of the arena before his stone platform. She kept sprinting at full speed without tiring. As she picked it up with a sense of victory, she heard Alænnor bellow with pain, and right as she turned toward the fight, she realized that there was no fight anymore.

Percival clutched her throat without warning, making her drop the broadsword. Alice rose into the air while gagging, her feet dangling a few centimeters from the floor as Percival held her high, her back tightly pressed against the wall. He snatched the diamond from Alice and let it drop to the ground. He raised his claw to finally execute his daughter. As the claws glinted against the torch above, Alice gazed into her father's fiery wolfish eyes, his muzzle quivering with a growl.

Percival halted his paw from touching Alice at the last moment. His snout momentarily stopped quivering, and as he stared into her eyes, Alice thought she could notice a subtle change in her father's eyes, as if they had somewhat softened; as if she knew that there was still a tiny shred of humanity left in him; as if he was still there, alive. For a brief moment, both stared at the other, as if in quiet reconciliation. Alice had to stop herself from asking aloud: "Father, is that you?" Percival suddenly released Alice from his clutch and closed his eyes with a deep scowl.

Alice fell to the floor onto her knees, gasping for breath and holding her throat with her hands while coughing hoarsely.

Percival began to growl painfully, clasping his head with both of his paws. During his internal struggle, he began to mumble unintelligible words, some of which Alice understood. "Don't... my daughter...Alice..."

All of a sudden, Percival was flung aside by Alænnor's tail as he swept it at them, missing Alice by a few centimeters.

Percival regained his consciousness and retrieved the diamond while dodging Alænnor's lashing tail as he attacked again. Alice realized that her father had forgotten what had happened a few seconds ago. She reclaimed her broadsword and bolted toward Percival, who was already being chased by the dragon, and after a brief moment, getting knocked to the ground. As Alice reached the spot where the diamond had fallen, Percival was just rising.

Alænnor flew back onto his stone pedestal and faced the center of the chamber. He hissed: "*Dovuúl aan Alæn!* (Swallowed in darkness!)"

His hulking ribcage expanded as he inhaled the air deeply into his flaring nostrils. Alice knew what he was doing: what every dragon does. He was charging his fireball. Alice lifted her shield. Percival readied himself to dodge. But instead of spraying fire, Alænnor opened wide his maw, releasing a large-scale cloud of sheer darkness, the pure essence of madness, a massive cape of black haze, engulfing both of his opponents in the pitch-black cloak as both unsuccessfully attempted to evade it.

By the time the blackness dissipated, Alice had lost her bearings, just as her vision became slightly blurry and the ground began to tilt from one side to the other, shaking to and fro before her sight. Seeing everything blurred and uneven, Alice bent on her knees, clinging on to sanity as madness began to take her over. The few skulls that were scattered around the chamber were clattering their molars in unison as if they were alive. The gold coins turned to gilt dust the moment she touched them. Glancing to her side, she caught Percival, who had lost his bestial form and was now wearing the Corvus cloak, staggering to his feet, but stumbling back to the ground after a few steps. She returned her gaze to the podium where Alænnor was perched, eyeing them with discernible amusement. Then she caught the glint of the diamond, a meager ten meters away from her.

Alice crawled onto her feet with difficulty, trying hard to keep down the scalding vomit that squeezed up through her throat. She tottered toward the diamond, nobody standing in her way; no one trying to kill her now as she crossed the line-painted floor. And as she neared the diamond, all of a sudden, a great wall rose from the ground five meters high, blocking all entrances, appearing from nowhere discernible. She pushed it with her fingers, but to no avail. To keep her balance, she kept her hands pressed against the strange wall as she staggered along it. And that is how she noticed how the trick worked. With every step she took, the wall kept rising further, materializing out of the bold lines drawn on the floor; however, it lowered back into the floor as she moved away, like a solid wave. And every line in the arena rose up as she came closer to them, enclosing her in an unpainted spot. The lines followed an intricate pattern: a maze that she would have to cross to retrieve the diamond.

As a final act of defiance, Alice drew out her bow and nocked one of her last three arrows from her quiver on the taut bowstring. Even though her vision remained impaired, she quickly locked on Alænnor, who stood still on his pedestal, embraced by darkness. The arrow whistled in the air and darted across Alænnor's body, crossing clean without a hit mark. The dragon's shape suddenly faded into a dark shadow and vanished from its spot. Alice quickly nocked another arrow and frantically looked around for her target, ignoring Percival as he struggled to stand up. Then she finally found the dragon; only instead of solid, he was a mere shadow against the walls and the floor, and the body was nowhere to be found.

Alice locked her sights on it, failing to find the bull's-eye as Alænnor's shadow began to slither nimbly across the wall, going from torch to torch, snuffing them out as it left each blaze. Alice released the arrow, but it only shattered as it crashed against the wall, and as the rigid bowstring rattled back to its normal posture, Alice lost her balance and fell down on her back.

The only way to free herself from the binds of madness would be to somehow dispel the darkness that consumed her. The same way she had defeated Geister's dementia, she would have to overcome Alænnor's induced madness. If she had defeated madness once, she would do it twice. Somehow she knew that the walls that rose from the floor where unreal; that she could pass through them like a ghost would. Alænnor's trick was to make her believe that she could not achieve what seemed impossible, but was, in fact, conceivable.

She closed her eyes and inhaled deeply. She stood up and when she opened them, her vision had somewhat reassembled, the world was even, and she could walk without tripping over. The wall rose as she approached the boundary. Alice pressed her hand against the wall and pushed hard, eyes closed, imagining that nothing could stand in her way. The wall reluctantly gave way to her fingers as they pushed through it to the other side. And gradually, her entire hand went in. Her chest went in, and her head, and finally her legs. Then as her entire body went through it, she took off in a sprint, traversing across every wall that rose to stop her, shattering them to strips of shadow that vanished on contact with her, like an unstoppable force.

Alice notched her last arrow while running, and as she came closer to the diamond, only two meters away, she felt a menacing presence right above her.

Everything happened in only two seconds. Alænnor materialized out of the murk above Alice, hurtling down toward her with his wings fully extended. And as he snapped his jaws open, right above her head, Alice thrust herself forward, jumping high and spinning one-hundred-eighty degrees in mid-air, turning around so she would fall on her back, facing Alænnor's wide open maw ready to gorge her in, and promptly aiming her bow at the inside of his mouth, released the arrow.

Alice fell on her back, the collision painfully jarring her body, leaving her without air, writhing momentarily before regaining her composure. Alænnor jerked back, flailing his head from one side to the other, bellowing and bawling with severe pain and gingerly groping his huge maw with one of his talons as if to remove the arrow that pierced his soft palate, almost the throat, which would have choked him to death.

Determined to take this final chance, Alice stood up sorely and scooped up the big diamond, forming a loop around it with her arm and shambling almost blindly toward the middle of the arena. And as she jammed it into the aperture without hesitation, she heard Percival's footsteps closing in behind her. The deed was done; the riddle was solved.

Alice turned around and the dagger made a shallow gash across her right cheek as she leaned back. Then she deflected Percival's following thrust. But Percival struck her with his bare left fist on her other cheek, throwing her to the ground and leaving her briefly defenseless. Percival lifted the dagger, the blade flashing against the little light left available, his eyes inexorable and cruel, and let the weapon plunge toward his daughter's heart…

¤¤¤

A sudden flash of light left Alice and Percival temporarily blind, and as soon as they recovered their vision, they realized that there was no arena anymore and that they were separated from each other. It had vanished and all that remained was a murky abyss, above and below and to the sides. It was all pitch-black.

"Welcome, welcome," Geister announced, "mighty Harbinger and mortal Alice, to my throne room! I must admit that you are the first humans to finish my trial in centuries."

The abyss cleared like a raging gale, the murk sweeping away in a heavy rush of wind. Both Alice and Percival stood upon an obscure cloud, high in the sky, overlooking the entire world of Arcadia kilometers below.

When Alice found out where she was, her heart jolted with awe, blood dripping down her face to the point that she had to gingerly wipe it from her brow and eye, all the while gasping for air. Her face was grimy, her eyes tear-filled and drooping, her hair stained and greasy. Her entire body armor was severely battered and dented, and some parts, like the pauldrons, were already bouncing loosely.

There were three distinct figure outlines before Alice and Percival. Alænnor lay curled up further across the cloud, almost off the edge with his long tail dangling in the air, his maw wide open as he struggled to breathe with ease and emitting low wails of pain. Off to the right, in the center of the cloud, a two-meter tall silhouette sat upon a tremendous throne, made of some kind of dark metallic material. And more to the right, Alice distinguished Sonja's shape behind the bars of an ethereal cage, formed by the vapor of the cloud. She was resting on the floor of the cage, her back leaning against the bars; however, as Geister spoke, Sonja reacted promptly by looking back at them.

Alice immediately took off toward her, but an invisible force pushed her back without warning, almost causing her to tumble down.

"We had a deal, bloody liar!" Alice shouted at Geister, who stirred on the throne and rose from it.

"And we still do," replied Geister as he rose up, the light of the star above illuminating his face. His entire body was draped in a dark robe. His face was disturbing. Only it was not his face, but a mask divided vertically in half; his mouth and nose were divided in two. The half mouth on the right side was curving upward, as if the mask were smiling, the eyebrow slanting up. And the left side had its half mouth arching down, its eyebrow turning downward, although the left side was brightly lit by some dark artificial illumination coming from inside the mask. The eyes seemed empty, completely devoid of life, as they stared vacantly at Alice and Percival. "Come hither, human!" he hissed, his voice somewhat muffled by the mask, raising his hand and making a gesture as if he were pulling something toward him. Some invisible hands suddenly began to drag Alice against her will toward Geister, her heels failing to stop the pull as she pressed them against the cloud below her. The unseen force released her and now she was facing Geister a meter away.

"You must be proud," Geister's voice seemed unaffected and devoid of any emotion, but Alice could feel anger emanating from it. He extended his arm and handed her a bloody arrow. "You nearly killed my poor Alænnor. I had to remove the arrow myself."

"If you use him as part of your games, you better be careful next time," Alice retorted coldly. "Because next time, he might just die."

"I admire your courage. Not even I would be so insane as to

defy a Lord," Geister snapped back. "Nevertheless, you have completed my final enigma," he announced, changing the topic. "But do not feel flattered, for there are still more Purging Trials pending, and you might not survive them all."

"I don't care about that right now," Alice snapped. "You owe me something, remember? Give me my prize," Alice demanded, nodding her head at Sonja. "I want no setbacks, no conditions, no excuses and certainly no more of your riddles."

"Something has arisen," Geister said. "Rather unfortunate, as a matter of fact."

Alice felt her blood boil like a furnace. "I said no excuses!" she snarled, unsheathing her sword in blinding speed and pointing the tip at Geister, who remained immobile, merely watching her without flinching. Alænnor rose abruptly from his place, trying to roar but coughing huskily instead, his back arched as he crouched in readiness to bolt at Alice.

"*Ezrakum, Alænnor,*" Geister hissed in a soothing serpentine voice, eyeing Alice intently as she grimaced at the sound of his alien words. "*Nud pastuúm.*"

"What did you just say?" Alice retorted, glaring fiercely at Geister.

"He told him to calm down; nothing happened," Percival responded from behind, a sharp scowl on his forehead. Alænnor curled up again on the edge of the cloud, warily observing Alice, carefully placing his head over his talons.

"What's your excuse?" Alice inquired, slightly lowering her weapon. "In case it is because you think this was a tie, you are wrong, because I was the one who inserted the eye where I was supposed to."

"Here is your reward." Geister waved his hand at Sonja's cage. The bars vanished into puffs of cloud and Sonja stepped out.

Before Alice knew it, her friend was already embracing her, Sonja's arms holding her tightly.

"I knew you'd make it," she whispered in Alice's ear. Alice felt relieved, as if a heavy burden had just been taken off her shoulders.

"And what about me, you bloody demiurge?" Percival snapped, losing it completely, unable to move from his spot. "Am I just going to turn into one of your ghost puppets?"

"There are more Trials ahead of you, Harbinger," Geister replied indifferently, dismissing him with a wave of his dark gloved hand.

"I hope this is some kind of a joke!" He raised his voice. "I have a mission to fulfill, and that is to cure the Hellgod of his curse, who happens to be your Lord as well, by the way. It is imperative that I return to the Overworld. I need to go back. Our plans are derailing; something has gone terribly amiss..."

"I do not abide by what Antares says, Harbinger," Geister said, raising his voice, although there was no feeling in it. "This is what makes me rejoice!" He laughed to himself as Alice glowered at him distrustfully, protectively swathing Sonja in her arms. Gradually, the left side of the mask, the one that depicted anger, began to lose its bright illumination; the right side, which represented joy, was lighting up. "Bedlam stories—just how I like to call them. O, my victims, how they suffer. All they do is plea, plea, plea, and...demand!" he exclaimed, throwing a glance at Alice, this time showing emotion. "Misery, sorrow, despair, anxiety, distress, pain, fear, anger, worry, trouble, grief; I just enjoy it when they are all inflicted upon them. Whenever I get to smite my pleading victims it feels like glory! And right now we are about to witness another Bedlam story!"

"Beware, Geister," Percival mumbled, his voice poisonous. "You do not want enemies, even less, powerful ones. Return me to the Overworld and you shall be spared, Lord of Madness. Otherwise you shall suffer Antares' wrath!"

"But I did not mean you, Harbinger!" Geister replied ecstatically.

Alice whipped around to face Geister's unreadable countenance, backing off while pushing Sonja behind her, drawing out her broadsword.

"You stay away from us!" Alice warned, her voice quivering. "We solved all of your enigmas. Now all you have to do is...send us to the second Trial..."

"Well, well," Geister snapped his fingers merrily. "Did I not say it? This is what I was talking about! Nonetheless, there is one teeny little problem...well, two in fact. The first one is that Lord Hades of the Dead gave me a rather grim message: Sonja Krauss, for refusing to obey clear wraith orders on the shores of the Lethe river, is sentenced to spend all of eternity in the pit of Tartarus. That is something you did not expect, am I not right?"

Alice's heart twisted within her as her world turned upside down and all turned to chaos and turmoil inside her mind, her thoughts racing and scattering away without knowing what to do next.

"No…," Alice hesitated, making up her mind and finally remarking firmly, "Punish me instead. I told her not to drink from the Lethe; I craved her to refuse. I am the instigator! It's my fault, and I will pay the consequences. Leave her alone and send *me* to Tartarus!"

Geister negated her with his finger. "That is the second teeny little problem!" he replied, enthusiastically. "Antares, the Hellgod himself, has requested that I send you to him forthwith. And even if he did not, you are still alive. There is no rule concerning living things. Hades will let you wander on your own."

Percival suddenly broke into a harsh laughter, thereupon regaining his composure and turning incredulous. "Her?" he exclaimed, pointing derisively at Alice, who perspired profusely as she clung to Sonja's arms. "Her and not me? I am the Head Harbinger!"

"It is time to say 'farewell,'" said Geister, ignoring Percival's complaints.

Alice turned to face Sonja, distraught and feeling unable to do anything to divert their dooming fates, unable to keep her promise of protecting one another and standing by her side to the end of things. As the odds stacked against her favor, Alice let her tears flow as Sonja hugged her one last time, before being harshly separated from each other as an unseen forced pushed them apart.

"Can I at least know what's next? Anything at all I should know, your demented Highness?" Percival asked sarcastically, anger present in his voice.

"Oh yes, indeed, Harbinger, why not?" Geister chuckled. "It is going to be wet!"

"Sorry?" Percival asked, evidently bemused.

Geister did not answer and a white heavenly nimbus materialized beneath Percival and Sonja's feet, the halos gradually enclosing around them as they rose into the air head-high. Percival was bound to finish the second Trial. Sonja was to atone in Tartarus, the infernal land where souls burned for eternity.

Geister was the only one enjoying the occasion as he took in his victims' suffering, dropping his arms to his sides and gazing skyward.

Alice could barely contain her despair and sorrow as she saw her final moments with Sonja zip by. Alice clenched her fist, feeling powerless once again, and found she still had the arrow Geister gave her in her palm, enclosing the wooden shaft in her fingers. Alice looked down at the arrow, a wild thought already forming in her mind. Would she do it, given the circumstances? The bloodstained arrowhead hungered for more blood; its fury had to be satiated. Sonja was well beyond her rescue now. Geister was distracted, thinking he had already won. Then Alice asked herself, *Why not?*

The hissing, bloody arrow pierced Geister's heart. His head sagged down, staring vacantly at the protruding shaft. The bright side of his mask lowered in intensity, and suddenly both sides began flickering in a maddening trance; all the while he held his unforgiving empty gaze locked on Alice, whose lips curled faintly with satisfaction.

And bedlam it was. Everything happened in a matter of seconds. Alice's grim gaze strayed to find Percival's unbelieving eyes, speechless, just as he began to fade from the realm of Arcadia and be transported to the second Trial. Then she glanced back at Sonja, who also began to fade and be transported to Tartarus, just in time to give her a look that bore a message only Sonja understood: 'I'm coming for you…count on it.' In no time, Alænnor was gliding full speed toward her, toward his master's murderer, producing grating coughs as he tried to bellow, but to no avail. Geister remained standing like a statue, his head sagging while coughing and chuckling unnervingly. He slumped down onto the ethereal canopy of dark clouds, his mask shutting down completely. Alice winced and braced herself to receive Alænnor's furious and ruthless strike.

All at once, a robed man stepped before Alice facing Alænnor as the Black Shadow-King hurtled toward them, indomitable and determined to tear Alice to pieces. His slit eyes burned with fury, and his speed was unwavering and precipitous like nothing Alice had ever seen. Right as the dragon got within five meters of them, the man spread out his arms and time seemed to flow slowly, smooth waves distorting the view. Alænnor stopped short as soon as he touched the invisible barriers. However, he did not stop at will. He was still trying to seize Alice, his wings beating heavily and hastily as he pushed forward with his head and claws, trying to produce bellows instead of raucous coughs, but an unseen force was all it took to shield them from him.

Alice was still transfixed by the battering dragon, her eyes wide with fear and her heart in her throat, when the man turned to face her. She did not have time to draw her broadsword. The red-headed man, with scarlet eyes that portended nothing but chaos, clutched her wrist with incredible strength and said: "Become."

A vortex tore open out of nowhere and a blast of wind rushed out of it. Viktor shoved Alice into the vortex and he followed right away, shutting the portal behind and leaving the realm of Madness, Arcadia.

And so, Percival was transported to the second Trial, Dædali, hoping to catch a soul. Sonja was delivered to the Tartarus warders, down the titanic black chasm. Tartarus' bottom was a world streaked with rivers of fire from the Phlegethon, volcanoes erupting massive amounts of lava and colossal maelstroms of ash, its inhabitants being the wickedest and cruelest of creatures that have ever trod the Underworld and the Overworld together, paying for their sins and crimes for eternity. And Alice, hauled before the feet of the dying Hellgod, Antares, enemy of humanity and destroyer of Earth, uncertain of his purpose, was just about to be at the mercy of mankind's most powerful and dangerous foe…

Epilogue: Dæmon

Arthur's eyes flicked open as sweat streamed down his face and neck. His head had a freshly changed bandage that covered his countenance where William had ripped open his flesh, although it was already stitched together. The wool blankets from his bed were wet from his constant sweating, and from the occasional wrung-out damp cloth that let some droplets of water trickle onto the mattress. Arthur felt hot and sticky, his head throbbing with pain. His fever was intense. He remembered his nightmare, in which he murdered an innocent man; the guilt consumed him. The fear that the authorities might discover his acts was unbearable as he rushed to hide all clues that might convict him to the gallows. It was only a bad dream, he thought. But in reality, he was emotionally damaged. When Arthur killed Duke William and realized that the young man actually had been innocent from the beginning, it dawned on Arthur, the factual measure of his actions, all against his personal principles and morals. Now he was going into his tomb taking with him the intense guilt he felt.

The room was obscured, its only window, high in the middle of one of the walls, small and barred, draped in a black cloth to keep out the sunlight. In the penumbra, Arthur lay on his deathbed, the poison of the reptilian eating away at his body, especially his arm, bluish and oozing pus. He lost sensibility and his fingertips tingled, some of them becoming outright stiff. Although he had long lost his appetite, he forced himself to gobble down the food he was offered there, at Amos' personal quarters.

Duke Jean returned to the throne in Normandy and promptly made amendments for the issues William's reign had given way to. The denizens of Rouen tried to return to their normal lives, except that many people were aiding those wounded in the demonic outbreak and the conflagration that burned away a big part of the city, combing the debris and ashes for survivors.

Amos led the rebels to defend themselves from the Dwellers that attacked the city, and had become a recognized figure. After the conflict ended, Arthur fell into a grave, feverish state and Amos resolved to take care of him in his personal quarters back at the tavern. Many people did not know who the real hero was on that crucial night; however, Amos considered Arthur the one. But that was not the only reason why he was taking care of his precarious health. Posters rewarding thousands of gold coins for Arthur's head were stamped against walls all around the city.

There was a presence in the room. Arthur could vaguely feel it as he wearily sat up against the moldy wall.

"Just…show yourself," he slurred.

"I've been looking for you," a familiar voice replied in a murmur. "You were hard to find. I come in peace."

"Valerie?" Arthur mumbled.

"Certainly. I do not know how critical your situation is, but I have come to ask you something. It concerns your new Viceroy, Vincent Blanc. You were right since the beginning. Blanc had nobody else to blame other than you and us, and blame us he did. I know you want revenge. I could see it in your eyes before you left the stronghold…"

There was a noise behind the door and Arthur heard Valerie's dress rustle as she went for cover in the corner. The door of the room opened just as much as one person needed to squeeze through it and closed with a thud. Antoine came over to Arthur's bed and sat down on the chair beside it, unaware of the third presence lurking in the shadows.

"Marshal, I thought you might want to hear this news," Antoine whispered, his voice clearly uneasy. "Things are getting ugly out there. King Philippe has finally declared war on England, and Edward will not be lenient. Raids and pillages have taken place in the county of Flanders. It will get worse than it is.

And the second news is that the High Pontiff, Benedict XII, has died in his Château de Avignon without any apparent explanation; an untimely death, only to quickly be replaced by a man called Salvatore Cavalieri." The name did not ring a bell with Arthur, but in his actual state of mind he could not afford to sift through his memories. "That's what I wanted to tell you. Not that we can do anything, but I just thought it would at least connect you with reality and the world outside."

"It reminds me of William Bloodthorn's usurpation," Arthur remarked.

"You might want to hear my news as well," Valerie said in low voice, standing a few meters from the knights. Antoine was startled and as quickly as he rose he already had his longsword in hand.

"Who are you?" he asked, straining his sight into the gloom.

"An agent of darkness," Valerie replied confidently. "I come unarmed and with an offer."

"How do I know you're not here to kill him?" Antoine asked, pointing to Arthur.

"If I were here to kill him, he would already be dead," she said grimly, hidden in the dark.

"What could you possibly offer me? You were going to assassinate me a few nights ago," Arthur cut in, his head pounding with pain.

"You were a contract," Valerie began to explain. "But not anymore. I can give you a future, a family, a life, one more chance to redeem yourself and to accomplish much more than what you have done."

"Why would you do that?" asked Arthur, his words slurring out of his tired mouth.

"Because we are both after the same target: Vincent Blanc. Because we also want to see justice restored in this world," said Valerie.

"We don't need your help, assassin!" Antoine retorted.

Arthur held up his arm, as if asking Antoine to remain silent. "What do you propose?" he asked.

"I am sure that what I believe is the same thing you do," Valerie replied. "That Vincent Blanc, as a Viceroy of the most powerful military, is a danger to Europe and to France itself. And I am sure you two want revenge as much as I do." She addressed Antoine, too. "The Cult of Tiberius calls for you. You are not knights anymore. Become assassins and cleanse the world from evil and sin: *Illuminat viam, ensis in tenebris.* That is our creed: 'Light the way, a blade into the dark.'"

"How would that help me redeem myself? How would joining your family help me accomplish more than what I already have?" Arthur drawled, lying down on his bed.

"Like I said, if you were to join the Cult of Tiberius, we would provide you with a secret shelter, something you desperately need at the moment. We would provide you with resources, weapons, supplies, horses, a new identity, and, possibly…with a cure. We deal with several kinds of poisons, and of course we also manufacture their antidotes. Besides, our healers are some of the finest across Europe. You'd be in good hands. There is nothing you can do other than wait for death. So what is your say?" Valerie said, getting a little impatient. "Do you accept the deal?"

"My quest for the Harbingers is still pending," said Arthur slowly. "If that is your creed and you faithfully intend to follow it, then my blade shall sink into the dark as well…"

¤¤¤

Hero of the people and killer of masses, fighter for freedom and repressor of liberty, everlasting tyrant warped by his lust for immeasurable power, whose body has been transformed and fused with fire.

Antares, the Sun, as he was often called, or the Crossbred, as his dissenters used to call him, lay agonizing against the fiery wall of the red mountain and upon his red-rock throne, blistering lava oozing down his colossal body as it erupted from the ever-active volcano above. The sky, overcast by dark crimson clouds and whirlwinds of black ash, was in constant turmoil, searing dry winds rushing across the red realm of the Hellgod.

A vortex ripped out of the air and Alice emerged through it and down on to the brown craggy ground, landing on all fours. Out the Harbinger came as well, standing a few meters away from her and remaining still as a statue of rock. Right away she began to feel the scorching heat of the place, not knowing whether she was in Tartarus until she peered up and found herself before the feet of the Hellgod. What could she do other than stare back at him and wish she were dead? Her quiver was empty, but still she figured that an arrow would not even sting him a bit. Using her broadsword against his feet would be like hammering a rusty and blunt dagger against a mountain.

A clamorous growl startled Alice and she turned to the right. What thing in either world could emit such a gut-wrenching noise? Only a gigantic beast, one that Alice had already seen before outside of Notre Dame. Kronnix the Sovereign, thirty meters at his highest, black and overpowering, was curled up on the ground beside his master, tiredly squinting his huge golden eyes, overall weakened by the removing of his soul to save Antares from an unexpected stroke that could have killed him; but only half of his soul was removed, therefore he was still alive.

The giant Antares moved. An unseen force pulled Alice from her feet into the air and she rose upward at least half a kilometer, coming face to face with the Hellgod, her feet dangling in the air.

Antares' skin had darkened, turning a smoke black color, and become rough and shabby from the passage of time. Some parts of his body, his broad chest, for example, were glowing red, as if they were made completely of fire.

Antares glared at Alice with his draconic eyes, his long claws splayed above her as she levitated beneath them. Alice could not move her gaze away, nor was she able to perform any kind of movement other than to stare directly at him, unblinkingly. The heat was gradually turning unbearable and she was perspiring streams of sweat, struggling to breathe. She could almost feel her hair singeing off, her lungs burning.

"Art thou a worthy warrior, or art thou not?" he croaked, with a voice that made Alice shudder; piercing, deep and hoarse. Without waiting for Alice to respond, he went on, slurring his words. "I *need* more souls, and thou shalt bring them unto me unquestioningly." Antares placed his other giant hand in front of Alice a few meters away and she began to writhe in pain, unable to fight back. "Receiveth the Kiss of the Fiend!" Antares proclaimed. "The foundations of men shall cease to exist. Mountains shall crumble and kingdoms shall topple in thy wake. Rob the powerful of their wealth and dethrone them. Reap the souls of the innocent, the sheep, and give them eternal rest." His rumbling voice sounded poisonous. Alice continued to writhe, groaning and crying, until the pain stopped and she remained inert in the air, her eyes closed. "Now goeth forth, my Harbinger, and bindeth the world in darkness!"

Alice's eyes opened and her irises had a new scarlet hue, her lips curling with malice. "Yes, milord..."

In ignorance there is bliss. In knowledge there is power. And power corrupts the greatest of minds.

The End

Acknowledgements

I want to thank Chris Sansom, for guiding me through this hazy and unknown world called 'the publishing process'. Lucy Irving, for creating such a great, eye-catching cover. I want to thank the entire team at Authoright for helping me achieve my dream.

Derek P. Chase, who revised the manuscript at its early stages, for without his keen eye and feedback, it would never have grown to such scope. Kirk Boys, my dear mentor, who willingly dedicated his time to see me grow as the writer I am today.

My friends, for being so supportive and sticking with me. My grandfather, Alberto, who gave me the means to make all of this possible, and for giving me a good book when I needed it most. Nichole, for believing in me and always wishing me for the best. My brothers, Juan Pablo and Rodrigo, for being so noisily and annoyingly fun. And Zarina and Sergio, my mom and dad, who have always been there for me when I needed them most, who taught me how to live in this world, and whose unparalleled love has kept me going forward.

www.ingramcontent.com/pod-product-compliance
Lightning Source LLC
LaVergne TN
LVHW091123080826
845145LV00008B/2021

9781909477148